The AGE of MIRACLES

The AGE of MIRACLES

Catherine MacCoun

THE ATLANTIC MONTHLY PRESS
NEW YORK

Published in Great Britain in 1989 by William Heinemann Ltd.
Published in Canada by Little, Brown Canada Ltd.
First Atlantic Monthly Press edition, June 1989
Printed in the United States of America

Library of Congress Cataloging-in-Publication Data

MacCoun, Catherine.
The age of miracles / Catherine MacCoun.—1st ed.
ISBN 0-87113-312-1
I. Title.
PS3563.A2658A74   1988   813'.54—dc19   88-39299

The Atlantic Monthly Press
19 Union Square West
New York, NY 10003

Design by Laura Hough

FIRST PRINTING

for Malcolm MacCoun,
with love and gratitude

Acknowledgments

I would like to thank Joe "Windhorse" Spieler for his unsurpassable confidence, his solicitude and his skillful means.

The primary editor of this book, Anne Rumsey, was sensitive, clever and tactful beyond all reasonable expectation. I feel very lucky.

Kate Bertrand, Ron Bognore, Bill Burton, Charley Custer, Richard Engling and Gary Koningsfeld of the Chicago Writers' Group were the first readers of this book. I am grateful for their many helpful suggestions and for their jolly companionship in good times and bad.

I would also like to thank Larry Zimmerman and Allan Yamakawa, my daytime employers, for their patience and support.

This is the story of a failed saint. Church history records the miracles she performed in 1345, then lapses into silence. Documents detailing the inquisition into her subsequent conduct have long been suppressed, and in secular history there is only one mention of her: that in 1348 she was exiled from England, for an unspecified crime.

PART ONE

One

When the man was injured so near their gate, the nuns said it was God's will. One might well wonder—they didn't, but one might—whether anything ever happened that was *not* God's will. They would have replied that it was a matter of degree. Under normal circumstances the will of God flicked over human affairs absentmindedly, like a cow's tail. It was only rarely that it snorted and stamped and charged and impaled a man on its horns. Theologians debated whether it would do so without provocation. The man thought so, but then he was always one to give himself the benefit of the doubt.

The man. That is how they referred to him at Greyleigh. Coming from Dame Agatha, it was an intentional insult, calling him "the man" as if he did not merit a Christian name. The others called him that because they were never told who he was. They breathed the word with hushed and titillated respect, as one might whisper "the dragon." He would have been flattered if he had known.

He introduced himself to Ingrid as Jacques Brigand des Cœurs. ("Please excuse me. I don't speak French very well," she apologized, in perfect French. "Neither do I," he admitted. "It's a stage name. You can call me Jack.") Though he was famous all over England, no one at Greyleigh had ever heard of him. They gathered that he was some sort of performer. Under a wreath of dark curls his face had the kind of charm that invites one to become a co-conspirator in some delicious mischief. It was the animated look of a professional entertainer, not an ordinary expression at all, and Ingrid judged it even more immodest than his lurid and abbreviated costume.

The accident happened as he was on his way to join the king's hunting party at Woodstock. Jack did not hunt, but he was looking

3

forward to his stay there. The ladies of court would be left idle, and he would have the long golden days to harvest the longing he sowed in the evenings with his stories and songs. At court he would broaden his peasant accent, the accent that early in his career he had labored so hard to lose. For ladies, he had learned, were beguiled by the knowledge that he had started life as a plowman. They liked to imagine that they could still feel calluses on his well-kept hands and that his expensive shoes still smelled faintly of manure. And so he would coarsen his speech a little at Woodstock. Perhaps he would look away, abashed, after letting some beauty catch him in the act of picking his teeth with his knife. Feigning clumsiness with the complicated hooks and laces of her gown, he would, perhaps, tear an eyelet. Just one. In his peasant impatience. And she, how she would finger that tiny tear in her bodice, never allowing her maid to mend it . . .

Yes, he would have a good time at Woodstock. But he must hurry, for the sky was fast growing dark. It was not the dingy opaque white of the usual English rainy day, but steely, angry, voluptuous with threat. He quite liked it. He could smell the coming rain and sense the excitement of the birds.

Briefly he considered taking shelter at Greyleigh, the convent he'd just passed. The place had become something of a sensation recently. Ladies flocked there on holy days to pray before the new crucifix, which was nearly life size and sculpted, it was whispered, from a live model. The thing, which was inspiring paroxysms of piety in the gentle sex, had been donated by Lady Ladbrook, who claimed to have been miraculously cured of her paralysis by one of the novices. This novice was reputed to be a living saint. The fashion, it seemed, was to praise the place for its fidelity to all the old monastic values, gape at the crucifix, make a decent donation and leave before one could be depressed by the pervading gloom of the abbess, who was said to hate men even more than she loved God. Naturally one did not send one's surplus daughters there to take the veil. There was Godstow for that.

He did not like the look of the place with its heavy masonry, its cowering gray arches and shuttered windows. A man, particularly a man of his calling, would find no comfort there. Maybe if he rode very fast, he could make Woodstock before the storm broke. He liked the idea of arriving at full gallop, his cloak flying behind him, the thunder announcing him.

During his convalescence he would remember this fantasy often, wondering whether it had made him the object of divine ridicule. For the thunder came, sure enough, and the horse reared dramatically—throwing him off. He heard his leg crack like the splitting sky.

Shooting pain and cold rain assaulted him at once. For a moment he was stunned, and then, instinctively, he reached for his lute. It was unharmed. He tried to stand and his leg screamed in protest. The horse was stamping uncertainly beside him, and he lunged for the reins. It whinnied and trotted out of reach. The man cursed.

He dragged himself along the ground toward a sapling, noticing with dismay that he was soiling his fine clothes. Bracing himself against the trunk, he raised himself on his good leg and with both hands grasped the branch nearest his head. The wood did not easily surrender its young life and he had to pause several times to catch his breath before he succeeded in snapping it. With a few more rough twists he had torn it from the trunk. He used his knife to strip it of twigs and leaves, then hauled himself to his feet with it. The slightest pressure on his left leg was agony. He would have to make his way hopping on one foot. Lustily he cursed God, the sky and his devil-begotten horse.

The gatehouse was some two hundred yards from where he had fallen and it took him an age to reach it. Another age seemed to pass before his insistent clanging of the bell was answered by a small, blinking nun. "Good sister," he began, doffing his sodden cap. His vision blurred, and he had to steady himself against the doorframe. He must have appeared drunk, for she attempted to slam the gate on him. He caught it, forcing his way in. The nun let out a little squeal of panic and made a run for the main building. He hobbled up the path after her, panting "Please . . . please . . ." but she vanished inside.

In her agitation she had neglected to secure the door, and he lurched through, out of the rain at last. He paused and wiped his wet face with a wet sleeve. Should he venture farther or call out or simply wait? Dizzy from exertion, he leaned against a wall and slid slowly down till he was sitting on the floor, his head drooping between his knees.

Dour saints glared down at him from their niches in the damp walls. They were lit from below with candles so that one saw too much of their nostrils, and their weird wavering shadows were thrown upward. The cloths draped across the unglazed windows to keep out the storm puffed in and out, and there were puddles on the flagstones. The place smelled of mildew, cheap lamp oil and fish.

He heard rustling. Another nun was coming. This one was dark and glowering, and she walked fiercely, kicking her black skirts out with each step. He staggered to his feet and managed a wobbly bow. As he bent forward, water dripped from his hair to the floor. Distinct drops. Plop. Plop. Her eyes followed them and made a scornful journey back upward, taking in his muddy shoes (their stylish pointed toes now sagging despondently), spattered hosen, clinging tunic and saturated cloak.

"Good lady, forgive me for upsetting your household. I am injured and beg your hospitality for the night."

"Injured?" She eyed him suspiciously.

"My leg. I was thrown from my horse." Leaning on his make-shift crutch, he dangled the offending limb in front of him. She frowned and he could tell she was scanning her mind for a Christian alternative to taking him in. Finding none, she snapped, "Very well. Please follow me," and led him through the cloister at a pace that, to a man in his condition, was little short of breakneck. The grunts that issued from him with each hop were very loud in that cavernous space. He felt ridiculous: his syncopated hop-drip-grunt, hop-drip-grunt laboring behind the efficient snap of her skirts. They passed the parlor and the open doors of the refectory. Inside a score of identically dressed women sat erect at a long table. No one was talking and the clink of spoons echoed in the bare, vaulted chamber.

He fell behind, and she paused to let him catch up, her lip curling at the muddy tracks he was leaving. He thought it unfair of her, since there were already puddles all over. "Can you manage?" she asked, without conveying concern.

They turned down a narrower hall, at the end of which was a low door that opened onto the outdoor passage to the infirmary. Rain pelted them through the open arches of the covered walkway, but the distance was short. The nun, who he had concluded by this time must be the dreaded abbess, paused in the antechamber. Through a half-open door he could see a row of cots, some of them occupied, and hear low conversations. "Sister Ingrid," she called from the doorway.

The infirmarian came out at once, closing the door to the ward discreetly behind her. She was uncommonly tall and looked very clean. She also looked too young for the responsibility of her post—she could not have been more than eighteen. Instead of the cowl, scapular and veil, she wore an apron over her dark gown and a plain linen kerchief tied low and indifferent over her handsome brow. She listened gravely as the abbess explained the situation.

"Has anyone gone after your horse?" she asked. He could have hugged her, for she had raised the concern uppermost in his mind.

"He followed me here and was just outside the gate when I came in." His voice sounded strange to him. Unbelievable how much effort it cost just to get the words out. He was swaying, his knuckles white from gripping his staff. If he did not lie down soon, he would fall.

Ingrid turned to the older woman. "Maybe someone should be sent to fetch it before it runs off," she suggested.

The floor was beckoning him. "I'm afraid we'll have to put you upstairs," the girl was saying.

He followed her glance to the steep, winding stairway. Holy Mother of God. "I can't . . . ," he started to protest, but she clasped him around the waist and drew his free arm over her shoulder.

"Go ahead and lean," she encouraged. "You're not heavy." Her voice was like milk. She bent down to cradle the injured leg behind the knee. Thus entwined, they thumped up the stairs.

"Goodness, you're shivering," she exclaimed.

Warm milk.

Two

Half the tunic was magenta, the other half scarlet—outrageous colors for clothing, or for anything. He had worn it with a brilliant blue shirt of fabric finer than any she had ever touched, and violet hosen. His cloak was of a more sober midnight blue, but lined with scarlet and gold stripes. Soaked and muddied when he arrived, this garish ensemble had been a bit subdued and it was only now, after she had laundered and dried everything, that she experienced the full visual assault.

What was even more striking to the few who had seen him before he could be hidden away was the immodesty of his costume. The tunic was so short it scarcely cleared his buttocks. One wondered what would happen if he should bend—but such speculation was an occasion of sin, and Ingrid steered her mind clear of it.

She pressed her nose to the bundle of clothing. The odor of it had been so strange: perspiration, leather, horse and some faint and intoxicating perfume. Now it smelled as all the linens in the convent did—aggressively clean.

She shifted her burden onto one arm and with her free hand withdrew a rusty key from her apron pocket. The room had long been out of use, and the door was difficult now to unlock. Each time she entered, she was afraid her patient would be awakened by the rasp of the key.

Dame Agatha had ordained that he be locked in, for even if his broken leg kept him from wandering about the cloister, there was the danger that one of the older students, learning of the troubadour's presence, would attempt to get a glimpse of him. The wisdom of this was clear to Ingrid once she became acquainted with the man. In the two days since his arrival she had heard more curses than in all of her eighteen years combined. Even her father had not, to her recollection, cursed like that. She feared for the man's soul and hoped that God would make allowances for the fact that he was, through no fault of his own, quite drunk. So drunk that most of the time he seemed not to know she was there.

Maybe she should not have given him so much herbed wine. Dame Agatha had been upbraiding her lately for dispensing too many pain-relieving infusions, reminding her that pain was humanity's inheritance from the Fall and that, if offered up in a spirit of penitence, was pleasing to God. But every time the man returned to consciousness, he moaned and wailed and thrashed about like someone damned. The patients downstairs would start to cross themselves and bite their nails, and Ingrid was so distracted that she was useless to all of them. So the man got his medicine.

All day he had been writhing on the cot, neither awake nor deeply asleep, sweating under the twisted blankets that she kept doing her best to smooth. The room smelled like the inside of a wineskin. The shutters on the only window had been bolted for years. She struggled for several minutes before they gave way, all at once, to fresh air and light.

The setting sun cast a streak of gold across the floorboards and over the man's dozing form. His right arm was thrown across his face, and Ingrid could see the deep armpit with its fine, moist hairs. His skin, which took on the color of the fading light, was stretched taut over his bones, the rib cage lifted gently by his breathing. Since she last looked in on him he had kicked the blankets off, and now they covered only his splinted leg. The good leg bent inward in such a way that his pelvis protruded sharply and she could see the pale smooth crescent of his buttock. The sight of him evoked a queer tenderness, a seasickness in her womb. Though she had never seen a naked man before, something about the slight palmward curl of the fingers, the plaited muscles, the jutting bone of his hip—something about this sight and this tenderness was not unknown to her.

The blood rushed to her face as she realized what it was. The man reminded her of the crucifix in the chapel, the one Lady Ladbrook had given them. Dame Agatha detested it, and Ingrid was furtive about her own feeling for it. The straining body against the uncompromising geometry of the wood seemed to her all the rebellion in the world, and all surrender. The sad face, the feet curled one atop the other, the bones so raw they seemed to bruise the flesh from within—she wanted to take it all into some safe, secret part of her own body, to cherish and heal it.

The moment the crucifix was unveiled she had grasped for the first time what she had always been taught: that God had been a man. The gospels she had memorized as a child became animated with this discovery—that this God, who seemed to regard his creation from the sky like a spectator, had felt it with his feet. As hot sand, as cool grass, as pebbles on a riverbed. The taste of a grape in his mouth was the same as that taste in her own. When he healed lepers, he, too, must have smelled their breath. Perhaps he, too, once shuddered when the blind, the lame and the pox-scarred tugged on his robe, and wished to rest his weary sympathies in a place where all were whole and pleasing to look upon. Betrayal had broken his heart, and nails had broken the bones of his hands. He had been alive.

Before making this discovery, she had expected to meet God in the next life and regarded her present existence as a kind of waiting period in which her one task was to keep her soul unsullied for its divine rendezvous. But if God had become man, he must yearn for humanity as humanity yearned for him. It must be possible to join with him in this life. This union became her only desire.

And she could not achieve it. She would stay awake all night gazing at the crucifix, tears running like rivers down her face, tears of utter frustration. The dry wafer through which he was said physically to enter her left her hungry and thirsty. She believed it must be subtle and hidden sins that hindered her and she searched them out with a ruthlessness that itself began to seem a sin.

There were moments, ecstatic moments when her frustration, her remorse, her temptations and her longing ignited into a great bonfire, a burning devotion. The light of it would dispel all doubts, and the heat of it was all the nourishment her body and soul required.

Afterward, she was left with ashes. Her head would ache and her limbs drag with fatigue. It was as if the very solidity of the physical world were bruising her. Tables, chairs, walls, and everyday objects took on a kind of menace. They were dumb, dense, arbitrary, yet absolute. And like her body, they imprisoned her.

She began to believe that she must die after all to be united with Christ, and she prayed ardently for an early deliverance. She wished that this were an era of martyrdom. As now she burned and was rent by terrible devotion, she wished that real beasts might tear open her breast and free her spirit, that real flames might consume her flesh and allow her soul to ascend in smoke.

Instead, she was being fed, living, to the sick. They were waiting for her now. Foul smelly towels, chamber pots and blood bands, all the insulting accompaniments to incarnation nagging: Do this in remembrance of me.

She looked once more at the sleeping troubadour. She saw the faint bluish traces of veins on the underside of his arm. The sun picked out copper threads in his dark beard. Fine beads of moisture clung to his curls and caught the amber light.

Three

Jack was awake, painfully and irrevocably awake. He closed his eyes, threw his arm across his face and willed himself back into oblivion, but to no avail. Sunlight was slamming at his forehead, and the knowledge of where he was and why was cutting through his pleasant delirium.

What was that queer sound? It had been in his dreams, that sound, in recurring dreams that he was a prisoner in a hive of insects buzzing, humming around his head. Now he identified it as women's voices, chanting. It had been going on and on . . .

The crucifix on the far wall had also been in his dreams. A lurid thing it was, badly sculpted and crudely painted, with an elongated torso and abbreviated legs. The flesh was chalky, with great splotches of red paint dribbling down from the hands, feet and side. There were also red droplets splattered around the crown of thorns on its melancholy head. The eyes and mouth slanted downward in an expression of such morose and impotent patience that Jack could understand the impulse to taunt it with a vinegar-soaked sponge. He had been dreaming that his foot was being nailed to a sapling in the rain and that red paint was running down his chalk white leg.

His ankle! God, what had they done to it? He flung off the blankets. The calf had been splinted and bound, and the foot seemed to be back in its proper place. He compared it with the good leg to make sure. Aye. That was how a foot should look. He tried to flex his toes and found it painful but possible. Sighing, he fell back against the pillows. The girl had known what she was about.

He suspected he owed her an apology. The sight of it had been so nauseating—the discolored ankle swollen to double its normal size, the foot veering off at a grotesque angle. Even when treated by good doctors, injuries like that left men crippled. What indignities would he suffer at the hands of a well-meaning schoolgirl? For the rest of his life he would be dragging the mangled limb behind him, the silk-clad object of desire now an object of pity. No more would he leap nimbly to a tabletop as he sang, no more prance and swagger and crouch and pounce. No more travel, no more fame, no more easy money.

So he had railed and babbled about riding on to Woodstock to see the king's physician. He had demanded his horse. It was hard to remember with the drugs he had been given, but he was pretty sure that he had accused her of wishing to maim him for life. The one clear impression he had was of the girl's unwavering gaze and the mesmerizing way she had told him, "You will not be lame." Was she pretty? He could not even remember that.

Still squinting against the light, he took in the rest of the room. It was spacious, with a high, beamed ceiling and plank floor. An assortment of disabled and forgotten furniture was jumbled in one corner, and buckets had been set in various spots to catch drips from the leaky roof. His clothing, saddlebag and lute were arranged on the table at his bedside, and the stick he had used to hobble to the convent stood near the door.

He wished someone would come. His mouth was gummy and bitter and his empty stomach was chewing on itself. He shifted on the cot, trying to find a position in which his leg did not hurt. Across the room the deformed Jesus looked down indifferently. "If thou art truly the son of God, come down from that cross and fetch me a nurse!" Jack challenged.

As if in answer, he heard a key in the lock. "It may please you to know that you have just demonstrated the divinity of Christ," he said as the young infirmarian entered with a tray balanced on one arm.

"I beg your pardon?"

"Never mind. I am glad to see you. I thought I was going mad. I hear chanting all the time—even in the middle of the night."

She set down the tray and poured out a cup of wine for him. "You're not going mad—we do chant at midnight."

"Every night?"

She nodded.

"Why?"

"It comes from a psalm: 'Seven times have I sung thy praises. At midnight I arose to confess thee.' "

He accepted the wine. It had a medicinal smell. "Do you mean to tell me that your whole life is based on a line of poetry?"

She considered this soberly. "I've never heard it put that way, though I suppose you are right."

"I like that, in principle. But I would have chosen a different line."

He expected her to chuckle at this, but she did not even smile. Her expression was vague, as if they were speaking a language in which she was not quite fluent. Her timing was like that too: a long pause and then a lurch into speech. "You seem to be feeling better."

Actually, now that he was conscious he felt worse, but he wanted to be polite. "Aye. Thanks to your most kind ministrations. I fear I have been an impatient patient. Please forgive me my ravings these last few days."

"There is no need to apologize. The devil often speaks through the lips of those who are abandoned to pain. You were much in our prayers." She lifted the blankets away from his injured leg and sat down to examine it. "The bandages are loose. That is a good sign. It means

the swelling is down. I'm going to have to tighten them. Don't worry—
it won't hurt much. I've already done this twice while you were
sleeping."

"What day is it?"

"Friday."

"Friday! And I arrived when? Tuesday?"

"Yes. You have had a fever."

"I'm sorry to have imposed on you for so long. I will be on my
way just as soon as I get over this blasted headache."

She looked horrified and for a second he wondered whether
she objected to his language. ("Blasted" was a substitute for something
coarser, but with nuns, who knew?) "Oh no! You must not travel, not
for at least six weeks. You must not even leave your bed."

"Six weeks?" He let it sink in. "Six weeks is impossible." He said
it calmly—a matter of indisputable fact.

"No doubt you are worried about your family. We can write
them for you—"

"Nay, I have no family. But I can't stay here for six weeks.
Obviously."

It was not obvious to her. She stopped her work to study his
face. "We must beg your forgiveness for making you feel unwelcome.
You see, we are not used to having . . ." She hesitated, as if there were
something indelicate about the phrasing, and finally abandoned the
sentence altogether. "Men usually go to the abbey, you see. But of
course, in your case that wasn't possible, so—"

"Well, there it is," he interrupted. "It's as bloody inconvenient
for you as it is for me."

She was blushing. "Please . . . what I meant to say was that
you are welcome here."

"That's very kind, but I'm leaving." He gulped down all of the
wine at once and banged the mug on the table.

For a moment she said nothing, and he was distracted by the
strong, sure movement of her hands as they unwound the bandages.
Large for a woman's, long fingered, careful but not in any way
tentative, they inspired trust. And when she spoke again, it was with
unexpected firmness. "You cannot ride with a broken leg. It won't heal

straight, and you will end up lame. Please understand that I have no reason to deceive you about this."

That much was true. He groaned. Six weeks! In six weeks the golden autumn would have given way to winter. The king would be gone from Woodstock and with him the ladies. In six weeks Jack would be mad, driven insane by boredom, loneliness and piety. There had to be an alternative.

"Look, I have heard talk of miracles at Greyleigh—miracles of healing. Maybe this saint they speak of could help me."

He felt a sudden break in the rhythm of her movements. "Your leg will heal naturally. That is miracle enough."

She said this coolly, but he noticed that her fingers faltered as she resumed her work. The subject was awkward for her. Why? Maybe she regarded the saint as a rival. After all, who wouldn't resent someone coming in and, with a wave of her hand (or however it was done), accomplishing what one worked so hard to achieve by natural means? Jack could understand her jealousy, but he was not about to let it stand in his way.

"Would this saint consent to visit me nevertheless? I would find such a meeting edifying."

"I know of no saint here, though many of the ladies are holy and devout. Perhaps you have confused this place with someplace else."

"Is there not a large crucifix here donated by Lady Ladbrook?"

"Yes. There is." The answer came unwillingly.

"Then this is the place. I've heard the story more than once—of how a young novice cured the lady of her paralysis. And many were cured after that."

"Stories become exaggerated."

"Aye, they do. But I met a man not long ago who claimed to have been cured of leprosy. I could tell he'd had it once, for some of his fingers were gone. Yet he was quite sound."

She looked up, attentive. "Was he? Do you remember his name?"

"Nay, that I don't. Do you?"

She shook her head—sadly he thought. "There were many. Many who came, I mean. I think not many were cured."

"You were here, then. You must know this girl."

She hesitated for a moment, then stood up, her work finished. "I'm tiring you with all this talk. You must have your breakfast and then rest. Would you like another cup of wine?"

"I would like an answer to my question."

There was another pause, and when she spoke he could sense her irritation.

"The answer to your question, sir, is that all healing comes from God. And it is all a miracle."

Four

Ingrid's mother had died giving birth to her. Her father, who had been fond of her mother, was not fond of children. Ingrid felt rather apologetic about her existence. The nuns described this attitude as meek.

It was when she was six that her father had taken her to the convent to be educated. She never saw him again. This saddened her, but not for long. The fallible man who had sired her was no match for God, the just and loving father whose protection she had gained. At home she had never known when her father's huge hand would descend on her without explanation. For her, the nunnery was a haven of safety and justice.

To be sure, there were many rules, and infractions were punished severely. Guilt, persistent and unremarked as a shadow, followed each resident through the corridors of Greyleigh. The sin could be anything: too little diligence, too much pride, a stain on one's tunic, a word mispronounced. The girls were taught obedience, not reason. They found it hard to distinguish a small fault from a great one. So one was equally careful in penmanship and in prayer. Dame Agatha, that black-eyed, hawk-nosed angel of judgment might swoop down at any moment.

For Ingrid, the world of guilt was at least a world of order. One could avoid punishment by being perfect, and she managed to mimic perfection convincingly. To worldly sensibilities, she might have appeared grotesque: this little girl with the solemn face and ramrod posture, a child who never giggled, who could kneel for hours without fidgeting and knew the scriptures by heart. But in the convent this freakish behavior was expected of children, and Ingrid's conformity was held up as proof that the expectation was not unfair. Her rejection by other children had been assured.

She would approach a conspiring huddle of girls and find that their whispering stopped as soon as they noticed her. They would greet her stiffly, all the while smirking at each other. She saw these glances—she was meant to. She would stand there in an agony of embarrassment, knowing they were waiting for her to leave so that they could resume their secrets. "I'm sorry," she would stammer, "I must go study my Latin now." Then she would blush, realizing that she had made things worse, for she was already the best student in Latin. Their giggles were like knives in her retreating back, and she would straighten her spine to conceal her shame. "Saint Ingrid the Stuck-up" they called her, when they thought she was out of earshot.

It would not have occurred to her to feel sorry for herself, for she knew that she was exceedingly blessed in everything but friendship. Her mind was a reservoir that caught learning like rain. Her steady hand produced penmanship of great elegance, and her steady will kept her upright through all the canonical hours. She was the favorite of Dame Agatha, who called her into rooms of glittering adult strangers to recite, to answer tricky questions of theology, to bow her head modestly as they praised the accomplishments that came to her without effort.

At a loss for what to do during recreation, when no one would play with her, Ingrid had begun to follow the infirmarian on her rounds. Sister Phillippa (or Sister Pipp, as she liked to be called) was plump, with a gap between her front teeth, frowsy hair that frequently transgressed the boundary of her wimple and eyelashes so pale they were invisible unless one looked close. Her skin turned very pink when she went out in the sun or laughed. Often she laughed at Ingrid, always at moments when the child felt most holy or obedient or helpful. What pleased or impressed other adults seemed, at best, to amuse the infirmarian. The converse was also true. Ingrid had committed the only crime of her childhood in the herbarium and it had gone unpunished.

She had been eight, maybe nine. The work table that now was level with her waist had been at shoulder height and she had used a high stool to reach it. There she dissected a dead mouse she had found in the kitchen. First she chopped off the head, legs and tail with the kind of good clean whacks that Sister Maude, the cellarer, employed beheading fish. She had not known how to proceed with the torso, and her clumsy slice down the middle had left her with a mash of slimy, undifferentiated tissue and fur. When the infirmarian came in and discovered the carnage, Ingrid was already in tears, not from fear of punishment, but from grief over the pathetic mutilated pieces that would yield no meaning to her butchering investigation. She felt irredeemably clumsy and unworthy, looking at the tiny head with its eyes smaller than rosary beads, the pinprick nostrils on its pink snout, and toes as fine as eyelashes.

Sister Pipp had not reproached her. Instead she helped Ingrid wrap the dismembered creature in a cloth and bury it in the herb garden. "An honorable end for the humble mouse," she pronounced. "First he teaches you how dissection is *not* done, and then he gives his body to the soil, where it will nourish insects and plants." She made the sign of the cross over the little grave and rose from her knees with a groan of effort. "I'm getting old," she declared, as if noticing for the first time. "Someday I shall be too old for this work, and a younger nun will have to replace me. Who knows? Maybe it will be you."

That was how Ingrid's apprenticeship began.

Sister Pipp taught her that God never created an ailment without also creating its cure and that it was the task of humankind to seek out these remedies. Sometimes God left broad hints, such as the heart-shaped leaves of the wild pansy, which were used in a cardiac tonic, or the nodules on the roots of the lesser celandine, which resembled the hemorrhoids that plant was so effective in curing. Other clues were more subtle: the pimpernel's petals closing at dusk, like the eyes, whose ills it was used to treat. Adder's-tongue relieved indigestion because the fern was ruled by the moon, and the moon was ruled by the sign of Cancer, and the sign of Cancer ruled the alimentary system.

She began to accompany Sister Pipp on her foraging expeditions. Together they browsed the pasture for cowslip, eyebright, toadflax and yarrow, poked in hedges for foxglove, feverfew and thistle. The marshland at the bottom of the pasture, near the river, yielded comfrey, bog myrtle and meadowsweet, and on the riverbank were horsetail and loosestrife, skullcap and watercress. Sometimes they ventured into the woods, which were forbidden to inhabitants of Greyleigh—adults and children alike—for the forest had never been, and could never be, converted to Christianity. Ingrid stayed close to her teacher then, frightened by the huge spiderwebs with their drying victims and by the green-black shade that seemed to lure her deep into the web of the forest itself, there to be caught forever in the chaotic net of roots and vines. Sister Pipp warned her away from a circle of toadstools that she called a fairy ring. ("If you step inside, you won't be able to get out unless someone breaks the enchantment for you—which *I* certainly won't.") It made her shudder. But the greatest wonders were to be found in the woods as well: wild raspberries which they munched while harvesting the leaves, velvet mosses, mushrooms and the wee, perfect bells of lily of the valley.

After gathering the herbs Ingrid sketched them for her medical manual. Each plant had to be depicted at all stages of its annual cycle, and these drawings were accompanied by rather gruesome renderings of the herb's application to suppurating wounds, projectile vomiting and the like.

Then there was the work of drying, crushing, grinding, steeping, straining and decanting—which Ingrid enjoyed as much as their excursions. The medicines were arrayed in earthenware jars, identical and inscrutable as nuns until they were uncorked. Then how magical the hidden textures, the murky colors, the smells like the perfumes of angels and demons! Even the names were magic, music: betony, barberry, bistort and borage; agrimony, fumitory, tansy and twitch; henbane, vervain, heartsease and horehound; cowslip, coltsfoot, clubmoss and dodder; wormwood, mugwort, figwort and feverfew; hyssop, honeysuckle, fenugreek and rue.

Not all of her training was so idyllic, for these medicines were applied to living—and dying—patients, and she was expected to give equal attention to the varieties of human excreta. Sister Pipp maintained that diagnosis was the work of all five senses and that no physician who would hesitate to inhale a patient's breath or taste a patient's skin in quest of information could hope to succeed. There was plain hard work as well: beds to make, trays to prepare, baths to give and endless laundry.

The most common surgical procedure at Greyleigh was phlebotomy. Each nun was bled several times a year on dates appropriate to her personal horoscope. Most of them looked forward to it as a sort of holiday, for they were allowed to eat meat, linger in bed and enjoy hot baths until their strength returned. This was the first surgery Ingrid learned. Sister Pipp rolled up her sleeve and presented her own rosy freckled arm for the apprentice to practice on. Biting her lip in concentration, her hand quivering, Ingrid began her incision, only to be stopped by a ghastly scream. She looked up, horrified, already determined never, never to wield a scalpel again—looked up to confront Sister Pipp's manic, gap-toothed laughter. The infirmarian poured them both a stiff cordial and the operation was attempted again. When Ingrid's confidence fell short, the cups were refilled, and before long both of the woman's arms were crosshatched, and the claret jug was empty. Then Sister Pipp, the ruddiness of whose countenance was not at all impaired by her heroic sacrifice of blood, instructed Ingrid to open her own vein. "Won't hurt a bit," she promised, and it hadn't.

Ingrid was in the herbarium when Jack's singing began. She could hear it through the open window. It was astonishing: so intricate compared with plainsong, and so loud! The sun, too, was coming through the window, throwing a yellow trapezoid across her worktable. Somehow the warmth of his voice and the warmth of the sun seemed to her the same, so that she might have described his voice as yellow and the sun as loud. She looked up and saw that the treetops were swaying to the rhythm of his lute and her arm, working the pestle, moved to it as well. He was not imposing a rhythm, only making audible one that was always there, unnoticed by her until now. A thrill like holiness ran through her. She saw how the trees grew toward the sun and bent to the wind with a kind of devotion though they did not know it or will it or even feel it, and the same fervor swelled the man's voice—a goodness irrelevant to the state of his conscience. And it was in the motion of her arm, and nothing she could think or will could increase or diminish it. She did not think this in so many words, but swayed to it like the treetops, flushed with it as with the sun.

The patients in the next room would be able to hear the singing. She was glad, particularly for Sister Elizabeth, who suffered from acedia. Or, one might say, was *guilty* of it, for, strictly speaking, this deadly combination of melancholy and ennui, of gloom and sloth and irritation, was a sin. Awakened by the bell for matins or prime, the sufferer could see no reason to begin a day identical in every respect to the one that had gone before and the one that would follow. She must exert herself then and begin it nevertheless, must swim vigorously through the succeeding hours to escape the undertow of futility, lest she drown in despair. Sister Elizabeth's case was severe: Ingrid had bled her, given her meat, sweets, tonics, even flowers, and the woman just stared at the wall.

But no one could remain indifferent to Jack. This morning she herself had awoken with a succulent feeling of expectation, as if it were Easter. The recollection of their difficult visitor dawned with the sun. When she brought him his midday meal, he complained that the food was inedible, but he had had a way of eating it that gave *her* an appetite—he was all strong, carnivorous teeth and greasy lips, and she had thought suddenly, oddly, "This is what it is to eat." When he scratched, it was with such ardor that she found herself wondering why they did not all scratch more often. Even when he suffered, his robust complaints were like a celebration.

Once, when she and Sister Pipp were gathering nettles, Ingrid had been badly stung. Sister Pipp tore off a large dock leaf that grew nearby and rubbed away the sting. "God always plants the antidote near the poison," she explained.

Jack was the natural antidote to acedia.

Five

Admittedly, his selection of *Chanson de la Nonne* was tactless. The gist
of it in English was:

> The nun is complaining
> Her tears are down raining,
> She sobbeth and she sigheth
> To her sisters she crieth
> Misery me!
> O what can be worse
> than this life that I dree
> When naughty and lovelorn and
> Wanton I be?
> All night long I unwillingly wake
> How gladly a lad in mine arms would I take!

And the verses got bawdier after that. Between them a chorus
of *hey nonny la's* showed off his vocal nimbleness and range to particular
advantage, but mischief had been his motive in choosing it.

He had decided he might as well cheer up. No matter how
much he drank, he would not be able to remain asleep for the rest of
his convalescence. And it was only a matter of time, he was convinced,
before the saint took pity and sought him out.

It could be worse: He could be recuperating in a monastery. At
least twenty women lived in this house as well as an indeterminate
number of students: sweet young things already aflutter with curiosity
about the troubadour locked in the infirmary. One would be clever
enough to procure a key and then the days would pass quickly.

Since he was expecting visitors, he made an effort to look

presentable. He pulled a wrinkled linen shirt from his saddlebag. He could not get his hosen on over the bandages, but the shirt was cut large and fell halfway to his knees. Patiently he worked the tangles out of his sleep-matted curls and smoothed his close-cropped beard. He used his knife to clean the dirt from under his nails.

The man was not really handsome. His features were too coarse, particularly his large imprecise mouth, and his lithe body lacked mass. Nevertheless, he was able to wrap the illusion of beauty around himself like a cloak and herd the aimless longings of women into its folds.

And there was his voice. If a lion could sing, it would sing like Jack: in a lusty tenor with a growl in it to raise the down on ladies' arms. Unleash it in these hushed corridors, and it was sure to come back with its lamb.

He held the lute's smooth belly close to his own and coaxed each string to pitch with a lover's patience. When it was tuned to his satisfaction, he struck an assertive chord. He threw back his head for joy as he strummed the chord again, then followed it with a shimmering arpeggio.

He was on the last verse when the door was flung open. The ugly abbess stood on the threshold. "Kindly remember that this is a house of silence and of prayer!" Her fists were clenched at her sides and she squeezed the words through her pinched mouth like acid from an eyedropper.

"I beg your pardon, madam." He bowed his head with exaggerated courtesy. "It has always been my custom to repay hospitality with song and I regret that my song does not please."

"Our hospitality is given in the name of Christ and the proper repayment is prayer," she said stiffly. "It is for this that you were struck down at our gate, that you might repent of your pagan lusts, not celebrate them at the top of your voice!"

He was flattered by the part about pagan lusts. Could he extend his lust to her, he wondered. Twould be a mercy. It was Jack's conviction that a maidenhead left too long in place poisoned a woman's blood. But this one was so far gone that even his magnanimous sexual imagination fell short.

He bowed a second time. "Thank you, madam, for instructing me in this matter. I shall repent forthwith."

"See that you do. We shall pray for you." She delivered this last as if it were a curse on the next twenty generations of his descendants, then turned on her heel.

He called out to her. "Good lady, your dismay at having me for a guest is exceeded only by my dismay at being that guest. Nay— a moment, please." He held up his hand to halt her incensed retreat. "What I mean to say is that our interest in my speedy recovery is mutual, *n'est-ce pas?*"

"It would be unchristian for us to wish you long suffering," she replied.

"Precisely," he agreed, a lawyer now, leading his hostile witness. "Therefore I am confident that you will grant my request."

She waited for him to come to the point.

"Send me the saint," he concluded triumphantly. "Have her work a miracle."

For a moment she looked dumbfounded. Then a subtle smile— secret, ironic and unfriendly—altered her tense features. She shook her head as if amazed that this victory had been dropped in her lap. "Sir, you are even more of a fool than you look."

As a matter of fact, Agatha was not a virgin, though Jack had been right about her disposition toward members of his gender. The only surviving child of the earl of Winderton, she had been heiress to a considerable chunk of Oxfordshire. But her twenty-third birthday found her unwed and with little inclination to change her condition. She was plain, with a prominent nose, thin lips and a bad complexion, and there was nothing in her equally daunting character to distract a man from her appearance. Still, her father could not die without somehow disposing of his daughter and his fortune. His last will bestowed both on Roger Fleming, the son of his best friend.

Never had a marriage of convenience proved more inconvenient to the participants. Five years her junior, the groom was handsome, rowdy and affable. Drinking, hunting and whoring appeared to be his only interests, and Agatha suspected he was illiterate, for he would sign documents concerning the management of their lands brusquely, without reading them. This did not entirely displease her, for she considered the Winderton portion of their estate to be rightfully hers and was glad to channel her formidable energies into its administration. Nor was she displeased when the bailiff came to her, cap in hand, "meaning no disrespect to his lordship," to question one of Roger's incompetent orders. She was not at all offended, she assured him. After all, Lord Fleming had more weighty matters on his mind than the collection of rents, the low yields that year due to the unseasonable cold and the consequent destitution of some of their tenants. These trivial matters were more properly the concern of the sportsman's wife, and she urged the bailiff to come to her directly whenever he felt the need.

For the first year after the obligatory consummation of their marriage, Roger left her alone: He was content to find his pleasure elsewhere. Agatha had not cared where, not until tenants began to grumble that he was corrupting their sisters and daughters. Her keen sense of *noblesse oblige* was offended by this, and she took him to task.

"Well then, Agatha," he said, with an amiability that made her feel shrill, "be a wife to me." Something in his gaze made her shy from it. He laughed. "Don't look so scared."

"Afraid of *you*? You flatter yourself, Roger."

"Not afraid?" He sprang to his feet and began to bark at her. "Woof!"

She flinched but held her ground. "Don't be absurd."

"*Woof!*" He was all around her ears. "*Woof, woof, woof!*"

Her hands flailed, swatting ineffectually at him. He took this for encouragement. "*Grrrrrrr! Woof, woof, woof!*"

"Roger, for heaven's sake, stop this."

"Scared?"

"No."

"Good, then," he chuckled. "Off we go to bed."

Sometimes she bolted the door to her bedroom, but he made such a row threatening to break it down that she feared the servants would overhear, and she ended up admitting him, night after night. He smelled of horses, ale and sometimes of other women, and he took her crudely, folding her into positions which she found obscene and humiliating. She bore it with clenched teeth, refusing him the satisfaction of a struggle. One night, though, a spasm rocked her hips upward against him and unthinkingly she had clutched him, as if for balance. A genial smile broke across his face. "Aye, girl, there you go!" he had exclaimed, not unkindly, as he slapped her cheerfully on the flank.

She had seen him make the same gesture with his favorite horse. It could not be forgiven. As soon as he rode out the next morning, she packed a bag and went off to take refuge in the convent.

She had not supposed that Roger would regret the loss of her. But Church law forbade his remarrying as long as she lived. Her departure deprived him not only of a wife but of an heir. So Fleming and his ruffian friends stormed the convent, to the delicious terror of its inhabitants. Agatha sped to the chapel, and her husband, who had not hesitated to break into the nunnery, was not so reckless as to violate the sanctuary itself. He and his men settled themselves outside the door and waited, for she could not remain inside forever. Agatha was equally determined. It looked as if the siege would go on for days. Luckily she had had the foresight to bring with her the deed to the Winderton portion of their estate, which Roger, in his mindless illiteracy, had signed over to her. She used this to bargain for his promise to withdraw and never set foot in the nunnery again.

Greyleigh had been quite a different place then: financially sound but spiritually bankrupt. Although the divine office was still recited, most of the nuns had learned the Latin by rote and did not understand what they were saying. The misericord, where the sick were fed the red meat from which the healthy were expected to abstain, had come into such common use that the main refectory was closed. The nuns wore whatever clothes their families were generous enough to provide, and most families were generous indeed to judge from the satins, brocades and furs on display. Many of the nuns kept small dogs, even bringing them into the chapel, where their yelping drowned out the listless chanting of the psalms.

Agatha hated it. The triviality, the pointlessness of her days filled her with fury. Her aristocratic nature would not permit the outlet others found in complaining and bickering clique against clique. Though different factions courted her at first (for the drama that attended her arrival had made her a sort of celebrity), she snubbed them all.

Her misery was the more acute because she longed to live by the Benedictine rule. She saw in it not a static code of law, but a road map for a journey of the soul. Its single theme was obedience, not as a guarantee of order, but as a liberation from self-will. Fight the rule and monastic life would be an endless series of privations, thwarted preferences. Surrender, and the walls would no longer confine; the convent would be an inexhaustible ocean of silence, of peace. With every surrender, the soul would become emptier and into that emptiness God would rush. This was the glory that the nuns had given up in exchange for gossip, leisure and baubles.

Agatha might have lived out the rest of her days in lonely frustration if it had not been for the scandal of '27. In the spring of that year, Sister Alyce Rowse was brought to bed of a healthy baby girl, sired by the chaplain, Osbert Gray. The unfortunate Alyce was not Gray's only conquest. It was rumored that the abbess herself had dallied with him. The affair was too conspicuous to be covered up, and word reached the bishop, who was obliged to intervene.

He interviewed each nun in private, listening wearily to the usual jealousies and petty grievances, gaining overwhelming confirmation of the rumors he had hoped were exaggerated. He had been impressed with Agatha, for her account of conditions was scathing yet fair, precisely observed and free from vindictiveness. One month after he left Greyleigh, he wrote to inform the residents that their abbess was being demoted and Agatha Fleming appointed in her place.

Her reforms were uncompromising. The misericord was closed and vegetarian meals served to all in the silence of the refectory. Partitions that had subdivided the dorter into private rooms were torn down. Plain habits were woven for each sister and all other garments given to the poor. Dogs were banished. Latecomers to the chapel were punished. The randy Osbert Gray was evicted, and a doddering old priest imported once a week for mass.

Whatever the spiritual effects of all this, the financial consequences were devastating. Nearly half the residents applied to other houses, taking their endowments with them. The departures meant a staggering loss of revenue, and privately the bishop tried to persuade

Agatha to moderate her zeal. But he could do little to curtail her formally when everything she did had been prescribed by the founder of her order.

Those who stayed fell into two categories: the few who had become nuns because of a genuine vocation, and the many who had nowhere else to go. They were the disinherited and the dowerless, the ugly and the half-witted, widows and others, like herself, escaping intolerable marriages. She gathered this small band around her in the chapel like the ragged survivors of a shipwreck and tried to inspire them.

She told the nuns that God had chosen them to revive the dying Benedictine ideal, that without them it would vanish forever from the earth. "You may lament the circumstances that brought you here," she said. "You may feel ill-used by men or by nature or by fate. But you should thank God every moment of every day for that apparent misfortune. God has marked you with it, marked you as his own. You are one of twenty women—'mere women' some will say— who, in the face of obstacles that would daunt brave men, will reinstate the Benedictine way of life. A way of life more rigorous, more holy, more rewarding than any that has ever existed. Therefore rejoice that you have no husband. Rejoice that you have no wealth. Blessed are you who are rejected of men, for you shall inherit the kingdom of God right here in this forgotten corner of Oxfordshire!"

Speeches like that came easily to her in those early years, and with them she had managed to win the loyalty and cooperation of most of her sisters. Yet she knew that none of them really understood the rule. They wanted to please her, or at least to avoid her displeasure, and they did not see that she was merely the instrument of their own salvation. Greyleigh had the form of Benedict's vision, but she doubted it had the spirit. She reproached herself for thinking it, but the fact was that they were dull. Every last one of them. It seemed to her a bitter irony: She was the one woman in the convent who knew where the rugged journey of obedience might lead her; and she was the one woman there who could not undertake it, who instead must be obeyed.

In time she lost her ardor. Even in the chapel, her mind was tethered to administrative concerns. But now there was Ingrid. Ingrid was the vindication of all her efforts. Agatha had been the gardener, cultivating the thorny vine of discipline; Ingrid was the flower that vine had at last produced.

Six

Hour followed identical hour. Jack's hungry senses grasped at what few sounds there were: the creak of a well that seemed to be right below his window, splashes of used wash water being thrown out the kitchen door. For a short time in the afternoon there had been the squeals of children liberated from their studies. And then the bell that called them back and a sharp woman's voice scolding stragglers.

Mostly there was the chanting. It did not so much break the silence as frame it, emphasize it. Surely God himself must crave a respite from this incessant praise!

The psalms they sang were once shrieked in the desert by prophets hoarse with longing and despair. Born of dry heat, they must have torn the plains, stirring the dust with their accusation and their praise. Now, sung in soft and circumspect Latin in this dark and humid land, they cloyed and dripped like the moisture on the convent's gray walls. Songs of longing still, but sedate, melancholy.

The sound reminded Jack of eternity. And nothing terrified him like eternity. It was not that he feared his damnation (which he had pretty much assured). No, he dreaded heaven as much as hell, for he imagined both to have a bleak, never-ending sameness, a numbing lack of contrast, like Greyleigh. While most of his contemporaries conceived of life as a brief ordeal that tried one's fitness for eternal bliss, Jack saw it as a short-lived diversion before damnation to eternal boredom, a sweet moment of significance before a man was dwarfed and crushed by bullying infinity. As he lay drifting in and out of dreamless sleep, he felt as if he had died already and welcomed the occasional throbbing of his leg, which told him he had not.

By evening he was desolate, and he rejoiced at Ingrid's knock, followed by the scraping key. She greeted him kindly, but with more reserve than before, not looking at him as she placed the supper tray across his thighs. He could tell that she meant to leave quickly.

"Sit with me awhile," he pleaded. "You can't imagine how lonely it is here."

She looked perplexed, as if she really could not imagine this. "Do you not pray?"

"Not much."

"You should do. No one is alone in the presence of God."

"If so, he's a jolly dull companion."

She seemed a little worried by this. "I will pray for you since you do not pray for yourself."

He shrugged. "As you wish. But you'd do my soul more good if you would just pull over that stool and keep me company."

"I'm sorry. We must keep the silence."

"For the love of God, woman, where is your charity? I lie abed in dreary silence for hour upon hour, my poor weak mind at the mercy of Satan's wiles—and now you would deny me the solace of a few moments conversation with one of God's own!"

Ingrid sat down warily and pretended to study her interlaced fingers. *The abbess has warned her against me,* he thought.

"Your superior does not like my music."

"Please do not be offended. Secular music is forbidden to us."

"You do not like it either?"

"No. I mean, I found myself quite distracted by it, and this makes me understand why it is forbidden."

Jack laughed with real pleasure. "I'll take that as a compliment."

He turned his attention to the supper tray. Half a loaf of tough bread, a morsel of hard cheese and some rather nice figs. He ate the figs first.

"Your superior also seems to think that I am lucky to have broken my leg," he said as he smacked on the fruit. "A peculiar notion of good fortune, wouldn't you say? She told me that this was the strategy God had used to wrest my soul from the clutches of the Evil One."

"Sometimes grace comes in unexpected, even unwelcome forms," she pointed out.

He tore into the bread. "Do you not find it revolting to think that God and Satan fight over our souls like two dogs over a scrap of meat?"

She looked both vague and startled, like a child who has been awakened in the middle of the night. And then she seemed to withdraw from him, her eyes lowered, her fingers fretting over the weave of her apron. He studied her frankly, fascinated that a woman could come so close to beauty and yet miss, miss completely. He admired her strong, chiseled chin, her straight nose and serene gray eyes. Yet the way her features were set, firm and serious against her pale, lackluster skin, spoke of austerity, brittle virtue.

"You know what you look like? You look like one of those statues in the cloister." Suddenly it was obvious. The abbess was right: He was a fool. "It's you, isn't it! You are the saint they speak of."

If he had any doubts, her evident discomfort dispelled them. She chose her words carefully. "There are rumors about me. I think they are mistaken."

"Then you do not believe you are a saint?"

"No more than you believe it."

The directness of this response took him aback. She's cleverer than she lets on, he thought. "What makes you think I do not believe it?"

"Would you talk to me this way if you did?"

"I might. I have a sacrilegious nature." He ran his tongue over his teeth, getting rid of the sticky cheese and figs. "Do you really work miracles?"

"God works miracles."

"You know what I mean."

She sighed. "They are attributed to me."

"You answer like a lawyer." Or like a criminal, he thought. "Are you just being modest?" He gave her a penetrating look. Nay, it was not only modesty. She had a secret.

"What I really want to know, you see, is why, if you can work miracles, you won't work one for me." He said this in an offhand, half-jesting way, and he himself was not sure how seriously he meant it. But Ingrid answered in earnest.

"You don't understand what you are asking for."

"Does it cost you so much, then?"

She shook her head. "It isn't that. It would cost *you*. You do not really want God to touch you, and that is why he keeps his distance. Don't you see? It is out of deference to you."

This was sweetly said. He wondered later why he responded with such asperity. " 'Tis a very civilized God you have around here," he said. "But then I suppose the abbess keeps him in his place."

That night Ingrid shunned her bed and kept a vigil in the chapel. She felt guilty of sins she didn't even know the names of. The most obvious was her dishonesty with Dame Agatha. Fuming on the threshold of the herbarium, the abbess, who had come straight from Jack's room, had said, "You'll be relieved to know I've put an end to that iniquitous bawling." Ingrid had dropped to her knees, her head bowed and her fist poised over her breast in the stylized gesture of repentance that all the nuns observed when being rebuked. "I should have stopped it myself," she murmured.

"Yes, well, never mind," the abbess excused her. "I can see why you were afraid to. I'm sorry you have to be exposed to such blasphemy at all."

Ingrid had let her leave without disclosing the real fault: She had been enjoying the song. For that sin she would fast all the next day.

It had not always been like this. For years she had confessed even undetected sins and every flicker of temptation. Now she was afraid. It was a small fault, maybe—liking the music—but potentially deadly, like the single dropped stitch that could unravel an entire knitted stocking. The trouble seemed to be that she lacked a sense of right and wrong. Obedient she could be—she was the very perfection of obedience. But left to her own conscience, often as not she would err. She had taken care to learn every word of the Benedictine rule, every statute of canon law, and in most situations she got by. But when something arose that the Church Fathers had not foreseen, she could not, like Dame Agatha, reason her way to a moral conclusion. Her nature was unreliable. She feared it was corrupt in some basic way. The newest and most persuasive evidence of this was that she liked not only the man's music, but the man himself.

She had heard of imbeciles who could add twenty figures in their heads before you could blink an eye, and her healing powers struck her the same way, as some freak talent bestowed on a moral idiot. The exercise of it brought her joy—how could it not? But she knew that God had not meant to imply by his use of her that she was a saint. She was like a conduit through which his grace flowed, and when it poured into the people she touched, there was not a drop left inside her.

Since all the fuss had started the older nuns deferred to her. Even Dame Agatha hesitated to correct her. If she protested, "I am not worthy," they took this as evidence of saintly humility. That was what saints were supposed to say—"I am not worthy"—and Ingrid did not know what tone to take to convey that she really was unworthy. There seemed to be no choice left open any more but to conceal her faults as best she could and pray for the grace to live up to her inflated reputation. Sometimes she wondered what they would do when they realized their mistake.

Seven

The accounts were keeping Dame Agatha up late again. As usual, there was not enough money to get them through the winter. She would probably end up writing the king again to seek a reduction in taxes. And the entire clip of wool would have to be sold, with none held back to clothe her nuns. They could live with fraying hems and threadbare elbows for one more year. The glazing of the cloister windows would have to be put off again as well. The repair of the guesthouse roof could not wait though: more of it was falling in with every rain. Not that she wasn't glad of the excuse to turn dignitaries away. But that could not go on forever.

Maybe a papal indulgence could be granted to laymen who donated their labor to the reconstruction. She was sure the bishop would be only too happy to intercede for her. On his brief and rare visitations his only comments concerned the poor quality of the food and lodgings. "Let me send you some hangings, Agatha, to cut the drafts. It's no wonder no one sends his daughters here—the place is like a dungeon." She would shake off the arm he had draped around her shoulder and tell him to send books instead, for the meager library was the convent's true disgrace. "No daughters, no money," he would remind her. "You're going to starve this last stronghold of the Benedictine ideal right out of existence." She could not miss the irony in his smile.

But they had not starved. The convent was like the gnarled trees that live on wind-lashed cliffs: stunted, hideous, twisted inward, but indestructible. It was a place where women could carry themselves without vanity, a place where the tongue, freed from frivolous chatter, could rest, where eyes did not flirt and could see plainly. The body was imprisoned so that the soul might adventure. Dreary, dilapidated and forbidding, the convent was nevertheless a palace for aristocrats of the spirit.

Bishop Locke had written again this week to nag her about Ingrid. Agatha had promised two years ago, when it seemed the time would never come, that her famous novice would resume public life soon after she took final vows. Her consecration had been in August, and petitions for her help arrived almost daily, both at Greyleigh and at the bishopric in Lincoln. There was no escaping it: Ingrid was an adult now and could no longer take a child's refuge from God's demands on her.

Word of Ingrid's first miracle—the Ladbrook healing—had traveled fast, luring an endless procession of ragbound suppliants to the gate. They could not be received on a daily basis without compromising the peace of the cloister, so Agatha had decreed that

Ingrid would bestow a general blessing on Pentecost and at scheduled intervals thereafter. It had seemed like a practical solution at the time. But the event was more chaotic than she could ever have anticipated. Days in advance, vendors began arriving, camping just beyond the gate. Even in the cloister they could be heard hawking their wares: meat pies and ale, cakes and dried fruits, slivers of the true cross and nail parings of the Virgin. Pilgrims, beggars and invalids camped alongside them, and amid all the laughing and talking, singing and squabbling, one could hear racking coughs and low moans.

As if that weren't trial enough, every clergyman in the Midlands had wanted to share in the glory of Ingrid's celebrity, and the house was full to bursting with bishops and their bejeweled entourages. Locke had even taken the precaution of bringing his own cook. The aroma of roasting meat had filled Dame Agatha's vegetarian house, arousing no little resentment among its fasting residents.

Ingrid had been a few months shy of sixteen—still growing, and too young to fast as she had for an entire week. Too young to be subjected to sights which Agatha herself could hardly endure. When the gate was opened on Pentecost, all the misery on earth seemed to pour in. The chapel, usually so cool and bare, heaved and oozed and stank of infection and decay. By some curious intuition about the etiquette of such situations, people exposed wounds and deformities normally hidden, as if for a physician. Stumps of limbs, empty eye sockets, festering sores, boils, tumors, rashes, ulcerations, blisters, scars and all manner of disfigurement. Agatha had been moved to see the way Ingrid touched without squeamishness, the soft way she asked each person about his troubles, her sweet attention to the answers. As the procession wore on, she swayed slightly and her voice grew hoarse. At one point she turned to the bishop, who stood at her side, and whispered, "I'm so cold . . ." but when a cloak was brought for her she seemed not to notice, allowing it to slip from her shoulders as soon as it was placed there.

She had blessed nearly everyone when a legless man approached, dragging his trunk down the aisle with thick, over-developed arms, a look of elation on his simple face. Though his progress was faster than one would have imagined, and seemed to cause him no embarrassment, the sound of his belly sliding over the floor was hard for others to bear. Ingrid looked troubled, and he smiled cheerfully at her, as if to reassure her. Returning his smile, she seemed to have decided to walk toward him. But as soon as she took a step forward, she turned back toward the bishop with an odd, questioning look. Her hand flew up toward his brocade sleeve, then wavered as if lost. She collapsed, unconscious, on the chapel floor.

For the better part of a fortnight she was delirious. The whole convent shuddered at her screams. In her lucid moments she beckoned Agatha close to her cracked lips and demanded in what was left of her voice to know the fate of each person she had blessed. Agatha did her best to find out. As was always the case with miracles, some cures were complete and final, others partial or temporary. The percentage of cures was better than at Canterbury—most impressive, Agatha thought—and of those who remained afflicted none complained. But Ingrid would sob for hours over her failures.

All during that time, as Agatha kept vigil over the girl's fever-racked body, she chastised herself. If Ingrid had died, no amount of penance could have expiated her guilt. She could not forget the look of incredulity on Ingrid's face when she first learned what was being planned for Pentecost. "God forgive me if I have misled even you!" the girl had said. "I am no saint. Madam, you know that I am not."

"Whether or not you are a saint, it appears God has chosen you as his instrument."

But Ingrid had become agitated. She sank to her knees, as if trying to offset with the humility of her posture the defiance of her words. "No, no, he has not!" she insisted. "I *know* that he has not! I did nothing to make Lady Ladbrook walk. I was just in the room. You will see, I will fail. God will strike me down for my presumption. He will strike me down!"

Agatha had known a moment's anxiety. What if Ingrid was right? There was potential for scandal. But as soon as she perceived her own hesitation, she knew that she must overcome it. There was no worse failing to her than cowardice. By then the child was doubled over, sobbing, clinging to the hem of her gown and saying, "Don't make me do it! Please don't make me do it!" as if pleading for her life. A stone would have wept in sympathy. Agatha was made of something harder than stone.

"Ingrid, get up," she had said. "Stand up straight and stop that shameful carrying on."

"Madam, *please* . . ."

"Stop it, I say. You are thinking only of yourself and how people regard you. If you are humiliated on Pentecost, so be it. It is of no consequence. God has asked this of you and you must do it. Try to think of the people who need your help."

Was that so wrong? Ingrid had pulled herself together. She had done penance for her defiance and never again spoke of her fear. Her bearing, that Pentecost, would have done a queen proud. And many were healed. Surely it had been right to demand that best of her.

No one who saw her the day her father brought her could have guessed what Ingrid would become. A skinny weed of a girl, hair in her eyes, thumb in her mouth. Agatha had reached out to pat her head and the child had flinched. When she glanced at Fairfax he looked down at his shifting feet, shamefaced, and Agatha had seen how it was with them. He promised to visit his daughter at Michaelmas, but she could tell from the size of his gift to them that he meant never to return. Ingrid had known it too, and wept dirty tears.

One could see her uncommon intelligence in the eyes which peered out through that veil of stringy hair—alert, watchful, wary. Agatha had mistaken this look of cunning for guilt until close surveillance failed to uncover any misbehavior. Then she attributed it to fear. She took care never to threaten or beat the child, and indeed, Ingrid's sensitive conscience made punishment redundant. In time the girl stopped cringing, learned to stand up straight and carry herself with dignity. But even now that wary look sometimes reappeared. It had flicked across her face this afternoon in the herbarium.

Agatha sighed. What did it matter, really, these scars that all of them bore? Phillippa had fussed over it. "The child knows the *Summa* by heart, but she hasn't the first idea of how to play! Can't you see how lonely she is?"

Of course she had seen. But what did it matter? It was in Ingrid's nature to be lonely, as it was in her own nature. The soul was ageless, it knew no childhood. "If Ingrid dies tomorrow, she will not meet her maker in a little girl's body." That had been her reply to Phillippa. The infirmarian had gone all red in the face from self-righteousness and told her she was heartless. That was what they all thought. What did it matter? Ingrid was a saint. It was that greatness in her that Agatha had nurtured. That and only that. Phillippa had gotten through her life relying on her "tonics." But all the stinking tisanes and cordials and poultices she could invent were useless, ludicrous when applied to Ingrid's sort of pain. Let the girl once discover her own weakness and she would find it fathomless. Ingrid would be a saint, or she would be a suicide: There was no middle course open to her.

Agatha sank back in her chair and pressed her fingers to her throbbing temples. Phillippa had been dead three years—what was the point of this heated mental argument? She should get some sleep. Too late now, really. Almost time for matins. At least she could lie down. Wearily she closed the account book, wiped clean her quill and blew out the lamp.

Ingrid was still up—she could feel it. Often the girl kept a vigil in the chapel after the others went to sleep. Agatha would open the great door a crack and watch her there, her long body prone on the floor, her shoulders shaking with inaudible sobs. That kind of emotion was unknown to the abbess, who loved God with a kind of blood loyalty: noble to sovereign. She watched it with a mixture of awe, parental pride and faint distaste. Was this what mothers felt for their grown children? She had presided over nearly every moment of that girl's life for thirteen years, only to find that, finally, the results were inscrutable.

Eight

They must have known what they were doing when they deprived him of his music; they must have known that alone and in silence the man he had constructed would fragment and scatter to the winds. It was others who made him Jacques Brigand des Cœurs. Without their eyes to make him handsome, their ears to hear his voice and their voices to pronounce him marvelous, he was a nameless, faceless, aching animal. This is what they were plotting—to reduce him to abject sniveling, and then to smother him in the fat sweaty bosom of Our Holy Mother the Church.

But his resources were greater than they imagined. He would stave off the temptation to piety with a litany of curses. He would offer novenas of erotic fantasy. He would guard his soul with the reliving of good memories. Six weeks was not an eternity, however long an hour might seem to be.

Over and over he told himself his life story, beginning in the great rolling sentences of an epic and then, because he was feverish and could not concentrate, losing the meter or the rhyme or the sense and having to start over. Before long he would sleep, dream, twist the blankets and make them clammy, throw them off and wake from the chill, only to begin the tale again, indifferent to the boredom of the walls and the furniture, the captive boredom of the long-suffering, paint-splattered Jesus.

Jack was born a peasant's son, doomed to work the land. A hero to his oxen, an ox to his careworn wife. Bound to the soil, bound to days of toil, but born for the outlaw's life. Not for Jack the six days of filth, the well-scrubbed, humble Sunday. Not for Jack the toil and the envy—the bitter envy. Let them envy him! He the free man—outside the laws of men, outside the laws of God, sworn only to

39

defend the laws of love . . . Was that how it went? Jack was born a plowman's son, doomed to work the land. Bound to the soil, to a life of toil. Bound to the lord, the cruel, cruel lord who . . . the cruel, cruel . . . thief of hearts, the bandit of beauty, the pirate of tears . . . ah, the tears of women, the sighs, the moans, the tears of women like laughter in the face of indifferent . . .

He was singing for a huge crowd, resplendent in gold and scarlet silk. His voice slid over the curves of the sweetest melody he had ever composed. The ladies were dewy and swayed toward him. Eyes in the audience misted as he sang. But then the sound became distorted. Fissures opened up between the words, and his voice strained to leap from one to the other, slipping, falling, falling lower with each note until it sounded like the growl of a monster. He looked down, and there was Elaine, clutching desperately at his leg. She was wailing, her cries like those of an infant or a cat in heat. The audience was recoiling. He kicked hard, trying to throw her off, but her nails dug into his calves and tore his flesh. Tears were drenching his hosen and making a puddle beneath him. The ground was turning to mud. It covered Elaine's face and breasts and dripped sluggishly down her thighs. Slowly he began to sink in this mud made of tears. It crept, cold and cloying, up his legs, enveloping him. Panic-stricken, he appealed to the audience for help. They assaulted him with laughter. Their merriment seemed to increase with every inch he sank. The slime was up to his chin now. It would fill his mouth and nose, suffocating him while his eyes were still uncovered, able to see the audience to the last, able to see his own death in their eyes . . .

He awoke with a gasp. He could not remember where he was, and in its thick darkness the room gave no clue. His heart pounded in his ears. For a moment he believed he was in hell. Quiet terror had a hold on him.

He felt certain that if he did not leave at once he would go mad. He groped in the dark for his tunic and hosen and began to dress. The leggings would not go on over the bandages, so he abandoned them and slipped his bare feet into his shoes. His left leg throbbed. But no physical pain could match the inner distress that compelled him to move. He pulled himself to his feet, careful to favor his right leg. On one foot he hobbled to the corner by the door where his walking stick was propped. Darkness hid the stool in his way and when he stumbled against it his weight fell for a moment on his injured leg. Blinding pain shot through him, bringing tears to his eyes. Unheeding, he found the crutch and dragged himself to the door. He lifted the latch and pulled. It did not move. He yanked harder and the door still would not yield. The scraping key . . . "Damn it to hell, they've locked me in!" He slammed his fist against the wood in impotent rage. Then, knowing it was useless, he staggered back to his cot and fell on it, still dressed.

He was *not* cruel. Or if he was, it was the unstudied cruelty of nature, without malice. He lived by the morality of beauty. He loved women, all women. His connoisseur's eye caught the special detail which made a woman unique; he celebrated the interesting flaw with the same rapture he devoted to the classic profile. A woman learned from him to love her long nose or freckles or crooked teeth; she came to full bloom in the sunshine of his admiration and could never afterward make a case against him. He abandoned them often, always, but not in restless pursuit of someone better, for each of his women was perfect to him. He sought only one more of the infinite variations on perfection, one more goddess to worship, serve and gently forsake. In city and village, castle and cottage, women faithfully awaited the return he never promised. They suffered, aye, but they suffered gladly to know the riddle of his strange loving. They immortalized him in heartache as he immortalized them in song. Women hoarded the brown petals of deceased flowers, squashed them under their pillows, inhaled the powdery perfume of their decay. But Jack was brave, cruel with nature's cruelty and sinless against the morality of beauty.

Elaine's face came back to accuse him: he lied. Her sorrow had none of the sweetness and inevitability of a fading flower. It had been inflicted on purpose in an act of revenge.

Ah, revenge—what a silly, squalid thing that had turned out to be! For more than a decade he had waited to strike. When, at times, the tumble of events threatened to bury his grudge, he would dig for it, sucking the root of it to revive its bitter taste. For Selwyn had deprived him of his wife, his home, his very honor, and no man who called himself a man could let such a crime go unavenged.

He had honed his voice like a weapon, honed it till it could inflict gooseflesh at his command. To test it, he had chosen the roughest tavern he knew, had stood up and sung a simple melody, without accompaniment, without words. All of the women and half of the men had wept, and when he passed his cap, he collected enough money to buy himself a lute. He sang his way from inn to inn, and travelers spread his fame along their routes. Before long merchants were inviting him home with them. He picked up better manners and a little French, and manor houses opened to him. Then castles. Two years after leaving Lord Selwyn's bondage, Jack, the serf, was formally introduced to his past master by the queen. Of course, Selwyn did not recognize him. To noblemen, peasants were faceless.

They met from time to time over the next nine years, outwardly remaining on the most cordial terms while privately Jack kept his hatred sharpened, never finding the fatal target at which to aim his blow. Then, this spring, gossip had revealed the longed-for opportunity. The first Lady Selwyn had died, and her successor was a girl of sixteen. By all accounts, the marriage had been motivated by love. This was a subject of gentle merriment: a man of middle age and such ruthless practicality that he would levy taxes against his own mother, gone soggy over a girl younger than his daughter. It was perfect. Jack set out at once to call on the newlyweds.

It gave him particular satisfaction to visit this castle, remembering the times in his childhood and youth when, pausing in the fields to mop his brow with a dirty sleeve, he would look up and see it, majestic and mysterious on the high ground. As a child his mental image of heaven had been that same castle, planted in the clouds. He used to sit in a tree by the road that led to the drawbridge and watch the splendid lords and ladies riding out to hawk, feeling an envy not yet tainted with resentment.

Today he was an honored guest. Lord Selwyn sent for him the moment he arrived, eager now that he was in love to make a confidant of love's most famous spokesman. The old warrior was in the armory, where his bride never entered, for he wanted to surprise her with a huge bouquet of roses. At least a hundred of them were heaped in his shield, which rested saucerlike on the earthen floor, and Selwyn was sitting crosslegged in the midst of the most menacing assortment of weapons Jack had ever seen, pinching the thorns off one by one. If the man had not been his enemy, Jack might have succumbed to the charm of that portly face, alight with naive wonder and a little sheepish, knowing what an ass love had made of him.

"I'm not fool enough to think she loves me the same as I love her—how could she, a man my age? I give her everything she fancies—what else is money for?—and I do believe she's fond of me. Lets me come to her every night with none of those silly female complaints, none of that female whining. A cheerful lass she is. 'Tis not a bad thing for a man of my years to get the fire back in his loins, eh?" He looked to Jack for confirmation with a mixture of embarrassment and knee-slapping heartiness, and Jack forced his features into a grin of agreement, remembering bitterly how that fire had incinerated all he once held dear.

Selwyn's feeling for Elaine was easy to understand. She was dimpled and peachy, the sort of girl made to be tumbled in a hayrick. Now that she was lady of the manor she was trying—without much success—to outgrow giggling. Selwyn had given her a great deal of jewelry, and she wore all of it at once. How charming to scold her for her improprieties, to lecture her, feeling himself mature and solid and stern, scowling as she perched adorably in his lap!

Selwyn had written a poem, a very bad poem, trite and overblown, with the usual analogies to flowers and gems, and making Elaine the equal of every mythical beauty from Helen of Troy to Guinevere. He wanted Jack to set it to music. Only too happy to comply, Jack performed it after dinner one night in the great hall, singing earnestly, as if every ridiculous word were being wrenched from his heart. At one point (he had rehearsed it carefully) his voice got husky, threatening to crack, and Elaine, who had been rapt throughout, stopped breathing altogether. So far so good. When the song was over, Jack bowed almost to the floor. As he arose, he allowed his eyes to catch hers for the briefest instant, one of his brows lifted with unmistakable sarcasm.

After that he flirted openly with every woman in residence except Elaine, his avoidance of her polite, yet pointed. She was obviously irritated, and she began to taunt him a little, in company. He allowed it to pass twice. The third time he shot her a black and dangerous look.

The following morning he made sure he could be seen pacing

moodily in the garden beneath her window. It was not long before she joined him. At first she attempted the kind of arch and mannered exchange she knew to be fashionable among sophisticated men and women. His responses were sullen and distracted. He strode brusquely along the shaded path as if he had a destination, so that she was almost running to keep up. Then, breathless, she gave up, coming to a dead halt. "Why are you so mean to me?" she blurted, with tears in her voice.

A breeze blew her hair across her face, and she brushed it aside. Her small hand was dimpled like a child's and so heavy with rings he marveled she could lift it. He replied with pained formality. "Forgive me, lady, if I have shown you less than the courtesy due you as my hostess."

"You have," she said petulantly. "When you are not ignoring me, you are glaring at me. What have I done to make you dislike me so?"

They stood near the garden wall. He could see over it, down into the valley where he had spent the first twenty-two years of his life. His own hut was not visible from here, but there were others like it. Small figures moved with an industry that looked as odd, as meaningless from this vantage as the flustered and self-important exertions of ants. He yanked a handful of leaves from an overhanging bough and tore them to bits.

"It is not dislike that causes me to avoid your eye, my lady. Quite the contrary. And now, I beg you, give me leave to go before I betray my host and my foolish heart."

"Your heart?" she prompted, hopefully.

"I beg you, excuse me now."

"I will not. Not until . . ." She paused, wondering whether she really had the nerve. "Not until you kiss me."

"Very well." He acquiesced with a reserved brush of her cheek. Then, as if overcome, he took her lips in a long, voracious kiss. When at last he drew away, she clung to him and tried to pull his face back. Gently but firmly he disengaged himself.

"Alas, it cannot be," he said with a sigh. "You are the wife of my host."

"He need not know."

"You would deceive him?"

"He would deceive himself."

This was astute. Jack suppressed a smile. "Ah, faithless woman. Then you would deceive me, too." With an exaggerated sigh, he strode away.

After that it took all of his ingenuity to contrive moments alone with her while at the same time appearing to avoid her. He would kiss her until her chin was rubbed raw by his beard and she was swooning in his arms, begging to be taken, and then, abruptly, heartlessly, he would shove her away, pretending (it was not always pretending) to be fighting for self-control. Overnight she lost her coltish high spirits. She looked drawn and miserable.

One evening, the ladies retired from the great hall after dinner to convene a "court of love." Jack, as an expert, was torn from the robust boredom of male camaraderie and invited into the solar to arbitrate.

Elaine watched him anxiously as the arguments were presented. The majority held that a married woman might allow her lover to visit her in bed without being considered unfaithful to her husband, so long as the lovers stopped short of consummation. The minority maintained that while a woman might offer her lips and, in extreme cases, her breasts, she could not permit her lover to lie in the bed she shared with her husband, no matter how chaste the paramour's activities.

Jack listened judiciously, warming his vanity by the heat of their competition for his approval. "Heartless ladies," he said, when the time came for his ruling. "The question has been ill posed, for it speaks to the rights of the husband with no consideration for the far more delicate sensibilities of the lover. If a husband is cuckolded, his pride may be injured; he may suffer a loss of esteem in the eyes of his friends. Compare this trifling mishap with the wound sustained by the jealous lover. Does the husband lose sleep? Nay! He snores like a bear while the lover keeps his vigil on a cold, hard pallet, tormented by the thought that his love lies curled in another man's bed. And the husband—does he miss a meal? Nay! He chomps down his meat. He gulps down his wine. He belches and farts mightily while the lover wastes away." In illustration, Jack opened his cloak to display his own slender form and gave his flat middle a whack.

"A further example," he continued. "Suppose a lady wishes to offer her lover unmistakable proof of her affection. What does she give him? A caress that leads him to the very border of her chastity or perhaps—" he glanced over his shoulder at the door, as if assuring himself that no husband was spying on them, and lowered his voice to a stage whisper "—perhaps *beyond.* Forgive me if I go too far, ladies. Forgive me if I cause you to blush—" They were rapt, breathless. "But let us suppose that, moved by a love too fine, too rare for this uncomprehending earth, she allows her lover to slip his hand under her skirt. Scarcely able to believe his good fortune, he ventures upward. She does not arrest the journey of his ardent fingers as they glide over her silk hosen and come to rest on the soft—oh, such infinite softness, such excruciating sweetness—the soft, warm, inviolate inside of her thigh."

The room shivered. Elaine was biting her pink baby's underlip. He thrust a finger into the air. "Is the lover satisfied? Nay! My ladies, let us be candid: We all know that he is not. Grateful, aye, more grateful than a thousand prayers could begin to express. But satisfied he is not. Why? The reason, my ladies, is that he knows that her husband may lay his crude, unknowing hands on those same sacred limbs any time he chooses. And does the husband's hand tremble? Nay, we know it does not, no more than it trembles to touch his cattle, his tables and chairs, his coat of mail. For that thigh is his property, and what one owns one can never truly love. As you can see, if you follow my reasoning, there is no assurance a lady can give her lover that will put him out of his misery, because whatever she offers, she has given a hundred times over to one who loves her less.

"That is why I would propose that fidelity to a lover is a subject too urgent for this court to ignore. And I would suggest to you, merciful ladies, that there is only one just conclusion by the laws of love: What a lady gives to her lover she must be willing to withhold from her husband."

He had spoken in contradiction of his own true opinion (which was that women should do whatever they pleased, so long as they pleased him), and his statement was so outrageous that most of the ladies thought he was joking. They laughed nervously, all except Elaine, who had gone pale.

"But a wife has a duty to her husband," she protested. "It says so in the Bible. It isn't a matter of love . . ."

Jack scalded her with his eyes. "Nay, with whores it is not a matter of love."

Several of the women gasped. He put on an agonized expression and bowed out of the room, muttering, "Forgive me, I beg you . . ." with a nice touch of enigmatic suffering.

Knowing Elaine would follow him out to the garden, he arranged himself in a brooding pose by the wall. Her footsteps were tentative: She was afraid of his anger. He did not look up.

"Jacques?"

No response.

"Jacques, do you really think of me that way? As a . . . you know."

The trees rustled under the moon and there was a scent of roses. They could have been lying on the cool grass together. It made him sad.

"Nay," he said listlessly. "You do what you must."

"Aye," she agreed, encouraged. "What I must. It isn't love, you know. I mean, when I married him I was very young. I didn't know what love was."

He had to struggle not to laugh—the wedding had been four months ago. At the same time he felt a despair quite separate from the despair he was faking. "Never mind," he said. "I have no right. I am not a wealthy man like your husband. I cannot give you what he—"

"Don't say that!"

"—gives you. I cannot afford to buy you jewels."

She was weeping now. "You make me so ashamed," she whispered between sobs.

He, too, was ashamed, for he was teaching Elaine to hate in herself what he liked best about her—her innocent vulgarity. Looking out over the wall, he tried to make out his village. Vague silver light and shadow. Tonight his rage eluded him. That did not mean he forgave.

The roses were past their prime, dropping their petals, but he saw one that would do. He plunged his hand into the bush. Thorns scratched his wrist and the back of his hand, and he inflicted several bleeding cuts on his fingers as he yanked and twisted the tough stem. "I have nothing to offer thee but this," he said solemnly, giving her the flower.

It pricked her too. "Owww!" she protested, holding up her finger with its black dot of blood. "You left the thorns on it."

He twisted his features into a bitter smile. "I thought you were a woman, Elaine. I see now that you are but a child. My mistake." He bowed curtly. As he walked away, sucking his bleeding fingers, he could hear her crying.

The next morning he was awakened by a sound like a wounded bear. Servants were rushing about, to no particular purpose, whispering and wringing their hands. The cry had come from Selwyn. Elaine was gone.

Jack dressed hastily. As he was rolling up his featherbed, which had been spread on the floor of the great hall, he found her letter. It had been tucked under the mattress, among the rushes. There was a blotch of grease on it where it had come to rest next to a chicken bone. Looking around to make sure he was unobserved, he broke the seal.

> My only love,
> I cried for a long time last night because I saw that you were right though I did not want to admit it at the time. About marrying Selwyn for his money, I mean. But it was not only that. He was very good to me. He used to give me the biggest bouquets of flowers which do not cost any money and I know his friends did not think much of me but he always stood by me and did not hold it against me that I was young just like I did not hold it against him that he was so old and had hair in his ears. But it is true that I was too greedy for jewels which I am giving up now, all except the sapphire necklace which is my favorite. It reminds me of your blue eyes please don't be angry that I kept it. I tried to think of how to keep Wynnie away from me so that you would not suffer any more and be afflicted with jealousy and heartache. He would not believe it if I told him it was my bad time of the month every night so I wrote him a letter saying that I cannot bear children and we

should not lie together if we cannot procreate. I had to tell him that so he would not blame you and smite you down and slay you with one blow of his mighty sword which I have heard he can do when he is full of wrath and which impressed me before but now I am sore afraid of him. I have stolen away in the cloak of night to take refuge among the good nuns at Aylesbury until you come for me and that is where I will be when you read this. It will be easier for you to abduct me if you have a horse which I know you do not at present since you are as you say a carefree rogue so I am leaving you Damascus. He is mine Wynnie gave him to me but then he would not let me ride him because he is too skittish so he bought me a mare instead which is the one I have taken just to be safe even though she is really too slow. But I am sure you can handle him. Damascus, I mean. He's tied up behind the mill. Now you can see that I really do love only you and that I am truly a woman. You should not have called me a child but I forgive you since you had a broken heart. I will act very holy until you come and then won't they be amazed when they see the handsome and famous troubadour who has come to abduct me! Godspeed, my love.

Elaine

The handwriting started out large and loopy, reaching the bottom of the page long before the message was completed. The remainder climbed up the right margin and coiled in spirals of ever-diminishing letters around the border.

Jack threw the letter into the fire and watched it burn to ashes. Selwyn's yelps of grief were echoing through the castle. They gave him no satisfaction.

Nine

In his dream he was running home. He was chilled. Anne was already warming his bed, and his cold skin was eager to fall against her, to be wrapped in her long fragrant hair. He could see her small, perfect body glowing in the firelight. He ran hard but she got no closer. His blood was beginning to freeze in his veins and his heart was an iceberg in his chest. Only Anne could thaw him. But his limbs were leaden and could not span the distance between them. She remained remote, yet her eyes were right there before him all the time. The idea came to him that he could dive into them and reach her that way. Then he was no longer running, and she was very near. In her nearness, all details were sharpened, as if by merciless light. A purple bruise glared obscenely from her swollen face and dried blood rimmed her nostrils. Ice blocked his throat, imprisoning his scream. "I will kill them!" he whispered. But her eyes accused only him. "Nay, it was not me!" he protested again and again, but the reproach remained in her eyes. He was strangling on frozen tears. "Anne, please, I did not hurt you. It was not me!" In disgust she turned away and began to walk toward the soldiers, her hips swaying. The men stared their own condemnation of him as they enclosed her in their ranks. "It was not me, Anne," he still moaned, his heart torn. "Anne, you must believe me . . ."

Gradually the dark, suffocating web of the dream was broken by the light from Ingrid's candle. His fingers relaxed their fevered grip on his pillow and his eyes opened to the sight of her. She stood there calm and neat, and his heart rose in gratitude for her plainness.

"Were you having a bad dream?" she asked kindly.

"Aye." He sat up wearily, rubbing his face, and brushed back the hair plastered to his sweaty forehead. The bedclothes were snarled, and the air in the room was dense and fetid, as if still drenched with his nightmare. She handed him a cup of ale. It was cool and reassuring in his hands—a solid connection with the waking world. Opening the shutters, she let in a bleak dawn. The air was muggy, and the sparrows sounded overwrought.

As she turned from the window, Ingrid saw for the first time the overturned stool, the discarded hosen and the staff, abandoned in the middle of the floor. He answered her questioning look with an embarrassed shrug. "I got wanderlust."

"It's a good thing we locked the door."

"It's a terrible thing you locked the door," he retorted sourly. "Am I a beast to be kept in a cage?"

He watched her as she set about rearranging the room. The contours of her body were impossible to discern beneath her habit, which was a drab, old-fashioned garment, its heavy folds falling in unbroken lines from shoulder to foot. She must have grown since the gown was first made, for the skirt stopped several inches shy of the floor—a detail that would have stirred his tenderness had he been himself. Though her arms and legs were long, her movements were curiously confined, as if she considered it an impertinence to occupy space, and her head was inclined diffidently, her eyes cast downward. This irritated him. Everything irritated him. In truth he *felt* like a beast, like a snarling vicious dog. He attacked his breakfast.

"Sir?" She sounded uncertain.

"I told you—call me Jack."

"I thought I might read to you while you have your meal."

"Read me what?"

"This morning's service." She held up a psalter.

He rolled his eyes. "Dear lady, I just woke up!"

She looked hurt. "All right then. I will come back in a little while to collect your tray."

He cursed under his breath. "I didn't mean for you to leave. Please—don't go."

"I just thought . . . We seem to lead one another into rather frivolous talk. That's why I thought it would be better to read."

He gave an exasperated shrug. "Go ahead then, read if it makes you feel better."

She settled herself on the stool beside his bed and, finding the page, began: *"The lord is merciful and gracious, slow to anger and abounding in steadfast love. He does not deal with us according to our sins . . ."*

Jack was ignoring the words, chewing his bread and speculating about her body.

". . . nor requite us according to our iniquities . . ."

How he would like to redden that prim mouth, to make that long, straight back arch and yearn!

". . . for as the heavens are high above the earth, so great is his steadfast love toward those who fear him . . ."

What would it be like to hear that measured voice howl? What would it take to make her laugh? To make her cry?

"As a father pities his children, so the lord pities those who fear him. For he knows our frame, he remembers that we are dust—"

"You know," he said. "When you die, they will hack up your body for relics. Good thing you're tall—they'll get a lot of bone fragments out of you. Think of it—at about a shilling a sliver, your corpse'll be worth a king's ransom!"

Ingrid was so flustered she dropped the psalter. As she stooped to retrieve it, he said, "Being a saint's a bit of a disadvantage, isn't it? You've got to read me the good book instead of bashing me with it, as I'm sure you'd like to."

She stood up, clutching the psalter to her chest. "I don't want to bash you," she said levelly. "But I think I should go. Father Bonaface is coming tomorrow to say mass. Shall we send him to hear your confession?"

"No, Goddamn it!" The fury in his voice surprised even Jack. She crossed herself, making amends to heaven for his profanity, which only enraged him more. Before he knew what he was doing, he had hurled his cup across the room. It hit the wall beneath the crucifix and clattered empty to the floor. Ingrid stared at him, stunned.

"You want me to confess? All right, I'll confess. But you must be my confessor."

She was backing away.

"Sit down!" he thundered.

She perched on the stool as if it were the rim of a bottomless well. When he looked down at his hands, he saw that they were shaking. I must seem like a madman to her, he thought. He combed his fingers through his unruly hair and made a surly stab at apology.

"I didn't mean to scare you."

"It's all right."

Of course she would say that. You could flay her alive and she would just look at you sadly—sad for your soul, not for her skin—and say, "It's all right." It was enough to drive a man to murder.

"Look," he said. "Something does weigh heavy on my conscience. I do not confess it to God because it was not God who was wronged. And anyhow, he knows all about it already. But I would confess it to you, if you will hear it. Will you stay?"

She nodded.

He rubbed his beard, searching for a way to begin. "I was not always the blasphemous scoundrel you see today. At your age this man was a hardworking, God-fearing youth called Jacob Rudd. A plowman. Six days a week he labored in the fields of Lord Selwyn and the seventh he devoted to his Lord Jesus Christ. Even your abbess would have found no fault with him.

"He fell in love with a girl named Anne. She was a beauty—so small and delicate he could lift her with one arm. Her hair was raven black and her eyes put the sky to shame. Swans would have felt clumsy in her presence. She was sweet natured as well as beautiful, and to this man's everlasting surprise and gratitude, she loved him too. They became betrothed.

"Now there is a custom you may have heard of, a wedding custom. When a peasant marries, the lord of the land may 'sample' the bride first, if you get my meaning. Usually the lord can be persuaded to dispense with this rite, for a price. In fact, the custom is really no more than another tax. One of many. Jacob—or Jack, as his friends called him—Jack worked hard and saved for a year to make the payment so that he and his bride could be married with nothing to blot their happiness.

"And it was a happy marriage. They had a little cottage to themselves, and every night they would make love by the reddish glow of the dying fire. You couldn't see much farther than the bed in that kind of light, you couldn't see that the room was poor. He often thought that what he saw at those times was no different from what the king saw when he went to bed. Or better, for Anne was much prettier than our lovely queen. So you see, however backbreaking were his days, by night, in the arms of his beloved, Jack was a king.

"After a year of these amorous nights, Anne had not conceived a child. The couple went to church often, prayed and made offerings. And nothing happened. Eventually both came to believe that Anne was barren. This was hard to accept, but Anne reminded him that Elizabeth, in the Bible, had given birth to John the Baptist after decades of infertility. So they prayed for a miracle.

"One day when Jack was off working on the common, Lord Selwyn and a party of his soldiers came riding through Jack's fields. They used to do that for a lark—go tearing through the fields and spoil a man's crops without a thought. They stopped for refreshments at Jack's cottage, where Anne had remained that day to do the baking and the washing. She gave them the day's milk and the bread she'd just baked. They thanked her by . . . by raping her. All of them." His voice faltered, was barely audible. "Jack comes home to find his wife cowering in a corner, terrified of him. Her dress is in shreds, and she is so badly bruised that there is no part of her that he can caress without hurting her. But the worst is, she's terrified that he will be angry with her, that he'll turn her out because the other men have had her. Men do that sometimes—I've never understood it. Jack is only angry that she could have so little faith in him . . ."

He stopped. He had never told this story aloud before, yet the words had been with him for years, memorized until they replaced the memory, became the memory. He was startled now to discover that they were not true. An image untamed by words was rising up to make a liar out of him. He was standing in the doorway of his cottage and Anne, who usually ran to greet him, seemed not to know that he was there. She was sitting on the floor, hunched over, trying to mend her torn bodice without taking it off. Her inefficiency was bizarre and terrifying. "Anne?" His voice came out like a strangled scream. She looked up abstractly. "They tore my dress," she told him, without emotion. Her eyes were vacant. "Anne!" he cried, and all at once the daze broke. She reached up for him, letting the needle and thread dangle, and he scooped her into his arms, pressing her tight to his chest as she sobbed. There had not been a moment's doubt that he

54

would comfort her: She had trusted him as if he were her guardian angel.

It was later that she cowered from him. Six weeks later. He had not hit her, but his fist had been raised. Her arms had flown up to protect her face and then he had seen this fist . . . His.

His eyes smarted. He blinked and swallowed hard. "For a time after that Anne lost the joy of lovemaking, so they lived together as brother and sister. During that time they discovered that the 'miracle' had happened. Anne was with child." He glanced at Ingrid. "You know what that means, don't you?

"Jack was ashamed, overwhelmed with shame. He could not protect his wife. He could not even get her with child. But most shameful of all, he had not the courage to bear his shame. So he left her."

He paused to rub his face. His eyes were dry now, and when he spoke again his voice was hard. "The priest told him that he must not lie with his wife again, that sterility was his cross to bear and he would be rewarded in heaven. Well, Jack bore crosses for years, and what was his reward? Who is to say that God will be any more just in the next life than he is in this one? So Jack forsakes God's stinking justice for poetic justice. Do you know what that is? When a man turns his curse into a blessing, when he takes advantage of his useless seed, for instance—that is poetic justice. God told Eve that her daughters would pay a price for their pleasure. Well, not with me, they don't. I talk and sing and charm my way into noblemen's homes all the time, and I have their wives like they had mine. No, not like they had mine—their wives are willing! Their wives pine for me!"

His voice sounded very loud to him. He fell back against the pillows, suddenly tired. Ingrid got up quietly and retrieved his cup from the floor. She refilled it and handed it to him.

"Thank you." He drank deep, for his mouth had gone bitter and dry.

"Just before I came here, I took revenge on Lord Selwyn." His tone was subdued now. "To hurt him I had to hurt his bride, who was four years old at the time Selwyn raped my wife. And he is hurt, all right. Not as badly as Anne or myself, but he is hurt. He thinks of me as a friend—doesn't know what he did to me or what I have done to

55

him. He cannot comprehend what has happened—it seems to him the random cruelty of the universe. Through his tears he might cry, 'What have I done to deserve this?' and the last thing he would expect, or want, is to be told the answer.

"Anne does not know she has been avenged—nor would she be glad if she learned of it. In fact, I think she would be ashamed of me. She is remarried now, for after a few years people were kind enough to persuade her that I must be dead. I'm told her husband provides well for her.

"So you see, my poetic justice has contributed handsomely to the sum of human misery and subtracted nothing at all." He shrugged. "There is my confession. *In nomine patris et filius et spiritus sanctus amen.* And now, dear lady, let us have your absolution."

As soon as he said it, he was sorry. It was the kind of thing he said sometimes for the symmetry, for the charm of the words themselves. But he regretted it, for he had given Ingrid an opening for some pious platitude. She would intone a stupid little homily about God's mercy and he would want to break her teeth.

He steeled himself to look at her and was touched by what he saw. Her face was smudged with sadness, at once full and contained. There was not a shadow of censure on it. The naked meeting of their eyes gave him a thrill like no meeting of naked skin had given him in years. "I see you understand," he said softly. "Oh, you blessed angel . . . Come to me. Please."

He extended one hand to her and with the other patted the spot on the bed where he wanted her to sit. She came willingly and gave him her hands to hold. Full of tenderness, he raised her fingers to his lips, turned her hand and kissed her palm, folded back her sleeve and kissed the delicate underside of her wrist, all the while gazing at her as if to keep her forever with his eyes. Then he brought her hand to his chest and slipped it inside his shirt, to rest against his heart. She looked down shyly but did not move away. He took her face in his hands. "Gentle lady, have mercy on this poor sinner."

He meant to kiss her lightly, moving ever so slowly as one would approach a deer. But when he met her lips and found them softly parted, unknowing and defenseless, his passion flared. He kissed her deeply, hungrily, until she wrenched away. She regarded him with wide, startled eyes. "Don't be afraid," he soothed.

"You are seducing me!"

He chuckled. "Well, that's putting it rather baldly . . ."

She shook her head as if she could not believe she had been betrayed in this way. "I touched you out of pity."

It was as if heaven had smiled at him and then turned cold. A sourness seeped into his mouth. "Did you now? And when you stared at my body—was that, too, out of pity? Oh, aye, you thought I was asleep, didn't you? But I felt you there. Staring at me. Breathing hard, out of pity."

Her color flamed so hot it must have hurt her. "I touched you out of pity," she repeated in a whisper.

Jack sighed. "Then I accept your pity with humble gratitude, Saint Ingrid."

Ten

Ingrid made a quick, neat incision on the inside of her elbow and held it over a small bowl. She was impatient at first, tempted to cut again, for the blood came slowly. She had too much blood.

The hair shirt had raised wicked red bumps on her skin. It was hard to keep her free hand away from the irritations. A rope wound tightly around her waist constricted her breathing. She had fasted to the brink of starvation and still she burned. She had too much blood.

Right after it happened, she had run to Dame Agatha, intending to confess. But the conversation had gone all wrong. As always, she knelt for the abbess' blessing. She stayed on her knees, staring at the floor, searching for the right words. Before she could find them,

Dame Agatha said, "I'm glad you've come. There's something I must discuss with you. Come, be seated."

Still on her knees, she appealed to the older woman with her eyes. Dame Agatha was impatient with slow compliance and with stammering. She flicked her hand toward the chair beside her desk. Ingrid obeyed.

"How does the man fare?"

"I think his leg will heal all right. But he is unhappy. And—" she faltered.

"This is not his sort of place," the abbess observed with unkind amusement.

"No, I suppose not. I tried to read to him, as you suggested. It only made him cross. He—"

"That is to be expected. He'll try to scare you off, if he can. The wicked flee from the righteous. But he can't flee, can he? God has got him trapped. So he snaps and snarls. But he's no match for you, my child."

Ingrid shook her head helplessly. Dame Agatha's confidence was like a wall erected against her confession. How could she begin to explain? It was she who was no match for Jack. She knew his story that morning had been full of blasphemy and error, yet she couldn't conceive of correcting him. His pain silenced her. In his presence she felt young and ignorant. Each time she entered his room she was eclipsed, fading to a thin pale light like the moon at dawn.

"I am a little afraid of him I suppose. Or, perhaps not afraid. He is . . ." She paused, trying to get it right, determined to tell the truth. The only word that came to mind was *beautiful*. She couldn't say it. And anyway he wasn't beautiful, exactly. He was hot. He was bright. Her face burned as she recalled his keen blue gaze, the warmth of his skin inside the shirt, the rise and fall of his breathing. The kiss, chaste at first, cool lips sour with ale. And then the shock of his tongue, full in her mouth. She had pulled away only because she was startled and it had taken her a moment to know what to accuse him of, or even to wish to accuse. The sensation had been like a hot liquid, drunk so deep the heat went to her knees, and it returned now, just from remembering.

"He is vulgar and worldly," Dame Agatha pronounced. "You

have grown up protected from such people, so no doubt you are intimidated. Perhaps you are even fascinated. Is that it?"

"Yes," she agreed quickly, relieved to have it said for her. "It is true, madam. I become fascinated."

Dame Agatha sighed. "That is unfortunate. But inevitable, I suppose. Satan is no fool. He does not come to us looking ugly on the surface. It is in those things which we find most attractive that we should suspect his presence. It is only on further acquaintance that the ugliness, the evil shows itself."

This was a familiar argument. Its familiarity consoled her. Satan prospered in confusion. To strip off his disguises was to render him harmless.

"Do not be afraid of this man," the abbess continued. "As you come to know him the fascination will soon wear off. You'll see he's little more than an animal dressed up in silks. What does he do but eat, drink, and fornicate? Oh, his speech is facile, but there's no soul in what he says. His soul is atrophied with neglect, his body rotten with sin."

The devil played with Ingrid's mind then, for she wondered how an atrophied soul could create music. She scanned her memory of Jack's body, searching in vain for the rottenness of sin. She wanted, suddenly, to defend him.

Dame Agatha went on, quoting from the Psalms. " 'Transgression speaks to the wicked, deep in his heart: There is no fear of God before his eyes, for he flatters himself in his own eyes that his iniquity cannot be found out and hated. The words of his mouth are mischief and deceit; he plots mischief while on his bed and spurns not evil.' "

During this oration, a ray of sunlight, like an arrow shot with great accuracy through the narrow window, illuminated Dame Agatha's face. Ingrid could see the enlarged pores on the woman's nose, the faint dark moustache over a mouth tense with disdain. As evil could be beautiful, so virtue must have this hideous aspect. She could not trust her senses. Her body felt hollow. She wished she could lie down alone somewhere and sleep.

The abbess changed the subject. "I have had a letter from the bishop. As you know, we had agreed that you should not receive visitors for awhile. Requests for aid have continued to come almost daily. I have not spoken of them till now because I felt you should be allowed to complete your novitiate in tranquility."

Ingrid's hands tensed in her lap. She knew what was coming.

"We have both come to see that we were unwise to handle it as we did last time. Throwing open the door to all comers created a great deal of confusion—for Greyleigh, and for you. What I intend to propose—and I have no reason to think his grace will object—is that you see people a few at a time. No general announcement will be made. I've tried to sort these out somewhat." The abbess picked up one of two thick rolls of parchment that rested atop her ledger. "These are the more serious cases, as far as I can determine. I'd like you to read them and select the ones you'll see first. I should think no more than a dozen to start."

Ingrid stared dumbly at the roll of letters she had just accepted. It was tied with a black ribbon. The ends of the ribbon were slightly frayed. She pulled at the loose threads, making a fringe. Dame Agatha was saying something about writing to the people she selected, telling them when to appear. She heard "feast of the Epiphany."

She looked up, stricken.

"I don't know how to make it any easier, Ingrid."

"No . . . This is fine." She ventured a weak smile. "I'm not going to make a scene."

"Of course not." The abbess exhaled with relief.

"They have been waiting a long time, these people?"

"Some of them. Yes."

"Then I must see them soon."

She had spoken firmly, hoping that conviction would follow. It was like the apostle Peter, walking on the surface of the sea: The trick was not to become self-conscious. Don't look down at the churning waves of doubt. Think of the people who need your help. Keep your eye on the suffering people and don't look down.

Dame Agatha was watching her closely, her brows knit with concern. "Ingrid, we have not discussed this for quite some time. I shall not reprimand you for speaking freely."

Ingrid pulled another thread from the ribbon with her fingernail. "I can't think what to say. I should like to say that I feel ready, but . . . I shall make myself ready." The fringe was growing longer.

She caressed her fingertip with the soft end of it. After a moment she looked up and said with attempted casualness, "Might I be permitted to wear a hair shirt?" The words were startling said out loud. She blushed, as if caught in the act of impersonating a saint.

Dame Agatha gave her an assessing look—Ingrid couldn't quite meet it—then went to her cupboard and took out a length of coarse brown cloth, tied up with twine. Even at some distance Ingrid could see the sharp fibers sticking out of the weave. "The rope goes around your waist, over the cloth but under your gown. It's meant to be tight."

So Agatha had worn this. She hadn't guessed.

"It's rather awful, isn't it?" she said with a nervous laugh.

The abbess returned a dry smile. "That is its function."

She'd had the queerest longing to weep then. To have a mother and weep into her apron. Afraid of displaying her weakness, she asked, abruptly, to be excused.

She had left without confessing the kiss.

Her conscience kept returning to that omission as the tongue returns to a sore in the mouth. It could be rationalized. She knew Dame Agatha had been worried that she would balk at further healings, and she was anxious to demonstrate her willingness. In the light of the momentous business ahead of her, the incident in Jack's room seemed trivial, something to be managed privately and without fuss. She did not wish to appear to be fabricating a crisis. And if she'd told, the man would have been evicted at once, to the detriment of his health. That was neither necessary nor fair. He had apologized for his rash act. She knew he would not attempt it again.

Those were the honorable reasons, and they were true, as far as they went. Harder to admit was the way she hoarded the memory of that kiss. Her mind kept returning to it, questioning it as if it were an urgent message in a language she did not understand.

Temptation—that's what the abbess would call it. An impulse to be conquered with a simple act of will. Ingrid had no fear of temptation. Her self-control was so despotic that her eyelids scarcely blinked without express permission. Still, she was afraid. Not of what she might do, but of what she might know. Did know.

She remembered with shame the many nights she spent alone in the chapel. There on the cool moonlit stones in the great overarching emptiness of the nave, she would commune with the crucifix. Fat tears would roll down her face in what she took to be the rapture of prayer, the incessant and voluptuous longing for union with Christ. She knew that the word *mystic* was whispered behind her back. But it was Jack who had taught her the true name for what she felt. She saw now that if she were to bathe Christ's feet with her lips and hair, it would be for the sake of the feet and the lips and the hair. What, then, was her soul, her celebrated soul?

She would never find out until she snuffed out this fire in her veins that posed as a soul. She had too much blood.

The bowl was brimful now. Ingrid pressed a clean cloth to the wound and leaned back. Better. Her head was too light to think and below it she felt nothing at all.

Eleven

Jack saw that he did not have to wait for death to face the emptiness of eternity. It could ambush him in the hesitation between the end of one thought and the beginning of the next. It was there in the transit of the sun across the walls and ceiling each afternoon, there in the routine of anticipations and disappointments that made up his days. Sometimes it depressed him. And sometimes, facing it square on, he felt braver than a knight. He told himself that if he could keep his sanity through the next five weeks, nothing need ever frighten him again, neither heaven nor hell, and each night he slept the honest sleep of accomplishment.

Anticipation and disappointment attached themselves most particularly to two aspects of his day: meals and the appearances of Ingrid. Meals were simple. He never failed to look forward to them, not only out of hunger but out of boredom, and they never failed to daunt his appetite. The staple was something called stockfish. At first he imagined there must be a disagreeable seagoing creature called a stock fish, but Ingrid had explained that the dish was all different kinds of fish hammered together and kept between layers of burlap for— well, for generations, to judge by the dryness and the smell. He was sure none of it had breathed water since the reign of Arthur. There was also a very dense bread, the chewing of which was his only exercise. The warm, yeasty smell that wafted across the yard promised better, and he took his own stale loaves personally until Ingrid explained that the nuns went to the precaution of baking their bread a week in advance of its use. For what eventuality they were stockpiling it she was unable to say. Finally there was a dreary pease porridge. Substituting the bread for stones and the porridge for mortar, one could have built a very sound little cottage. A stockade for stockfish.

He daydreamed incessantly about Ingrid. In his fantasies she was moist and yielding, all of her like his one brief taste of her mouth. For hours he would marinate in the heavy sweet syrup of desire, waiting for her to arrive. Then she would appear with her chapped hands and her drab complexion, her disciplined spine. It was a shock, an affront at first. But soon he ceased to believe in these apparitions. That body was a lie. A ghost. Her true body was in his keeping.

After he kissed her she stayed away for a whole day. His meals were brought to him by a nun who was old enough (they must have reasoned) to be safe from his "pagan lust." He reproached himself for moving too fast and was afraid he would never see her again. But the next morning she was back. Her manner, at once formal and kind, gave no indication that anything personal had passed between them. So he apologized, not because he was sorry (he had stopped being sorry the moment she reappeared) but as a way of reminding her of their fleeting intimacy.

"There is no need to apologize," she said. "Indeed, I should thank you. No one here dares show me the truth about myself. Perhaps that is why you were sent."

She uttered this odd speech with great earnestness. There was no doubt she meant it—whatever it meant. Immediately afterward she found an excuse to rush from the room. He wanted to ask, *"What truth?"* And, damn it, no one had sent him. But the next time she came in, she took refuge in her duty to him as if no longer a woman, only a nurse.

But it was as a nurse that she was most a woman. The intimate nature of her services to him never appeared to dismay her. Absorbed in her work, she forgot her self-consciousness. Her movements were graceful then, her touch assured and pleasing. She seemed to know even better than he what he needed. When his legs went dead from inactivity, she rubbed the sensation back into his feet. When his dreams hovered too long around his pillow so that his whole bed was stale with sleeping and waking obsessions, in she would come with folded sheets to make the bed crisp and fresh again.

There was a day of deep blue sky and rustling yellow leaves, the day he most mourned missing the autumn. That day she brought him a perfect apple, newly fallen. He almost wept. In his helpless condition, gratitude became like a bedsore. Women had always been so kind to him! His idle hours were haunted by memories of all he had so thanklessly received. The pain of old injuries, even his huge grudge was dull compared with the inarticulate tenderness of his newly swollen heart. He wished to fling himself on the breast of the earth which he, great baby, had so mindlessly sucked, cry for mercy when it was mercy which he had never been denied.

Once a day she sat at his bedside and read to him to stave off his boredom and loneliness. He could see that this was hard for her the first few days. She moved the stool out of his reach and kept her eyes fixed on the page, which rattled when she turned it. Gradually, though, they got used to one another. All day he would wait for her, thinking how good it would be to exercise his voice, and then, when he had his chance, nothing seemed to need saying. Her presence stilled the clamor of words in his head, and he was content to let the placid stream of her voice wash over him or just to sit with her in silence.

The window of his room overlooked the yard between the infirmary and the convent proper, but from his bed he saw only a bit of roof, a smudge of distant hills and the sky, which, more often than not, was overcast. As October lengthened and the weather grew colder, he had to endure chill and damp in exchange for this indifferent view, but he refused to give it up until the sun had set—and sometimes not even then if the stars shone clear. Ingrid kept adding blankets to his bed, until there were five in all. The weight of them was oppressive and one day he gave up and let her close the shutters. He could not hear the chanting or the children or the well then, and the walls seemed to press in on him. The isolation was worse than the cold, and after that the window stayed open all day, no matter what the weather.

He loved it when birds flew close and he could see the exertion of their wings. He imagined himself in flight, the wind breaking against his breast. Once he saved some of his bread from breakfast, tore it into small pieces and asked Ingrid to put them on the sill. Sparrows came and fussed over this largess, and he took such absurd delight in it that from then on the bread offering became a daily ritual.

There was another storm during his fifth week of convalescence. The thunder woke him in the middle of the night, so he was lucid when Ingrid tiptoed in with her candle. How often did she come in when he was sleeping? The thought that she might watch him every night made his hair stand on end. At the same time he found himself hoping that he slept in flattering positions, that his mouth didn't hang open or drool and that he didn't snore when she was there.

"Hello, Saint Ingrid," he greeted her in a low voice.

She started: She had not realized he was awake. "I came to make sure the window was closed," she hastened to explain.

It was. The sky had been rumbling at dusk and she had come in at compline to fasten the shutters. He saw no reason to point this out. Her eyes looked as if she had been weeping, and there were dark rings beneath them that seemed to go halfway to her chin. The night he arrived he had guessed she was eighteen. Now he might have said thirty. Her face was haggard, gray and hollow-cheeked.

"Don't you ever sleep?" he asked roughly.

"Nighttime is my only chance to contemplate."

"So it's contemplation makes you look like that."

"Like what?"

"Unhappy."

At this, tears started to spill from her eyes. The candle wobbled in her hand, its light darting around the room like an agitated ghost.

"Put that down before you drop it."

She obeyed. He thought she would have a good cry then, but she took a conclusive shuddering breath and wiped her cheeks with the back of her hand. "I'm sorry . . .," she murmured.

"You're always apologizing."

"I'm . . ." She caught herself in the act of apologizing for apologizing, and this made them both laugh.

"Better?" he asked.

She nodded.

"Good. Sit down then. Or have you come to share my bed?"

That was clumsy of him. He was certain she did want to share his bed—why else had she come?—but she must not be asked to admit it. Women were the only creatures on earth who must be tricked into attaining their heart's desire. When he saw her alarm, he added quickly, "Nay, I see I am not to be so fortunate. But stay awhile. Do."

She took her bedside seat, and Jack arranged himself more comfortably on the pillows. Outside the rain fell in a steady hiss, and the candlelight gave the room a cozy feeling. The roof leaks splashing into their assigned buckets were a cheery melody. He smiled at Ingrid and she smiled shyly back, and he noticed that he was as happy as he had ever been in his life.

"Tell me a story," he demanded, like a tucked-in child.

"I don't know any stories. Unless you mean Bible stories, or the lives of the saints."

"Tell me the life of Saint Ingrid."

"That would be a very short story."

"You can tell me how she came to work miracles."

"You seem to have heard that already."

"Only the official version."

"Which you do not believe."

"I will believe it if you say I should."

She studied his face for a moment. He had the impression she wanted very much to confide in him and was wondering whether she dared.

"You seem to be a man who is not easily scandalized."

He laughed. "I daresay that is one of my few virtues."

She took a deep breath. "Then I will tell you the truth. There was a—a misunderstanding. A little girl, the daughter of the cook who worked for the Ladbrook family, was helping her mother in the kitchen and cut her hand. It was not a deep cut, but it was long and bled a great deal, so the mother became alarmed and brought the girl to the infirmary. Normally a wound is cauterized before being bandaged, but in this case I neglected to do so. Nevertheless, the wound healed quickly."

"Why did you not cauterize it?"

She paused. "The reason causes me shame. At that time I suffered from temptations."

"Temptations?" Jack asked hopefully.

"Yes. The first came when I was about to open a vein for a bleeding. Suddenly I had an impulse to slash the entire arm from wrist to elbow. I could actually see the gash in my mind. The image was so strong I could hardly believe that I would *not* do it. And there were many other impulses after that. For every ministration in the infirmary, a vile counterpart arose in my mind. Naturally I confessed this at once, but as there was no one to take my place, I was obliged to go on with my work."

"Did you ever actually hurt anyone?"

"No. By the grace of God, I did not. Everyone was praying for me. The closest I came to hurting anyone was the cook's little girl. I had cleaned the wound and was heating the cautery iron and I felt a cruelty in myself. It was almost a glee at the pain I was about to inflict." Ingrid looked down at her hands. "As I say, this causes me a great deal of shame. I put down the iron and crossed myself and thought the temptation had passed. But when I picked it up again and took her little hand in mine, she looked at me with such fear. She was trying to be brave, poor thing, but still she tried to pull her hand away, and the feeling of cruelty came back, stronger than I'd ever felt it. At the last moment I managed to shove her hand aside and burned my own instead."

Jack winced.

"It was not as terrible as you might think. I remember seeing the washbasin, cool with still water, and the white cloth I'd used to clean the wound, all vivid with blood. Sunlight was coming in on the table and the sight—I saw only ordinary objects, but in that moment of pain they affected me like a vision from heaven. A vision of such

goodness . . . I'm sorry, I am not used to speaking of these things."
She looked abashed.

"You speak honestly and well. Please go on."

"Well, after that, I could not bring myself to cauterize the child's hand. I simply bandaged the wound and sent her home. As it happened, it healed quickly—long before my own, in fact. And the mother, who had seen me burn my hand, she thought it was some kind of magic, I guess."

"And how do you explain it—the fact that the child's hand was so speedily healed?"

Ingrid considered for a moment. "I don't mean to excuse my negligence, but it may be that the cut never needed to be cauterized to begin with. There are so many things which God sets right with little interference on our part. Your leg, for example, will be as good as new by Christmas if you have the patience to rest properly, and there is not much I can do to help it."

"So Lady Ladbrook heard of this?"

"Yes. She was so desperate, you see. She had consulted the best physicians, and they had been unable to help. In truth, I thought it cruel of Dame Agatha to encourage her in her hopes. I was sure I could do nothing and that she would leave here despairing of God's grace. It is all the more miraculous that he would choose as his instrument a person of such weak faith, and I never cease to give thanks that my superior exceeded my own limited vision."

"How did it happen?" Jack prompted, impatient with this pious digression.

"She was in the guesthouse, all wrapped in furs. She was young and quite pretty, though very pale. I asked to be left alone with her. For a long time neither of us spoke. I was not sure how one went about performing a miracle."

Jack's eyes danced. "It *is* hard to imagine oneself doing such a thing with a straight face. I mean, if you'd said, 'arise and walk,' and she'd just lain there, crippled as ever, it would have been damned embarrassing, wouldn't it?"

A grin cracked the symmetry of Ingrid's face and she giggled. It was only for a second and then her brittle composure returned, but Jack reeled with curious delight, as if an icon had winked at him.

"Happily it was nothing like that. After a very long silence she told me about the baby she'd had at the end of her first year of marriage. It was born after forty hours' labor, with arms and legs that were mere stumps, almost like fins. Nothing about it was quite human, except its eyes, which—which seemed to speak to her. Almost wise they were. She loved this creature with all of her heart. Her husband, who was young and proud, tried to take it away from her, meaning to strangle it or dash it to the floor. She wouldn't let go of it; she clung to it for hours until it died naturally, less than a day after it was born. Afterward the baby often appeared to her in dreams, speaking to her in a voice of sweetness and strange wisdom."

For the second time that night Jack's hair stood on end. Ingrid was clutching an imaginary infant to her breast and rocking back and forth on the stool, seemingly unconscious of him. He tapped her knee and said her name and she took a ragged breath and went on with her story.

"The next time her husband came to her, her legs were very stiff, and within a few days she was unable to move at all. As she told me this, she was crying, and I was sitting beside her, stroking the fur covers over her rather absent-mindedly. She said 'That feels good.' I think it took a moment for either of us to notice that there was anything strange about that. I pulled the covers off and started to rub her legs and feet and gradually the feeling began to come back. A little while later she could move. She couldn't really walk properly— the muscles were wasted after six years. But I held her up and she sort of stumbled around."

Ingrid glanced at him through her lashes and smiled. "You would have laughed, because it wasn't at all like miracles in the scriptures. We were both a bit giddy, and when Lady Ladbrook tried to walk she looked like a drunk. Then Dame Agatha came in, and Lady Ladbrook's confessor, and we both realized we should be looking solemn, but when we caught each other's eyes we started to laugh, and neither of us could stop."

Jack slapped the mattress in hearty enjoyment. "Oh, that's marvelous! Marvelous! What happened next?"

But fear had darkened her face like the shadow of an evil wing. "I have been talking so long!"

"Aye. At last."

She shook her head. " 'In much speaking thou shalt not avoid sin.' "

He stopped himself from responding in exasperation, reaching over instead to clasp her hand. She did not retract it. Outside the rain had slowed and he could hear a steady splash from the gutters. A small puddle had formed beneath his window, despite the fact that it was closed. The cloister must be flooded.

He could feel Ingrid's pulse racing, but she made no attempt to leave. She had a lost look, as if the long conversation had disoriented her and she was waiting for him to tell her what to do next. He could have her now: It came to him all of a sudden that she was as easy as any woman he'd ever had.

Too easy. It made him too gentle.

"You'd better go," he said, squeezing her hand. "Try and get some sleep."

She arose in her obedient way, her skirts sighing as she went out, taking the candle with her. Jack, finding himself alone and wide awake in the dark, cursed.

Twelve

Ingrid stared at the letters stacked on her worktable. There were dozens of them, sorted into three piles: Yes, No and Maybe. Maybe was the thickest. Cradling her head in her hands, she began to read again. Some of the letters were crudely printed in charcoal, smudgy now from repeated handling. They broke her heart.

She had attempted the task many times during the past few weeks, each time using different criteria. She had tried choosing the most painful illnesses. Or those most likely to be fatal. She had tried assessing the degree of faith. That was hopeless: Each letter expressed a naive and unwavering conviction that her touch would cure all. Her latest idea was to choose those which moved her most readily to compassion. But she mistrusted this notion. Surely, the fate of these people should not depend solely on her emotions.

A vague and persistent headache—the result of fasting—blurred her vision. She glanced out the window, resting her eyes. Outside, thatchers were going up and down the ladders propped against the guesthouse, great bundles of straw balanced on their shoulders. They were getting it ready for her visitors.

She clasped her hands together, resisting once more the urge to scratch. If she waited, the individual prickles resolved themselves into an overall burning, which gradually receded from consciousness—for a while, at least. She wanted to think of cool water. But that defeated the purpose. The function of a hair shirt was to be awful.

Concentrate, she exhorted herself. She'd been given these letters weeks ago and ought to have finished in a matter of days. She kept making excuses. There were herbs to harvest before the winter, medicines to be replenished, and the extra patient demanded more of her time. But the truth was she simply couldn't concentrate. The roiling doubt kept pulling her under.

Jack was well now. He was leaving tomorrow. Perhaps she would be able to think then. But the odd thing was that these days she only knew peace when she was in his room. She didn't have to pretend with him. He was profoundly unimpressed with her sanctity—if anything, he found it ridiculous. Nevertheless, he seemed to like her, for no reason at all. He smiled when she came in and listened with amused tolerance when she read from the scriptures. For her sake, he tried to watch his language. Sometimes he tried to make her laugh. And she did laugh, over the stupidest things. In his room, fresh bread was better than stale, stockfish stank, and a good night's sleep was good. There were no second thoughts.

She turned back to the letter in front of her. *"I stay here because it is better than outside where people hold their noses, and I have many leper friends, so I do not complain. Only I cannot see my children. They were small when I got it and now they are big. I would like to kiss them some day. But I would not want them to be disgusted . . ."* She put it on the Yes pile, and picked up the next.

"To tell the truth I was never one for shrines and relics and all, and I have committed many sins. Now I do not commit those kinds of sins because I am crippled. If this saint heals me, maybe I will sin again. So I suppose she won't. My brother says I am a fool to tell the truth like this. But I figure if she is a saint she will be able to see through lies, so I had better. If she will not see me I will understand, but would you ask her to keep me in her prayers?" Another Yes.

The next one was written on expensive parchment in an elaborate hand. The style was elaborate, too, and hard to read for all the flourishes. Something about boils. Her vision fogged again. This time tomorrow, Jack would be gone. Winter would be long and dreary, and spring after it. God, as always, would be silent, aloof from her outcries. Her emptiness was a sponge for the suffering of others. Its capacity seemed boundless. With sudden decision, she moved all the Maybes to the Yes pile. After a moment's hesitation, she added the rejections as well.

Jack was standing by the open window. His dark blue cloak was drawn tightly around him, for the air was chilly. In the late afternoon sun the blue burned like cool fire, and a red nimbus seemed to form around the edge of his curls. Pausing in the doorway, Ingrid almost winced, as if wounded by the colors. His face wore none of the manic expressiveness that had been so striking when he arrived, and the tormented look of the first two weeks was gone as well. Now it was simply a face at rest, a face that had forgotten itself. Looking at him, she felt a longing she could hardly bear—though what she longed for (to have him? to be him? to forget him?) she did not know.

He turned and smiled. "I saw you coming across the yard. I wanted you to look up so that I could wave."

There was a hard, swollen ache behind her eyes. She swallowed and said in a dull voice, "You'll tire your leg."

"Aye, but it's so good to stand. I feel like the tallest man in the world."

He was exultant to be leaving. She should be happy too, to be rid of him, his curses and his blasphemy, the way he disturbed her senses and stirred up confusion in her mind.

"I shall miss you, Saint Ingrid," he said, and she loved more than anything the derisive way he called her "Saint Ingrid." No one else would ever do that.

"Will you keep me in your prayers?" he asked.

"Of course."

"Nay, don't say 'of course.' I don't ask such a thing as a matter of course."

"What should I say, then?"

Something glinted from his blue eyes that could almost blind her—a naked look. "What I would like you to say you cannot say, even if it is true."

The silence that followed had none of the peace that silence was supposed to have. She tried to remember what she had come for.

"Your horse will be brought 'round after breakfast tomorrow."

"Aye, thank you." His hand emerged from the folds of his cloak holding a large gold coin. "Please give this to Dame Agatha and express my thanks for the care Damascus and I have been given." With a nod she accepted the coin, dropping it into her apron pocket.

"And you, sweet lady. How can I ever express my thanks for all you've done?"

His warmth was unbearable. "You may express your thanks to Christ, for it was done in his name," she replied. It reassured her to notice how much she sounded like Dame Agatha as she said it.

For an instant Jack stiffened, as if struck. Then he shrugged and said, "Well then, I wonder if I might impose on Christ for a mirror and scissors. My beard has grown shaggy, and I'd like to trim it before I present myself to the world."

"We have no mirrors."

"Really!" he marveled. "A house full of women, and no mirrors?" He looked at her intently for a moment—or, rather, he mimed looking at her intently, for the artificiality was fast returning to his face. "So that is why you have never discovered your beauty."

Now it was Ingrid who was offended. How impersonal, this suave appeal to her nonexistent vanity! What a ridiculous man he was, after all—how foolish, foppish and glib! All at once contempt for him presented itself to her as a kind of solution. She felt fortified by it and invigorated. "Only the wicked are beautiful," she declared with an air of finality, and turned on her heel.

But Jack was quick. He caught her wrist, delaying her escape. "Show me your wickedness, lady, and I'll show you your beauty."

She shivered. Satan would say such a thing. Satan's voice would sound like that, like the low sounds that cats make. She must hold on to her wits. "Words come easily to you," she accused.

"Aye," he said. "Perhaps too easily. Do not hold it against me. In all that comes easily to me I place myself at your service."

"Let me go." The croaked words sounded unconvincing even to her. It was like nightmares she had sometimes when she wanted to scream and no sound would come from her straining throat.

He tightened his grip. "It's time, Ingrid. You know it's time. Don't run from me."

Satan's words would resonate like that, not in your mind or your heart, but in your stomach and bowels. He would take you over from within, so that your own body betrayed you. She groaned in despair as, with one swift motion, he yanked off her veil. Her short hair fell across her eyes. As she raised her free hand, reflexively, to push it out of her face, he caught that wrist too. He heaved her back against the wall and leaned into her with the full weight of his body, pinning her. She jerked her head, trying to elude his kiss, but he grasped her head in both his hands and brought her mouth to his. Somewhere her palms were straining against his chest, but the kiss was seeping into her like a drug, and her muscles were weak, so weak. Her knees were giving way, and she was falling, falling with his tongue in her mouth. She clutched at his cloak, falling, fell so soft and slow that the floor was a cloud or a cradle, and she rocked on the soft floor, drinking deep of the drug from his lips.

Something stung her. Jack winced and drew back. She tried to close the gown, but too late. He shoved her hands aside and yanked it open to confront the penance of horsehair and rope.

His look of horror shamed her. "*This* is wicked!" he hissed, crushing the fabric into his fist. "Do you understand, Ingrid? It is wicked!"

Ingrid did understand. Her shame at having it discovered told her that there was something perverse about her penance, something twisted and foul. He was saying what she dared not even think. She felt at once condemned and reprieved.

Still fierce with disapproval, Jack reached for his knife. She held her breath as he cut the rope that seemed to have grown into her waist. He pushed the habit off her shoulders and then, taking care not to scratch her, eased the scapular over her head and tossed it across the room.

She could feel his eyes on her, intent with curiosity or lust or even disgust. She could not bring herself to look up and find out which. Just when she felt so dizzy she thought she might be sick from shame and desire, he took her into the folds of his cloak and pulled her hard against his body, arching her back and tilting her head to bare her throat. She felt his breath coming fast and an urgency in his muscles. "Do you want me?" he whispered, close to her ear.

Wedged tight between fear and longing, she could not bring herself to consent. She could only let her will go limp, to be molded by his. This was not enough for him. "Tell me you want me," he insisted.

A bell ringing in the distance pierced the dream cloud and she woke to the hard-edged world where she was a nun. "Vespers!" she cried.

He held on. "You don't have to go."

"I do! I do!" she protested. Bells regulated her life like her heartbeat, and she could no more disobey them than arrest her pulse.

"Stay."

"I mustn't!" There was panic in her voice.

His grip loosened. "Very well. I will not force you." He pulled the habit back over her shoulders. It stung like a rejection.

When she tried to refasten the hooks, she found she was trembling so hard that her fingers would not work. Jack helped her. He retrieved the fallen headcloth and tied it for her, his excessively controlled movements letting her know he was annoyed.

"I'm sorry," she said faintly.

To her surprise he laughed with genuine good humor. "A lady never apologizes for withholding her favors."

They both stood up unsteadily, and Ingrid fidgeted with her

habit, trying to reassure herself that it was tightly closed. Her fingers traced the edges of her veil, certain a stray lock of hair would betray her. Jack watched with undisguised amusement.

"Don't worry," he chuckled. "It's written all over you, but none of them knows how to read it."

Blindly she propelled herself toward the door. As she fumbled with the latch she could feel his voice, low and insistent at the base of her spine. "Come to me tonight. I will wait for you."

Thirteen

Dame Agatha shivered and thrust her numb hands into her sleeves. She was tempted to light the brazier, but if she gave in to the cold this early in the season, she would be hopelessly susceptible by January. It was this awful damp. The puddles scarcely dried from one storm before the next deluge brought more. Blankets were heavy and cold and smelled of mildew. In the chapel the host was soggy and limp.

She rose and paced in an effort to warm up. The floor was tile—thousands of small, smooth chips laid in an Arabian design, the gift of a returning crusader. Costly. Too bad there was no way to exchange it for food and fuel.

She was worried about Ingrid. More than a month had passed and the girl still hadn't decided which of the suppliants she would see. The job could have been done in a day, as far as Agatha was concerned. The delay smacked of resistance. Still, she hesitated to apply pressure. She'd forced the issue last time and look where she ended up: at Ingrid's bedside, witnessing the last sacraments.

Ingrid looked terrible—grayish, with the glassy eyes of fever. At vespers this evening, her hands had been trembling. Too much fasting, probably. Too many sleepless nights in the chapel. Perhaps she had better call a halt to the penances for a while.

There was a passage in the rule which always made her uneasy. Concerning monks who were ostracized in punishment for severe faults, Benedict wrote, "Let the abbot send brethren of mature years and wisdom who may as it were 'secretly' console the wavering brother and induce him to make humble satisfaction, comforting him that he may not be overwhelmed by excessive grief." What bothered her about this advice was that she never would have thought of it, or anything like it, herself. The tender solicitude implied was foreign to her nature. She knew how to challenge Ingrid—and the girl responded admirably, with courage, intelligence and the discipline of a soldier. But when she faltered, Agatha didn't know what to do. Her heart went cold at such times. She felt only impatience.

There was a tentative knock at the door, which Agatha recognized at once. "Come in, Ingrid."

The girl fell to her knees and the abbess had to suppress a smile. Ingrid had a way of dropping down all at once, instead of lowering herself with decorous unwillingness as the older nuns did. Just now it struck her as overdramatic. After a perfunctory blessing she said, "It's good you've come. I was about to send for you. Please, be seated."

That wary look again. Perhaps she expected to be scolded about the letters. Agatha sat down herself and said amiably, "Tell me first what you have come about."

Ingrid reached into her apron pocket and drew out a gold coin. "Master Rudd is leaving tomorrow. He asked me to give you this."

"Rudd? He told me a different name. Something French."

"He was baptized Jacob Rudd. The other is a stage name."

Agatha weighed the coin in her palm. "Most generous. Or does he want change?"

Ingrid was not amused by this. "He made me promise to tell you how grateful he was for your charity," she said. There was a peculiar emphasis in her tone, as if she were defending him.

"Presumably his leg has mended well?"

"Yes, ma'am. It was a clean break."

"And his soul?"

For a moment it looked as if Ingrid was about to laugh. Then she hunched over, one fist to her breast, the other pushing hard against her lips. Agatha noticed for the first time how flushed she was.

"Ingrid, look at me." She took her by the chin and tilted her face toward the lamp. A fine film of perspiration shone on it. Her eyelashes flickered and her eyes darted away from the close scrutiny. "How warm you are! Are you ill?"

The girl shook her head, wresting it free. "Just tired," she mumbled.

"You're fasting too much. And sleeping too little. A hermit might be permitted such excesses, but you are needed here. You must look after your health."

"Yes, ma'am." Now her expression was opaque.

"It's been a strain on you, taking care of that man. He may not appreciate it now, but someday he'll realize what you've done for him."

The corners of Ingrid's mouth twitched again, and she dropped her gaze.

"Child, what is it that's troubling you?"

She shook her head as if to say "nothing" and then blurted, "Madam, I didn't help him at all in the way you think. I couldn't answer his doubts and I—" She bit down on her knuckles and rocked forward with a faint moan.

"Never mind," Agatha soothed. "It's too soon to tell. Don't be hard on yourself."

Ingrid shuddered and seemed about to weep. All at once, she recovered herself. She sat up straight and looked the abbess in the face for the first time. "You have a headache," she observed. "Is that why you were sending for me?"

This had happened too often for Agatha to be astonished any more. Sometimes Ingrid would take her head in her hands and draw the pain out. But Agatha's conservative nature disapproved of miracles on an everyday basis, so her usual reply was the one she made now. "God has sent me this gift, and I'd be rude to refuse it. No, I just wondered how you were coming along with the letters."

"I've finished."

"Oh, good. Good! I can start sending out replies at once then. How many have you chosen?"

"I'm going to see them all."

"Oh dear."

"Is that not all right?" Ingrid asked, dismayed. "I thought you'd be glad. Sooner or later I must see them, so I thought better to just get on with it. Isn't that so?"

"I don't know that you *must*—"

"But you said—"

"—Not all at once, in any case. We mustn't have you collapsing on the chapel floor again."

"What does it matter? I don't care. I really don't care." There was a hysterical edge to her voice. Agatha had never seen her quite like this—giddy, and yet also abandoned to something like despair.

"My dear, you are exhausted."

"Yes," Ingrid agreed with a sigh. "I suppose that's it. I'm sorry."

"Have you finished in the infirmary for the night?"

"Not quite."

"Well, go to bed as soon as you have. Sleep through matins and lauds if you can. And break your fast tomorrow."

Ingrid's eyes widened. "Madam, it isn't necessary. I'm all right. Prayer will restore me sooner than sleep."

"Not tonight. If I see you at matins, I'll send you right back to bed. Now run along, finish your work."

The girl arose slowly and stood there, as if waiting for something else to happen. "Madam, I do beg you—let me come to matins."

"That's enough, Ingrid. Do as you are told."

With a look of wonder, Ingrid bowed her submission and quietly left the room. Agatha relaxed in her chair, pleased with her uncharacteristic leniency. For once she felt like the benevolent superior in Saint Benedict's rule.

Fourteen

The bedtime routine in the infirmary was maddening that evening because it was no different from any other night's. It seemed as silly to Ingrid as sorting laundry during the Apocalypse, but she carried on. There was a sleeping potion to prepare for Sister Elizabeth, who still refused to leave her bed though she could sleep no more than two hours a night unless drugged. Little Agnes Bennington was sitting cross-legged on a cot, complaining cheerfully of stomach pain. Ingrid had noticed that the malady recurred right before supper whenever dried sardines were on the menu. So she announced that all patients were going to be purged that evening, and Agnes, having taken a sudden turn for the better, scampered off to her own bed in the dorter.

Sister Emily had wet her bed again and needed fresh linen. This happened almost every night and each time the frail woman would clutch Ingrid's arm and say, "I'm so ashamed—that never happened before. I don't know what could be the matter with me." And Ingrid, shifting the little nun's body easily from one side of the bed to the other as she changed the sheet, would soothe her saying, "As it happens, I was just about to change the linen anyway." Sister Emily would smile through her cloudy eyes and say, "You're a good girl, Phillippa. God bless you, child." Ingrid stroked her arm where the skin was as fragile as a butterfly's wing until the old woman fell asleep, smiling.

Then there was the laywoman, Maggie Cooke, who had been a servant at Greyleigh in its wealthier days and was bedridden now due to a weak heart. She told the same stories over and over again about the glorious disgrace into which the convent had once fallen. "To the ninth month she carried it—aye, she did—and no one suspected, I swear they never suspected till they heard it squalling in the root cellar. Aye, in the root cellar, can you imagine?" Ingrid sat patiently through a quarter of an hour of this until Maggie came to the inevitable coda: "And now, praise God, I've lived to see this house I served for five and thirty years produce a saint. And I thank the Lord for my affliction, aye, that I do, for I'd sooner be a sick old woman with thee at my bedside than a blooming girl of twenty. Aye, that's a fact. Bless me now, lest I meet my maker ere morning."

With Maggie solemnly blessed and snoring, Ingrid's work was nearly finished. She had only to collect the used supper dishes and return them to the kitchen. She gathered all but Jack's and piled them on a large tray.

When she stepped outside, a chilly wind blew up her sleeves and caught the edge of her veil. The moon was sharply etched against the sky: Jack would have clear weather for his journey tomorrow. She glanced up at the second story and saw faint light through the crack in the shutters of his window. He was waiting.

How extraordinary that she had been excused from matins! Since she slept in the infirmary rather than the dorter, it meant that she would not be missed if she spent the night in Jack's room. Such a coincidence could only be the result of supernatural intervention. She was being tested. But why? God could read the secrets of her heart, knew the precise measure of her devotion and her frailty. Why, then, the need for this literal and heavy-handed trial? To prove her faith? Prove it to whom? "Lead us not into temptation"—those words mumbled daily were a shocking secret, hidden in plain view.

The darkened kitchen, so full of steam and clatter during the day, was eerie in its stillness. She could hear mice fleeing her footsteps. She set down her burden but did not return to the infirmary. She tiptoed through the refectory, bumping into an out-of-place bench in the darkness. The scraping sound echoed in a way that emphasized the vastness and silence of the room.

The cloister was lighter; moonlight from the courtyard reflected by the flagstones, a votive candle flickering beneath each statue in its niche. She knew every stone, every statue, every sound by heart. Along one wall was a single row of small desks where the schoolgirls took their lessons. The desks were placed close to the large arching windows, to take advantage of the light. Many of the panes had been broken by Roger Fleming's men long before Ingrid came to Greyleigh. Others had been blown out by storms. In summertime, the breeze that wafted in was scented with the tangle of grasses, vines and wildflowers that grew unchecked and uncultivated in the courtyard. Humming and buzzing with insects, it was an upbaptized Eden that always made Ingrid restless with a longing she could not name. On November days like this one, the dry brown skeletons of summer weeds shivered in the wind of coming winter. She could remember studying at these windows on such days, stopping frequently to breathe warmth onto her numb fingers. It was usually late December before Dame Agatha gave in to the need for artificial heat and light. The windows were covered over with canvas then, and the cloister was cozy with oil lamps and braziers.

She ran her fingers over one of the desks, recalling the pattern of the grain, which her eyes and fingers had traced so many times in childhood. She had outgrown the little bench—if she tried to sit at it now, her knees would bump the desktop. She felt an ache of tenderness for the child she had been—seeing that scrawny and earnest little girl as a separate person from the self she was now. A vivid memory came to her of a theology class in which she had been taught the difference between mortal and venial sin. To sin mortally, the sinner had to understand the gravity of the offense and, with forethought and free will, choose to do it anyway. With uncharacteristic boldness she had thrust up her hand to argue that mortal sin could not possibly exist if this was its definition. For who would be so wicked?

Now she knew.

Theology was thin as parchment. The heaving of a man's chest, the prickling of his beard, the challenges and succulent rewards of his mouth were a dimension unknown to those who had written it. Flat laws written on flat surfaces, applicable only to what was flat. The shallowest of Jack's kisses was deeper than her deepest thought.

Tomorrow he would leave, and the memory of him would gradually flatten and fade. Then it was her penance that would have a shape: the whisper of skirts passing over her as she lay prone at the entrance to the chapel, her bare feet icy on the flagstones all through the winter, her outstretched bowl begging table scraps in the refectory, the only food she would be allowed. These images did not distress her. They even brought a kind of peace. Shame would enclose her like a heavy mantle, visible to all, yet concealing her within its folds.

Even now she was certain she could resist the temptation she had been sent. Stubbornly, doggedly, she could outlast these beckoning hours. With Jack safely gone, she would confess her near fall, and her resistance would be counted a triumph. The lives of the saints were full of such melodramas of nocturnal torment, survived and conquered to the greater glory of God and the saint in question.

But in her heart she knew that such a victory would be a bitter transaction between her and the Almighty, a cowardly and loveless bargain.

Jack was sitting up in bed, strumming idly on his lute. Above the blankets he was nude, his skin golden in the lamplight. Ingrid felt awed by the easy grace of his arms, the unabashed beauty of his body. She could imagine no act that would satisfy her yearning for it.

He saw her hesitating in the doorway and a slow smile spread across his face. "Come in, my lady," he greeted her, laying aside the lute.

She paused to remove her veil, pushing her short hair behind her ears as plain women will. "It's smoky in here," she remarked, glancing fretfully at the brazier, which he had heaped with coal.

"I didn't want you to be cold. Come," he coaxed, extending his arms. He drew her down to the bed and embraced her. The dizzy momentum of the afternoon was gone, and enveloped by his warmth and the warm smoky air, she still felt cold—not at the skin but at the center, as if her intestines were full of snow.

Jack sensed her restraint. He gripped her by the shoulders and held her roughly at arm's length, scanning her face. "It's not too late to leave, Ingrid, but it will be soon. I won't stop this time."

"I want this." Her voice was quiet and resolute.

"Then take off your gown."

She shot him a look of panic, for his voice was hard. He stared back implacably. She rose and fumbled with the hooks, but his merciless attention was too much for her.

"Will you look away?"

"Nay." His tone was impersonal, almost stern, and he watched her as a snake might watch a mouse.

"Why must you make this so hard for me?" she pleaded in a whisper.

The reptilian gaze continued for a moment, and then, all at once, he softened. "My poor little saint," he said. "We all demand so much of you."

She had no idea what he meant by this, but it comforted her. And then, to her relief, he extended his arms and brought her down to lie with him, still clothed. He held her with her cheek against his chest and when he spoke she could feel his voice rumbling against her ear. His smell reminded her of fresh wood shavings and salt.

"There is a story I've been meaning to tell you," he said. "It is about a nun called Beatrice, young and pretty like you. She was the one who took care of the candles and incense for the altar—what do you call that?"

"The sacristan."

"Aye, the sacristan. Like you, this nun had a lover, a troubadour in fact. She eloped with him, but after a while he abandoned her and she found other lovers, leading what you might call a life of sin. Fifteen years later she was moved to repent. She returned to the convent expecting to suffer shame and to be forced to spend the rest of her life in the most extreme penances. But to her astonishment no one had detected her absence. You see, our Lady had taken on Beatrice's form and tended the altar for her all those years."

"Did you make that up?"

"Nay. It is a well-known story on the continent."

"Is it true?"

"I don't know. They say, though, that our Lady has a soft spot in her heart for troubadours and sneaks them into heaven when God has his back turned. I expect that's the only way I'll get in. But what good is heaven, eh, if we don't have the earth and our bodies to love with?"

"Our bodies are the source of loathsome suffering," she said, with some vehemence. "This is not just what I've been taught—I have seen it."

He sighed. "Aye, the lepers and all. I know. A few weeks ago, when my leg was hurting me so, my thoughts ran the same way. And perhaps tomorrow along the road I will see a rotting corpse hanged from a tree, and think it again. But tonight, lying here with you, I forget all I ever knew about the degradations of the flesh. And you, my sweet, know too much of the body's embarrassments and not enough of its joys."

"Saint Benedict says that 'death stands close at the door of pleasure.' "

"Aye, love, for once your Saint Benedict has got it right."

"You feel it?"

"Often."

"I think if I really felt it, I would not be here seeking pleasure."

He looked at her quizzically. "Is that why you've come?" She could not tell whether he was teasing or really asking, and there was no time to find out, for he had begun.

How could his lips and hands know all this? How could they call down sensations from the dream world, strange drenching dreams from which one awoke longing to return to the dream? How could he know—when she had not—that the dreams were stored in her flesh? Dreams that never answered her summons answered his, as if her dreams and her flesh had been his all along.

Having no knowledge of these things, Ingrid thought she was meant to lie still: Her body's pitching and swelling of its own accord alarmed her and shamed her. When he put his tongue to one of her self-inflicted wounds, tears sprang to her eyes. She could not bear this solicitude for her woe-begotten flesh. He paused, looked up at her with a bemused smile, and her shame overflowed. She tried to hide her face in the pillow.

"Nay." He laughed softly, wiping her tears away with his thumb. "Nay, see how you please me?" He disengaged her tense grip on the bedclothes and held her hand over his ribcage. She could feel his heart pounding as hers pounded. Then he led her shy fingers down his torso and wrapped them around his engorged sex. "See how you please me?" he repeated.

It felt like nothing she had ever before touched: weighty and tough, yet springy, as if poised to leap from her palm. It seemed both threatening and rather silly and she found herself torn between a gasp and a giggle.

He was watching her reaction without anxiety, his eyes smiling. There was a luxurious availability in the way he lay still, inviting her to look and touch. Moved by his simplicity, she found the courage to disrobe. His smile deepened and he wrapped the blankets around them both.

She had been cold as long as she could remember. Without the warmth of his skin she would never have known even that. She looked at him with adoration, as if he were the sun.

And then the sun went out, and the room was black with violence. All of a sudden he was single-minded and intense, frightening her with his groaning insistence. She searched his face in panic and found it savage and unfamiliar. He clamped his palm over her mouth to stifle her cry and for an instant she thought he meant to kill her. A moment before, his body had been the very Garden of Eden; now it was nothing but the power that drove this terrible weapon. She tried to shift her hips, to get out from under him, but he bore down ruthlessly. Phrases of reassurance came out of him in little grunts, but as he did not pause for an instant, they only underscored the selfishness of his passion.

A drop of sweat fell from his curls onto her face, and then another, and he exclaimed through the fury of his panting, "Aye, then, fight me!" She glared at him with the purest hate and he threw back his head, laughing, "Fight, then," he urged.

She slammed the mattress with her fists and thrust her hips up to throw him off. There was a gash of sensation: Scarlet ripped into her eyes. He reared, ceased to breathe, caught a cry in his throat. The tendons stood out on his neck and shoulders and his lips pulled away from his teeth like those of a warring stallion or a dying man.

And then it was over. He fell back heavily, sucking in great lungfuls of air and running his fingers over his damp chest in a little gesture of self-congratulation. Her thighs were trembling, and between them was a throbbing rawness. When she explored the damage, her fingers came back bloody. She held her hand to the light and gazed at it with puzzled neutrality.

Jack caught her fingers and kissed them, staining his lips. "It can't be helped the first time," he said, and his face was gorgeous with sadness.

Ingrid did not know what to think.

Fifteen

The room was blue-gray with the diffuse light of dawn. Matins and lauds were long past, and the bell for prime had not yet sounded. Ingrid slept on her back with her long legs aligned and her arms crossed over her midriff, like an effigy in a cathedral.

He was propped on his elbow, studying her in the gradual coming of daylight. The hands he already knew well: strong, slender fingers with reddened knuckles and short, immaculate nails. As she slept, they curled slightly. Her hair might have been beautiful, given the chance, for it was thick and wavy and finely threaded with gold. But her haircut was beyond belief. It looked as if someone had gathered the whole mass into a fist and whacked it off with a resounding snap of gardening shears. He thought of her kneeling on the floor the day before with her gown slipping off: the bareness of her neck and shoulders had been freakishly alluring and he'd felt himself on an edge between repulsion and desire, an edge so fine it could cut him.

There was a rash over much of her body from the hair shirt and several sores at her waist from the rope she had wound there. Her skin had a translucent pallor—blue veins were visible in her breasts and her eyelids, too, were blue tinged. She is tired, he thought, more tired than she knows. He wanted to take her out riding, to see her ruddied by the sun and the wind. He wanted to buy her a silk shift to wear against her abraded skin. He wanted to keep her feet warm and feed her meat. He wanted to cradle her small breast in his palm like the breast of a bird with its tiny rapid heart.

Moving carefully, so as not to wake her, he parted her legs. The hairs were sticky and matted with his seed. Flecks of dried blood clung to some of them. He separated the folds with his fingertips and bent down to taste her. It puzzled him that it should be called unnatural, this act so pregnant with the taste and terror of nature. Blood and salt, seed and sap clung to his lips and tongue like pollen, and he fancied he could recall the moment of his birth.

She murmured in her sleep, then started awake with a gasp. He did not pause. She moaned and tried to close her thighs, but he held them in place. She lay still then and he could hear her ragged breathing as evidence of her pleasure oozed into his mouth, his moustache and his beard.

He reared up as her whole frame began to shudder. She was biting deep into the flesh of her hand to keep quiet and tears were running unheeded into her hair. Gently he moved her hand away and put his own mouth over hers, bringing her taste to her.

He had not meant to take her again so soon, for fear of hurting her, but now his flesh awoke to challenge his good intentions. Entering with great care, he rocked within her, and it was she who raised her knees, urging him deeper. He watched her face as she caught the thread of pleasure only to have it severed by the jagged edge of pain where she was as yet unhealed. Diligently, she would try to pick it up again, rising to meet him, then falling back with an expression of bewildered defeat.

He put a stop to it with a regretful kiss of her forehead. "Too soon," he explained. He wiped his chin on the bedclothes.

Sorrow came rolling in on them then like a great slow wave, breaking in her voice. "I shall never see you again."

Here was the familiar temptation, so many times subdued. He did not say, "I'll come back."

"Hurry and dress," he said. "They mustn't find you here."

"Not yet," she pleaded. "Another hour—what does it matter?"

"You will be missed." He sat up and combed his hair with his fingers, demonstrating his resolve. "Come, make haste."

"Jack—" She steadied her voice with an effort. "Please. Just half an hour longer. It is too cruel like this."

He clasped her hand and brushed his lips across the knuckles. "I daren't, my love. They will find you here."

"What does it matter? In a few hours everyone will know."

"Not if you make it to the chapel on time."

"Not then, but later, when I confess."

He was so appalled that, at first, speech failed him. Then he began to throw up objections, almost at random, searching for the real one, the one prodding his heart.

"What will they do to you?"

"They will pray for me. And for you, too."

"I don't want their prayers! It is our secret together—you have no right to tell others!"

"I have been secret too long, Jack. It is better that I should be known for what I really am."

Worse than her words was the disembodied serenity with which they were uttered. He could hardly believe that this was the same woman who, only a moment ago, was begging him not to leave their bed, the woman whose smell was still on his beard.

"They won't just pray for you," he said. "They will punish you."

"There will be penances, yes, but—" she laid a soothing hand on his knee, "—It will not be more than I can bear."

Suddenly he felt he could not endure to be naked in this place a minute longer. He snatched his shirt and pulled it over his head and set about putting on his hosen. As he bent to put the stockings over his feet, he saw, protruding from under the bed, the horse-hair scapular. In a fury he wadded it up and threw it into her lap. "Put it on, then. Now. Let me see you in it."

Ingrid was silent. She looked attentive and respectful, like someone who has just been slapped. He relented a little, sitting back on the bed and taking the hair shirt from her. He looked at her searchingly. "Do you think me a villain?"

"No." It was a good, firm no. He took heart.

"They'll have you calling me one before the week is out. And you can say it, for all I care—what they think means nothing to me. It's your thinking it I can't bear."

"I won't ever think it," she promised.

"Oh, but you will. How else can you repent?" She was beginning to look confused, and something warned him to stop now. Where could this argument lead them, after all? Against all prudence, he went on. "Will you shuffle around with a bowed head, secretly entertaining thoughts of our lovemaking? How many times can you fondle the memory before you wear it out, do you think? It will grow tattered, you know, misshapen and dirty. You will end up making it dirty."

He was dead accurate. She recoiled, as if from a physical blow. "I will pray to God to remove the memory and to make me repentant. What else can I do?" she whispered.

Here was where the argument led, into this temptation. He took a deep breath. So be it.

"You can leave this place," he said. "You can come away with me."

Sixteen

Usually Jack did not admire the countryside as he traveled. His peasant origins prevented him from being out-of-doors without a nagging guilt, a feeling that there was something he ought to be doing. Mountains and seacoasts he liked—landscapes to which he could not be expected to contribute. But the tame and fecund Cotswolds, past ripe now and on the verge of rot, had no more charm for him than a demanding wife.

Still, it was so good to breathe air uncontaminated by fish and mildew, so very good to see anything at all that he not been staring at for hours and weeks, that Jack was exalted all the way to Woodstock. To guide his horse over the rutted muddy road, ducking a low branch now and then, brought him the blissful absorption normally afforded by far more challenging tasks, and each new breeze was an event of some magnitude.

Woodstock was a small, unfortified town. Not much to it but a high street of overpriced shops and taverns. Its economy was driven by the annual visits of the king to his hunting lodge. When the royal party was in residence, business thrived; when they departed, shops closed early if they bothered to open at all, and the principal industry was drinking. There was a false prettiness about the place that Jack had never much liked, a self-conscious rusticity served up for sophisticated visitors. Even the whores were done up as milkmaids.

Giffard was out in the yard when Jack rode up to the Swann. He let out a low whistle. "Is that Jacques Brigand des Cœurs on that fine mount?"

"Indeed it is, Giff. How do you do, man?"

"Very well. His majesty has just left the lodge, but business was brisk while he was about. What kept you? We thought we'd see you six weeks ago."

"Aye, so did I. This 'fine mount' was seized with the desire to have me *dis*mount rather more hastily than I would have chosen to myself. Broke my ankle. I've spent the hunting season flat on my back in Greyleigh infirmary." Jack eased himself off Damascus, careful to keep most of his weight on his good leg.

"Looks like it still gives you a bit of trouble."

"Not too much. Thought I'd be crooked for life if it were left up to the nuns, but it's healed quite straight. Just needs a bit more time. I thought I might rest awhile here at the Swann."

"Splendid." The innkeeper beamed. "Kate'll be glad of the chance to fatten you up. You know what she'll say: 'skin and bones, lad,' and I daresay this time she'll be right."

Jack groaned. "Convent food—it's beyond description. Tell Kate I'll eat anything but fish. If I even smell the sea again, I'm likely to puke." He put his hand on the other man's sleeve. "Listen, though, there's a matter to talk over before we go inside. I need a private room this time, Giff."

Giffard chuckled. "Same old Jack. Fast on your feet, broken leg or no. Who is she—if you don't mind my asking."

"Well, that's just it. It's a matter of some delicacy."

The innkeeper smiled craftily. "When is it not?"

Jack made a show of glancing about to make sure they could not be overheard. "She's a nun, Giff."

"A *Greyleigh* nun?"

"Aye. Had her right there in the convent while the rest of 'em were chanting their dominus vobiscums!"

The innkeeper whistled. "Christ have mercy! You're a menace to decent society, man."

Jack lowered his head modestly. "You flatter me."

"So how was she? All pent up and panting for it, I'll wager."

"Well, it wasn't so easy, with her tortured conscience and all, but oh, when the dam burst . . . Worth the trouble. Definitely worth the trouble."

Giffard shook his head in admiration. "Well, you've really surpassed yourself this time, eh? Still," he added seriously, "you don't really mean to carry her off."

"Aye. There's a lot to be said for conquering virgins, don't get me wrong, but the real fun—"

"Bloody hell, man! Have you taken leave of your senses?"

Jack laughed. "Aye, probably."

" 'Tis no laughing matter. Have you any idea what the penalty is for seducing a nun?"

"Priests do it all the time."

"Aye, maybe, but for a layman it's a different story. I heard of a chap in Wiltshire, got caught with a nun. For his penance he was to be beaten 'round the church in his shirt on three consecutive Sundays, then beat 'round Salisbury market on three Tuesdays. Then he was to go to Wilton and repeat the whole business—three Sundays 'round the church and three market days through the market. And that wasn't all. When that was finished, he had to make a pilgrimage to the Holy Land and stay there for three years. On pain of excommunication."

"Christ almighty! I think I'd just take the excommunication and be done with it."

"That's what this chap thought. Left town as soon as he heard the judgment. The king's men caught up with him and threw him in prison for three years."

"It's a sobering thought, I'll admit."

"Aye. I suggest you sober up fast, my man."

They went inside, and as predicted, Kate lamented what she considered Jack's emaciation. Kate required eaters in the same way that Jack required listeners. On his previous visits to the Swann, he had been conscious of disappointing her, for praise of her cuisine meant nothing to her: She would accept no tribute but gluttony. This time he was able to oblige. Before the midday crowd arrived he picked clean the carcass of a leftover pheasant, accompanied by half a loaf of soft bread, still warm from the oven. "Oh, Kate, such bread!" he exclaimed with his mouth full. " 'Tis like a cloud come down from the sky."

Kate glowed. "Wait till you taste the steak-and-kidney pie I've got going for you."

"Ah, meat! 'Twas all I could think of lying there all those weeks—nice bloody red meat. You are too good."

A serving girl sidled over with a fresh tankard of stout. The head spilled over as she plunked it down, leaning over so that her bosom frothed over her gown. "That was *all* you could think of?" she teased.

"Nay, beautiful, you've just reminded me what else I thought of."

She lowered her eyelids. "Still thinking?"

"There's a lot to think about," he replied, staring where he was meant to stare.

She laughed and turned back to the kitchen. "Save an appetite."

The pub was filling up fast, for Giffard had lost no time in spreading the news that the troubadour had arrived. Jack sniffed the air—he had forgotten that crowded, unwashed, human smell. The unruly sound of spontaneous laughter. The click of dice and the clatter of pewter. He licked the grease from his fingers and stood up like Lazarus risen. "A song, man!" someone called.

Jack feigned confusion. "A song? Is there a singer here?"

"A song!" Others took up the chorus. "A song! A song!"

"And what will you give me for it?"

A coin was thrown from the far end of the room and he caught it neatly, midair. "Pass me that lute, angel," he said to one of the milkmaid tarts who had installed herself at his side. A quick adjustment of the strings and then a chord. Loud. He wanted to sing *loud*. To break silence. He threw back his head of wild curls and sang like a barbarian.

He sang and drank and sang and drank and relished the roar of protest when at last he set down his lute. "Nature calls louder," he explained, heading for the door. A pretty girl stood in his way. He caught the tail of her long braid and she shrieked, pulling away, her face red with pleasure. Deftly, he coiled the braid around his wrist, once, twice. Thrice and she was close enough to kiss. She accepted his tongue.

Outside it was quiet, the chill air a relief. He hobbled toward the stable, his leg hurting a bit.

"Jack. A word if you don't mind." It was Giffard. Jack waited for him to catch up.

"You want Molly, I daresay she's yours."

"Who's Molly? The one with the . . ." Jack described a large bosom with his hands.

"Aye. Or there's that redhead who was sitting at your elbow."

"Or the giggler with the braid," he added impatiently. "What of it?"

"You don't need to be bothered with this nun."

"I'm not bothered."

"Look, Jack, I don't need to be bothered with her either. She's trouble, that's what I'm trying to tell you."

Jack shrugged, unconvinced. "Aye, maybe. You needn't concern yourself."

Giffard sighed with exaggerated patience, like someone trying to reason with a child. "That's just where you're wrong. I run a respectable establishment—" At this Jack's eyebrows shot up in comic amazement. "So maybe when a man arrives with a woman I don't ask him to swear by all the saints that she's his wife. One takes a gentleman at his word—" He saw that Jack could hardly repress his laughter and rushed on. "And that's why it wouldn't do to have the sheriff's men barging in and inquiring into matters that are between my customers and God. Now you know I'd do anything for you, Jack, but I'm sure you can see that it won't do to bring her here. It won't do at all."

"Look, Giff, I've got to piss."

"Say you'll think about what I've said."

"I'll think about it."

Alone behind the stable, Jack watched the steaming arc as it hissed and puddled on the cold ground. What would Giffard say if he knew *which* nun, he wondered with a touch of smugness. The famous miracle worker of Greyleigh—aye, he had surpassed himself all right. If they caught him it would be more than beatings 'round the church. He'd never again see the light of day.

And what would he do with her anyway? What would she make of a place like the Swann? Women were not made for traveling—they were meant to stay put, like roadside shrines. His heart was like a map of England, each shrine marked with a sweet little ache. Each ache in its own proper spot. Let the marks bleed onto the roads and the whole map would be a muddle.

Giffard was right: This was stupid. If they got caught, Ingrid would be in trouble too. Serious trouble. All the power of the Church had conspired to make her a saint whether she liked it or not. She didn't stand a chance against them. He remembered her look of mute appeal that night she'd told him about the miracles. That rainy, cozy night. Do something, her eyes implored. Rescue me. He'd seen that look before, on the faces of unhappy wives: Rescue me.

Sorry, my love, he thought as he straightened his clothing. Sorry, love, but I'm not a rescuing man.

He went back into the pub, waving off the crowd that clustered around him. He didn't feel like singing right now. He needed a drink. Kate set the promised meat pie before him and he dug in dutifully, though he wasn't hungry anymore.

He thought of Ingrid as she had looked that morning in the blue light: the dark circles under her eyes, the horsehair scratches all over her shoulders and breasts. She'd made a miserable bargain. A life of penance for one night of pleasure. And not much pleasure at that— not for her. He should have won her sooner. He should have loved her many nights in his narrow bed and made good memories to sustain her when he left. As it was, he'd taken too much and given too little.

He dropped his spoon with a clank and felt the blood drain from his face. It was too late. If he didn't return, Ingrid would confess.

They would come after him anyway. Oh, how could he have been so stupid?

But no, he'd made her promise not to tell. Not because of the danger to him (that hadn't even occurred to him) but because—what? Because he couldn't bear the thought of her in that hair shirt. Because he didn't want the nuns to get their nasty minds around . . . around the very thing he hadn't hesitated to boast and joke about to Tom Giffard. "If you confess, you betray me," he had told her. Solemnly she had taken his hand. She would never betray him.

"Haven't lost your appetite I hope." Molly's breasts were inches from his face, the cleft between them damp with sweat. Jack drew back with sudden loathing.

"Where's Giffard?"

"Don't worry about Giffard."

He stood up abruptly. "Where is he?"

Molly shrugged, offended. "In the cellar, I guess."

The innkeeper was draining a keg of ale. "Gone bad, I'm afraid. Hope they didn't serve you any."

"Two days, Giff, that's all I need." Giffard started to protest, but Jack cut him off. "Nay, listen. The girl leaves with me tonight. It is morning before her absence is discovered. The abbess sends her bailiff and maybe a few trusted nuns out to search discreetly. She suspects me, certainly, but In—the girl was seen hours after I'd left, and the abbess can't be sure she didn't just wander off while collecting herbs, something like that. Say by nightfall she decides that the girl is definitely missing. One day has passed already. She writes the bishop, but there is no one to carry the letter to Lincoln till daybreak. Let us suppose she finds a courier at dawn and he rides at breakneck speed so as to arrive in Lincoln by nightfall. The bishop reads the letter and writes immediately to the king. Another day passes before the king receives his message. Now assume—and this is a dubious assumption—assume the king considers the matter as urgent as the abbess and the bishop consider it to be. He allows it to take precedence over all other business and writes without delay to the various sheriffs. Yet another day will pass before these messages are received and who knows how many days before the sheriffs rouse themselves to begin searching.

Two days, Giff," he urged. "I need that long to have clothes made to disguise her."

The innkeeper was wavering. "Kate won't like it . . ."

"Kate will love her. The girl looks absolutely starved."

At this Giffard could not help smiling. "I don't know, Jack."

"Come on, man. You know I have only to tune my lute and your trade doubles. On top of that, I'll give you half of what comes into my cap."

Clearly torn, Giffard scratched his head. "Jack, this thing's no ordinary sin . . ."

"It is *my* sin, Giff. Mine alone. And two days is all I ask. I'll sing myself hoarse and you can have three quarters of the take."

"Aye, then," the innkeeper relented. "Two days. But mind: If you're not out of sight by noon on Thursday, I'm turning you in myself."

There. It was settled. As he set off down the high street to do his shopping the sun was so bright, the sky so clear, that it was impossible to believe himself menaced by God or man. Giffard was the worrying sort, always had been. After all, he, Jack, had been bedding married women for years and never once been injured by a jealous husband. His luck would hold. Our Lady, patron of troubadours, would look after him.

They could stay with his friend Roger, who had an estate just south of Oxford. Roger was a law unto himself, too powerful for any sheriff to tangle with, and known to thumb his nose at the Church now and then as well. Harboring them was just the sort of challenge he would relish. The only problem would be disguising Ingrid on the journey there. Her short hair was a dead giveaway. Unless . . . unless he could pass her off as a boy. Aye, that was it! After all, she was tall as most men, and flat-chested besides. It would be fun.

The cloth merchant had closed up early. Jack had to lure him from the tavern next door with a shake of his full purse. He deliberated a long time over his purchases. Jack himself loved all shades of red, but he knew Ingrid would feel too conspicuous. Eventually he settled on pine-needle green for both tunic and hosen, and fawn-colored linen for the shirt. He splurged a bit on the cloak, choosing a double-woven worsted of deep russet: She must not suffer from the cold. After carrying his booty to the tailor (and laying down a bonus for quick service), he browsed the shops for a man's cap and some well-made gloves. Shoes would have to wait till she could be measured by the cobbler.

The brilliance of the afternoon had faded by the time he set off for Greyleigh. He paid particular attention to the road, as he would have only the moon for illumination on the return journey. Sodden leaves muffled his horse's footfalls, a few of them flashes of clear yellow amid the brownish decay. Other leaves still clung to the branches above his head, their shivering a death rattle as the wind swept through the bones of the forest. The sun was but a weak and wintry smudge, yet here and there it gilded a leaf, a twig, an exposed root to blinding dazzle. There were harvest fires in the fields, their smoke pervading the countryside like incense offered to the old gods.

It was dusk when he halted at the crest of a hill. At the foot of it was Greyleigh, huddled in the valley as if seeking protection. In the waning light he could make out the main structure—a quadrangle with a courtyard at its center—and the thatched roofs of the infirmary and other outbuildings. He must wait until dark and an hour beyond, then she would meet him just outside the gate. He dismounted and settled himself comfortably on the ground with the supper Kate had sent with him.

Already he was quickening with desire, and with deep satisfaction he daydreamed about the nights to come. Some women loved the rituals of love—the caressing glances, the poetry and stolen kisses—and in exchange were willing to endure the artless entreaties of his flesh. They left him grateful, worshipful and hungry, and they prompted him to write his most shimmering verse. This was not the feeling Ingrid inspired, Ingrid who mistrusted his artfulness and craved only his body; sweet, avid Ingrid who did not yet know how to satisfy her own craving. He would show her, and she would sleep sound, spent and tangled in his arms.

When it seemed enough time had passed, he remounted Damascus and descended the hill by the light of the rising moon. The half-barren trees rustled but faintly and he could hear his own breathing and the creak of his saddle. When he reached the gatehouse she was not there. He assumed he was too early. The moon rose higher and still she did not come, and he thought she must have been delayed by a patient, but the fear that she had changed her mind was beginning to creep under his skin.

The moon slipped behind a cloud and he felt suddenly how cold the night was. She was not coming. He had been a conceited fool to think that after one night in his bed she would forsake her home and her work and her very soul for—for what? One night in a castle, the next on the dirty sheets of an inn. A love that might last a year or two years or no more than a fortnight and could never lead to marriage.

But Ingrid did not weigh things out that way. He remembered her stark, touching bravery as she stood in his doorway, shyly removing her veil. Either she was suffering genuine remorse, or she was unable to make her escape. He would not leave until he knew which it was.

He tied up Damascus and removed the saddle and blanket from the horse's back. Though the day had been fair, the ground was so saturated by recent rains that he had to search a bit to find a spot dry enough to spread the blanket. He drank a little more from his wineskin, made a pillow of his saddlebag and, drawing his cloak tightly around him, tried to convince his body that it was in bed.

All night long his mind played increasingly frenzied variations on a single fear. No doubt other women had disclosed their liaisons with him to their priests, but the thought of Ingrid confessing and repenting of their lovemaking drove him to madness. It was obscene. It made him hate her as he had hated her, just for a moment, when he discovered the hair shirt. And just as a moment later his hatred had melted into tenderness, his blood warmed now with a desire to cherish and protect her. If she had confessed, he would forgive her. It was not her fault: She could not stand alone against all of them. He would rescue her.

Resolved, he took another gulp from his wineskin and settled down to sleep. And he did sleep, for a few minutes at least, before he bolted awake again, newly horrified, newly enraged. He had a terrible dream in which she, naked, wantonly embraced lepers and cripples in screaming ecstasy and he, in the dream, felt his sound flesh to be shameful and ugly, and he could not stop weeping. When he awoke, his throat was tight with dream tears.

By then the sky was beginning to lighten, and he felt a little better, for the sun was always on his side. Probably she had simply been unable to leave without being detected. She had missed him at the appointed hour and did not realize that he would wait. Calmed, he slept without interruption for more than an hour. He awoke in full daylight and stood up to stretch his stiff limbs. His bad leg ached as he stamped gingerly to warm himself. He drained the last of his wine in a few fast gulps and ate a little bread and cheese. Faintly he could hear prime being chanted. After prime she always returned to the infirmary, bringing breakfast to her patients. Maybe he would be able to catch her then.

He chose a tree close to the wall and scaled it with some difficulty. Just as he had hoped, his perch afforded a clear view of the yard between the kitchen door and the small side entrance to the infirmary. The chanting ended, and a quarter of an hour later the kitchen door swung open. He readied himself to shout. But the figure, though it carried a large tray, was too short and stout to be Ingrid. His heart sank. Perhaps he had simply missed her, for the front entrance, the one approached by the covered walkway, was not visible from here.

No. The figure had borne a tray. Ingrid must have been removed from her position as infirmarian. She must have confessed already. The stout nun came back out into the yard and was joined by two others from the kitchen. They stood by the well, talking with great animation. He could not make out the words, but the talking itself was notable. During his recuperation he had been attuned to every available sound, and never had he known anyone to gossip in the yard. They must be talking about Ingrid.

He had another idea. He eased himself down from the tree and hobbled back to his horse. Fishing in his saddlebag, he found the gloves he had bought in Woodstock. Hastily he combed his hair with his fingers and smoothed his sleep-wrinkled tunic. Then, leaning on his staff, he approached the gate and rang the bell.

The same nun who had answered six weeks before opened the

gate slightly and poked her head out. Again she looked frightened. Probably it was her habitual expression.

He cleared his throat. "Sister, as you know I have been well cared for in your house. I am particularly indebted to Sister Ingrid, and I would like to present her with this gift. In person."

"Sister Ingrid cannot see you." She tried to close the gate, and just as before, he forced it open.

"I require only a moment. To thank her."

"She cannot see you," the nun repeated. "Go away."

"She *will* see me!" His voice was taut and dangerous and strange to him. Brushing past the indignant nun, he sprinted up the path. He was wild, insane with rage and a desperation that was hard to distinguish from joy.

The sun fell in patches on the floor of the cloister, alternating with slices of deep gloom. "Ingrid!" he bellowed. His footsteps clattered on the flagstones as he ran to the refectory. He threw open the double doors and cried, "Ingrid!," his voice echoing. A solitary nun looked up in alarm from her sweeping, but he turned back to the cloister without a word to her.

The chapel—she would be in the chapel. He half-ran, half-limped toward it, rending the convent hush with the clamor of his footsteps and his harsh breathing. The chapel door groaned as he shouldered it open.

"*Ingrid!*" The cry tore his throat and shook the windows.

A nun was kneeling on the floor of the sun-washed nave. She gave a startled glance over her shoulder, then arose with dignity and came toward him. It was Dame Agatha.

"What have you done with her?" he said hoarsely.

"Not in here," she whispered, and her composure made him more aware of his own derangement. But he did not care. Letting his walking stick crash to the floor, he seized her by the shoulders.

"I want to see her! Where is she?"

"You desecrate the chapel, sir. Let us step outside."

Defeated by her cool manner, he let his hands drop and followed her back out to the cloister. Little girls gaped at him through the windows at the other side of the courtyard. Agatha kept walking, her finger pressed to her lips, leading him to the parlor. Once inside, she shut the door and locked it.

"She is not with you, then?"

Her voice was lowered discreetly. "You know that she is not—"

But it was plain that she had not known, for she crossed herself as if in relief, whispering "thank God." Her whole demeanor sagged. He saw that she was worried, so worried that she forgot even to be cold toward him. She spoke confidingly, as if it were a shared crisis.

"I don't know where she is. She has not been seen since compline yesterday."

Seventeen

Agatha's voice was shaking. "When she didn't come to matins, I thought she must be sleeping too soundly to hear the bell—it's hard to hear in the infirmary, and she's been so tired . . . or a patient might have detained her. But when she didn't come to prime . . . Her bed hasn't been slept in. The patients hadn't seen her all night. One of them said—"

"What? Said what?"

"She thought Ingrid had gone with you."

"Why? Did Ingrid say—" He stopped himself. "Why in heaven's name would she think a thing like that?"

Agatha looked up at him with helpless appeal. "So it isn't true? You didn't . . ."

"Didn't what? Seduce her—is that what you think? My God, woman, what do you take me for?"

The abbess seemed near collapse. Jack took her elbow and steered her to a chair. He sat across from her, leaning forward, his elbows on his knees. "I don't know what Ingrid may have said to you," he said quietly. "But she struck me as a very unhappy young woman."

"What do you know about it?" Agatha snapped. "You blame me, I suppose."

Jack struggled to suppress his impatience. "None of this matters right now," he said softly, urgently. "Have you sent anyone out to search for her?"

"No."

"No?"

"I don't know whom to send. Master Rudd, you must understand my position. There is a great risk of scandal."

He sprang to his feet. "Risk! Have you any idea how dangerous the roads—"

Agatha put a detaining hand on his arm. "Please, not so loud," she entreated, with a glance at the door.

"Don't they know?"

"I said she'd been called away on an emergency. The Ladbrook's newborn."

"I see. And then you retired to the chapel, thinking maybe if you prayed hard enough some angel would swoop her up and carry her back to you."

"Not some angel. Her conscience. She will come back."

Jack rolled his eyes. "For Christ's . . . Madam, the countryside is teeming with outlaws. You think they're going to leave her in peace while she examines her conscience?"

Her grip tightened on his sleeve. "What can I do? If word of this were to get out, the scandal—it would mean the end of us."

"Of course," he said coldly. "A scandal must be avoided at all costs." He shook off her grasp and strode toward the door, then turned back to her. In a milder voice he said, "Look, she can't have gotten far on foot. I'll find her. And you're right. It's best we keep this quiet."

A spike of pain was driving itself between Agatha's eyes. She tried to focus on what she had written. *"Your grace,"* the letter began. *"It is my unhappy duty to inform you . . ."* However could she word it? *"Ingrid Fairfax has disappeared."* As if reporting something misplaced or stolen. She could imagine the bishop sputtering, "Disappeared? How can a nun in your care simply disappear?" "*It is my unhappy duty to notify you of the possible apostasy of . . .*" Of the girl we've been claiming is a saint. There was no way of wording it that was anything but damning, utterly damning.

Maybe the letter need not be written. Maybe the troubadour would bring her back and . . . and what? She had been thinking that if Ingrid returned by nightfall, or even within a few days, the fiction of the Ladbrook emergency would hold. But it was barely holding now. There was whispering, already a fraying at the edges of convent discipline. I will lose control of them all, she thought. And in what condition would the girl return? In what state of mind? And finally, what folly to think the man would bring her back at all—certainly not against her will if her will was to leave! Should lawmen be sent to retrieve her by force, the living saint dragged back to the convent in chains? The scandal was unthinkable. Unthinkable. The spiritual well-being of every Christian who had believed in Ingrid's sanctity was in peril. Agatha knew the man thought her cold, but she was right, right to consider that peril ahead of any physical danger Ingrid might face. "*Your grace, what am I to do? God help me, what am I to do?*"

I must get hold of myself, she thought. The way to handle a crisis was to break it down into manageable pieces and solve them one by one. Begin with the infirmary. That problem was well-defined: Ingrid had no apprentice.

She hurried across the yard, her head thudding with each step. The sickroom was in chaos. Unwashed breakfast dishes were scattered about, and there was a stink of brimming chamber pots. Sister Emily was calling for Ingrid: a thin, plaintive cry. Maggie Cooke was snoring noisily. Agatha stood over Elizabeth's bed, arms folded. "Get up," she commanded. "You've got work to do."

Elizabeth just lay there, coolly returning her gaze.

"You've done nothing but lie about like a lazy sow for months. You must have seen what Sister Ingrid does around here. So get up and do it."

Elizabeth stayed put, smiling a little. "Aye. I've watched. And listened."

"Get up!"

"Don't you want to know what I observed?"

"So help me . . ." Agatha threatened in the low voice she reserved for her coldest anger.

"Our little Saint Ingrid performs all the corporal works of mercy. Oh, aye, she took care of the man, that she did. Every night."

Tremors of controlled rage shook Agatha's slight frame. In one sweeping movement she denuded the malingerer's bed of its covers, exposing flabby legs sticking out of a scrunched-up nightdress. "Move!"

The background noise of Maggie's snoring stopped, and the old woman's eyes opened in surprise. Emily, who had been humming to herself like a vague, senile bird, began to weep. But Elizabeth, with a sangfroid that Agatha could not help but marvel at, held still for a breath or two before hauling herself up and stretching languorously, as if she had been meaning to get up anyway.

"You can start by clearing away these dishes. And I swear, if you ever repeat what you just said to me, I will beat you within an inch of your wretched life!"

Elizabeth just smiled.

"Ma'am, I'll be needing my medicine," Maggie Cooke said.

Agatha sighed. "What sort of medicine does she give you?"

"Don't know, ma'am, other than it tastes like it came off the floor of a barn."

"I'll see if I can find it."

The worktable in the herbarium had been swept clean of its usual clutter of decanters and drying weeds. Now there was only an open book—open intentionally, for the pages were weighted with a pair of shears. Agatha scanned greedily, hoping for a note, an explanation. Ingrid had left painstaking instructions for her successor: formulas for medicines, a schedule for bloodletting, dates for harvesting needed herbs and anecdotal information on the health of each resident of Greyleigh. But there was neither prologue nor postscript to explain the writer's disappearance. She leafed through the rest of the book in search of a clue. The early pages were full of the naive drawings Ingrid had made as a child. Each sequence began with the gruesome and literal depiction of an ailment, then showed its remedy being applied by a cheery nun and ended with the manic smile of the successfully treated patient. Later pages substituted neatly written notes in Latin for these pictorial narratives and were accompanied by botanical illustrations of scrupulous accuracy. The last of these drawings was subtly different from the rest, and Agatha pondered it for some time. The other sketches were flat, as if an idealized specimen of a plant had been pressed between the pages. In the last one, the leaves curled, half hiding their faces, their undersides in shadow. The berries drooped with real weight. Instead of imparting the accumulated knowledge of *Solanum dulcamara*, this drawing documented the fleeting appearance of one stem of bittersweet on a late autumn day. If the manual contained any clue to Ingrid's defection, Agatha felt, this was it. But what it meant, or why to her it bespoke rebellion, she could not have said.

She leaned on the table, cradling her aching forehead in her palms. There was something disturbing about these instructions Ingrid had left. They were so deliberate, so premeditated, so oddly responsible—like a thief tidying up after he's ransacked your storeroom. How long had she been planning to run away? She recalled Ingrid's weird smile two nights before. A brittle smile, like a warning crack in a pane of glass. A treacherous smile.

She took care of the man, that she did. Every night. Could it be true? Ingrid had been looking so tired, clearly had not been sleeping these past weeks . . . but no, it was to pray. Agatha had seen her on the chapel floor night after night, weeping . . . *a very unhappy young woman* . . . but saints do weep at prayer. Night after night, except that last night, the night she'd been excused from matins. She'd not been in the chapel that night—Agatha had checked. *That* night it was just possible. Oh, the scoundrel! How could she have let herself be duped by him? She sped upstairs to his room. There would be a stain, a red-brown stain on white linen, unambiguous as ink on parchment. This was *his* fault!

The rusted hinges screeched as she pushed open the door. The room was dim but for a crack of sharp light between the shutters, and thick with the odor of settled smoke. Not an oil or charcoal smoke—this was foul and acrid, diabolical. Something evil stirred near the floor. She shuddered: a bat. But no, it was only some light object disturbed by the draft. She crept closer to investigate. It was resting on the brazier. She touched it, recoiled, then lifted the thing: a wad of charred horsehair. An act of vandalism by the man, she thought, enraged. Her rage grew as she noticed the velvety black ashes beneath it, feathered like the leaves of a burned book. And their library held so few! But what book, and how did he get it? She opened the window to let in more light and saw on the floor a scrap that had escaped immolation. "erbury but" it said, and below that, "o relief."

"I visited the shrine of Canterbury but alas, I was granted no relief." This was one of the letters she had given Ingrid. The fire had been of her making. This can't be happening, Agatha thought. Soon the matins bell will ring and wake me from this woeful dream. Moaning, she sank down on the cot. The sheets had been stripped from it, and the ancient mattress was a noncommittal dun.

Eighteen

Sin took over more rapidly than Ingrid would have imagined possible. It was like watching the decomposing of a corpse: awful but not without scientific interest.

It had been dismally easy to fool her sisters in the hours between Jack's departure from Greyleigh and his promised return. She had taken care to expunge the evidence from the sheets and to follow her usual schedule, but she could not help feeling contemptuous of them for their failure to scent the change in her. Ignorant as sheep they were, falling for the wolf who wore their uniform. They did not see her, but she saw them as never before, as if sin were an acid eating away the varnish that till now had begummed her world. Had they put on laywomen's dress and mingled in a London crowd, she would still have spotted each one of them by that ignorant look they had. Their very flesh was ignorant, like wax.

At terce she had almost lost her nerve. Until Dame Agatha

nudged her, she had forgotten that she was the day's assigned reader. How could she possibly read scripture aloud? Surely toads and serpents would leap from her mouth. Surely she would be struck dumb. Approaching the lectern as if it were a scaffold, she felt the souvenir ache of new challenged muscles. She opened her mouth. The syllables rolled out round and sensuous and opaque as pearls.

Deception was so easy! It gave her more respect for God, seeing what he was up against. The cosmic contest was not, as she used to suspect, rigged in his favor. Like a balanced equation, its elegance gave pleasure.

Late in the afternoon, she went into the herbarium to make some notes for her successor as infirmarian. There, on the worktable, were the letters, the four dozen Yesses. No, she heard herself say aloud. No. She gathered them together and dashed upstairs to what she still thought of as Jack's room. She locked the door behind her, just to be safe. Stooping over the brazier, she set fire to them. The bright flames made her giddy with defiance. Too much of the body's embarrassments, he had said. Not enough of its joys. She could see his face clearly through the rising smoke, the face of her savior. There was something else he wanted. What was it?

The hair shirt. One of them had kicked it under the bed. It was still there, with its nasty twine belt. She fed it to the fire. The smouldering horsehair gave off a foul odor and after a moment it killed the flames. She tried to relight it but soon gave up.

How hot she was, prickling with sweat under her wool habit as if it were July! She went to the open window. This was where he was standing, this time yesterday, in a blue mantle, haloed by the autumn sun. She savored the memory cautiously, for there was something in it, like a bitter stone in sweet fruit, that she did not want to taste.

"That is why you have never discovered your beauty," he had said. But she had known then and still knew that he did not mean it. The ease with which such a lie came to him, the unthinking grace of it, was like her own ease with a scalpel, a kind of professionalism.

She looked down at her large, plain hands, which had always served her so well, looked at them not as her hands, deserving of her loyalty, but as aesthetic objects. The rest of her, she knew, was like her hands. In sinning, Eve had discovered her nakedness. Ingrid's discovery was worse. Outside of Greyleigh there would be mirrors, and she foresaw how relentlessly she would interrogate them. For her lover was beautiful and loved beauty. And her lover was a liar.

Oh God, what if he did not return for her? That morning he had dressed briskly and without regret. He had set off at a gallop, without looking back. She would wait an hour, two hours, the bleak certainty settling on her. She would postpone the moment, and postpone it and postpone it and postpone it, but finally it would come—the moment when she would turn back to the convent. She would make it to the chapel for matins. She would change Emily's urine-soaked sheets tonight, and every night. She would still be staring at these gray walls thirty years from now, when she herself was gray. Her flesh would be wax.

But no. He would come. He would. "Courage," he had urged as he took his leave of her. "If you are tempted to confess, think of me and how I shall make love to you tonight."

"*Thou hast turned for me my mourning into dancing; Thou hast loosed my sackcloth and girded me with gladness.*" His skin was warm against hers. His tongue was sweet on her sores and scratches. He would smile when he saw her by the gate.

At compline she found herself staring at the cruifix. A detail till now overlooked began to bother her. Had Jesus lain down willingly to be nailed? Did they have to tell him how to arrange his hands and feet, or did he know already and do it without being asked? She tried to imagine him giving over his warm living hand so that another man could drive a nail through it. She tried to imagine what it was like to be that other man. What a sordid business it was! Jack would never have held still for it. A dozen men would have been needed to hold him down and his curses would have rung out all over Judea.

Like an outgrown schoolgirl crush, her devotion to the crucifix embarrassed her now. All those hours in the chapel yearning after an unresponsive God had been nothing but disguised craving for the love of a man. She was grateful to Jack for showing her. He would fill the emptiness where her soul should be. His love would make her whole.

A doubt clawed its way through her ribs like talons, seized her heart and ripped through the meat of it. Not Jack either, said the doubt. It is not he. If God himself could not support her longing, how could a mere man? Her longing was too great: it would consume him.

She eloped with him, but after a while he abandoned her and she found other lovers . . . Lovers. Not *the* lover, or even *a* lover, but *lovers*. What a world of despair there was in that plural! In blind hunger she would take them, these faceless men, would grasp at anything to fill this gaping where her soul should be. Oh, it was ugly, this longing! It was sin and damnation together. It was the vast sky turned hostile and it would shake her bones till they snapped, would stare back in mockery while she howled at the moon. She was damned, doomed to wander the earth till her spirit starved to death. Compared with such a fate, the caldrons and horned beasts of conventional hell seemed reassuring, like figures from a child's fable.

At the same time her realization had a bracing, bedrock quality. It was even seductive, the way hard truth is seductive to the brave. She would stare it down. She would ride into it as into a cold wind. Alone.

PART TWO

One

It was that sodden time again, the conjugal bed a leaky rowboat bobbing on tides of blood and tears and milk and night sweats. A mudlike afterbirth smell mingled with the smell of milk and permeated their little house, and all of the children mewled like infants. Matthew shuffled about with a hangdog look that made Gillian want to tear his throat.

As the saints were his witness, he would have borne the children if he could. He was so big and Gillian so small—when they walked together during her pregnancies, he felt as if all eyes reproached him. Matthew Sturges, the ungallant empty-handed, letting his wife stagger under the burden of his begetting.

After each of the births she had wept enough to fill the baptismal font of St. Martin's. By now he should be used to it. He should have learned not to feel that each tear was a needle of blame being driven into his testicles. His mother-in-law used to pat his hand and say with that tender, mocking, men-are-such-babies bravado, "Don't take on so. All women cry afterwards. It's nature's way." And Gillian, too, when the floodwaters at last receded, would tenderly, mockingly reach up to him with her doll-like arms and say, "Silly old bear." This was supposed to make him feel better. It made him feel anxious and helpless, like a child who senses that adults are concealing from him the whole awful truth.

His shop was the front room of the house. A few years before he had knocked down part of the wall that separated it from the kitchen so that the downstairs was one large room. Most of the time it was a happy arrangement. He liked to have the children nearby as he worked, and Gillian liked to chat with his customers as they lounged by the hearth. But today it irked him to find a rag doll sprawled across his workbench, to search for an awl and discover that it now served as a flagstaff for a building-block castle. The children had learned a new nonsense song, something about piggy-wiggy and ho-ho-ho. Matthew suffered through twenty choruses before he threw down the shoe he was working on and stomped upstairs. He heard Bartholomew whine, "Why is Papa mad?" and Jocelyn answer him in hushed responsible tones.

Gillian was sitting in bed with the baby at her breast. The damp downy hair on the infant's head promised to be red, like the others'. Gillian looked up with red-rimmed, moist eyes, her face composed in a beyond-caring way. He was conscious of his hands hanging stupidly at his sides and of his stooping—necessary because the ceilings upstairs were low—which must nevertheless be hideous to her.

"I'm going for a shave."

"The children need to get out," she said in a mild, tired voice. "Take them with you, why don't you."

He sighed, agreed and lumbered back down the stairs. He sighed some more through the half-hour search for three pairs of shoes, stockings that matched, cloaks and hats and mittens. But his irritation could not last long as he combed out the tangles in those three tossled heads and pushed fat pink feet into little stockings. He was a giant made helpless by anything small. "Piggy-wiggy ho-ho-ho," he sang in a solemn gruff baritone, and the children shrieked for joy. He went through the usual futile exercise of asking the very young to anticipate the needs of their bladders, received the usual assurances and off they went into the Oxford streets.

The first snow of the winter weighted the clouds and made the town quiet. Though it was still midafternoon, lamps burned in the shops and houses. Night would be falling even before the church bells rang vespers. The heads of his children, like gay gallant flames, made people smile as they passed.

The warm, sheltering smell of cinnamon beckoned them from a pastry shop. "On the way back," Matthew promised.

They halted in front of Lucas Pratt's.

"Papa, I don't like that place," Celia fretted.

"Me neither," said Jocelyn.

"Me neither," her brother said, no less vehemently, though he did not know to what he was objecting.

He told them to wait outside while he had his shave. "No one is to move more than five paces in any direction from the barber pole," he admonished Jocelyn who, at seven, was the eldest.

"Five of your paces or five of my paces?" she demanded.

"Daughter, you are one of the fine legal minds of Oxford."

The children were vastly amused by this, repeating "five legal minds of Oxford" and laughing more each time they said it. To his children, Matthew was a wit.

Ducking his head so as not to bump it on the lintel, he entered the shop. The truth was that he had never liked this place either. It had a boozy smell, and a nastiness of dirty jokes thickened the air like brown smoke. In the front room, hair clippings muffled the floor and clung to customer's shoes long after they left. A greasy curtain separated this area from the even darker room where surgery was performed. About this back room there were evil rumors. The Chequer crowd hung about Pratt's, and what little crime in Oxford was not monopolized by the scholars originated at the Chequer. Now that he was constable, Matthew felt he should maintain a presence here.

Two young clerks were sitting on the waiting bench and another was being dabbed clean in the high chair by the window. Pratt, who was not at all pleased to see him, greeted him with false heartiness and insisted on taking him next, ahead of the waiting youths. Ever since Matthew's election, he had been accorded this sort of deference. Usually he declined special treatment, but the thought of having to wait half an hour while his children grew cold and cranky outside led him to accept. With an apologetic nod to the clerks, he seated himself in the barber chair. They snickered and complained to each other in Latin. Matthew flushed, wishing he had waited his turn after all.

As Lucas lathered his broad, homely face, Matthew glanced out at his children. Jocelyn and Celia were intent on a game that involved the intricate arrangement and exchange of small stones in accordance with rules abstruse enough to confound a scholastic. Bartholomew, the youngest, squatted beside them, ceremoniously offering some pebbles he had gathered, careful of his balance and his infant dignity. The girls were not at all appreciative of this donation. "Barty!" Jocelyn wailed. "Get out of the way. You're messing everything up!" The little boy arose, wobbled a little but caught himself and stood watching his sisters from a respectful distance.

"Heard the wife just had another one," Pratt remarked.

"Aye. A girl. Night before last."

"Long labor?"

Matthew sighed. He did not even like to bring his loved ones' names into this shop. Luckily they were interrupted by the cowbell on the door. The apparition that stood on the threshold brought all conversation to a halt.

She wore a dark cloak, heavy with damp and muck. Beneath it bare feet were visible, gray with cold. Her hair was so snarled and matted that it looked like felted wool or the nesting place of foul creatures. He might have taken her for a beggar or a madwoman, but her tall, dignified stance forestalled pity. It was as if she had been eating locusts for years and now was come to screech repentance at them. Matthew was ready to fall to his knees.

Not Lucas. "Clear off!" he said.

She blinked at him for a moment as if she were not sure whether this had been addressed to her. "Ex—" Her voice cracked. She cleared her throat. This time she managed, "Excuse me. I'm looking for Lucas Pratt" in what was, unmistakably, the accent of a gentlewoman.

Both men were startled, and Matthew got nicked. Lucas dabbed at the cut with a dirty towel. "'And what would you be wanting of him?" he said uneasily. "If this is a female matter, you'd best come back another time. Saturdays are no good—I've got shaves all day."

"*You* are Lucas Pratt?" She seemed to doubt it. "The surgeon?"

"Aye."

"I heard you were looking for an apprentice."

Lucas paused, holding the soapy razor aloft. "Aye. Boy I had ran off. You know someone I can use?"

"Yes. That is, I want to apply for the position myself."

"You!" He shook the foam off the razor and wiped the blade on the towel.

"I have some experience," she added hastily. "Sutures, cautery, phlebotomy, setting fractures—"

"Did the lads at the Chequer put you up to this? They did, didn't they?"

She looked blank. "The Chequer?"

"The Chequer?" Pratt mocked. "Tell them I said 'very funny.' "

She frowned, concentrating. "You think I am joking. But why would I joke?"

"You do it with a straight face, I'll say that for you."

One of the students spoke up, mock serious. "Why don't you ask her to demonstrate what she can do?"

"What—on you?"

"God save me!" the young man protested, warding off the very idea with his outstretched palm.

But the girl took this as inspiration. "I would be happy to demonstrate," she said. "On myself."

The students whistled and clapped their approval, but Lucas went back to shaving Matthew. "Very funny," he muttered.

"It was not meant as a joke," she insisted. "Please—name the vein."

Lucas said something in Latin that Matthew did not understand, but evidently the girl did. She blushed, saying "Not here, sir," and suggested an alternative.

The barber stared at her, impressed. "Aye," he said. "Show me then."

She glanced around the shop and, seeing an unoccupied stool, moved it over by the window where the light was better. Lucas passed her the shallow wooden box in which he kept his instruments. There was soot in the corners of it and a couple of dead flies. She lifted a knife and inspected it. Even from his seat a few feet away, Matthew could see that it was freckled with rust. She dropped it back in the tray and selected another, pursing her lips with dissatisfaction.

"Haven't you a sharp one?" she asked.

"Stalling for time, eh?" Lucas jeered. She ignored this. "That razor is sharp," she observed as he made the last quick strokes on Matthew's sideburns. "May I use it?"

The barber shrugged rather elaborately, wiped it on the limp towel and handed it to her. "Be my guest."

She seated herself on the stool, pushed her cape back over her shoulders and rested her bare left arm, underside up, on her thigh. The students leaned forward, all attention balanced on the blade's edge. The girl opened and closed her fist a few times, till the veins stood out clearly through her translucent skin. Matthew winced as she made a swift, decisive incision, as if drawing a thin, straight line of blood. She showed no fear, no pain, only—as he marveled to Gillian later—a kind of contempt, as saints are said to have contempt for the flesh.

Keeping her arm horizontal so that the blood would not run off, she raised it for Pratt's inspection. "Have you a blood band?" she asked calmly. Lucas had not yet recovered from his amazement and he passed her a strip of gauze without a word. She wrapped it twice around the arm and tied it deftly with her free hand and teeth. "Am I hired, then?"

"Where did you learn that?"

"My father was a surgeon."

"I say, Pratt, give her the job," one of the students urged.

"Maybe she can sharpen your knives," his friend added.

"I could," she agreed, not realizing that they were jesting. "And I could keep your linens clean and see women when decency prevents—"

"Impossible," Lucas said, folding his arms. "The surgeon's guild doesn't admit women. You should know that if your father was a barber."

She looked downcast. "I see. That is true all over Oxford?"

"It is true all over England."

Her reaction to this news was curious. Disappointment or even anger, Matthew would have expected, but it seemed to him that she was scared. With a little gasp she gathered her cloak around her, mumbled something to Lucas (the only audible word was "sorry") and rushed out the door.

There was nervous laughter in her wake, but Matthew did not join in it. Without stopping to think how odd it must look, he jumped to his feet, paid Lucas and bolted from the shop. The children clustered around him. "Wait here. I'll be right back," he told them as his eyes scanned right and left. He saw her dark shape retreating rapidly in the direction of St. Edward's and ran after it. Her shoulders contracted at the sound of his slapping feet. "Wait, please!" he called, and at that she began to run. "I won't hurt you!" he yelled.

How funny to be saying that: His harmlessness and his bulk were a single, indivisible truth that anyone would know in a glance. It had never before needed saying.

She slowed her pace and he was able to overtake her.

"I just want to tell you—" He was breathing hard. "I'm sorry about what happened in there."

She glanced sidelong at his face, trying to read from it whether he could be trusted. The one thing everyone in Oxford knew about Matthew Sturges was that he could be trusted. But she was a stranger.

A stranger! What a thrill there was in that word! Possible danger, possible discovery. Possibly the flat familiar earth might split open at his feet, show fruit of unimagined colors to the worm who dwelt on its skin. Possibly he might take off and fly with wings he never till then noticed he possessed. Anything could happen in that moment before she made up her mind to trust him.

Which, of course, she did. His weight caught up with him then, and there he was, planted like an institution in St. Edward's lane. Himself.

She halted too, facing him. He noticed for the first time how dirty her face was. "Is it true that women can't be surgeons in Oxford?" she asked.

"Aye. Nor anywhere else that I know of."

"Then he never had any intention of hiring me?"

"Nay," he admitted. "We let it go too far. That was cruel."

She frowned, seemingly more puzzled then annoyed. "Then why did he let me open my vein?"

Matthew rubbed his freshly shaved chin. "Well it was—entertaining. Not that that's any excuse."

"Entertaining." Still frowning, she pondered this for a moment. "Oh, yes, I see!" she exclaimed all at once, and smiled. Matthew could not see what there was to smile about, but he was glad for it. Smiling she was less uncanny, more ordinary, even, conceivably, pretty.

"I *am* sorry."

She shook her head. "No harm done."

"I'm Matthew Sturges."

He extended his big hand, and she seemed ready to jump back in alarm. But she caught herself and then gaped at the hand, as if wondering what was expected. Belatedly she raised hers and let it hover outside her cape for a moment, for by then he had let his drop. Both of then half smiled. She did not offer her name.

The children, against orders, had been creeping up on him. "Papa, the sweet shop will be closing soon," said the ever-practical Jocelyn, ignoring his companion. Bartholomew clung to his legs and from that refuge peeked out at the strange young woman. It was left to Celia to come to the heart of the matter.

"Papa, that lady has no shoes."

Matthew reddened and hushed her, but the stranger was not offended. "I lost them," she explained.

"Oh," said Celia, satisfied.

"Papa," Jocelyn said again.

"Aye, sweetheart, we'll be going in a minute." And then, to the woman, "Look here, do you have a place to stay?"

"Oh, yes." She ducked her head in a diffident little bow and turned to go. He was certain she was lying. "The thing is," he blurted, "my wife just had a baby, and we could use a little help. It would only be temporary, you understand, and we couldn't afford to pay you. But you'd have your bed and board and—" He almost said, "someone to look after you" but amended this to "a pair of shoes. I'm a cobbler, you see."

She hesitated, but he sensed that she wanted to accept. "Come along," he commanded, as if she were one of his children. Without giving her time to argue, he swung Bartholomew up to his shoulders and turned back toward the High. To tease Jocelyn, he pretended to pass up the sweet shop.

"Papa!"

"Aye, daughter."

"Aren't you forgetting?"

"What—have I left a child behind?" He counted them up ostentatiously. "Nay, it's three I set off with and three I'm bringing back." But he could see his eldest was in no mood to be toyed with, so he smacked his forehead. "Ah, the pastry shop. Mustn't forget the pastry shop." He winked, but she was slow to forgive. High-strung like her mother she was.

Mistress Davies, the baker, greeted them warmly. Matthew was struck by the contrast in her manner toward the young woman, who was huddling in her cloak and averting her eyes as if that would make her invisible. "What will you have?" the baker demanded with an impatient edge.

"She's with us," Matthew said, his glance urging tact. He wished he knew the girl's name so that he could at least introduce her. He rubbed the back of his neck self-consciously. Mistress Davies' reaction led him to speculate for the first time about Gillian's. She would not be pleased. He felt like a small boy hoping his parents will allow him to adopt a mangy puppy.

Back on the street the girl drew up beside him as if she had read his thoughts. "Maybe your wife won't like it that I've come," she said softly. "I'm very dirty."

He thumped a friendly hand on her back. He was not a boy after all, and it was, after all, his own home. "You can have a wash before supper."

She peered at him as if to say "Are you sure?" In answer he gave her the parcel of cakes to carry.

"What was that she called you, in the shop?" she asked.

He had to stop to think. "Constable?"

"Yes. I thought you were a shoemaker."

"I'm both. Constable's an elective office—for two years only. Lucky thing, too, for it leaves me little enough time to earn my living. But the guild helps out." Matthew was used to adding this complaint about his time to conceal the pride that welled in his chest whenever he thought of his office. He was the sort of good man whose virtue arises not from sanctity but from citizenship. His plain, fair, factual mind was made to serve on juries. He was the sort of man who counts his blessings, the sort of man who does more than his share.

By now they had reached Shoe Lane. Shoe-shaped signs rocked over the street, their chains creaking mournfully in the evening quiet. They halted in front of a flat wooden boot with an unfashionably round toe that read "M. Sturges" from the west and "Shoemaker" from the east. Matthew sent the children in through the front but guided the woman through the alley leading to the back yard.

He had built the washhouse himself, and it was more luxurious than the family's modest means would have led one to expect. It had a chimney and a miniature fireplace, so that it was toasty, even in wintertime. An iron caldron for heating water hung over the fireplace. Since the shed doubled as a laundry room, it was crisscrossed with clothesline. A shelf held towels, combs and a bowl of dried herbs with which Gillian liked to scent her wash water.

One evening a week Matthew bathed himself and all of the children together. On those occasions—when his naked ruddy children danced giddily around his own shaggy nakedness—he would not have traded places with a king. He was not only happy then, but conscious of being happy, as if he were looking back in nostalgia for the moment at the same time he was living it. Last week Jocelyn had announced that she was too old to bathe with her father, now that she was seven. Already he was losing her to that sad privacy of grown women. He was sorry for her, bathing alone, and sorry for himself.

As he stooped to light a handful of kindling he could feel his guest standing behind him, still in her cape. "There's a hook for your cloak," he said over his shoulder. "See—there beside the shelf."

"My dress is awful," she confessed with obvious chagrin. "I'm not even sure it's a dress."

"Never mind. We'll find you something."

He got a little fire going and rose heavily to his feet. By then she had taken off the cloak and was reaching up to hang it. She had not been exaggerating about the dress—it amounted to no more than several colorless sacks sewn together, bunched in at the waist by a length of rope. The sleeves were not proper sleeves at all—merely the overhang of the shoulders and so loose he could see her ribs and one scant breast. How easy for someone to slip his hand in and slide it down her hard, corrugated torso. A girl like that, a nameless ragged stranger, was somehow off the record. No father, no brothers— someone could take advantage. It's a good thing I found her, he thought.

There was an assertive tap on the door. The blood rushed to

his face, as if he had been caught at something furtive. It was Jocelyn. "Mama wants to know when you're coming in."

"Tell her in a minute. Listen, run to Papa's workshop and get my smock for this lady to put on."

Jocelyn looked with disapproval at the woman's bare calves and ragged hem. "I told Mama we had company," she said with a certain unkind significance.

"Your mother will be very glad to have some help with the baby," he said, warning her with a frown that he would tolerate no dissent. "Run along now and get that smock."

He shut the door to keep the heat in and turned back to the young woman. He felt he should say something to make her feel better. "My name is Jane Basset," she said without preamble, as if she had just thought of it. Her timing disconcerted him. He was irrationally convinced that she had read his thoughts a moment before, misconstrued them and now was presenting her name as a kind of chaperone.

"Jane Basset," he repeated. "I am Matthew Sturges." He flushed, realizing that he had already introduced himself.

"Yes. *Constable* Sturges. It is lucky for me that I met you."

Was she mocking him? She met his eyes for just a second and then looked diffidently away, clutching one bare arm and biting her lower lip.

He forgot to duck on the way out, and bumped his head.

"Who do you think she *really* is?" Gillian asked later that night, whispering so as not to wake Celia, who slept between them. They always kept a child between them at night, like Tristan's sword, for Matthew did not like to rely too heavily on his will power. On the rare occasions when he lost command of himself—usually when he'd had too much to drink—Gillian bore him with good grace. She would even soothe him in his remorse, saying, "I'm your wife, Matthew. You have every right." But love was not a matter of rights. If you loved your wife, you considered her well-being above all. So he did what he could to stack the odds in her favor.

Gillian was propped on one elbow, looking at him with the

bright, eager inquisitiveness that was characteristic of her except when she was robbed of it by childbirth. Her cocked head reminded him of a listening bird. He was lying on his stomach, his chin resting on one fist, feeling very relaxed now that Gillian was herself again.

"She said her father was a surgeon."

"If that were true, she would have known better than to try to get hired by one."

"Maybe it's different where she comes from."

"Where *did* she say she comes from?"

"She didn't," he admitted. "But it can't be denied she knew what she was doing."

"Oh, horsefeathers!" Gillian said. "How much do you have to know to cut up your arm? I'll wager she's a runaway serf. You said she was in rags, after all."

"Her dress was. The cloak looked expensive."

"She stole it."

"What about her accent, then? You have to admit she talks fancier than we do."

"Anyone can fake an accent." To prove her point, she thrust her nose into the air and gave her rendition of aristocratic speech. Matthew laughed. The heaving of his stomach shook the bed, and Celia fussed a bit in her sleep, rolled over and snuggled closer to her mother.

"Aye, but why fake that kind of accent?" he wondered. "She surely doesn't need it to get a job in Oxford. And why a surgeon's job, of all things?"

"Aye, you're right. I hadn't thought of that. The whole thing is curious, isn't it." He could see that the curiousness of the whole thing delighted her. Her wilted spirits were entirely revived.

She frowned and said seriously, "I can't say I really want her staying here, though."

"I thought she could help you."

"Oh come, Matty, you thought no such thing! You just wanted to help her and save her pride while you were at it."

Matthew looked sheepish, but it was too dark for his sheepishness to be obvious and he hoped that his silence might be taken for inscrutability. Gillian was not fooled and the knowledge that she had won her point enlivened her still more.

"Maybe we can foist her on the Greenes," she said.

"Gillian! That's no way to talk." His wife's lack of pretense never ceased to shock and attract him at the same time. Half-consciously, he always egged her on, offering his stolid, foursquare candor as a backdrop for her impertinence. Eight years of this had turned them both into caricatures of themselves.

"Matty, I'm serious. I don't want her to stay here. And Sabina would be so glad for any help at all—she won't care if the girl's a bit strange."

Sabina and Henry Greene were the proprietors of the Cross-roads, one of Oxford's largest inns.

"She's not the sort Henry will be pleased at having around," Matthew pointed out.

"Aye, and so much the better!"

"That's not how I meant it. Henry's as faithful as they come, never mind what he likes to pretend."

"That's not how I meant it, either. But look at the dimwits he chooses when the hiring's left to him. There must have been half a dozen of them in the last two years. There wasn't a one of them could add up a tab without counting on her fingers, and if the bill came to more pennies than they had fingers, why the difference was on the house!" Gillian was warming up to her subject. "The one talent all of 'em had in common was snaring young clerics and letting them do themselves right out of a living."

"You're exaggerating."

"All right," she conceded. "They weren't all clerics. The more sensible girls got themselves married to aging merchants. Either way, Sabina gets stuck with the work. I've a mind to take this Jane—if that's even her name—I've a mind to take her 'round tomorrow and let Sabina decide it."

He sighed. "You're not up to it."

"You do it, then. Will you? Tomorrow?"

Again he sighed, as if to say, "If you insist."

"You must talk to Sabina though," she cautioned. "Not Henry."

Their voices had gradually risen, and that, or hunger, had

awakened the newborn, who started to bleat. With a good-humored groan, Gillian got up, took the infant from its basket and brought it back to the bed to nurse. Celia stirred again at the loss of the mother's body warmth and burrowed against Matthew instead. Lulled by the baby's noisy sucking and his wife's deep, even breathing, Matthew drifted into sleep. Some time later, after she had nursed the baby back to slumber, his wife shook him. "Matthew, are you awake?"

"Nay."

"I think I've got it. She's a runaway nun."

He opened his eyes and shifted to face her. "A nun!"

"Aye. That explains everything, don't you see? The accent, the short hair. And where does a woman practice surgery without the backing of a guild? There's only one place, Matty—in a convent."

He could not dispute the logic of this, but it shocked him. "But why would she run away?"

"Why?" she repeated, incredulous that he did not know. "The only reason. She was seduced. And abandoned, poor thing, from the looks of it. Seduced and abandoned," she concluded with something very much like delight.

Matthew was thinking of the way Jane had looked when she first stepped into the kitchen after bathing. She had worked some miracle with her hair so that it was slicked back smooth and close to her head, damp, with the comb marks still visible. Between the place where the hair abruptly ended and the neckline of the smock began he could see the uppermost bump of her spine. His mind kept fixing there. After dinner he had outlined the soles of her feet directly onto the shoe leather with a bit of charcoal. They were long, fine boned and white, with a blush at the toes. He imagined angels would have such feet.

He shook his head despondently. "It can't be true," he said. "She's too nice."

His wife reached over and gave his head a pat. There was scarcely suppressed laughter in her voice. "Oh Matty! Promise me you'll never grow up."

Two

Jane Basset had been a classmate of Ingrid's at Greyleigh. She had long glossy eyelashes and wore velvet gowns every day. It had seemed to Ingrid that her very nerves must be covered in velvet, for nothing ever threatened her poise. She was the only person Ingrid had ever met who could stare down Dame Agatha. This singular ability won her many followers and, had she dared, Ingrid would have been one of them.

For a short time, when they were twelve or thirteen, Jane had taken an interest in her. At that age many of the girls were leaving school, having achieved all the education considered necessary or desirable for a young lady. The fact that Ingrid would be staying on fascinated Jane. "To live here all your life!" she would exclaim in an awed tone. "Never to see what's a mile down the road! Never to be kissed by a man! How can you stand it?" Though Ingrid had not ever considered objecting to any of this, "standing it" took on an aura of accomplishment, even of heroism. She began to see her own life in a romantic light.

Only a few weeks after elevating Ingrid to this new status, Jane left Greyleigh to be married to a knight. Alone once more, Ingrid did not take long to recognize that there could be nothing heroic in remaining, since she had no other choice. For a week or so she attempted to pine for some gallant youth who would glimpse her over the wall, be smitten with love for her and carry her off straightaway. But as she had never laid eyes on a single youth, gallant or otherwise, it was hard to flesh out the fantasy. Soon she gave this up and went back to dreaming that she was Mary Magdalene, with a yard and a half of red-gold hair tumbling over the feet of Christ.

She had not thought of Jane in all these years, but as Matthew waited tactfully for her to introduce herself and she realized she would have to come up with a name, Jane's was the first to come to mind. The curious thing was that along with the name, she seemed to take on some of its original owner's gaiety and confidence.

The simple happiness of her everyday life in Oxford was the last consequence she would have imagined of her defection from Greyleigh. Vaguely she could recollect the feeling she had had, that last day, of being singled out for a unique damnation, but it seemed like a story she had been told long ago, about someone else.

That first night, the night Jack had been waiting for her, she let herself out the kitchen door and headed for the woods. The dewy grasses of the pasture slapped at her ankles and she had expected the slow rustle of branches in the wind to gather itself at any moment into the reproachful voice of God. She had offered herself to the forest as if it were her fate, stepping into it briskly and deliberately. When it thickened and blocked the moon, she felt her way with outstretched hands till she walked straight into the sickening caress of a huge spiderweb. She fainted, thinking this was her death.

The next thing she knew silver rods of sunlight were penetrating the morning fog like arrows shot by the dawn. She thought at first they were angels. She was lying on a bed of damp leaves, looking up through gentle boughs, arms that reached out to accept her. The trees were like parents standing over her crib. They were whispering kind things about her. Trusting them, she arose and walked into their midst as if she were another shaft of light.

With each step she expected that the earth would withdraw and allow her to be sucked under, to sink right through it and plummet into hell. But no, in the most patient and long-suffering way, it interposed its cool, firm surface between the sole of her sandal and the yapping jaws of purgatory. All day long she tested it and it never failed her. By nightfall, she lay down with full confidence.

Certainly if God had wished to punish her, he need not have gone out of his way. Wandering without destination in the countryside, she might easily have succumbed to starvation, exposure or outlaws. Instead, she found accommodation everywhere. The woods abounded in edible things and nothing she ate poisoned her. She slept on the ground some nights, but on the coldest nights there was always a shed or cellar or barn to sneak into. She avoided roads, cutting instead through fields and woods, her main object being to elude pursuit. Reluctantly she exchanged her habit for a lice-infested rag she found in a shed. It wasn't warm enough, but in it she was less likely to be recognized.

She was not recognized because she was never seen. As she plodded on, without destination, she scanned the landscape. A faint, far-off voice, a human-looking speck on the horizon would send her into the nearest hedge where she would crouch, sometimes for hours, listening to her own heartbeat. She lost count of the days, but they amounted to weeks, and in all those weeks she never spoke to anyone. The sunlit hours were short and full of occupation—hiding, searching for food and shelter, walking to keep warm. But the nights were long and growing longer and colder. At night she knew she was losing her mind.

She found herself high on a hilltop, overlooking insentient, repetitive countryside with a sudden clot of humanity in the middle of it. The town was walled, and despite the acres and miles of unoccupied land that surrounded it, the inhabitants had preferred to layer themselves, to tuck in their elbows and suck in their breath to fit within the wall's confines. Ingrid did not wonder at this. She, too, wanted to be contained by that wall of soft golden stone, sagging leniently here and there but warm and encircling as a mother's arms, firm and reassuring as a father's law. She ran most of the way there, and once inside, spent hours wandering the streets, breathing in the warm stench of the open sewers, the polluted streams, greasy cooking and unwashed youths. The rude, man-made colors were hot against her eyes, and all around was the throb of language.

She was surprised to learn that the town was Oxford, for weeks of wandering had taken her less than twenty miles from Greyleigh. It was a risky place for her: The university chancellor and other Oxford dignitaries had been present for the Pentecost healings. At first she thought she would stay only until she had earned enough for a few good meals, shoes and warmer clothing. But from her meeting with Matthew onward, all she seemed to encounter was inexplicable kindness, commiserating looks she was at a loss to understand and a universal enthusiasm for adding pounds to her wasted frame. She listened for rumors of her apostasy, which she imagined had created a huge scandal, but she never heard the slightest allusion to it. Either Dame Agatha had managed to keep it a secret, or else people simply did not care. And the longer she stayed in Oxford, the more distant and dreamlike that former life became. Her name was Jane. She was a servant at the Crossroads.

The inn took its name from its location at Carfax, the intersection of the main north-south and east-west thoroughfares. Entering town by the north gate and proceeding down Cornmarket, a traveler would see its high painted fence—alternating pickets of red and yellow and green—on his left, facing the more sober edifice of St. Martin's. During the day the inn's gate was always left open and through it one entered a courtyard. The unpaved ground was dust or mud, depending on the weather—usually mud, stamped to a tolerable firmness by the traffic of horses and men. A well stood in the center, a trough and hayrick off to the right. Pompous chickens strutted about, clucking their indignation at the wild children and dogs with whom they were obliged to share the yard. The rambling structures of the inn—tavern, guest rooms, living quarters, stable and outhouses—bordered three sides of the compound, with the fence making the fourth. The buildings had a random look, having been added to as needed, out of whatever materials were at hand. No architect had been allowed to thwart the exuberance of the carpenters, which burst out in doors of every shape and size, not only at ground level, but one and two stories up. These were reached by rickety stairs and undulating catwalks.

The inn was a favorite with merchants on the Oxfordshire circuit, who filled the guest rooms on Tuesday and Friday nights in anticipation of the Wednesday and Saturday markets. It had a reputation for vermin-free beds and discouraged students as lodgers, though they were welcome to drink there. Tradesmen made up the bulk of the clientele and, because the Greenes had five children, they maintained a wholesome atmosphere. In the summer, when other taverns languished due to the university's long vacation, the Crossroads thrived by importing nightly entertainment. Minstrels, jugglers and jesters played from the outdoor galleries to crowds that packed the courtyard.

Henry Greene was responsible for making everyone feel welcome, and his talent for this was unsurpassed. His wife, Sabina, was responsible for everything else, including the care of their five boys. Though the two were the same age, she looked ten years older and had a resentful air. Once, in church, the priest had read the gospel story about Martha, who fussed and fumed in the kitchen while Mary sat at the feet of Jesus, having a nice chat. Martha had stomped out, hands on hips, demanding justice, but Jesus had taken Mary's side. When the priest read that part, Henry had elbowed Sabina in the ribs. Sabina's faith had never been the same after that.

Though she took Ingrid on mainly as a favor to Matthew, within a week Sabina was giving the constable his drinks on the house out of gratitude, for Ingrid was the best worker the Crossroads had ever had: tireless despite her appearance of ill health, uncomplaining, and so conscientious one would have thought her life depended on not making a mistake.

Ingrid, on the other hand, considered her new life luxurious. The food was good and abundant and there were no bells or patients to disturb her sleep. In addition to her meals and the little room that she shared with Henry's younger sister, Isobel, she was given two dresses and a small weekly wage. Since her basic needs were already provided for, she had at first regarded the coins Henry gave her every Friday wih some puzzlement. But one day, as she wandered dreamily through the market, her eye was caught by the flutter of multicolored scarves. She lingered at the stall, fondling the thin silk and marveling at the brilliance of the dyes, which brought on a bittersweet recollection of Jack. The vendor noticed her wistfulness and quoted her a price. For the first time she made a connection between her hoard of meaningless coins and a desirable object. She mulled it over for a full week and then went back to the stall and became the sole owner of a yellow silk scarf. Having been raised to consider private property an evil, she felt a little guilty about her acquisition and kept it hidden under her pillow. At the same time she began to see the market with new eyes. Everything in it was a possible possession. Though some of the things she bought were useful, it was always for their beauty that she chose them: two silvery needles stuck in a tiny scrap of deep blue velvet, three yards of red ribbon, four mother-of-pearl buttons, a beeswax candle, a rabbit's foot, a tiny vial of oil of clove. She arranged

her treasures lovingly in a spice box handpainted all over with gryph-
ons, unicorns, elephants and other strange beasts.

The Greenes' five boys were first introduced to her as Griffen,
Benedict, Osmund, Stephen and Peter. She had bitten her lip in
concentration, trying to memorize the names and attach each to the
appropriate grimy urchin. She needn't have bothered, for none of
them had been called by his Christian name since baptism. They were
actually called Grunt, Dickie, Ozzie, Quart and Pint. They were spiky
and uncultivated as weeds, and she soon got used to them as a big
sister is used to her little brothers.

Henry was more difficult to win over than Sabina. In his view,
conveying food and drink to the table was the least important job of a
serving wench. Much more important was the sway of her hips, the
warmth of her smile and the liveliness of her conversation. Not one
woman in his establishment came up to his standards. Sabina's efforts
were too effortful—she made one feel a little ashamed to be sitting
there drinking while she worked so hard. His sister Isobel, once one
of the beauties of Oxford, had grown less beautiful from keeping her
beauty to herself and now was regarded by everyone as a frightful
snob. The innkeeper's complaint about Ingrid was that she did not
talk. Though the most attentive of servants, she never initiated a
conversation and reacted to casual overtures like "How are you today?"
with mild alarm.

Nothing in Ingrid's upbringing had prepared her for the social
demands of her job. Having been silent all her life, she was baffled by
the ceaseless chatter of ordinary people, baffled too by the require-
ment that one have an opinion about everything that transpired in the
world.

"You've got to chat people up," Henry urged, taking her aside
one day. "That's what they come for."

Even as Jane Basset, Ingrid could not hear herself reprimanded
without becoming excessively worried. She hung her head and plucked
at her apron. "I'm sorry," she mumbled. "If you'll just tell me what you
want me to say, I'll be glad to say it."

Her abject posture annoyed Henry, who could not stand to
hurt anyone's feelings and generally held it against them if he did so

accidentally. "I can't tell you what to say!" he shouted. "You have to make it up yourself. Talk to the customers as if they were your friends."

Since Ingrid had never had any friends, this advice was not particularly helpful. "What exactly should I talk to them about?" she whispered, on the verge of tears.

Henry threw up his hands. "Talk about the bloody weather for Christ's sake!"

Sabina overheard them and came to Ingrid's rescue. "Hush now, Harry, you talk enough for all of us. Somebody has to slice the meat and draw the pints and wash out the tankards."

"I'm not trying to turn her into a magpie," he argued. "But she has to say something to people, or they'll feel like they're drinking in a bloody nunnery."

Ingrid blushed violently at this.

"Watch your language," Sabina scolded. Then she turned to Ingrid. "It's enough to talk about the weather. That's all you have to do."

"What should I say about it?"

Sabina raised her eyebrows. "Say whatever you think about it. Take today for instance—what do you think of today's weather?"

There had been a blizzard that day such as seldom came to the Midlands. The market had been forced to close early and everyone was driven indoors, where they sat drinking and singing around the hearths. The world seemed festive and covered in jewels. So Ingrid felt safe in saying, "The weather is wonderful today."

"You see?" Henry said to his wife. "She's hopeless."

But Sabina adoped a patient air. "Nay, think. What have you heard others say about the weather today?"

"Um . . . 'hideous storm' . . . 'worst I can remember.' "

"You see? That's all there is to it."

Ingrid frowned. "But I can't just repeat what others have said."

"Sure you can. Why not?"

"Well, what's the point, if it's already been said?"

It was Sabina's turn to throw up her hands. "You're right," she conceded to her husband. "She's hopeless."

But then came a day when Ingrid had something to say without any prompting at all. Several students, ill-clad youths about her own age, were complaining rowdily in Latin about the food and drink and service. She had not been in Oxford long enough to know that the antagonism between scholars and townspeople went back generations and that, as few Oxford natives spoke Latin, this was a favorite way for students to taunt them. The townsmen knew they were being talked about, but could make no retort. She was ignorant of all of this when she overheard one of the boys compare the Crossroads' ale to dog's urine.

Inspiration struck in the form of a memory. At Greyleigh Latin had been taught by the sardonic Sister Frances. She expected little of the students and was lenient compared with the other nuns. Once, when the original Jane Basset was disrupting a lesson with her giggly asides, Sister Frances had remarked drily, "Take care you don't nick the desk with your sharp wit." Wordplay was so rare in the convent that this remark had made a strong impression on Ingrid. After all these years she remembered it verbatim.

She thought it applied well to the present situation. So she glided up alongside the complainer, leaned over, and with a pleasant smile murmured in Latin, "Take care you don't nick the table with your sharp wit."

For a moment the fellow just gaped at her, and she looked around uneasily, afraid she had made a mistake that could cost her her new job. But as his companions took it in they doubled over, stamping and pounding with laughter. The novelty of a serving girl speaking Latin would have made any retort at all an automatic success. What made this one particularly apt was that she had unknowingly punned the victim's name.

"I say, Nick," one of them urged, giving Nick's shoulder a shove. "Buy the wench a drink."

At once Nick's dumbfounded face became animated. "A drink? A drink? I shall lay all I possess at her feet!"

"Better close your eyes, girl," his friend warned, "for he possesses naught but the clothes on his back."

Nick flung himself on his knees before her and slobbered all over her hand as he kissed it, crying, "My queen! My queen!"

"Buy the queen a drink," another of the friends suggested. "She talks like a scholar, let's see if she drinks like one."

"Aye, a peg tankard! All scholars, having passed their Latin, must pass the test of the peg tankard."

Nick stood up and fished in his purse. "Have we got the price of one between us?"

Henry, who had been looking on with amusement, bellowed, "Never mind the price. If it's for Jane, it's on the house."

"Harry, don't encourage this," Sabina warned. But her husband ignored her and dashed down to the cellar to fetch the requested item while Ingrid just stood there, flushed at being the center of attention, and confused.

"What's a peg tankard?" she asked.

"Ha! You'll see, you'll see," the lad who had first suggested it exulted.

"Nothing a girl should be concerned with," Isobel told her at the same time. "You don't have to go along."

But Ingrid, though apprehensive, wanted very much to go along. They had some ordeal in store for her and she wanted to pass it, for the approval of these lads was better than the best tonic Sister Pipp had ever devised. She looked from one to the other with bright, excited eyes.

Nick sprang to the tabletop and hoisted her up after him. Their heads were near the ceiling. Henry passed him the tankard. It held two quarts and was overflowing. Pegs had been driven through it at half-pint intervals. Nick held the mug aloft and pointed to the uppermost peg. "Now, most esteemed scholar, wit, queen of my heart," he began, bowing to her, "I shall set forth the rules of the ancient test of the peg tankard. Your task, milady, is to tip this vessel and drink off precisely one half-pint of the dog piss inside—pardon me, I meant to say one half-pint of this most excellent beverage— precisely half a pint at one go. When you lower the cup, the remaining ale should be level with this peg here. If you've taken more or less, you have to drink down to this next peg here. Do you follow me?" Ingrid nodded. "The contest continues till you get it right, or pass out, whichever happens first. Agreed? All right. We begin."

He passed her the tankard. It was so heavy she had to support the base with her left hand. Scanning the room from atop the table she saw thirty or forty faces looking up at her in mirthful encouragement and curiosity. She raised the cup and drank slowly and carefully, without pause, until she estimated she had drawn off enough. She handed it back to Nick.

"Oh, milady!" he exclaimed, in mock disappointment. "A very poor showing. Not even close." He stooped and allowed his companions to inspect the results, then passed the tankard back to her. She had only gotten halfway to the first peg. She would have to drink three quarters of a pint to make it to the next one.

"A little encouragement for the lady," Nick exhorted the crowd. They began to pound the tables in rhythm with her swallowing. This time she drank faster, gulping down as much as she could with each swallow. When she lowered the cup, she was gasping for breath. The pounding stopped while Nick judged the results. She had missed the peg, but not by much. "A noble effort," he declared.

On her third try the pounding seemed to get faster and Ingrid got a little reckless. Ale spilled over and ran down her chin, but she drank on to the thumping beat. At last she lowered the cup and laughed as she wiped her mouth and chin with the back of her hand. Nick whacked her on the back, and she belched aloud. The crowd applauded, and Ingrid gave a low, theatrical bow. On the way back up she swayed and Nick had to steady her with a hand to her elbow. "How'd I do?" she asked him.

"Why you greedy thing, you! You drank too far. Look."

She had indeed. "Oops," she squeaked. "Have to try again."

"*C'est dommage,*" one of the scholars commiserated.

"*Oui,*" she said. "*Tant pis.*"

"*Tant pis,* indeed," said Nick. "Get on with it, then."

With dauntless fortitude, she made two more attempts and would have had the hang of it by then but for the effects of her earlier tries. With this particular skill, practice did not make perfect—practice made impossible. But the crowd was very sympathetic, she thought. It was lovely the way they wore such colorful clothes—very kind of them. They had such kind clothes and such colorful faces. She was moved to make a speech. "I would like to comment on the weather," she announced with some difficulty, as her tongue seemed to have gotten fat and lazy. "B-Beastly weather we've been having lately. *Comme il fait mauvais."* She squinted at Nick. *"Mauvais? Oui, il fait mauvais.* Why, it's rain—it's raining cats and dogs! How'm I doing, Harry?"

The innkeeper raised his own cup to her. "Splendid, my girl. Keep up the good work."

"I will," she promised jauntily. *"Hideous* storm! Worst I've seen in, in, in centuries! And furthermore . . ." She swayed. Nick clasped her around the waist and steadied the tankard, which was drooping in her hand and about to spill over. How nice that no one in her audience had a skin disease, that they all had four limbs. "Thy faith has healed thee," she addressed them solemnly. "Go in peace. I drink to your health." With that she dispatched another half pint. Nick checked the cup. The ale was precisely level with the second-to-last peg.

Henry himself put her to bed, slinging her over his shoulder and carrying her upstairs. "Good show, Janie," he said, as he tucked the blankets around her.

Her adventure with the peg tankard won her not only Henry's approval and minor fame, but the friendship of Nick and his friends Nigel—whom everyone called Owl, because he looked like one, and Tom—whom everyone called Toad, for reasons that were by now obscure. They lived crammed into a tiny, unheated room at the top of Cary's Inn. They were so poor that they had pawned one of their academic gowns and had to take turns missing lectures, since no one was admitted without one. Books were out of the question and even parchment had to be rationed, so they became adept at memorizing, cramming their minds while their stomachs went empty. They were, in fact, ascetics, but their asceticism was concealed by a public frivolity that bordered on the dangerous. Ardently they violated curfew and other unimportant rules, as well as rules no one had yet thought of. They had a knack for intoxicating each other, so that they always appeared to be drunk, though they could not afford much beer. Conspicuous in mischief, they were secretive about their virtues. No one would have guessed from their bawdy manners that they were chaste. But as clerks they were sworn to celibacy, and having given their word, they kept it.

It was this sworn celibacy of half its residents—all of these celibates male and most of them under thirty—that gave Oxford its everyday atmosphere of impending riot. Released from their lectures, the youths burst forth in garish costumes and every sort of gaudy behavior. Bands of them would stalk the perimeter of Godstow, hoping to be entertained by its nuns, get drunk on the way back and vault over the broken town wall after curfew, crowing like nocturnal roosters. Roofs were for scaling, windows were for breaking and statues were for ironic defacing. Daggers, though outlawed, were ubiquitous. The scholars came from all over Europe, and Beaumont playing field was a literal battleground for international conflicts. Even murders were not unknown.

Governance of the town had been bled drop by drop from the mayor and council while the university grew and gained power. As members of the clerical order, scholars could be tried only in ecclesiastical courts, which more often than not regarded their crimes with boys-will-be-boys indulgence. The townspeople felt so besieged that they had crenellated the tower of the Church of St. Martin, turning it into a quasi fortress.

So it was an unusual town-gown alliance when the three roommates adopted Ingrid as an honorary chum. They were entertained by her combination of improbable booklearning and a naïveté about the ordinary world that would have embarrassed a child of six. On her afternoons off the four of them could be seen walking arm in arm through the clamorous streets. She saved day-old bread for them and occasionally forgot to charge them for a round of drinks; they included her in their earnest discussions and let her in on their private jokes.

"You'd better be careful of that lot," Isobel warned. "They'll amuse themselves with you, but in the end they're wed to their careers."

They were in bed. Isobel's disembodied voice was ominous in the dark. "I don't know what you mean," Ingrid said truthfully.

"Come. I've seen how you look at Nick."

Nick had long, wavy, beautiful dark hair, about which he was rather vain, and the face of an archangel. Ingrid did stare sometimes, wondering that this utterly accessible mortal could be so graced. "Everyone looks at Nick," she replied, a bit defensive.

"And Nick looks at you," Isobel persisted.

"You mean—how? With desire, do you mean?"

A dry chuckle. "You don't mince words, do you, Jane?"

Ingrid chewed her lip, suddenly uncomfortable. She hadn't thought of Nick that way—as a man. He touched her often—the others did too. And yesterday he had kissed her: a slurpy, ridiculous kiss that he and Tom had fought a broomstick duel for. It had all seemed very innocent, very chummy. Nothing like . . . No, better not to think of it—that catastrophic hunger, the world going dark and dizzy . . .

"But Nick is a cleric," she said. "He can't have women that way."

"Aye, and don't you forget it, and don't let him forget it either."

"He won't. There's no thought of—"

Isobel went on, ignoring her. "I learned this the hard way, you see. I fell in love with a scholar once."

"Did you?" Ingrid rolled to face her roommate in the dark, propping herself up on one elbow. "Who was he?"

"It's not important. His name was Christopher. He used to drink here. He'd bring his notes and sit in the far corner by the stairs. He said he couldn't study in the library, that the noise here settled his mind. After a while he couldn't study here either. He'd just be watching me. Once I snuck out after curfew, and we went out to Beaumont field and lay looking at the stars—he knew the names of all of the stars. We went mad together that night. We were going to get married. But of course, that meant giving up his work. God only knows how he would have made his living. He's brilliant, you see—it would have been a terrible waste. So I don't blame him. Nay, I don't blame him."

Ingrid knew she was being told something sad yet she was heartened to hear it. Isobel had known a man, too. Perhaps, her own secret was not so dark after all. She could confide it. *My lover's name was Jack. He was a troubadour. He used to tease me, and I liked to be teased by him. Sort of a rascal, really, but . . .* "So you and Christopher lay together?"

Isobel gasped. "Oh no, not like that! What do you take me for?"

Ingrid sank back on her pillow. Decent women did not do what she had done. Decent women didn't even think of it. She pulled the covers up to her chin. My name is Jane Basset, she told herself over and over again. I am a servant at the Crossroads.

Three

Roger Fleming rushed the length of the great hall to embrace him. He had the large gestures of a man who spends most of his time outdoors, a warmth springing from unconquerable physical vitality. His fair hair was going a little gray, his skin a little weathered around the bright blue eyes, but apart from that he looked but half of his forty years.

"It's been so long—oh, it's good to see you, good to see you! You look awful, but never mind, cook's got a splendid boar roasting— bagged it myself, I'll have you know—and we'll break open a lovely Burgundy I've been saving and catch up when the rest of 'em have gone to bed. What do you say? Oh do brighten up, man, and say you're glad to see me."

"Never been gladder, Roger, truly." Jack tried to force his tired features to show his gladness but had to settle for a warm clasp of his friend's hand.

"You'll be wanting a bath. I'll send Gwendolyn to see to you— mind now, she's under my protection, so look but don't touch—don't want to have to run you through before Madeleine's had a chance to see you—she'll be so pleased—too pleased, so watch yourself there, too. But what am I talking about? You look too fagged to lift a finger much less any other part."

Alone in the bathhouse, Jack examined his reflection in the looking glass. There were dark circles under his eyes and a gauntness about his cheeks. The dust of a month of travel had robbed his curls of their sheen. Wearily he shed his wrinkled clothing. It was cold. He climbed quickly into the tub. When Gwendolyn came in with towels and fresh hot water to rinse his hair he realized the extent of his fatigue: a pretty girl and he could think of nothing whatever to say to her.

Supper at the Fleming's was always a boisterous, torchlit affair, all yapping hounds and rowdy young men, with Roger and Madeleine beaming like dual suns at the center of it. There was no discernible order of precedence. Squires and vassals rubbed elbows with millers, peddlers, friars and the odd ragged persons Roger characterized as "Madeleine's waifs." Conversation, if it could be called that, was a loud overlapping of exclamations in which Jack's pensive silence went unremarked. As the pudding was served, Roger made his way over and clapped a hand on the troubadour's shoulder. "Let's hide in the solar," he suggested, swiping a jug and two cups with a complicitous wink.

The solar had a feminine air—spindly chairs draped with sewing-in-progress, the carpets littered with bits of thread and tangled skeins of embroidery floss. "Watch out for pins," Roger warned. He tossed some plump needlepoint cushions on the floor near the fire and made himself comfortable. Jack followed, grateful for the warmth: His leg was aching from the chill of the great hall.

"Now tell me, what's ailing you, my friend?"

"May I?" Jack reached for the pitcher and poured himself a tall drink. "I came here because I'm being followed. I think I've shaken them, but I need to hide out for a few days."

Roger gestured expansively. "As long as you like. That needn't be said. So what is it? Some trouble over a woman, I'll wager."

Jack nodded.

"And who's following? Her husband's men? Her father's? Perhaps you've bedded the queen and it's his majesty who's after you. That was a joke," he added, when Jack didn't smile.

"I don't know who they are, exactly. Two clowns in friar's garb. I first saw them three days ago, at Endstone, with their cowls drawn up, though the fire was roaring and the pub was stifling hot. In the morning I see one of them taking a piss out behind the kitchen. When he hikes up his robe there's a concealed dagger. Didn't think too much of it till the next night I'm at another inn twenty miles away, and there they are. Maybe just a coincidence. But aren't friars supposed to travel on foot? How'd they cover twenty miles? So last night, yet another inn, and this time I check the pub before going in. No sign. I eat, go up to bed, then go back down again on a hunch. And there they are.

"Since this trouble came up, I've been trying to travel on the quiet—which is pretty much the reverse of my usual way. But I ran out of money and, as you know, my way of earning money is damned conspicuous. So it seems they caught up with me. Anyway, I took matters in hand. Went bounding up to them like an overfriendly dog, saying 'What an amazing coincidence, you're everywhere I go. Bet I know what you're after,' I say. 'You're selling pardons and you figure me for the perfect customer.' Then I go into a full accounting of my sins, which took long enough to get them good and drunk at my expense. Told them I was staying another day and we could discuss the pardon then. Once I knew they were sleeping soundly, I rode off. Oh, and for good measure, I asked the stable boy directions to the London road. He said down the lane and turn right. I went down the lane and turned left."

"Well done!" Roger said, slapping his thigh with pleasure. "I should think you've lost 'em. And if not, hell, you know how I love a good fight. Still," he added seriously, "there's something else. A little scrape like that wouldn't steal your spirit. That's just a good day's fun for the Jack I know."

"Aye, there's something else." Jack stared broodingly into his cup. He wanted very much to confide but did not know how to begin.

"I broke my leg in September," he said at last.

"Ah. Dreadful to be reminded that we break, isn't it? Like a little taste of death. Still, you seem to have mended just fine—didn't notice any limp."

"Aye, the leg's all right. I fell near the convent of Greyleigh and—"

"Greyleigh? Imagine that. The abbess is a, you might say a relative of mine. A *distant* relative."

"Who—Dame Agatha? I wouldn't have guessed. There's no resemblance."

Roger chuckled. "I'm sure she'd say the same. Did you meet this young protégé of hers, the one they're calling a saint?"

Jack sighed. "Aye, Roger."

Fleming looked at him closely. "Oh. Oh dear."

"I—maybe I was just bored. I mean, I *was* bored, as well as randy, of course. You can get all caught up in thinking of how to accomplish something without ever stopping to think whether it ought to be done in the first place. Anyway, I asked her to leave with me."

"She refused, of course."

"Nay, she agreed."

Roger let out a low whistle.

"I was careful—as careful as you can be doing something so utterly foolhardy. I left and then came back for her late at night. She was to meet me outside the gate. But she never came."

"Well, at least one of you showed a little sense," Roger said with a look of relief.

Jack shook his head. "She ran away. All by herself."

"What?"

"I know. It's very strange. I don't know what to think."

Roger threw another log on the fire and stood poking it. "This is going to sound heartless, but I have to say it's probably lucky for you. They'd have your head on a platter if ever you got caught with her. Hell, Jack, what were you going to do with her anyhow?"

"I hadn't really thought it through."

"Aye, that's certain. I'll wager your cock was doing the thinking, and that's one job it's not made for."

"Spare me."

"Sorry."

"So," Roger said after a pause, "did they find her?"

"I don't know. But I suspect not. The rumor is she's gravely ill, that the doctors said she'd never recover at Greyleigh because of the damp and they've taken her away somewhere. Now if they've brought her back against her will, they're surely going to lock her up and spread a story like that to cover. And if they don't know where she is, well, the same story will serve, won't it? What makes me think she's still at large are those spies. Nothing was to stop them from arresting me if I'd been implicated. I figure they were watching to see if I'd lead them to her. Luckily for Ingrid, I have no more idea where she is than they do.

"I thought sure I'd find her the first day," he continued. "There's only one road from Greyleigh, she was on foot and I was on horseback.

But I rode ten miles in either direction. No one had seen her. And off the road—Christ, she could be anywhere. You know this country—if someone wants to disappear, it just soaks them right up. Still, I must have pounded on every door in the county. I've gone into woods so thick I had to leave my horse behind, found hermit's huts that God himself has never heard of. And what I fear the most, Roger, is that I'll find her corpse in some ditch. How can she possibly—"

A sudden defection of Fleming's attention told Jack they were no longer alone. Madeleine stood in the doorway, flushed with gaiety. Like Roger, she was tall, blond and comely. "There you are! We're getting up a pantomime and we need Jack here to play the role of Satan."

"I think not just now," Roger said gently.

"Oh, I see—there's a man-to-man talk under way. Now, don't be giving my husband any ideas, Monsieur Jacques," she said, laughing. "I've had quite a time settling him down, and I'll not have you leading him back to his old ways."

Fleming looked at her like she was the most splendid creature on earth. And by the light of that gaze she *was* splendid. "Nay," Roger was saying. "I'm resigned to my bondage. Besides, as you never tire of telling me, one false move and you'll murder me in my sleep."

"That I will."

"Come then, murderess, and give your poor prisoner a kiss."

She bent to comply, her loose hair falling forward like a curtain over the kiss, and Jack felt a rare pang of sexual envy. It wasn't so much that he wanted Madeleine—though he could have wanted her easily. It was the calm, steady burning of that domestic fire. To be loved as she loved Roger, which was not the way she would have loved Jack, even if he'd won her. He stared glumly at the hearth and waited for it to be over.

"You're a lucky man," he said when she had gone.

"Aye." Roger looked longingly at the space she'd just left. "Lucky." He poured Jack another cup of wine, as if to make up for his kinder fortune. "I'm sorry. Where were we?"

"Nowhere. Exactly nowhere. I can't find her, and I can't give up the search."

"You know, if she's the least bit clever she's gone to London.

Easy to hide there—no one knows his neighbor's business. Or cares to know."

He hadn't thought of that. He didn't like the thought. "London's a cesspool. And she'd have to have money—there's no such thing as charity on the streets of London."

"A pretty young girl would have no trouble finding employment."

"She's in a habit, for God's sake."

"That's no obstacle. We men have our vile fantasies . . ."

Jack's jaw tightened. "I ought to kill you for that."

"Well, *you* did, now didn't you."

Roger gazed steadily at him, not condemning but holding his ground. Jack couldn't take it. He got up and poked viciously at the fire. "And someone ought to kill me for it," he said in a subdued voice. "Pity Ingrid doesn't have brothers. Defenseless as a rabbit, she is. But that doesn't make us kind to rabbits, does it? The rabbit's flight just stirs the blood of the hunter."

"I'm sorry, Jack."

"Nay. You just hit the mark, that's all. I've got to find her, Roger. I've got to set it right somehow."

"Perhaps she doesn't want to be found."

"What else can I do?"

Both men fell into a ruminative silence. Faint shouts and laughter from the great hall floated on the sad air. The fire crackled.

"Jack, you're going to hate me for saying this," Roger said gently. "But what can you give this woman? What real good can you do her?"

The image that haunted him hourly came again: Ingrid at the door of his room, taking off her veil. Trembling. Jack took a ragged breath. "It's just the way she . . . the way things . . . things got wild— you know. There's a way you can make things go wild and I almost had her like that. If it had happened then, all in a rush and she half-resisting . . . I think if it had happened like that I could forget her. But I stopped. I wanted to go on and I couldn't. She went away. And then she came back. For her it was this terrible sin, this life-shattering sin. But she took it on. She took it on because she wanted me."

"Are you sure, Jack?"

"She came to me. She thought about it and she came to me."

"It's just that . . ." Roger hesitated. "I don't know what her life was like. I do know Agatha, and I can make some guesses. What I mean to say is, perhaps it was the other way around. Perhaps it was the sin itself she wanted, and you she took on to get it."

Jack's throat went dry. He saw what his friend was extending him—a moral reprieve. He'd played his role, and now it was time to leave the stage. A minor player. Accept the bitter truth, and the truth will make you free. He poured himself another cup of wine and drank it down fast, like medicine.

Four

Suppose God orders a man to stop loving him. If the man obeys, this is proof of his love and therefore he has disobeyed. If, on the other hand, he persists in loving God, he has disobeyed and cannot be said truly to love him. This was the paradox to which Simon Malverthorpe, Doctor of Theology, had devoted twenty years of intellectual labor.

Some theologians dealt with the problem by maintaining that God could not issue this sort of logically impossible command. Malverthorpe opposed that solution, because it undermined God's omnipotence. God, to be God, must be exempt from the laws of logic. That God had never in human memory given such an order was agreed by both sides to be entirely beside the point.

As philosophy, feeling its oats, began to raise more and more of these challenges to theology, keepers of the academic peace were moving to separate the two disciplines as they would separate the antagonists in a tavern brawl. Early in his career Malverthorpe had foreseen that this intervention would prove fatal to church authority. There could be but one truth, and theologians must be its keepers.

His ambition was to slay the dragon Philosophy and for this feat be acclaimed the greatest knight of the Church since Aquinas.

Every day for twenty years he had led his mind to the brink of its ordeal, and every day it had come to a dead halt, there on the brink, like a horse that refuses to jump a fence. He knew that there were men who used paradox as a sort of catapult into mysticism. Just as extreme torture of the body was rumored to lead to ecstasy, so this racking of the mind was said to give way to direct experience of the divine.

But for Malverthorpe, intellectual extremity relieved itself in fond recall of the good Burgundy he had sipped at dinner, the imagining of odd faces in the grain of his desktop or plans to be measured for a new pair of shoes.

Teaching was a consolation, for dull as he suspected himself to be, in the lecture hall he could always prove that others were dimmer still. He had a predator's unerring instincts, so that a student in a morning lecture who was generally prepared and never called upon would be asked to recite after the only night all term he'd been drunk. Or, if the unhappy scholar had memorized nine paragraphs out of ten, it would be the tenth Malverthorpe wanted of him. Logic, which he had set out to subdue in God's service, proved to be such a formidable enemy that Malverthorpe ended up paying it homage. It was more real to him than God and, fighting on its side, he was invincible. God help—yes, leave it to God to help—the truth-seeking lad who argued from conviction, from feeling or from fact.

At the age of forty he was appointed proctor. Had the appointment come a few years earlier he would have taken it as an insult, for no master whose work might bring credit to the university would be saddled with such an administrative chore. But hungry by then for any distinction, Malverthorpe basked in the dubious glory of his office. Each night he patrolled the streets with his "bulldogs," collaring students who violated curfew and bringing them to justice. To know that the sight of him inspired fear gave Malverthorpe a small thrill.

His power over the town's innkeepers was even more satisfying. Residents of Oxford had long compensated themselves for the disruptive presence of the university by overcharging its members for everything. But after a particularly bloody riot the clerics gained the upper hand, for the king declared that inns and taverns would be inspected by the university proctor. This gave Malverthorpe the authority to fine a publican for an offense such as selling in short measure and to put repeat offenders in the pillory which stood in front of St. Martin's. But he seldom went that far, for his power could be best savored if only the first transgression was punished. He never solicited bribes, but he accepted "gifts" and liked the obsequiousness that accompanied them. Odious as innkeepers found it to do him homage, it was cheaper than replacing all their false-bottomed tankards. And so it had gone for seven years.

Several of the inns of Oxford—most notoriously the Chequer—provided for the temporary relief of celibacy. In theory, Malverthorpe's duty was to prosecute anyone who extended this sort of hospitality to clerics. But, it was in everyone's interest that he overlook it. The chancellor himself had once hinted at this, when he had a good dinner and a bottle of wine in his belly. "No harm in a lad sowing a few wild oats," he had mused. "The trouble comes when he stays around for the harvest."

Malverthorpe was well into his forties when he lost his virginity to one of the Chequer girls who was offered to him in exchange for his tolerance. She had been no more than eighteen, but all the time she'd had this sly look, this shrewd, knowing way. He had tried another and with her it was the same—the feeling of being seen through and laughed at and manipulated, and all of these disagreeable impressions tied to the most exquisite physical release. He became addicted, and the more addicted he became, the more he loathed the girls and the act itself. And the more he loathed it, the more addicted he became. Soon he was going to the Chequer every night, entering by the back door after he had made his rounds. The girls dreaded his appearance. He began to indulge in small cruelties toward them. More and more often, whichever girl he requested would plead illness, and the girl he ended up with would be the one who owed the others a favor. He would overhear these negotiations behind the curtains, and far from being discouraged by them, he soon came to require them, or some other evidence of his partner's reluctance, to become aroused.

One night when no one else would have him, he found himself alone with an aging and complacent trollop who had till then managed to elude him. He made his ritual speech—equal parts abuse and threat. And she yawned. When he intensified the abuse, she let out a short cynical laugh. His desire withered, but he could not leave it at that. Hardly knowing what he was doing, he grabbed his belt and began to beat her with it. She screamed—more in fury than in fear—and Tychenor, the proprietor, burst through the door and expelled him. "Don't come back unless you want the chancellor to hear of this," he warned, but he need not have said it. Malverthorpe's sense of disgrace was so great that two years later he still crossed the street to avoid walking in front of the Chequer.

After that he no longer visited whores, and for a while he lost desire altogether. But lately he had been thinking that his big mistake had been his pursuit of professionals. What he needed, he decided, was a girl with little or no experience, a girl who would have proper respect. And so it was that Ingrid became the hapless object of Malverthorpe's attentions.

They met on a day in early March when the sun had burst forth with unseasonable gaiety. The heavy drab air of an Oxford winter was congenial to Malverthorpe's inner climate, but spring put him out of sorts. All morning long he prowled through the town scowling and handing out citations to students who violated the dress code with parti-color satins and extravagant displays of bright young leg, or played football in the street, or broke into song too near one of the town's twenty churches. With his gray hair in flattened waves over his ears, his lonely haunted look and his slinking walk, he reminded one of a wolf. He knew that the scholars ridiculed him behind his back, so when he was out he cultivated deafness, and he kept the windows and door of his room sealed so he would not chance to overhear them.

Worn out by his morning's labor of harassing high-spirited young men, he stopped at the Crossroads for refreshment. Henry Greene's pints were a full two ounces short, so he could be counted on to be doubly obsequious.

Some of the tables had been moved out into the yard, and these were crowded with the midday trade. Greene was sitting in the midst of the crowd, regaling them with some raucous story. A shadow of dismay crossed his face when he saw Malverthorpe, but he recovered quickly and tried to make room for the newcomer at his table. "I'll sit inside, if you please," the proctor said curtly and stepped into the reassuring gloom of the tavern. Greene was obliged to leave the sun-basking circle outside and followed him indoors with a barely concealed sigh. Once inside the host struggled to keep up the pretense of friendly conversation while Malverthorpe glowered at his food and drink, refusing to hold up his end.

He first saw Ingrid framed by the doorway, outlined in light, laughing over her shoulder at something that was shouted to her from outside. She set the empty mugs she was carrying down on the serving table and began to wash them, dipping them into the basin one by one and drying them with a vigorous snap of white towel.

For an instant too fleeting for him to be fully conscious of it, he felt as if *he* were a lighthearted girl, flushed with laughter on the first day of spring. On the heels of this impression came a bitter envy and then, just as swiftly, a desire to punish her. She felt him staring and looked up. The smile that lingered on her face faded and she looked away with a shyness that had nothing coy in it, like a shy animal.

Henry noticed his interest and called her over. "If Jane were a lad, she'd be one of your scholars," the innkeeper boasted. "She knows Latin and French."

Malverthorpe made no response to this, assuming that Henry was exaggerating to impress him, but he looked intently at the girl and saw a flicker of fear. She tried to catch her employer's eye and shook her head almost imperceptibly, as if warning him. "I know only a few words—what anyone can pick up in church," she said.

"You see how modest she is," Henry said. "But you should hear her chattering away with her scholar friends. They think she's quite a marvel."

Malverthorpe could see that she was anxious to get away. He leaned forward with growing interest. "Is that so, my dear?"

"It is only a marvel because I am a servant. In a theology lecture I should be quite lost."

"And how is it that you know any Latin at all?"

"My parish priest taught me a little. And my father."

Malverthorpe was dismayed at the mention of the parent. "Does your father live in town?"

"No, sir. He is dead."

Good. One obstacle out of the way. "What parish do you come from?"

At this she looked even more anxious. "You probably wouldn't know it, sir. I come from a very small town, far from here."

So much the better.

She ducked her head in a self-effacing little bow. "We're rather busy outside. I should go."

"In a moment. Obviously you have an inquiring mind. Would you like to learn more?"

"Education would be wasted on a person in my position," she said. Though the words were demure, he sensed a stubborn resistance behind them.

"Come now, don't be so prim," Henry interjected. "You're always after the lads to tell you what they've learned in their lectures. She's especially keen on medicine," he said to Malverthorpe.

"Education is a good in itself," the proctor replied. "Even for a young lady. If you will permit me, I will tutor you myself."

"That's very kind, sir, but—"

"I have an hour free this very afternoon. Why don't you come 'round and have a Latin lesson. Surely Master Greene can spare you for an hour."

Henry, seeing the girl's consternation and wanting to please everyone, tried to take a middle course. "To be sure, we can spare her, but you are too generous, sir."

Malverthorpe waved his hand majestically. "Think nothing of it. I shall expect Mistress Jane two hours hence. My lodgings are in Lodelowe Hall."

Five

Ingrid knew the tutoring was just a ruse. Skewered by Malverthorpe's relentless gaze, she had felt her guilty conscience twitching like a fish on a line. He had recognized her, she was sure of it. There was only one question: Was *he* sure of it? Was he meeting her in private simply to avoid the scandal of a public confrontation, or was he uncertain of his identification and planning to probe a little to see whether she would confess?

He could not be sure she was the same woman. For one thing, she had gained weight. That very day Henry had given her rump an approving pat, saying "You're finally putting some meat on those bones, Janie." And sure enough, when she looked down, there were her small breasts jutting forth, full of their own self-consequence. Her hair had grown out a bit, and Isobel had cut it to fall more becomingly around her face. With a kerchief tying up the back, she looked like any other girl. She had modified her accent and picked up a serving girl's slang. He must have his doubts.

Dread slowed her on the way to Lodelowe Hall. It was market day, and High Street was all a-stink and a-babble with gaudy commerce. She thought of the bleak, musty corridors of Greyleigh, the damp dour walls and endless, laughless days there. Of course they would make her return, in disgrace. The stares, the whispers, the hard penances she would be given—all of that would be the easy part. It was when the scandal subsided, when they gave her back her job in the infirmary and allowed her to return to the choir, that her real sentence would begin. Then she would trudge, cold and color-blind, through the rest of her days, and nothing in her bloodless, unfelt repentance would move God to console her.

Past St. Mary's the market petered out and most of the buildings belonged to the colleges. Students with their long black gowns flapping over short tunics and bright leggings strolled in pairs and trios or lounged against the walls watching a game of football in the middle of the street. She could hear snatches of French, Welsh, Italian, and strains of an Irish ballad. They were sinners, too, some of these clerics, bound by vows they had no trouble shrugging off now and then. Oxford was full of sinners. Why couldn't she repent on her deathbed, as ordinary people did, repent after knowing the full savor of her sin?

Malverthorpe had instructed her to pass through the alley between Spicer's and Lodelowe and enter by the back stairs. Her heart was punching at the wall of her chest. She paused, trying to slow her breathing. *My name is Jane Basset. I am a servant at the Crossroads.*

She knocked. He answered at once. "Welcome, Mistress Jane," he intoned in his deep, furry voice. Ingrid thought she heard an ironic inflection, as if he were saying "You *call* yourself Jane."

Entering his room was like being swallowed. The chamber was dark, purple and hot as a throat. Velvet drapes banished the sun, and despite the warmth of the afternoon a small fire burned in the grate. There was a large oak table covered with a Turkish rug, flanked by two pompous chairs. The bed, swathed in heavy curtains, looked vain. The black oak wardrobe looked severe and domineering. And Malverthorpe, robed in garnet velvet, looked like his furniture.

He locked the door and put the key in his sleeve. *It's true then,* she thought. *He knows, and he's afraid I'll try to escape when he confronts me.*

"Am I a prisoner?" she asked with attempted levity. Her voice was high and strained.

"Of course not." His smile was as false as her joke. "I just don't want any of the lads to see you and become envious. Please, be seated."

He followed her over to the table and poured some wine into a heavy silver goblet, all the while scrutinizing her with such intensity it took all her self-control not to blurt a confession. At his nod she took a sip of wine. It tasted like the room—heavy, purple, velvety. Sweat broke out on her forehead and upper lip, and the moment she swallowed she was dizzy. Carefully she set the goblet down.

He set an open book before her and pointed out the passage she was to read. It must be a test. Latin was as natural to her as English, but the country girl she was impersonating would not be up to this text. So she read haltingly, underlining each word with her index finger, stumbling and mispronouncing to the best of her ability. He did not correct her errors, did not even seem to be listening, but his piercing, almost hostile stare never left her.

She dared not look up, nor could she hear him moving closer in that sound-muffling room, but she felt a sort of exhalation from his velvet robe and all the little hairs on her arms shivered as he stood behind her. She stopped reading. His harsh breathing seemed very near her ear. She pressed her finger hard against the page to stop its trembling. "How do you say this?" she asked him, pointing to a word, because she felt that if he did not speak soon she might scream.

He did not answer. She felt his breath at the nape of her neck. He fingered a wisp of hair that had escaped her kerchief. It was curly and damp with perspiration. "You are warm," he observed. And though she *was* warm, she shivered as his fingers traced a whispery spiral around her neck and twitched at the lacing of her bodice. The cord flicked out of the first eyelet like a snake's tongue. She was paralyzed. He groaned, and his other hand came up around her throat, his cold rings grazing it. Her neck was strained, her chin tipped back. His gray, wolfish face descended on her, lips parted, the inside of his mouth hanging raw like meat, his teeth unsheathed. Her own hand, still on the page where it had been tracing sentences, jerked out spastically and upset the goblet. She heard the splash of wine and felt it trickling into her skirt. She gave a little cry, and for an instant he drew back and she was able to jump to her feet, shaking her skirt and looking about for something to mop up the spill. "Leave it," he moaned. He grasped her wrist and attempted to draw her toward the bed. When she tried to wrench free, his fingers dug into her cruelly. Without meaning to, she screamed.

Immediately he let go, his face sick with fear. The scream had startled her, too. Her hands flew to her mouth, as if to hush herself. "I'm sorry," she gasped.

He recovered first. "I was only trying to move you away from the spill, my dear." There was a plaintive note in his voice. With an air of being misunderstood, he went to the wardrobe and took out a towel for her. She dabbed at her skirt and then at the stain on the Turkish rug, feeling much abashed.

"You startled me, that's all," she murmured. "I'm sorry about the mess."

"Never mind. Come sit here." He seated himself on the edge of the bed, and because Ingrid felt so bad about screaming and spilling the wine, she joined him there. His breathing was still labored and his hand hovered over her knee as if wondering whether to alight. When it did, she let it stay. So he did not suspect her identity after all! Relief made her magnanimous. Poor man, she thought. So hungry, so lonely, and at the same time so disagreeable. He had not been born ugly—no one feature was particularly objectionable—but over the years he had hammered himself into the shape of a gargoyle. If she'd met him at Greyleigh, she would have taken his poor, harrowed head into her hands and blessed it.

Malverthorpe was much encouraged by the mildness that had come over her face. "I'm not so terrible," he said, almost whining.

"Nay, you are not," she replied in her warm, milky voice. Feeling herself rich in the youth and cheerfulness that he lacked, she did not begrudge his hands what pleasure they took in her. She could afford it. She sat with a benign, patient, rather saintly expression on her face, hands limp as a martyr's, and let him touch her. But when, through her clothes, he took her nipple precisely between his thumb and forefinger, the nipple stood up like a traitor at enemy roll call. Ingrid shuddered at this defection of the soul from her flesh as she would have shuddered to pick up her own severed arm.

His face was moving closer, his lower lip hanging loose and a predatory concentration in his eyes. She turned her face aside and he jerked it back, squeezing either side of her mouth to force the lips apart. She could not help exclaiming in disgust as his mouth mashed into hers.

She was afraid she had hurt his feelings. Instead, he seemed almost pleased. He growled a low mirthless laugh. "Do I frighten you?"

"Nay, of course not," she lied. "But this is wrong."

She would not have thought that anything could scandalize her after what she herself had done, but Malverthorpe's reply shocked her into speechlessness. "Fear of sin need not deter you, my dear," he said. "I am a priest. I can absolve you before you ever leave this room."

He went on in a new, unctuous voice. "Have you studied the commandments, my child?"

"Yes, of course."

"Which commandment do you fear you will violate if we lie together?"

Puzzled, she answered, "The sixth, naturally."

"The sixth; that is correct. And which commandment concerns obedience to your superiors?"

"The fourth."

"Correct. As the fourth commandment precedes the sixth, so your duty to obey me comes before your duty to remain chaste."

Ingrid was flabbergasted. Did he really think her so simple? And if so, what a vile abuse of power to mislead her that way. But contradicting him would reveal more education than she was supposed to have. So meekly she bowed her head and said, "I will put the matter before my confessor, sir, and if it is as you say, I will obey you."

She thought she had outsmarted him then. But her self-congratulation lasted only as long as it took her to stride to the door. She had forgotten she was locked in.

Malverthorpe was right behind her. "Do you mock me, young woman? Do you mock me?" His voice was low and dangerous. Still struggling with the latch, she did not reply. "I will not be mocked, do you hear?"

She tried to keep her own voice calm. "Please, unlock the door. I was not mocking you."

He ignored her. "I am a doctor of theology. You do not ask some unlettered country priest to pronounce judgment on me!"

"Very well. I will leave it to God to judge you. Now please, open the door."

"I have not finished with you yet."

Trapped between this sinister utterance at her back and the unyielding door, she panicked. She whirled round to face him, her breath coming in a sort of dry sob. "Please," she entreated. "Please unlock the door. Please."

"My dear, there is no need to be so dramatic." As if to prove his point, he went to the table and casually poured them both a drink. "You are not in any danger. Come, sit down and hear what I have to say to you. I shall not detain you much longer."

His affected nonchalance could not conceal how her begging had gratified him. Even in her panic she saw it. The observation brought her back to her dignity. She took a seat and waited.

He handed her the goblet and sipped meditatively from his own. "Are you fond of your employers?" he asked her.

She wondered what he was getting at. "Quite," she answered, a bit defensively.

"Go ahead, drink," he urged.

"Why do you ask about the Greenes?"

He waved his free hand. "Just curious. Did you know that Henry sells in short measure?"

"Nay, I'm sure he doesn't. We fill the mugs to overflowing."

"That may well be," he conceded. "The mugs don't hold a pint."

Even as she started to protest, she felt a creeping doubt. It was not hard to imagine Henry cheating in small things. Somehow she had known this about him already.

"He's already been fined for it twice," Malverthorpe continued. "The penalty for a third offense is the pillory."

Henry would as soon die as have that happen to him, Ingrid thought. She remembered a day when the boys had snuck into the chicken coop and stolen eggs to throw at a man who was locked in the pillory across the street. Henry had been furious—it was the only time she had ever seen him strike his children, and this despite the fact that the intended victim was his closest competitor and certainly no friend. Now she understood why. It might have been he. "There won't be a third offense," she said.

"Alas, there already has been," he said with scarcely concealed triumph.

"I can't believe that. His children would be mortified. I can't believe he would risk it," she insisted.

157

The proctor shrugged. "Ask him."

"Why are you telling me this?"

"I just thought you might be concerned."

"Concerned enough to . . . to bargain for your mercy. Is that what I'm to understand?"

He gave a short, dry laugh. "Henry was right about you. You are not unintelligent."

Ingrid had never before encountered an evil that declared itself so frankly. A naturalist's urge to dissect it, to observe and classify it was for the moment stronger than her sense of revulsion. "You would really do this? You would not be ashamed?" she wondered aloud.

"My conscience is none of your concern," he said. "Do not inquire into matters that are beyond your understanding."

She looked at him with gentle, urgent appeal. "You are not so heartless," she coaxed. "You do not mean it."

"Indeed I do."

"But if I come to you under duress, how much pleasure can you have in it?"

His features twisted into an expression of irony and bitterness. "Enough," he replied. "Enough." And then, sneering, he added, "Should I have waited for you to fall in love with me? Do you suppose I don't know how repulsive you find me? No—don't shake your head like that out of flattery and fear. A sinner I may be, but I am not a self-deceiver. You will not be expected to feign pleasure."

This speech, managing as it did to provoke pity and refuse it at the same time, stuck to her like the stuff spider webs are made of. She was caught. "Must I decide now?" she asked in a whisper.

He had turned from her and was gazing into the fire. She had to say it again.

"You have three days," he muttered with an impatient, dismissive gesture of his goblet. Without looking at her, he took the key from his sleeve and placed it on the table. Then he turned back to the fire. She stared at the key, hardly comprehending that she was free to go, for the web still held her. After a moment he glanced over his shoulder at her but averted his face at once. "Don't stand there staring as if you thought you could stare shame into me," he muttered. "Shame is my food. "Yes," he repeated to himself with secret sullen amusement. "Shame is my food. Now go. Go!"

Outside the daylight blinded her. She had forgotten there was a sun.

Six

Ingrid made her way back to the Crossroads along the gravel path that lined the town wall, avoiding the main streets, for she dreaded meeting anyone she knew. Malverthorpe's airless purple room hung over her like a miasma. Demon wings beat close to her ears, made sudden fierce shadows before her eyes.

Common sense tried to make itself heard. Henry's predicament was his own fault, and her chastity too great a price to pay for his rescue. A decent woman would refuse Malverthorpe, would feel righteous and clean in doing so.

But Ingrid could never feel righteous and clean. Chastity? She had no chastity to protect. Her lost virginity was an open wound, vulnerable to infection. Malverthorpe must have known that—he must have chosen her for that reason. A fellow sinner could see through her disguise—her crisp linen apron and kerchief, her hardworking hands, the wholesome blush of Jane Basset's cheeks. Sometimes other men gave her looks that made her think they, too, saw through it, and she was afraid to meet their eyes. Malverthorpe had recognized the sinner in her, as Jack had recognized it.

She shuddered to recall the creeping, quivery response of her flesh to the proctor's touch. *Concupiscence*—that was the word for the soulless hunger of the flesh. A nasty word, she'd always thought. When she'd tried to apply it to the dream flush brought on by Jack's kisses, her mind had recoiled, had said no, there must be some prettier name. Sin with Jack was dew gilded and sweet as Eden fruit. Like Eve she might bewail the punishment, but she could never repudiate the taste. Malverthorpe, though, had the look of the serpent and the taste of poison. He came to her the way the devil would come when he'd dropped all pretense, when he knew you were his.

And yet, she felt such pity for him. For years she had forced herself to touch what was repulsive to her, and now it was a habit. This man was like a leper, a spiritual leper. The smell of his mind made her queasy. So how could she refuse to put her lips to his foul and festering sores? How could she stand off saying "Do not infect me"? He had infected her already. She could taste the corruption at the back of her throat.

I touched you out of pity . . . An upswelling nausea doubled her over, and she clutched her cramping stomach. She was sweating as though sick, and chilled.

"Jane?"

It was Matthew Sturges coming back from the tanner's through Smith Gate, a thick pile of hides balanced on one of his monumental shoulders. From head to toe he was a warm, reassuring brown, and if acorns had dropped from his russet hair, she would not have been surprised. "Are you all right?" he asked.

She wished she could bury her face against his sturdy chest, sob and tell him everything. His fists would clench, his honest jaw tighten in outrage against Malverthorpe. He would act swiftly to protect the decency of Oxford serving girls. A petition would be drawn up, justice demanded. Her maidenhood would become a rallying cry, a florid symbol of the peace of Oxford. And there she would be at the center of it all—a cankerous lie.

"Aye, I'm all right," she said, forcing a smile. "Just something I ate."

"Uh-oh. Not one of those sausage rolls from the booth by St. Mary's, I hope. They're being cited, you know."

She gave a sheepish little shrug. "They smelled so good."

"Oh, Jane." He shook his head sympathetically. "Since you ate one I won't tell you what's in 'em."

Yes, she thought with resignation, let him save his wrath for the sausage vendor. She looked wistfully at Matthew's simple, guileless face. Happy are the righteous, she thought.

They walked on companionably, chatting about the unseasonable weather and the littlest Sturges, who was teething. By the time they reached Cornmarket and their routes diverged, Ingrid was feeling a little better. Maybe Malverthorpe was lying about Henry's pints. After all, he had lied about the commandments. She hurried back to the inn, frantic with hope.

Her scholar friends were having a round in the pub. She greeted them abstractedly and went straight to the ale cellar, tying her apron as she walked. A quart measure—the standard established by law—hung on a peg by the door. She took it down and blew the dust off it, filled two of the Crossroad's mugs with ale and carefully poured them in. Malverthorpe had not been splitting hairs: There was better than an inch left at the top. She wanted to cry.

Henry had followed her down to the cellar, hovering silently, anxiously, while she came to her conclusion. She had been so absorbed that she didn't know he was there until he spoke.

"So he told you."

"Aye, he told me." The quart wobbled in her hand, but it was not full enough to slop over. She set it down and turned to face him.

"Everyone does it, Jane. The customers know it—no one is really deceived." His wheedling tone irritated her almost beyond endurance—she was ready to slap him in the pillory herself.

"He said you've already been cited twice."

"Everyone gets cited twice and that's the end of it, as long as you keep him happy."

Her heart sank. "You sent me to keep him happy, then. You knew . . ." The possibility of such a betrayal crushed her.

"Knew what? What happened?" To his credit, the innkeeper sounded sincerely alarmed. Maybe he really didn't know.

"Nothing happened," she said in a dull voice.

"The lesson went well? Are you going back?"

She nodded.

"You haven't made him angry, then?"

"Oh, no. We got on famously."

"Well, good," he said, a little uncertain. "I was afraid from the way you were acting . . . I can't afford to have Malverthorpe angry at anyone here, that's the thing." He smiled a sickly ingratiating smile and patted her shoulder as if he were afraid it might burn him. Ingrid almost let him get away, then changed her mind and caught him by the sleeve.

"Wait. What are you telling me?"

He steered her to the corner of the cellar, speaking in a low, confiding tone. "Jane, don't misunderstand me. I would never ask you to—to do something you felt bad about. If you've won Malverthorpe's favor, well, that's grand. I hope you can keep it. But if for some reason you have to cross him, believe me, no one here will blame you for it. I'll give you a good reference. You won't have any trouble finding another position."

So that's how it was. She had been thinking of the Crossroads as her home, of the Greenes as the family she never had.

At the top of the stairs Nick accosted her. "Jane—"

"Please, I can't talk now," she mumbled, blinking hard. She didn't want to cry in the pub.

"Look, I couldn't help overhearing—"

"Couldn't help overhearing!" Tom exclaimed. "Confess it man, you were crouched on the top stair straining to pick up every word!"

"It's Malverthorpe, isn't it," Nick went on. "He's putting the bite on you."

The thought that her friends knew only made matters worse. "Oh, God," she cried, and rushed blindly out into the courtyard.

They followed her. "Nick, leave it," Nigel was saying. "Can't you see she wants privacy?"

"If it's what I think it is, privacy's the last thing that's wanted. Jane, listen to me," Nick urged softly, putting his arm around her shaking shoulders. "Malverthorpe's notorious."

"Is he?" She sniffed and wiped her cheeks with her fingers.

"He's got every ale seller in town blackmailed, and he's a regular terror in the whorehouses from what I hear. Got thrown out of the Chequer, if you can believe that. Christ, you have to be half way to hell before they let you *in* to the Chequer. It boggles the mind to think what he had to do to get thrown out of it!"

"Buggery, that's what I heard."

"Toad, there's a lady present," Nigel reminded him.

" 'Twas a lady he did it to," Tom retorted. "Never heard of him going after a serving girl before, though."

"We must credit him with taste for picking our Janie," Nick said, giving her shoulders a squeeze.

"Oh, splendid," Nigel said sarcastically. "You really know how to make a body feel better."

But in fact they *were* making her feel better. Their frankness dispelled some of the shame that oppressed her whenever she recalled Malverthorpe's hot purple room. Nick was guiding her out through the gate. "Now you just come along with Uncle Nick and Uncle Toad and Uncle Owl," he crooned. "We'll work out what to do, don't you worry."

The sun was going down, and vendors were closing up their stalls as the four of them made their way down St. Aldate's to Cary's Inn, where the lads smuggled her into their attic room. It held three cots and not much more. Here and there was a dirty shirt, a pair of balled-up hosen, a few empty jugs. The prized scholar's gowns were hung reverently on a peg. The room had no dormers, and the eaves were so low over their heads that it was possible to stand erect only at the roof's apex. A smelly breeze from the nearby fish market blew in through the small window and mingled with the smoky residue of lamp oil. The odor reminded her of Greyleigh.

Tom reached under his cot and produced a jug of cheap wine. "Been saving this for an emergency." They sat cross-legged in a huddle on the floor, passing it back and forth. Under the influence of the wine and her friends' affection, the knot in Ingrid's stomach untied itself. Little by little she recounted the whole story, and in the telling it became more of a comedy than a tragedy. Malverthorpe's argument about the commandments doubled them over.

"I wonder what he'd say if one of us produced that in theology class."

"Good Lord, wouldn't that be rich!"

"So what answer did you make?"

"I told him I would take it up with my confessor."

"Good girl. Oh, he must have been livid at that."

"He was. He came roaring after me saying, 'I will not be

mocked. I am a doctor of theology. I will not be mocked!' " Her imitation of his humorless basso profundo set them off laughing again.

"So what did you say to that?"

This time she mimicked her own helpless entreaty. " 'Oh please, sir, please sir. Let me out. Let me out'," she piped. "And all the time he's just staring at me with those flinty eyes of his."

"Poor Janie," Nick said. He took a swig from the jug and passed it to her. "Well, gentlemen, what are we going to do?"

"Let's challenge him to a duel," Tom proposed.

"Can you fence?"

"Not actually. But I daresay neither can he."

"I wonder—can one be sent down for dueling with the proctor."

"Undoubtedly. Not to mention killed."

"There's nothing any of you can do," Ingrid said with a sigh. "I shall simply have to find a new job."

"Henry—in the kindest possible way, mind you—Henry made it clear that he would give her the sack if she disappointed Malverthorpe," Nick explained to the others, who had not overheard the conversation in the cellar. "The trouble is, Jane, that he can harass you anywhere in town."

"But he can only blackmail me if my employer is breaking the law."

"Good luck finding one who isn't."

"Really?"

"That's the way he wants it, you see. If the ale sellers were honest, what power would he have? They don't want reform and neither does he. It's a cozy arrangement. If you're to remain in Oxford—and don't you dare leave—we have to find a way to stop him."

"What if Jane were to put in a formal complaint to the chancellor?" Nigel suggested.

Vehemently she shook her head. She was certain the chancellor had been at Greyleigh.

"But why not?"

"I'd get Henry in trouble."

"What's that to you? He certainly hasn't shown *you* any loyalty."

"He doesn't want his children to see him in the pillory. How can I blame him for that? I don't want to see it happen either. And besides, it's my word against Malverthorpe's."

"You've got a point there."

"Unless there are witnesses!" Tom broke in excitedly. "Suppose one of us—or all of us, for that matter—concealed ourselves under the bed, in the wardrobe, out on the window ledge, anywhere we could, and sprang out at an incriminating moment?"

"Oh, wouldn't that be a coup!" said Nick. "Put him out of business for good."

"What do you say, Jane?"

"I don't want to get in trouble."

"You won't. Malverthorpe will."

"But wouldn't the chancellor want to question me?"

"I don't know. He might. Just to make sure you didn't lead the man on. We'd back you up—it's nothing to worry about."

She shook her head. "I don't want that kind of attention."

"But why not?" Tom persisted.

"I just don't. I'm sorry."

"You talk as if you're a fugitive from justice," Nick said.

"I am, sort of."

The admission had come out so abruptly it startled her as much as her friends. She gave a feeble belated chuckle, trying to laugh it off, but they were not so easily thrown off the scent of a juicy secret.

"Really?"

"Do tell."

She studied their friendly, curious, tipsy faces. Maybe it was no accident that she had let it slip. Maybe she had been wanting to tell them all along. She knew they would never turn her in. "Do you swear if I tell you it will never leave this room?"

They all swore eagerly and huddled closer.

"Jane Basset is not my real name," she began. That revelation did not create much of a sensation. They were waiting for her to say more, but already she was losing her nerve.

"Well? What *is* your real name?"

"Come on, out with it."

"You won't believe me."

"Give us a try."

"Give me a drink first." Tom passed her the jug and she took a good swig. "All right, you promise this is our secret?"

"You have our word of honor as gentlemen," Nigel said. "This secret of yours had better be good for all the fuss you're making."

She looked them over one more time and lost her nerve. "No, I can't tell. I'm sorry."

"What?" Nick exploded. "Lads, are we going to let her get away with this? Nay, my pretty, we're going to torture you till you confess all!" At that, the three of them wrestled her down to the floor. Tickling fingers scrambled all over her. Thrashing and shrieking, she at last surrendered.

"I'll tell, I'll tell."

The tickling stopped, but she was still pinned.

"Let me up."

"Confess now."

"I need another drink first. For courage. And anyway, I need to be sitting up straight for this. It's a very serious confession."

"What do you say, lads? All right," Nick said sternly. "We'll let you up. But mind—if you don't confess now, there'll be no mercy for you."

They let go and she straightened up, sitting on the floor with her back against a cot. Her kerchief had come askew. She pulled it off and combed her hair back with her fingers. "Pass me the jug."

She took a long drink and then quickly, before she could lose her nerve again, she asked them, "Did you ever hear of Ingrid Fairfax of Greyleigh?"

"Of course we have. The one who works miracles, right?"

"Funny," Nigel said. "You don't hear of her so much these days. She got sick of something, didn't she?"

"I am she. I am Ingrid Fairfax."

For a moment they just gaped at her. Then Nick burst out, "Oh, Jane, you really had us going there!"

She let out a wild giddy laugh and took another drink. She was vastly relieved to have said it and even more relieved that they did not believe her. Still laughing, she staggered to her feet. "Look," she said. "I'll prove it. I'll show you how I used to do it." She tied her kerchief low on her forehead, concealing all her hair, and assumed a solemn expression. "All right, Nick, pretend you're a leper. Nay, you have to kneel. Yes, like that, but try to look more pathetic. That's it. All right, now you must present the affected part." Nick thrust his arm up and dangled the hand. She took it between hers, looked him deep in the eyes and intoned a blessing. Theatrically, she concluded. "You may rise."

Nick rolled his eyes heavenward. "Praise be to God. I'm cured."

"Go and sin no more," she admonished him.

"My turn," Tom cried, throwing himself on his knees. "Oh help me, Saint Ingrid, for I am sore afflicted with impotence. Shall I present the afflicted part?"

At this they all laughed so boisterously that Cary came stomping up to the attic to hush them. "Quick, Jane, under the bed!" She flattened herself beneath one of the cots, eye to eye with dustballs and dirty hosen, as Tom went to the door. "Good evening, Master Cary, and welcome. To what do we owe this singular honor?"

"Did I hear a woman up here?"

"That was me, sir," Nick tweeted in comic falsetto.

She could hear a wink in Cary's voice. "Well, don't keep the house awake, eh lads?"

"All clear!" The blanket that had concealed her was lifted, and Ingrid scrambled out. By now they were a little tired from so much laughing, and they sat in a quiet, happy circle, passing around the last of the wine. It was dark, but their eyes had grown accustomed to it.

"You really are daft, Jane," Nick said, chuckling.

"And bloody sacrilegious," Tom added. "Imagine taking Saint Ingrid's name in vain like that."

She beat her breast. *"Mea culpa."*

"Never mind. We are going to be priests. We can absolve you before you even leave this room."

She felt Nigel's owlish gaze on her. He was not laughing with the rest of them. He knows, she thought. He knows it's no joke. His troubled, thoughtful look made her ashamed of the frivolous charade she had enacted, and she glanced away swiftly.

*   *   *

The next day Ingrid had a headache from worry and cheap wine. Henry made no reference to their discussion of the previous evening, nor did he reprimand her for leaving during the busy supper hour and sneaking back in after curfew. She was up at dawn, as usual, and worked hard all day, because she didn't know what else to do. Despite their promise to help, her friends had gotten sloppy and sleepy at evening's end without proposing any solution she dared go along with.

She would not go back to Malverthorpe. She had awoken that morning with a clear and unquestioning horror of it. That meant she had two days to leave town. Perhaps this was wise anyhow. She could move to a town farther from Greyleigh, a town less dominated by the Church, less populated by officials who might recognize her. Really, it had been foolhardy to stay this long.

But Oxford was site of the only real happiness she had known. That happiness was the product of coincidences which she regarded as magic and unrepeatable: meeting Matthew who treated her so kindly and influenced others to do the same; the way Sabina had come to embrace her as a sister; the inn; the Greene boys; the lively hum of Oxford learning; and most of all her friends—Nick, Toad and Owl—the only friends she had ever had. As for Jane Basset, she was a tenuous creation, made by Oxford the way Saint Ingrid had been made by Greyleigh. Remove her from her surroundings, and she would cease to exist.

Ingrid thought back to the weeks between Greyleigh and Oxford, the time when she had been neither Jane nor the nun. Who had she been then? A hunted creature, a succession of urgent needs—find food, get warm—a madness in the middle of the night. She had not suffered at the time, but she suffered terribly to think of it now.

How extraordinary that Jack traveled of his own free will! Often he had spoken of his love of the road, of something he called "freedom." She wondered whether he was the same Jack everywhere he went, and if so, how he managed such a thing. Who would she have been had she traveled with him?

Late in the afternoon Tom and Nigel came into the pub, accompanied by a gray-haired man she had not seen before. He wore rather threadbare priest's garb—too shabby to be a master of the university, too old to be a student. Tom introduced them. "Jane, this is Father Nicholas, your old pastor and confessor."

Ingrid stepped back and gaped. "Nick?"

"Yes, my child," he responded in a middle-aged voice. He had cut off his long curls (his beautiful curls!), enlarged his tonsure and powdered what was left of his hair. On close examination his face was unlined and youthful as ever, but his whole bearing—his expression, his voice, his mannerisms—evoked a man of fifty.

"I didn't recognize you!"

"Neither did Malverthorpe." His eyes were alight with triumph.

"You've been to see him?"

"I have indeed. Did I not promise you Uncle Nick would make it all better?'"

"But how?"

He looked around anxiously. "Is there someplace more private we can go to talk?"

It was Wednesday, which meant unoccupied guest rooms. She led the three of them to a small room on the third floor. They sat on the bed, while Nick paced back and forth, milking all the drama he could from his role.

"I went to his lodgings early this afternoon and introduced myself as Father Nicholas, the pastor of your home parish. The only trouble was, I couldn't remember what town you said you were from, so I had to kind of skirt that issue. I said I was on my way to Canterbury and had decided to stop in Oxford to see you, as you were always a favorite of mine. (Malverthorpe had no trouble believing that!) Anyhow, I said you'd mentioned his kindness in offering to tutor you. I went on about your scholarship and all, your thirst for knowledge—"

Ingrid was skeptical. "He believed all this?"

"Oh yes. Every word, so far as I can tell. I was very convincing if I do say so myself. Put on sort of a bumpkin accent and was very respectful of the 'great doctor of theology'. That was the main thing— how could he be suspicious of anyone who confirmed his own high opinion of himself? Well, I said the main purpose of my call was to thank him for his generous attention to you—you had spoken of him so warmly, so admiringly."

"Oh come!" Ingrid interrupted. "He didn't fall for that!"

"He did. He did, I swear he did. He puffed up like a pie in the oven. But here comes the good part—"

"Wait till you hear this, Janie," Tom said, elbowing her side.

"I said that I had another reason for wanting to meet him, for I needed his opinion on a moral problem that was perplexing me, a problem far too complex for an ignorant country pastor like me to figure out on my own."

"I bet he loved that."

"Oh, he did. The problem I posed was this: A young woman wished to become a nun but could not because she had to work to support her aging mother. So she settled for a secret vow of lifelong virginity. I as her confessor am the only living soul who knows about it."

"Why is the vow a secret?" Nigel interrupted.

"I don't know," Nick admitted. "Never figured it out. Luckily, Malverthorpe didn't ask. Anyway, this secret virgin has met a great man, a man she not only admires but also desires. She is honored by his interest in her, and when he invites her to become his mistress, she feels it is her duty to obey, for he represents the authority of the Church. But what about her vow of virginity? Greatly troubled, she has brought the problem to me, her confessor."

"Nick, this is so risky!" she said.

He shrugged. "I know. That's why I didn't tell you about my plan until I'd actually brought it off. You know what gave me the idea? It was your little pantomime last night. You were very convincing as a saint—rather virginal and grave and sweet. Oh, I know, it was just an act, but still, one could almost believe you did have a secret vow . . ."

"Owl here is still wondering if you *are* Saint Ingrid," Tom joked. Ingrid blushed and kept her eyes clear of Nigel.

"Well, back to my tale, which now reaches its exciting climax. The girl has brought her dilemma to me, and I rather suspect that this highly placed man she refers to would want to know of her vow, that he would not wish to transgress it unawares. I am tempted to tell him of it. On the other hand, I cannot do so without violating the seal of the confessional."

Tom nudged her again. "Isn't this brilliant?"

"It's insane."

"Hush, my children, here comes the best part. Humbly I asked, 'What, milord, would you do in my situation?' Well, he didn't answer right away. He paced a bit and his face was turned from me all the while, so there was no guessing what he was thinking. He made those sort of grunting groaning noises he makes. My heart was in my throat as you can imagine. Finally he turns to me and I see there are tears in his eyes."

"*Malverthorpe?*"

"Yes, yes, I swear it. Tears. He was all choked up and in this choked voice he said to me, 'I would do exactly as you have done.' And then he said, 'I thank you from my heart.' "

"One wouldn't have guessed he had one," Nigel said.

"I know," Nick mused with a softened expression. "I was rather touched, actually. So anyway, Janie, it looks like you're off the hook. Just don't let him see you kissing anyone. You've got a vow of virginity now."

Seven

Nick's plot had one serious weakness, and that was the improbability of Jane Basset's hometown confessor arriving on the scene the very day after Malverthorpe's attempt to blackmail her. Tom and Nigel had been sure the proctor would see through such a fishy coincidence. But as it turned out, the trick succeeded precisely because of this supposed flaw, for Malverthorpe saw in it the hand of God.

He'd watched through the curtains as Jane fled his room—half-running, probably in tears. The same girl who'd been laughing a few hours before, fresh, sweet and untroubled. *That* was the girl he had wanted, the laughing one, as if by bedding her he could enter an Eden from which he'd been barred. If only she had come over to him in the pub, taken his hand: "Come out in the sun, you silly old man. Come laugh with us." She would have drawn him outdoors and sat him beside her on a bench, patting his knee to reassure him in his shyness. She would have kissed his cheek, showing the others he was not so bad, and they would have accepted him. Because she liked him. As the wish welled up in him, he felt its impossibility, and he would have wept like a child, could he weep.

He couldn't have that laughing girl, because as soon as he came near she ceased to laugh. He found himself hoping she would not come back. Run away, child. Run fast. But she would come and he would drag her to the bed, and his flesh rose thinking how she would lie so still and scared and how he would hurt her, and he lay down on the bed and groped for himself.

In the desolation that followed, it came to him that he was a common blackmailer. He had never applied that name to his tyranny over the publicans. After all, he promised nothing, asked nothing . . . really, it was just a matter of keeping them in line, for what was a proctor for but to instill the fear that kept human affairs in order?

He never intended to threaten Jane. But *she* had threatened *him* with that talk of her confessor. He had to stop her. That was all he meant to do when he brought up Henry Greene. It was she who jumped to the conclusion. And when she'd wondered, Would he really do this? Would he not be ashamed? he'd known a sharp thrill of possibility. Yes, he would really do this and yes, he'd be ashamed, but he had no fear of shame and therefore, yes, therefore, all things were possible. He felt exalted with an expansive sense of evil, real evil, soaring high above the stunted, furtive mediocrity he had become. He saw that strength was what mattered. Strength, not goodness, commanded the respect of men.

So it had seemed then, with his blood stirred by lust. Now, lying clammy on his stained coverlet, he was queasy with anxiety. Common blackmail. If the authorities got wind of it, would he soar? Would he challenge them with his satanic defiance? Hardly. This was the small crime of a small man, and he was terrified to think how it could disgrace him.

Three days. If three days passed and she didn't come, he was clear. Of course, he would take no action against Greene. And if she did come, he would tell her she had misunderstood. Or else he would have her. He started to imagine it all over again—her passivity and her fear, the way her eyes would widen in the dark. His hand moved back to his flaccid sex. "You are not so heartless." He kept hearing her say that: "You are not so heartless." Hurt her, he urged. Think of hurting her. He tugged furiously, but his flesh refused to rise. He saw the pity in her look: You do not mean this. You are good underneath. He called to his demons: Slap her. Crush her. Make her cry. Still he could not obliterate it—that sad compassion in her gaze. It hovered, just out of reach, white and cloudlike. He moaned and rolled over and covered his head with the pillow.

The next day Jane's confessor called on him. God had seen her peril and, swift and vengeful, had sent this champion. Hadn't she said as much? *"I will leave it to God to judge you."* Malverthorpe was trembling as he invited his visitor to be seated.

He hadn't the manner of an avenging angel, this priest. He was modest, shabby and a bit befuddled. But his face, strangely youthful in its frame of gray hair, had a celestial beauty: elegant bones, huge dark eyes, the full red lips almost womanly. All through their conversation, a queer duality of presence put Malverthorpe on edge. Father Nicholas spoke like a country simpleton, yet there was a penetrating intelligence in his expression, a spark of outrage behind his bumbling self-effacement. He did not reproach, and that gentle refusal to reproach cut deep into Malverthorpe's conscience. The soul that had long been dead in him convulsed with the pain of returning sentience.

As soon as the priest had gone, he threw himself on his knees. "How is it you requite me with gentleness—I who have never been gentle?" He prayed, tears streaming down his face. "Oh, cut off the sinful hands that defiled this girl! Burn out these eyes that leered at her! Do not wound me with this mercy—I cannot bear it."

He had been blind to faith, so God had written large and plain. Out of all possible girls, his victim had been this one, a consecrated virgin. And out of all possible days, Father Nicholas had come to town today. *Today!* God had intervened not to punish, but to save him—he who was too far gone in sin to pray. This was mercy beyond mercy:

to answer a prayer that had never been spoken, an unuttered cry from the rim of hell.

He wept and prayed all afternoon. Then he got the idea of throwing himself at Jane's feet and begging her forgiveness. Like a penitent he would go, barefoot and bareheaded. He searched his wardrobe for something rsembling sackcloth. The closest was a black wool velvet, trimmed in sable. Even after he tore the fur off, it was too fine, but it would have to do. He rubbed ashes from the grate into the fabric and into his hair as well, and for good measure he streaked his face with soot.

To walk barefoot down High Street was a perilous undertaking, not only because of the open sewer and piles of garbage. A sort of slime covered even the cleaner patches, and there were pebbles and shards, animal bones, living insects, rat turds. All of his attention was concentrated on the ground, as if he were a worm, and he hardly noticed the looks he was getting. To touch the earth with his bare skin made him feel newborn, quivery and sanctified.

His arrival at the pub in this improvised penitent's outfit would have created more of a stir if a troubadour had not preceded him. All the patrons were massed around the table the singer was using as a stage, and Malverthorpe was able to slip into a dark corner unnoticed.

Jane was so busy serving the crowd that she did not see him at first. He couldn't seem to find the right moment for throwing himself at her feet, for it wouldn't do to accost her while she had three beer mugs in each hand, nor while she was taking an order or making change. He decided to follow her to the cellar and abase himself there in relative privacy. But just as she reached the stair, she recognized someone who seemed to be a friend—a large fellow with three red-headed children—and she became engaged in animated conversation with him. Then Greene came up and gave her a nudge and she nodded, excused herself and went quickly to the cellar.

She came back with a pitcher and began refilling cups, always with a look of concentration as she poured, followed by a sweet smile to the customer she'd just served. He saw that other men watched her, admired her supple grace, the doelike submissiveness of her bent head, the quiet joyousness in all her movements. And that big, rusty-haired man—his eyes followed her with the mournful longing of a hound, and his homely face reddened whenever she went near him. Easy to guess what was on his mind! How could Jane possibly preserve her chastity in a place like this?

All at once he realized what God wanted of him. He must become her protector, the champion of her secret virginity. As threats to it might arise at any time, he must be near her whenever she was in public, ready if need be to defend her at the cost of his own life.

As he was thinking this, she noticed him for the first time. It pained him to see the pleasure drain from her face. She parted her lips to say something to him, but just then Greene's wife came up and spoke to her. Jane nodded and seemed to forget him as she threaded her way through the crowd, picking up a toddler and rounding up several small boys whom she shepherded outside. From the groans and lamentations he gathered she was putting them to bed.

He followed them out to the courtyard. Feeling his presence, she turned and looked at him once more, taking in for the first time his penitential dishabille. Her face registered alarm and concern. Just as he was about to throw himself down, one of the smaller boys cried, "Who's that scary man?" Jane shook her head faintly as if she knew Malverthorpe's intention and wished to discourage him. The little boy tugged on her skirt. "Janie, I don't like him. Make him go away."

"Hush, Quart, you'll hurt the man's feelings." She clasped his hand and steered him toward the stairs.

"Why is his face all black?" an older one demanded.

Her back was turned now as she led them away, but he heard her say, "That is what people do sometimes when they want to tell God they're sorry."

"*I'm* sorry," the littler one asserted. "Can I put dirt on my face?"

"Nay, silly," she laughed. "You're dirty enough."

That was all he was able to hear, for they went into one of the upstairs rooms. She gave him an anxious look from the balcony before shutting the door. Disappointed and suddenly tired, he made his way home in the dark.

The next day he awoke in that state of elation one feels at the commencement of a journey. Right away he set about making arrangements for his new life. He hired a student to see to the sale of his fine clothing, jewelry and furniture, and the purchase of plain things to

replace them. The money left over was to be distributed to the poor.
He sent a letter to the chancellor, resigning his office. He bought
himself a sword. Then he walked to Cowley to make his confession.
Oxford abounded in priests, but all of them knew him, and Malverthorpe was planning to reveal everything. Everything.

As it turned out, the confession was something of a letdown.
The priest was old and a bit deaf, so Malverthorpe found himself
shouting repetitions of sins it was hard enough to disclose once and in
a whisper. Toward the end, the old man nodded off, and instead of
the tearful welcome back into the arms of the Church that Malverthorpe had envisioned, he got a perfunctory absolution. The priest
seemed relieved to see him go.

Back in Oxford, he donned the rough robe that had been
procured for him and took his new sword into the Church of Saint
Mary the Virgin. Prostrate before her altar and weeping for joy, he
dedicated body, soul and sword to the defense of Jane Basset's chastity.

From then on he kept his vigil without wavering, arriving at
the Crossroads before any other customer and remaining until curfew.
Of course, Jane must never know of his purpose. He must respect the
secrecy of her vow. When he followed her through the market he kept
his distance so that she would not detect him, but his hand was always
on the hilt of his sword, and his eyes never stopped scanning the
crowd, looking out for potential danger.

He feared his constant presence in the pub would arouse
suspicion, so he pretended to have become a drunk, sitting alone in
the darkest corner, consuming wine slowly, steadily, by the pitcherful.
The wine gave him an authentic look of dissipation. The bags under
his eyes got heavier, his lips slacker, his complexion more sallow. He
let his hair grow unruly, neglected his beard. Even his speech, on the
rare occasions when he spoke, was slurred. No one would have
guessed, to look at him, that he was a man transfigured. And he was
glad of this. His inner exaltation demanded this outward debasement.
His worldly pride had been like his black oak wardrobe: heavy and
dark, stifling and confining him. Now he hacked it to splinters with a
vandal's glee and made bright fire of it, and the smoke of his burning
pride was sweet as incense.

In a curious way, Jane became his—much more than any

woman he had physically possessed. Her way of wrapping her arm across her waist and clutching the opposite elbow, of blowing stray hair out of her face when her hands were full, of ducking her head and gliding away like a swan when she was shy—all of this was more familiar to him than his own body. The cadence of her speech was the rhythm of his breathing. Not a drop of her sweat went uncounted or unloved. He did not struggle against his desire for her but welcomed the torment of it, gloried in the knowledge that it would never be appeased. Renunciation turned the base metal of his lust into gold, and he mined it, heaped it on her secret altar. The secret of lovers and beggar saints was given to him—that nothing is base. He would have followed her into the privy. He would have subsisted on the gristle she spat out and called himself a glutton.

To see her kissing a little boy's skinned knee or rocking a child to sleep moved him to religious awe, and when he prayed to the Madonna it was Jane he saw in his mind. It gave him joy to know they were linked for life by their respective vows, and it grieved him sometimes that she would never know if it, that she, like everyone else, must think of him as the broken drunk in the corner, the failed theologian, the pervert who got thrown out of the Chequer. Often he imagined dying in defense of her virtue. He saw the two of them as a pietà in the courtyard of the Crossroads (an idealized courtyard without the chickens), his blood seeping into her apron, her eyes welling up with gratitude and regret as she bid him farewell with one chaste and burning kiss.

"Matthew, I'm not exaggerating. He follows me *everywhere*. Look outside—nay, don't let him see you looking. He's there, isn't he?"

The constable glanced out his shop window. Sure enough, there was Malverthorpe, across the lane, his hooded eyes fixed in their direction.

"He waits by the gate till we open, every morning, and he's always the last to leave when we close. But if I go out, he goes out. Whenever I look over my shoulder I see him, ten paces behind."

Matthew took a small nail from between his lips and poised it over the sole. "Has he threatened you?"

"Nay. He never speaks to me at all. He doesn't even order his drinks from me."

He drove the nail home with a light tap of the hammer. "And have you tried talking to him?"

"I can't."

"Why not?"

She looked distressed. "I just can't. Please, isn't there some law?"

"Well, that's just it," Matthew said, tapping in another nail. "If a man wants to sit in a pub all day staring at the waitress, there's no law that says he can't. Now if he touches you—"

"He won't," she said quickly.

He put down the hammer and gave her a close look. "You seem very sure of that."

"Yes, because he thinks I'm a virgin."

Matthew's eyes widened. He remembered Gillian's pronouncement: *seduced and abandoned.* Jane flushed deeply as she realized what she had said, and he felt his own face grow hot.

"I mean," she amended, "he thinks I have a vow."

He was seeing her small breast in the washhouse, a fleeting pink nipple. "Well, vow or no vow, you're not married, so of course—" He was making it worse. He fumbled with a nail, whacked hard with the hammer. The nail bent.

"I suppose you added the vow for good measure," he said at last.

"Yes." Her eyes were on the window.

"But after you told him, he continued to follow you."

She didn't answer.

"Is that right?"

"More or less," she mumbled.

More or less? What did that mean? One moment you were having a perfectly rational conversation with a perfectly ordinary girl, and then . . . a mist would rise from her pond-gray eyes, and your vision would blur and you'd feel like some foolish mortal who'd tried to shake hands with a wraith.

"Matthew," she said with soft urgency. "Please—I am afraid." Her nearness made him light-headed. He lost track of his feet. "You can't imagine what it's like," she was saying. "It's like he's eating me with his eyes. And it never stops. It never stops."

"He can't keep it up forever," he heard some sturdy citizen's voice reply. "Sooner or later he's bound to lose interest."

"A sane man would. But can't you see? Malverthorpe is mad."

She was right. The proctor had resigned his office. He went about in a shabby brown robe. His eyes were bloodshot, and he smelled.

"How can it end?" she whispered. "I am afraid of how it will end."

He put his hands on her shoulders because she was trembling— it was the natural thing to do. "I'll keep an eye on him," he promised. "No one is going to let him hurt you."

Jane was tall, and standing this close, her face was nearer than Gillian's would be. Her lips were pale and seemed very soft, and that fog was rising from her eyes, and his feet seemed very far away.

"Papa?"

It was Celia. His hands dropped abruptly and he didn't know where to put them. They felt large and guilty.

Eight

Rumor had it that the proctor appointed to replace Malverthorpe was an honest man, so all the ale sellers in Oxford were rushing to unload their false-bottomed tankards and buy true pints. Henry grumbled that the metalsmiths were exploiting the situation and decided he could get a better deal in London. Ingrid, Sabina and Isobel were left to manage the Crossroads on their own for a few days. Then Sabina surprised them by proposing to take a holiday herself. Ingrid encouraged her, for Sabina had been looking wearier of late. She wept sometimes without reason and she had taken to lying down in the middle of the day. So she set off early Sunday morning to visit her cousins in Wolvercote, and Ingrid found herself alone with Isobel on a quiet overcast afternoon.

"I noticed your admirer in church this morning," Isobel said as they were preparing the dough for the next morning's bread.

"Aye, as usual." By now Malverthorpe's vigil was into its third month. Time had not diluted his concentration, nor had Ingrid grown accustomed to it. His greedy, unwavering stare was like a spider on the nape of her neck. She had come to look forward to Sundays for respite, for the pub was closed then. He followed her to Mass, but once she got back to the Crossroads she could bolt the gate and not be bothered for the rest of the day.

"He should bathe now and then. Maybe he'd have better luck with you."

"Please." Ingrid hated it when Isobel took that arch tone. She slapped a wad of dough on the table and began to knead.

"Well I do wish you'd do something to get rid of him. I'm really getting tired of the man. Especially since I'm the one who has to serve him all the time. Thinks you're too good for it apparently."

"Come, Isobel, you know that's not my doing."

"No? You could tell him off. But then, you're too sweet for that, aren't you? You would never raise your voice."

Ingrid felt the dull beginning of a headache behind her eyes. Always these little barbs when they talked, barbs she didn't know how to defend against. She'd asked Sabina once why Isobel disliked her so. It isn't you, Sabina told her. Isobel is angry with the world.

And that was a great mystery too—how anyone so perfectly made could be unhappy. For Isobel was exquisite in every detail. Even her feet were lovely. Sometimes Ingrid felt quite stupid with awe. Sometimes in their room she would be so struck, she would want to say something, but didn't dare. She had seen with what contempt Isobel treated men who spoke their admiration—to admire her was an honor not to be granted ordinary mortals. There was something rather splendid in this feline scorn of hers. Ingrid, who felt obliged to drum up kindness when she didn't take to someone, wondered what it would be like to just arch her back and walk away instead. She thought it would be nice.

Once, in the bright sun, she had noticed the sketchy beginning of wrinkles around Isobel's mouth, the sort of wrinkles one gets from pursing the lips. On strict examination of her conscience, Ingrid recognized that this satisfied her somehow. So, she concluded, she was far from blameless in their difficulties, and she took Isobel's hostility as something deserved. But she regretted it. All through her childhood she had longed for the friendship of another girl. To whisper and giggle when the lights went out. She had hoped rooming with Isobel would be like that.

"I'm glad Sabina's taken this rest," she said, to change the subject. "I don't think she's looking well, do you?"

"She's probably with child again."

"Oh. I hadn't thought of that. Wouldn't she tell us?"

"She'd tell *you*, I would have thought. Seems to tell you everything."

Another barb. Or was it a clue? She wondered if Sabina and Isobel had been closer before she arrived. "I think whatever's bothering her, she wants to keep to herself. I asked, the other day—you know when she ran up to her room crying—and she didn't want—"

"Janie, look what I found! A rock with sparkles in it." Quart bounded across the kitchen and crashed into her apron.

She admired the chunk of gravel in his grimy palm. "Ah. *Lapis philosophorum.*" This was their latest game: the Latin naming of insects and weeds and whatever other debris Quart dug up from the yard.

"Lapis fossorum," he repeated.

"Almost. Philosophorum. Philoso—"

"Philoso."

"—phorum."

"Phorum."

"Philosophorum."

"Phisolophorum."

"Phi-lo-so-phor-um."

"Phi-lo-so-phor-um."

"Got it!"

"Oh no! I forget the first part now!" he cried, slapping his forehead in mock despair.

"Lapis. Lapis philosophorum. It means 'philosopher's stone.' That's what they use to turn metal into gold."

"Can we try it?"

"Well, that's rather complicated. Only alchemists know how."

"When I grow up I'm going to be an owcomiss."

"Well, then. You'd better hang onto that stone."

"Will you wash it off for me?"

"I'll do it for you," Isobel volunteered. "Jane's got her hands all full of dough." She tried to take it from him, but Quart closed his fist stubbornly.

"I want Janie to."

"Aunt Isobel's right—I'd just get it all sticky."

"Will you do it later then?"

She looked at Isobel apologetically and shrugged. "All right. Put it down there by the pitchers."

Quart set it down reverently and went back outside, leaving an awkward silence in his wake. Ingrid cast about for a safe topic. "What shall we make for supper tonight?"

"Oh, I don't know. We've got that leftover mutton."

"You could make one of your wonderful pies! The boys love them so."

"I suppose I could. All right."

Ingrid, noting a slight thaw, rejoiced out of all proportion. "You know," she said, in a rush of generosity, "I *would* tell Malverthorpe off if I thought it would do any good. I do loathe him."

Isobel raised an eyebrow, an expressive skill Ingrid thought would be handy. She wished her own eyebrows worked independently like that.

"Do you? I didn't think you hated anybody." She reached for a bunch of carrots and began to chop.

"It isn't charitable, I know, but sometimes I do hate—"

"You don't know what hate means," Isobel said sharply. "You don't have it in you."

From anyone else, it might have been a compliment. Ingrid could not understand why she felt such a compulsion to defend herself against this charge of not hating. "Do you imagine I like being followed everywhere I go? Being stared at from dawn to dusk?"

"How would I know? You don't do anything to discourage it. You even defend him."

"I don't!"

"Jane, I heard you with my own ears. Last week, when those fools from Brasenose were in here."

She had forgotten all about that. "They were mocking him to his face. It was too cruel. Anyway, all I said was 'keep your voices down.'"

"See what I mean? The soul of charity. You probably defend me, too, when I'm not looking." She whacked violently at the carrots.

Ingrid flushed. "Don't be silly." The fact was that she often did stand up for Isobel. She knew what it felt like to be called "stuck-up." She knew how that wounded. "Thinks she's too good for us," young men would snicker when Isobel refused to flirt back. "And she's right, too," Ingrid would assert, wagging a finger. "So mind your manners." She had learned a lot these past months about pub banter.

"Well, I don't care what they think," Isobel said sourly. "God, I hate this place!"

Ingrid kneaded in silence, not knowing what to say. "You know, a lot of men are taken with you," she ventured at last. "You could marry if you wanted. Then you wouldn't have to work in the pub."

"Marry who? The buffoons who come here?" She shoved the bits of chopped carrot out of her way with a contemptuous movement of her small hand. "The men in this town—they'll get you with five brats in as many years. Then they'll be in here drooling over some wench who looks just like you did, before they ruined you."

"They're not all like that. Look at Matthew Sturges."

"Aye," Isobel said triumphantly. "Look at him. You can look at him a lot because he's not at home, is he? He's here, drooling over you!"

"Nay!" She blushed under Isobel's hard scrutiny. She didn't want to know this about Matthew, and her skin prickled with the truth of it. And the truth about herself—she didn't want to know it was Matthew she meant to please with her new summer dress, her new way of braiding her hair. To sin in ignorance is not to sin. There was no *intention*.

"Matthew loves Gillian. And they love their children. You are leaving out love."

"Love . . . I have known love." Her voice trailed off sadly. Then her face hardened once more, and the little lines appeared around her mouth. "And what do you know about it anyway?"

Ingrid sighed. The headache had taken hold. She heard the boys shouting out in the yard. "I'm telling!" one of them cried. She supposed she should go break it up before noses got bloodied. She wiped her hands on a towel, then stopped. Someone was ringing the bell.

"Your admirer, no doubt."

She panicked, thinking the same thing. "Let's not answer."

"But Jane, have mercy," Isobel taunted. "He's dying of love for you."

Ingrid threw down the towel in exasperation. "Well, if he's going to die I wish he'd get on with it!" she snapped. Her temples were pounding.

The bell rang again.

"We really should answer," Isobel said with surprising gentleness. "It could be a lodger. Listen, Jane . . . I know you don't encourage him. Sometimes I'm a shrew."

Ingrid didn't trust herself to speak. She was on the verge of tears.

"Look. I'll get it, and if it's him, I'll say you're not here. All right?"

Ingrid nodded, grateful.

A moment later, Isobel came back into the kitchen, looking puzzled. "It's for you. Not Malverthorpe. A boy. He wouldn't say what he wanted. Shall I tell him to go?"

"Nay, I'll go out there."

The boy was in his early teens. She had never seen him before. "You're Jane?" he asked.

"Aye. What is it?"

"Come with me, please."

"Where? Why?" she demanded, suspecting Malverthorpe.

"Your mistress is asking for you."

Now she was alarmed. "What's happened? Is she ill?"

"I cannot say, miss," he answered. "Just come. Please."

"All right." She untied her apron. "I'll just go and tell Isobel I'm leaving."

"Nay, miss. Please, just come."

He led her rapidly through the deserted streets, but though she continued to press him, he would only shake his head dolefully, refusing to say where they were going. When they halted in front of Pratt's, the first thing she thought of was that sooty box of dull, rusted instruments. "She isn't here!"

"Aye, miss." He rapped lightly on the door and Pratt himself opened it, looking up and down the street to make sure they were unobserved. His sleeves were rolled up, and his face had a pinched, harassed look.

"You!" he exclaimed.

"Where is she? What have you done?"

He blew out a long-suffering sigh. "Before you see her, I want you to know it wasn't my fault. I told her to lie still, but—"

"Sabina!"

In response she heard a muffled moan from behind the curtain. She could smell the blood as soon as she entered the back room. Her eyes took a few seconds to adjust to the darkness, and then she saw the woman huddled into a ball on the operating table. The sheet under her was so thoroughly soaked that it was dripping on the floor.

Pratt had pulled back the curtain and was leaning against the doorframe, his arms folded. "You have to get her out of here. I can't have her dying here."

Ingrid spun round. "No, *you* get out of here! You get out!" When he delayed, she took a step toward him and stamped her foot as one does to scare off an animal. He slithered out, letting the curtain fall shut.

Sabina moaned again as Ingrid rolled her onto her back and attempted to open her bent legs. "Nay," she said in a hoarse whisper that had death in it. "He's right. Take me out of here, Jane. Don't let me die here. Henry . . . " She had to stop, for Ingrid was peeling the bloody sheet from between her legs, and the pain overwhelmed her.

"You're not dying," Ingrid stated in a tone that would brook no opposition. "Christ, it's dark in here. I can't see anything. Was it this dark when he did the abortion?" The word "abortion" came out blunt and accusing: She wished she had chosen a euphemism.

Sabina just moaned. As Ingrid looked around for a lamp or a candle, she noticed that the room had an outside door. She opened it, letting in wan sunlight from the alley. Once she was able to see the damage clearly, she could not help gasping. There were clumps of tissue mixed with the blood which washed fresh and warm over her fingers as Sabina's pelvis jerked in agonized spasms.

"Take me out there," she whispered, pointing to the alley. "I must not die in here. Tell Henry . . . Tell him it was a miscarriage."

Ingrid ignored her. She was searching the cupboard for gauze. All she could find was a limp towel. She tore off a strip, rolled it up and attempted to pack the wound, but before she got it in all the way it was soaked through. The woman's skin was grayish-white.

Sabina seized her hand. "Tell Henry—"

Ingrid nodded. "Aye. It was a miscarriage."

"Tell him my last wish . . . " She rolled to her side, doubled up from the pain. "Oh, it is terrible!" With sudden force of will, she managed to roll back again so that she could look at Ingrid. Her eyes were dry and lucid. "Jane, marry Henry. Tell him that was my wish. I know you will be a good mother to my boys."

"Don't talk like this. Don't give up. I can't help you if you give up."

"No one can help me now. I've done wrong and now I shall be punished." A stricken look came over her. "Oh, Jane, I am dying unconfessed. I shall burn in hell forever!"

Ingrid blotted the woman's damp face with the towel. "Nay," she soothed. "God is not so hard as that."

The idea of eternal punishment was raging now like a fever in Sabina's brain. "It's true, it's true! All the priests say so. I shall burn in hell forever."

"They don't know."

She said it as if she did know. A strange composure was coming over her. "Sabina," she said in a voice different from her own, a voice full of authority. "Be quiet now. You are going to live."

As if hypnotized, the woman did become quiet. Her convulsing limbs relaxed and she lay watching Ingrid with all her attention. Ingrid's hands felt hot, engorged with confidence. She placed them on Sabina's abdomen.

Later there would be questions: Had she meant to work a miracle? Was she praying as she did this? Did she call on God for help? And as she searched her recollection of this moment, she would come up blank. The truth was, she wasn't thinking much of anything. Someone dumped a slop pot from a second-story window—she heard it splash in the alley. A fly paused on the bloody sheet then flew off. Sabina's breathing slowed and deepened to match the rhythm of her own. That was all. After a while, she dabbed at the wound, then inspected the towel. There was only a trace of blood. She did not feel surprised.

"The bleeding has stopped. Nay—don't sit up. You've lost a lot of blood."

Sabina's eyes were wide. "And yet, I *could* sit up, I could almost!" she whispered, awed and rather afraid. "How? How have you done this?"

"God has done it."

"But how? How, after what I've done?"

Ingrid had forgotten what the sickness was like. It was coming on fast now. "Sabina, I've got to go. Promise me you'll never tell anyone about this. We will never even refer to it between ourselves. Promise."

How strange, this coldness, as if her veins were glass and empty. How far away the ground. She knew she didn't have long. "Pratt!" she called sharply, opening the curtain. He was sitting hunched on a bench, sulking. "She'll have to be carried back to the Crossroads. Send your boy to get the three scholars who live—" She steadied herself against the door frame. "Who live at the top of Cary's Inn. Tell them it's a favor to me. Get rid of the blood before they get here. You can tell them . . . Tell them whatever Sabina wants you to." His face was blurred and shifting. Nausea was rising up from her knees like the tide of a murky green sea. "And get some fluids into her," she concluded hastily. She let the curtain fall and ran out to the alley, where she was violently sick.

*   *   *

"No, don't lie there," came a deep, furry voice. Supporting hands slipped under her arms, preventing her from falling into the pool of her own vomit.

Her knees were buckling, and she was past caring where she fell. "I can't . . . "

"Just a few steps." He threw her limp arm around his neck and kept her upright long enough to stumble to a stone bench in the churchyard of St. Edward's. There she lay for most of the night with her head in his lap, wrapped in his dusty secondhand cloak.

He could hardly believe it—this blessing, this unmerited bliss. To hold her for hour upon hour. To stroke her feverish forehead. Had he died then and there he would not have complained.

She spoke Latin in her delirium, most of it unintelligible. Once he thought he heard part of a psalm: " 'The zeal of thy house has consumed me.' " And over and over again, "God's mercy." And once she opened her eyes and raised a wan hand to touch his cheek. "Poor Malverthorpe," she whispered.

Near dawn he dozed off, and when he woke up she was gone. He found her at the Crossroads when it opened, looking very tired but otherwise sound. As always, she ignored him. But for the sour smell of his sleeve, which he'd used to wipe the vomit from her mouth, he would have come to believe it had been nothing but a dream, the sweetest dream of his life.

PART THREE

PART THREE

One

The long, loveless winter of her life was over at last, Isobel thought. Seven years it had been since Christopher. He was a doctor of philosophy now. Sometimes she overheard scholars who were the age he had been then discussing his lectures in the pub. Most of the time they spoke Latin, but she caught the tone of respect. He had done well for himself, had Christopher, made the brilliant career that would have been closed to him had they married. She had always tried to understand and not to be bitter. But after Christopher how could she look twice at the louts who tried to court her—the blacksmith, the wool merchant, the journeyman tailor? Christopher had spoiled her for anyone else.

Oh, not physically. They had always stopped short of consummation. Otherwise, he would have been honorbound to go through with the marriage. She often thought that had been her big mistake. There were several times when it would have been easy to push things to the point where he would lose control. Instead, she had withheld herself, clung too tightly to her own honor till in the end her honor was all she had. And nobody cared a fig for it. Not even she.

She would not make that mistake with Jacques. If he wanted her this very night, he would have her. She would run off with him, escape this oppressive, vulgar, tedious town. As his wife she would dine with the king and queen, be received everywhere with respect. For the famous Jacques Brigand des Cœurs had chosen her.

How quickly it had happened! Evidently he had fallen in love with her at first sight. He had come in at the quiet time of the afternoon when she was alone in the pub, sweeping up. Sabina had gone to church to say her rosary—she did that every day now, had

191

gotten very pious since her illness in the spring. Jane was gone, too. She had taken the boys to Port Meadow for a picnic. She'll be envious, Isobel thought. All the girls in town will be envious. Well, maybe not Jane. She was a queer one. Several men in town were mad for her, but it went right over her head. She simply didn't notice.

He had come in and offered to sing for his supper, modest as you please. But his clothing was expensive, and that indefinable sheen about him told her he was a celebrity even before he said his name. There was no private room for him, this being a Tuesday, and that flustered her a bit. But he had taken the news with perfect equanimity. "Milady, I would consider myself lucky to have come to this place even if you put me up in the stable," he said gallantly, while his eyes, looking into hers, whispered, "We have known each other always." She led him to the room he would be sharing with two merchants, and he tossed his saddlebag and lute onto the free bed and asked about a bath. She must have given directions to the bathhouse but she could not remember it now. For just as she was about to make her exit he said, "Such lovely golden hair you have. Will you unbraid it for me?" She reached up to loosen it on the spot, but he caught her hand. "Nay, tonight. After the show. Can we meet then?" She nodded while he kissed her fingers, never taking his eyes from her face. "I shall be counting the minutes until then," he said.

Afterward she ran to her room, unfastened her braids and consulted the mirror from every angle to see how she would look to him later. The sun glanced off the rippling waves as if her hair were a golden sea. Now the long tragedy of this unadmired beauty was at an end. She experimented with various demure and smoldering arrangements of her features, then rebraided her hair and changed into her best dress.

Jack gave his performance from the rickety first-floor gallery. The town had been emptied of clerics for the long vacation, but the rumor of his appearance spread quickly, and before long the yard was packed.

He was wearing a short black tunic with long scalloped sleeves lined in scarlet. His hosen, too, were scarlet, his low-slung belt embroidered in gold. His hair, still damp from the bath, was slicked back. The August heat was his pretext for going shirtless and leaving the front of his tunic casually unlaced. Now and then he would touch his open breast, then sweep his hand out over the audience. This gesture gained in effectiveness as he worked up a sweat and his skin began to gleam. One could feel a warm collective sigh rustle over the yard.

He concluded the first round of his performance with a long and bloodthirsty Scottish ballad that he sang unaccompanied, bellowing with all the power in his lungs. He had a way of letting his voice stray off key, savage and seemingly uncontrolled, then bringing it back, against all odds, to true pitch. It was a trick he'd happened on by trying to imitate bagpipes, and it never failed to ignite the audience. They would hold their breath, then let it out in whoops and yelps of relief. This was what he was doing when he saw her.

At first he did not recognize her. He thought, How can a woman so young have so many children, and how can I get her away from them? Without knowing who she was, he wanted her. In that first instant, before she saw him, she was laughing at something one of the children had said. Her feet were planted apart, her hip thrust sideways to make a saddle for the littlest boy, whom she held with an easy peasant grace. Her skirt was hiked up, revealing bare, dusty ankles and feet. A day in the sun had gilded her light brown hair—which was coming loose in sweet thoughtless tendrils—and flushed her skin, giving her a burnished look.

Then she glanced up at him, looked directly into his face, but still he did not recognize her, because he had never seen such health and high spirits radiating from the Ingrid he had known. She recognized him though, and the sudden gravity and worry coming over her made her familiar.

Long ago he had given up the search. Often the memory of her came to him unbidden, with an uneasiness that was something like hurt feelings—she was, after all, the first woman ever to leave him—and something like a bad conscience. Then he would invoke Fleming's words: " 'Twas the sin itself she wanted and you she took on to get it. " With that one magic sentence he could draw boundaries around the ache. It belonged to Greyleigh, to the autumn of his thirty-fourth year.

Now here she was in another place, in another season. He felt trespassed upon. After all those months of worry, how dare she be someplace so ordinary? How dare she look so healthy? It irked him that she had become pretty without his assistance.

He heard loud applause, stamping, whistling. Somehow he had gotten to the end of his song. He bowed and promised to return after a short break. The lovely blond he'd had his eye on earlier—what was her name?—was waiting by the steps with a pint of ale. He could no longer see Ingrid now that he had descended the stage. " 'Twas the sin itself she wanted," he said to himself. "And me she put up with to get it." But whatever meaning the incantation once held for him was lost— it was so much gibberish to him now.

Ingrid rushed to her room, shut the door and leaned against it, breathing hard. She thought of hiding under the bed, of slipping out of the inn and running as fast and as far as she could. "Oh, dear God," she whispered, hugging her waist. A wild glad smile was breaking on her face.

Anxiously she interrogated Isobel's mirror. She was sunburned, and her hair was a mess. She threw off her dusty linen dress and put on her good wool one, lacing it up with the red ribbon she kept in her painted spice box. She wrapped her hair in the yellow silk scarf.

"Jane, are you in there?" Henry called, banging on the door.

"Aye. Just tidying up."

"Well hurry. There's a thirsty mob downstairs."

"Aye. Right away."

She studied the results of her efforts in the mirror but did not know how to evaluate them. She was hot in the wool dress, felt conspicuous in the yellow scarf. With a sigh she stripped the whole ensemble off, shook the dust from her original frock and put it back on. She tried to braid her hair but couldn't get it right and finally gave up in nervous exasperation. At the door she paused, making the sign of the cross before venturing out.

Jack had drawn the biggest audience the Crossroads had ever seen, and for the next two hours she had not a moment's respite. Until now she had not realized that he was so famous, that the mere mention of his name was enough to bring people running from the opposite end of town and even from beyond the walls. The inn's stock of ale was depleted long before closing time. Henry had to buy extra barrels from the Swindlestock for twice what they were worth. Yet, though five hundred souls stood elbow to elbow, when Jack sang a hushed love song the courtyard was quiet as a cloister. Like a magician, he raised storms of emotion. Women whom she knew to be industrious and upright and sensible were close to swooning.

And she was one of them. I fell for this, she thought, aghast. For this I broke my vows, perhaps have damned my soul. And what is it? A king of magic, and yet so commonplace. A democratic spell that enthralled dairymaids, seamstresses, bakers and websters as surely as it had undone a saint.

Dusk fell, and the torches were lit. All the church bells were ringing curfew, but no one would leave until Jack, pleading hoarseness, set down his lute. As he rose from his final bow, he caught her eye with an intense and questioning look. She shook her head slightly and glanced away. Someone brought him a pint of ale. He sat on the steps drinking it, shining his professional smile on the well-wishers who competed for his attention while his eyes continued to seek her. Without much conviction Henry was shouting, "Closing time!" but the crowd was slow to disperse. The summer night was charged as if with heat lightning. Ingrid bustled about, gathering up the empty mugs that littered the yard and praying that Jack would not rashly call out her name. When the crowd became too thin to hide her, she took refuge in the pub.

"Look at this mess!" Sabina complained. "Every mug we own— both the old ones and the new ones. We'll be a week washing up."

"Go on to bed if you like," Ingrid urged. "I can take care of it." Her voice came out high and giddy.

"Count the till, will you? We've still got to pay the Swindle-stock."

Ingrid spilled out the money box and began to count, glad of the excuse to be silent. The incident at Pratt's had put a strain between her and Sabina. Both had their reasons for wanting to forget the affair, and they never referred to it, but any time they found themselves alone together they felt its shadow over them. For Ingrid, the healing was a troubling reminder of the past she refused to reckon with. The number of thoughts she had to ignore each day to maintain the illusion of contentment kept growing, and her ignoring took on a stubborn, strident quality. Just because Sabina stopped bleeding when I touched her—, she would think, and the thought was never finished. She could not stand to be alone. She chatted up the customers all day long and drank to fall asleep. In the middle of the night she would bolt awake from a recurring nightmare, her chest heaving: The chapel was full of lepers and cripples—they had been waiting three hours already. But she was in the little room atop Cary's Inn, drunk, and it would take days to walk from Oxford to Greyleigh because she had to hide in the hedges, and she had burned her habit and had nothing to wear. And if she didn't hurry, all of the bishops would burst in, yank away the covers and find her with Jack.

She could not concentrate on the count. The Greene boys, up past their bedtime, had reached a pitch of giddiness that could not be sustained: Tantrums were impending. "Dickie, I'm not going to tell you again!" Sabina scolded. Quart was sprawled on the bench beside her, giving her flirtatious looks. She rubbed his stomach absently with her left hand and flicked pennies with her right. Eighty-one, eighty-two . . . "Did you tell Mama about the deer we saw on the way to the meadow?" Eighty-three . . .

A cap full of coins hit the tabletop with a loud clank. "I wonder if I might exchange all this for something more portable," Jack said.

A penny skidded to the floor, and she heard it spinning, spinning, spinning. Quart made a dive for it, and her left hand was suddenly marooned. Slowly she raised her eyes, unable to speak.

Isobel had her arm slipped through Jack's and was introducing him now with a proprietary air. He acknowledged Ingrid formally— "Mistress Basset"—as if it were really their first meeting.

Conversation went on and on around her, burbling from afar as if she were under water or asleep. Sabina was herding the children out. She said something about the washing up. Then it was just the three of them, and Isobel was saying, "You've had such a long day, Jane. Why don't you go on up to bed? I'll finish down here."

She realized that Isobel had the same plan she did—to wait till everyone else retired so that she could be alone with Jack. "Nay," she said firmly. "You go."

"But you must be exhausted after your outing with the children," Isobel insisted through smiling teeth.

"Not at all. I couldn't sleep now if I tried." She reached for Jack's cap, dumped the coins from it and began counting in a show of determination.

Jack, who had been watching their duel with amusement, now stepped in. "Well, I for one am quite undone. Lovely Isobel, will you show me to my room? I can't remember anymore which one it is." He wished Ingrid good night with a pleasant but impersonal smile and Isobel towed off her prize in triumph.

From the door of the pub she watched them. On the second-floor catwalk he paused to caress Isobel's cheek and bestowed a slow, careful kiss on her mouth. Jealousy—an emotion till then unknown to her—bit into her with its fierce beak. She drew back into the pub, afraid of seeing more. Isobel's beauty, so often contemplated with ungrudging wonder, was a torment now. He would touch that skein of golden hair and her soft thigh would know the tickling of his beard. He would admire her tiny hands and feet, her flawless skin, the shadow her lashes cast on her cheek. Isobel slept prettily, curled like a cat— that is what he would see when he awoke.

I have no right, she told herself. It was I who left him. Why? Was it as a penance that I made myself give him up? Did I think to please God with such a sacrifice? God does not care. No, she thought, with a stern and bitter realism, God will not assuage a lover's jealousy. He does not care for a lover in pain, and if he does not care for that he does not care for anything.

The clutter of empty cups echoed her dejection. She had to go back outside to draw wash water, but dread of seeing Jack and Isobel together again paralyzed her for a long time. Finally she ventured out with her eyes closed, humming loudly to warn them in case they were still on the catwalk. She stopped to listen and heard nothing. Cautiously she opened her eyes. There was no sign of them. Only the chirping of crickets, a moon and somewhere, far off, a dog howling at it. The torches still burned, throwing off a wild orange light. In such a light it was possible to feel one's loneliness as something fiery and brave; to be sad and tall under the moon had its own poetry. Pulling off her kerchief, she let the breeze console her.

She hooked the bucket to the pulley of the well and lowered it into the black water. She was hauling it up when she heard the low, intimate voice behind her.

"Saint Ingrid."

She gasped, spinning 'round. The bucket fell back with a far-off splash.

He was poised on the lowest step. The dance of shadows and fierce light, of wrath and humor and bewildered fondness on his face made her dizzy. She touched the well for balance. "Well, good sister . . ." he began. A false beginning. He closed his mouth and looked at her some more. A torch sputtered.

"Damn you."

In three impetuous strides he reached her and now he was crushing her in his arms. "Damn you," he said to her ear as he kissed it. "Damn you," he said to her throat. A low exultant moan rose from her as he kissed her and cursed her again and again. She kissed him back with wild avid inaccuracy—mouth, cheek, tunic, hand, beard. They were holding each other's faces, laughing, crying, kissing, all at the same time.

"Unhand that woman," someone said pompously. Jack tore himself from the embrace only to laugh, thinking it was a joke. "Who is this fellow?" he was starting to ask when Malverthorpe emerged from behind the hayrick, stooped, shabby and brandishing a sword. Jack still wanted to laugh, for the man looked ridiculous, but the concern on Ingrid's face told him to beware.

"If the lady dislikes my embrace, she herself has a voice to say so," he pointed out.

The man was in no mood to reason. He was advancing single-mindedly, his fist tight around the hilt of the sword, which he held at arm's length, stiffly.

"Look man, I am unarmed," Jack said, holding both hands up to prove it.

His challenger continued to advance with inexorable menace. "Prepare to meet your death then, knave!"

"Oh, bloody hell!" Jack said in exasperation. He began skipping backward with light-footed grace, his arms still raised as his eyes darted about in search of a weapon. The torch by the pub door—that would do, if he could get there in time. He skipped faster while his opponent continued his slow unwavering advance.

"Stop this!" Ingrid cried. Both men ignored her. She ran forward and put herself between them, facing Malverthorpe. She came so close to the blade that for a moment Jack thought she would be impaled. He was about to hurl himself forward and throw her out of the way when Malverthorpe lowered the sword.

"Give it to me," she commanded.

"I cannot," her would-be champion replied. "This scoundrel means you harm."

"Nay. He is a friend. Give me the sword."

The older man hesitated. "But my lady—"

"Give it to me," she insisted. Jack thought: That is the tone she must have used to work miracles. She could say "arise and walk" in such a tone, and no one would think of disobeying. The man was clearly in conflict, but he handed over his weapon. Then he fell to his knees.

"My lady, forgive me. Even to threaten violence in your presence makes me ashamed. But this man—"

"Oh, do get up, Malverthorpe," she interrupted with soft impatience. "This has really gone too far."

"Nay, my lady. I would protect you if need be with my life." He had seized her hand and was pressing his ardent lips to her knuckles. She tried to be gentle about withdrawing it.

"I do not wish to be protected from this man."

Malverthorpe was incredulous. "But your vow!"

"There never was any vow. It was all a deception. We never expected you to take it so much to heart or—"

"No!" His breathing was loud and raw. In his darkened expression Jack saw venom and Ingrid saw pain.

"I'm sorry. We just didn't know what else to do."

"No! It's a lie!" He was tugging his gown at the chest like someone suffocating. Ingrid took a step toward him, her hand raised to comfort him, and he backed away. His mouth gaped open, straining, emitting a sound like a death rattle. Clutching his throat, he turned from them and disappeared into the night.

Two

It was quiet now, everyone else long asleep. Jack and Ingrid sat side by side on a table top, surrounded by the flotsam of unwashed mugs, like survivors of a shipwreck. They were drinking flat, leftover ale.

"Why didn't you meet me that night?" Jack demanded after a long silence. "I waited all night for you."

She averted her face, not knowing what to say. "I'm sorry."

"Damn it, Ingrid, that's your answer for everything. You're bloody sorry."

The hurt in his voice shocked her. Jack to her was like the wind or the rain, the sun—an elemental force that could sweep her up, drown her or burn her but certainly could never be affected by her in return. He was The Man. "It never occurred to me that you would wait." This was the truth, but said aloud it sounded lame.

"I rode around looking for you for weeks. Do you have any idea how dangerous the roads—"

"You would have abandoned me," she blurted.

"Not on the road."

She went blind with pain.

He leaned nearer, his voice ardent, warming her hair. "Can you not feel how I desire you? I've never wanted anyone more than I want you at this moment. Now, Ingrid, now! May God silence me forever if I lie."

No, she thought. He couldn't be hurt by her. He wore his vulnerability like a costume. When the performance was over he could just strip it off. "Another one of your lyrics," she scoffed.

"Nay." He caressed her cheek with the back of his fingers. He had touched Isobel's cheek in exactly the same way less than an hour before.

"Aye!" she said hotly, removing his hand. "I don't want to be one of your ladies. I don't want to be in any of your songs."

She wanted to run to the safety of her own room, to nurse her wound in peace. But if she ran, she would want him to chase her, and if he did not chase her she would have to turn around and come back to him.

Jack was staring down at his cup. "The funny thing is that I *haven't* put you in any songs," he said thoughtfully.

"You'll sing about Isobel," she snapped. As soon as it was out she resolved never to forgive him for the fact that she had said it.

He shrugged. "Aye, maybe. There's something tragic about Isobel."

"And that's what you like? Tragedy? Maybe I should go drown myself in the Isis." Her voice was shrill. She was mortified. She pressed her fingers to her temples, just as Dame Agatha used to do. "Oh, I'm being dreadful, and I can't seem to stop it! I don't know what's the matter with me."

"Nay. You're a woman, that's all." He drew out the word *woman* with a sort of awed benevolence that melted her.

"What is that—a plenary indulgence?"

He tossed back his head and laughed his deep, relaxed laugh. "Aye. Aye, that's exactly what it is."

"I can't stand it, Jack."

She could not have explained what she meant by 'it,' but she didn't have to. He knew. Tenderly he drew her toward him and embraced her. "Never mind, love. No one can."

"*You* can," she accused with renewed resentment.

"Nay, love, I can't either. But what are we to do?"

"No, no, no!" Malverthorpe groaned, rocking back and forth on his cot. He clutched his shirt, the fabric wadded in his fist like the handle of a dagger he kept trying to remove from his breast. "No!" Jane—his lady, his love, his life. Jane—the only light in this dark, dark world, the only good, the only pure—Jane in the arms of that vile lecher, that godless scoundrel. She was in his arms now. Naked in his arms. Naked to his lewd gaze, his lewd hands. Whore! Wanton! Harlot! Deceiving witch! Oh, Jane, Jane, my life, my love! Thou harlot—I shall kill you!

Oh, to see her blood run! To slash her deceiving face, lay bare her deceiving heart, and stab and stab and stab it! To kill her and then kill himself. She was killing him, killing him. With every breath he felt the hot blade. He tried to rise—"I shall kill them both"—and the blade felled him. He writhed on the dirty sheets.

They were laughing at him. They were young and naked in bed and they were laughing at him. *We never expected you to take it so much to heart. We.* Who was that *we?* Everyone. The whole town was in on it. His long, dirty hair, his shabby, filthy robe. Lo, how the mighty are fallen! Where once he struck terror, now there was only pity. Pity and laughter. Oh, he'd heard them laughing. *"When I humbled my soul with fasting, it became my reproach. When I made sackcloth of my clothing, I became a byword to them. I am the talk of those who sit in the gate, and the drunkards make songs about me."*

Yes, the drunkards made songs: He'd heard them. Humiliation had been a love offering to his secret bride. The more they ridiculed, the more he . . . oh, vicious, ungrateful whore! He would never live it down. He could never recover his office, never return to the lecture hall. Nothing to live for but revenge—and he would have his revenge. He would show them all that Simon Malverthorpe was not to be trifled with. He knew the law. Jane would suffer for this.

He tried once more to rise from the cot and fell back, panting. No matter. He knew the law. He could do it from here. "Porter!" he yelled. "Porter!"

The day had begun without him: the sun coming in through his closed eyelids, chickens and children boisterous in his ears. It seemed to Jack that he had never had a better bed than that hayrick, and for a long time he lay in heavy, drowsy contentment, letting the busy sounds of the morning buzz around him. I am sleeping here for all of you who must work, he mused. My sleep is for all of you. His heart swelled with a profound mystical feeling as he dedicated his slumber to the whole of striving humanity. *Be at peace, all ye who labor, for I sleep.* Then a bug crossed his nose on its march through the hay, and he sat up sneezing.

He went, all rumpled and groggy, to look for Ingrid. She was sitting in the pub with a small child in her lap, feeding it morsels of bread dipped in milk, and at the same time directing the efforts of the older boys, who were washing and drying last night's mugs. She had a woman's way of doing two or three things at once while seeming to do nothing at all. When she looked up at him, her face happy and serene, he thought, "to see that face every morning . . . "

"Hello," she said to him.

"Hello."

Sabina, at the far side of the room, was kneading bread in her effortful way, sleeves rolled back from her flour-dusted arms. "Help yourself," she told him, indicating a fresh loaf at Ingrid's table. "Dickie, get Master Jacques a pint of cider." Jack tore his eyes away from Ingrid long enough to greet the other woman politely, then sat down at the table and tore off a chunk of bread. It was still warm. He fingered it with appreciation, but did not eat. "Hello," he said again.

"Hello."

"Next time you'll have to warn us when you're coming," Sabina scolded him. "We ran out of ale last night." It was hard to tell whether she was complaining or praising him. Jack nodded absently. There was a wisp of straw caught in Ingrid's hair. He reached over and removed it, showing it to her with a private little smile. She blushed and smiled back.

"Will you be staying on?" Sabina was asking.

Jack pretended not to hear, for he did not know what to say. A bit of bread was falling out of the toddler's mouth and Ingrid popped it back in with the tip of her long finger. The child reciprocated by smashing his small gooey hand against her chin. She removed it mindlessly. Her attention was on Jack. He wanted to say, "Forever."

What can you give this woman? What real good can you do her? No seed, no home, no possibility of the Church's blessing. He took a big bite of bread, and no matter how he chewed he could not seem to swallow.

203

"We don't open till noon," Sabina said sharply. Jack glanced up and saw an elderly man with red eyes and a redder nose standing on the threshold.

"It's on bishnesh that I come, madam," the man replied, with slurred consonants and an air of offended dignity. "I am John Thasher, the shummoner, come to shummon Jane Bashet."

Ingrid went pale. "I am Jane Basset," she said.

Thatcher wove his way to the table and presented the sealed letter importantly.

"What is it?"

"A shummons to the Chanshellor's cour', mish. I haff the honor of eshcortin' ya."

"Now?"

"Aye, mish. The cour' convenes in hav 'n hour."

Ingrid glanced swiftly at Jack. "It's a Church court," she told him. "But why am I summoned?" she asked Thatcher.

"It says in the doc-oo-ment, mish. If ya like I'll ree' ih t'ya."

"No, I'll read it." She used the bread knife to slit the seal and unrolled the parchment. The baby tried to grab it, and she had to confine the child with one arm and hold the summons out of reach with the other. As she scanned it, the parchment began to rattle in her hand.

"It's Malverthorpe," she said. "He's charged me with witchcraft."

Three

Documents which survive from this time indicate that Thomas Waler-and, commissary general and magistrate of the chancellor's court, was considered by his contemporaries the most capable jurist in England. Perhaps he felt a moment's excitement, seeing a heresy case on the docket, perhaps he thought, At last, a case I can get my teeth into! For Walerand was squandering the prime years of his career adjudicating the endless stupid squabbles that arose between town and gown. Here a petty theft, there a petty fraud, fist fights, food fights, imagined insults and undergraduate pranks. It was no accident that a brilliant and subtle mind had been assigned to such pennyweight matters, for Oxford tempers were quick to riot. Unchecked, a quarrel between town and gown could escalate into a standoff between pope and king. Walerand knew how to keep small conflicts small. He was above all a diplomat, with a knack for leaving the losing side convinced that his secret sympathies were with them. Both the bishop and the chancellor considered him their most trusted confidant, and students felt just as much at ease with him. He treated the mayor and constables with deference so that townsmen thought him jolly decent, considering he was University.

Today's heresy was not destined to rock Christendom. Martin Stone, the horse trader, had asserted that it would profit a man as much to be buried in a marsh as in a churchyard. Thatcher, the summoner, chanced to overhear him. Thatcher's job was to act as a sort of ecclesiastical detective, actively seeking out spiritual crimes to bring before the court. During the academic year he never had to exert himself, for the scholars created enough legal problems to occupy Walerand full-time. But things got so slow during the long vacation that there was a real possibility the court would convene only to find that it had no business. Thatcher was sitting in the pub thinking he'd better drum some up before his uselessness became obvious when Stone, who had several rounds in him, began to hold forth on the subject of a Christian burial. Rather a happy coincidence, Thatcher thought.

Court was held in the Church of Saint Mary the Virgin. The only university building large enough to hold a convocation of all its members, Saint Mary's was a symbol and a rallying point for clerics in the same way Saint Martin's was for townsmen. Laypeople entered unwillingly, suspiciously, certain, if summoned, of being condemned by laws that ran counter to common knowledge and common sense. Nearly a hundred of them had gathered in support of Stone. They stood fingering the hilt of their indignation, ready to unsheath it at the first sign of injustice. Portable barricades, not unlike cattle pens, held them back from the large rectangular area in the north transept where the defendant stood.

For his part, Stone found it much easier to be a heretic in the Saracen's Head than he did in the gloomy majesty of Saint Mary's, cold sober, with the registrar writing down every word he managed to croak out and the judge looking down from his dais, backlit by a very large stained-glass window. All things considered, the issue of a Christian burial was not worth becoming a martyr over, and he recanted without further ado. Walerand sentenced him to weed the garden in St. Peter's churchyard.

"Who's next?" the magistrate asked, leaning toward the registrar.

"Jane Basset, milord."

"The charge?"

"Witchcraft."

"Witchcraft! Thatcher, you've outdone yourself!"

"Nay, milord," the registrar corrected. "The case is a lawsuit brought by a member of the university."

The magistrate's eyebrows went up. "Who?"

"Doctor Simon Malverthorpe."

"Good Lord! Is he here?"

"Nay milord. He is represented by Reginald Baldwin."

"Tell him to approach."

As a student Walerand had been guilty of nearly every misdemeanor for which he was now expected to punish others, and because of this his sharp features had settled into a permanent expression of mild irony. Baldwin, a young lawyer who admired him, tried to imitate this expression. But he was too young to have earned his irony, and on his bland face it come off as a kind of smugness. Walerand, who was conscious of being imitated, would wonder, Am I really so insufferable? whenever he saw the younger man. Wycliffe, the registrar, with his acne-ravaged cheeks and his tactless passion for truth, was much more to his liking, much more what he thought a young man should be.

"I know it's summer," the judge whispered to the lawyer. "You could use the fee, and we both could use the exercise for our wits. But

I must warn you that never once in my career have I encountered a witchcraft charge that could be proved. Forgive my bluntness, but has Malverthorpe lost his mind?"

Baldwin flashed what he probably thought of as a conspiratorial smile. "Actually, yes, I believe he has. He blames it on the girl."

Walerand frowned. "He will come to his senses, though, and when he does he'll be mortified. Let's do him a favor and postpone the case. Give him a chance to rethink."

"I did advise him to delay, milord. He threatened to go to the Hustings tomorrow if we failed him today."

"He can't be serious!"

"I'm afraid he is."

For a cleric to go before a civil court would set Church autonomy back two centuries. It was unthinkable. "We should have to forbid it. On pain of excommunication."

"Is that what you wish me to communicate to my client?"

"Would he listen?"

"I expect not. I've never seen a man so bent on revenge."

"And who is this girl?"

"A servant at the Crossroads."

Walerand smirked. "Oh, for heaven's sake. Let's get it over with."

Baldwin gave a respectful little nod, sensible enough not to gloat over this minor triumph when a major defeat was just moments away, and stepped back to his place while Wycliffe read rapidly the Latin formula that declared him Malverthorpe's proxy.

"Would the defendant please step forward."

Thatcher opened a gate in the barricade, and a tall, slender shape glided into the foreground—to Walerand's myopic eyes a pleasant enough smudge, though nothing to drive a man to madness. He gave her a humane little smile to reassure her. "State the charges."

Baldwin spoke up in his best courtroom voice. "My client accuses this woman of malicious witchcraft in that she did knowingly and deliberately cause him to fall in love with her, endangering his celibacy, depriving him of his livelihood and jeopardizing his sanity."

Walerand pressed his first knuckle to his smiling lips and

pretended to clear his throat. "Mistress Basset, what answer do you make to this most grave charge?"

Because he was so nearsighted, the magistrate had learned to pay particular attention to voices. There was a quaver in hers as she answered, "It is false, milord."

"Master Baldwin, surely your client would not bring such a serious accusation before this court without proof. Tell us, please, what evidence the distinguished doctor offers in support of his charge."

The lawyer ran his finger under his collar, as if it were suddenly too tight. "After years of untroubled celibacy, my client found himself obsessed by lustful thoughts concerning the defendant."

"My, my, Mistress Basset," the judge interrupted. "It seems you made an impression." The spectators laughed. They were still venting their relief over his lenient verdict in the Stone case.

"There is more, milord," Baldwin continued, undaunted. "The defendant led my client to believe that she was bound by a vow of virginity. Shocked and ashamed to discover that he had nearly caused her to violate this sacred contract, my client devoted himself single-mindedly to her protection, to the extent of resigning his office and—"

"Wait." Walerand put up his hand. "Am I correct in assuming that your client made some attempt to assuage this lust which the defendant allegedly used supernatural means to arouse?"

Once again Baldwin rubbed his neck. "Uh, as I understand it, it was she who enticed him."

"Remarkable." He peered at the girl. "How old are you, Mistress Basset?"

"Nineteen, milord."

"Nineteen. And Malverthorpe is—what? Nearly fifty, I should think. My eyesight is not good, so I will leave it to an impartial witness to say whether the defendant is pretty or not. What say you, Master Wycliffe? Is Mistress Basset a pretty woman?"

The registrar flushed. "Yes," he muttered.

"So we are asked to believe that a girl of nineteen, who is on record as being pretty, employed magic to seduce an aging cleric. Tell me, young lady, do you see something in Doctor Malverthorpe that the rest of us have overlooked?"

Once again the spectators roared. Taking his query to be rhetorical, she did not answer it.

Baldwin was only momentarily nonplussed. "I do not speculate about the defendant's motives. But the damage she has done my client is plain to see. Two days after they met, he resigned his office, gave away most of his belongings and from that day on devoted his entire waking life to her protection, neglecting even his own health and appearance. Long before this case came to trial, the change in him was the subject of discussion by members of this university. With all due respect, milord, I have heard you refer to it yourself."

"What you say is true," Walerand acknowledged. "We all know that your client has not been himself of late. I will even go so far as to accept his obsession with the defendant as the cause of his difficulty. But if every time a man made a fool of himself over a woman we convicted her of witchcraft, well, my good man, there are not enough dungeons in the realm to accommodate the witches of Oxford!"

This won shrieks and guffaws from everyone except Baldwin and the girl. Even Wycliffe was smiling a little.

"Milord," the lawyer protested in an aggrieved tone. "I sense you are making light of my client's charge."

"You are mistaken, sir," Walerand countered, and all the mirth went out of his voice. "This young woman, whose only crime has been to catch the eye of a randy old cleric—this woman is being publicly embarrassed by your client's absurd charges. I do not take this lightly."

As he spoke, a commotion arose at the barricade. He saw the blurry image of a woman grasping the top of the gate with both hands while Thatcher held it shut from the other side, and another man tried to restrain her. "I must!" she was shouting.

Walerand raised his voice. "Madam?"

"I must testify," she called to him.

"In the case of Jane Basset?"

"Aye, aye," she replied impatiently, as if to say, "What other case?"

"Very well," he soothed. "But do calm yourself. No one is being sent to the stake. Thatcher, allow the lady to come forward."

When the gate was opened, she took a step inside and then hesitated a moment before hurling herself toward him. She stopped just short of the dais. Her face was red and her mouth distorted from weeping. Getting to the front of the room seemed to have used up all of her courage and now she looked quite spent.

"Kindly tell Master Wycliffe here your name for the record."

"Sabina Greene, wife of Henry."

"And where do you live?"

"The Crossroads Inn, milord."

"Then you are acquainted with the defendant."

"She worked for us."

He noted the tense. "She is no longer in your employ?"

"Well, not after today . . ."

She seemed rather at a loss, and Walerand thought he was coming to the rescue when he said, "Have no fear. Mistress Basset was about to be acquitted even without your testimony."

She did not look at all reassured. She glanced back over her shoulder at someone, then blurted, "But she is guilty, milord."

Walerand's eyebrows shot up. Baldwin shrugged to indicate that this was a surprise to him as well.

"I didn't realize till the charges were brought, milord," she was explaining. "I never thought she was a witch. God help me, I should have thought it, but it seemed only like kindness, you see. But nay, I should have known better, because she made me swear to tell no one, not even my confessor."

Walerand sat up a little straighter, his intelligence on the alert. Something about a sorcery trial, he reflected, brought on a stampede of imagination. You could almost hear it rumbling, stirring up a dust so hot and thick you could hardly see or breathe for it. There were parts of Europe where the discourse of reasoning minds could not be heard above the pounding and the dust defeated the sun. But this was England, sane England.

Little by little, she sobbed out the repellent tale of her abortion, near death and repentance. When she had finished, Walerand first directed Thatcher to serve summons on Lucas Pratt. Then, with great gentleness he said, "Mistress Greene, it is obvious that you feel much remorse over what you have done—"

"Aye, milord, if only it could be undone!"

He put up a hand. "Please, listen a moment. A troubled

conscience can be irritated by the smallest thing. In this case the irritant was Malverthorpe's charge against Mistress Basset. This is quite understandable. But we must not exaggerate the magnitude of the irritant just because the pain it causes is great. Do you follow me?"

She wrinkled her forehead to signify that she was trying, but had to admit that she did not follow.

"My point is that your remorse may have led you to exaggerate the events which followed the abortion. Now, when you say that Jane Basset stopped the bleeding, what precisely do you mean? Did she staunch the wound?"

"Nay, milord. She put her hands here." Sabina touched her aproned belly.

"Did she speak?"

"Aye. In Latin, though. She speaks Latin as well as a scholar."

The younger woman, who till now had been starkly silent, emitted a gasp and was shaking her head in vigorous denial. "What answer do you make to all of this, Mistress Basset?"

"There was no spell, milord. I did in fact staunch the wound with a bit of toweling, and I spoke only English, for Sabina does not understand Latin."

"What did you say?"

"I said, 'The bleeding has stopped.'"

"How did you know?"

"I could see."

"And you said nothing else?"

"Nay, milord, not that I can remember."

Walerand was inclined to accept this version, but Sabina burst out, in a voice throaty with conviction, "Tell the truth, Jane! I don't say these things to hurt you. You saved my life. But now we must both tell the truth and save our souls."

"*God* saved your life!" the girl returned, with equal passion. "Oh, surely you remember, Sabina, how I told you to confess as soon as you were well and to thank God for his mercy toward you."

"Aye. And then you said 'but say nothing about what I have done. That must be our secret. We will not even refer to it between ourselves,' you said."

Though Sabina stood so close she could have touched the table between them, Jane held to her original position a few paces behind so that Sabina had to turn backward to address her. Walerand wanted to scrutinize the girl more closely. "Mistress Basset, would you oblige me by stepping nearer?"

She moved forward a single step.

"Even closer, if you please."

As she came into focus, he was jolted by a sense of familiarity, though he could not have said how he knew her. Along with the feeling of recognition was a sharp but undefined anxiety. At first he thought she might be someone he had bedded in his wild youth; it took a moment to remember that this girl had been an infant in his wild youth.

"Is it true you swore Mistress Greene to secrecy?"

"Yes, milord. That much is true," she admitted.

"Why did you insist on that?"

"I don't know."

Somewhere before he had seen such a tall young girl, very frightened and very still, as if she were carrying her fear in a shallow bowl that she must not allow to spill over.

"Come."

"I was afraid." She had not once raised her eyes since she came into his range of sharp vision. This only added to her haunting familiarity.

"Of what were you afraid?"

"This."

She had whispered, *I am so cold.* When the cloak was fetched, it was he who had put it over her shoulders.

He leaned across the table and said in a low urgent whisper, "Do not speak again until I have cleared the court."

Four

Jack was the only member of the murmuring crowd who knew the meaning of their hasty evacuation. When Walerand first entered the church, Ingrid's grip on his fingers had tensed. "He was at Greyleigh," she whispered. "He will recognize me."

"Nay. I hardly recognized you myself," he had protested, to keep her spirits up. Walerand's early announcement of his nearsightedness had come as such good news he had almost laughed with relief, and his flippant handling of Malverthorpe's accusation was even more encouraging. Jack had actually relaxed, begun to enjoy the comedy of the proceedings. He thought of how they would chuckle over it later. But he saw the seriousness of Sabina's accusation even before Walerand saw it. He knew by the stiffening of Ingrid's back, by the unconscious return of her school-trained accent, by the angle of her neck, that she had reverted to the nun he had first met, ashamed of her very shadow. Now Walerand would know her.

When it happened, it happened very fast. There was only time for a quick glance before he was herded through the great doors with the rest of the spectators. Her tall, thin body reminded him of a spire on a vast, empty plain—that is how alone she seemed as she stood before her judge. Such a spire could tickle the moon. Such a spire could be stabbed by lightning. Keep low, he thought, keep low.

Outside the rumors swarmed around his ears. He wished everyone would leave and let him keep his vigil in peace.

"They say she tried to kill herself in Pratt's. Raving mad she was when Sturges first found her."

"Aye. Gillian was none too happy when Matthew brought her

home, out of her mind and crawling with lice. Myself, I'd have thrown her out that very night."

"Too good for his own good, is Matthew."

"A kinder heart you'll never find."

"Taking in a witch—that's going a little far, ain't it?"

"Well he didn't know. No one knew but Sabina."

"Poor Sabina."

"Poor *Henry*!"

"Well, if she's the one who put Malverthorpe out of business they should give her the key to the city, that's my opinion."

"Amen to that!"

"Imagine having a witch under your roof all those months and not realizing it. They had her taking care of the baby and everything."

"Those boys adored her."

"Maybe she put a spell on them, too."

"They say she's a runaway nun."

"I heard a runaway serf."

"Nay. She speaks Latin. It's a runaway nun she is."

Even a happy summer afternoon is slow, as if time itself is bloated by the heat. Suspense swelled this one even further. Thinking that at any moment Ingrid might come out, Jack dared not desert his lookout on the church steps. After a while his vision began to shimmer and his damp shirt clung to his back. He kept trying to guess at what was happening inside. He knew the sorcery charge that Walerand had ridiculed at first took on more serious implications in the light of the miracles in Ingrid's past. For once he found himself wondering just what powers she did possess. Had she really healed Sabina, and if so, what did that mean? Where had the power come from? But he was sitting in the sun and his thoughts kept shrinking and popping like drops of water on a hot skillet.

"Do you think they'll burn her?" someone wondered.

"It's only in Spain they burn witches. Very bloody minded, those Spaniards."

"I wonder what it smells like. Like meat, do you suppose?"

Jack whirled round, his fists ready. But the speakers were walking away, and they were just boys. When he closed his eyes again, he could see the capillaries in his eyelids.

Later—he could not judge how long it had been, but the sun was relenting a little, and the crowd was gone—later he thought he heard a scream. He pressed his ear to the heavy door, half-mad with imaginings. All he could hear was the thumping of his own pulse. Soon afterward the door opened with a great crack and Thatcher came out. Jack tried to question him, but he refused to speak as he hurried past and retreated down High Street. A quarter of an hour later he returned with a very large rusty-haired man, and the two of them reentered the church. When they opened the door he glimpsed Walerand and the registrar still sitting at their table on the dais. But he saw no sign of Ingrid before the door was emphatically shut. He had only another moment to wait, though, before she came out.

She was holding her arms in an odd, stiff way, and when she threw them up to shield her swollen eyes from the sun, they moved as one and he realized her wrists were bound together. The big man who had just gone in had hold of one arm above the elbow and he watched her feet with some concern as they descended the stairs. Jack had the impression that she would have stumbled if the man were not holding her up, that she might have allowed her body to fall out of simple indifference to it. He called to her. She did not respond—whether from presence or absence of mind he could not be sure, for he had carelessly called her Ingrid. He called out again: "Jane!" By then she had already passed him. She half turned and glanced over her shoulder. She seemed not to recognize him, or rather to mistake him for someone she feared. Averting her face, she huddled closer to her captor as if seeking his protection.

Jack was stunned. Like a soldier in the heat of battle, he could not feel the wound: He felt only rage at the sight of his blood. He would not let this happen. Had he really been a soldier he would have drawn his sword. But Jack was a performer. He would give the performance of his life.

Five

"I will forgive him," Isobel told herself again. "After all, he was bewitched."

"We can put this behind us. We can still go on."

"He respected me. He did not respect her."

Last night he had kissed her outside the door to his room. So sweet, that kiss. She thought he would ask more; she was prepared to give it. But he feigned a yawn. She knew it was feigned. She understood what it meant—that he dared not trust himself with another kiss. What she was prepared to give, he refrained from taking. So he meant to have her lawfully! Her joy bombarded the stars. "Till tomorrow," he said, brushing her cheek with the back of his fingers.

She rose early. Too, too early. The sun had scarcely chased the moon away, and by moon and sun she saw them. He, face down, his back and buttocks naked, hosen in a tangle about his legs. Jane, covered by his body, just a face in chaos of hair and straw. And one bare calf. Her eyes closed again the moment they opened. But a slow smile of triumph spread across her face.

Witch.

Hadn't she always suspected? Jane could have discouraged Malverthorpe. Hadn't she always said so? Jane *wanted* his obsession. She fed off the man's blood. How gratifying, to be wanted endlessly and never to give. Never to give and still to be wanted. To make a man forsake his life's work for you. To cause a cleric to give up his vows. To steal his soul with the mere dream of your body. And all the while to remain intact. That was the aim of her witchcraft.

Jane covered her designs with a show of sweetness, but she, Isobel, was never taken in. No one is that nice. No one on earth.

She had gone back in her room after seeing them, too stricken to face another human being. When, hours later, someone tapped on the door, her heart beat wildly. Should she comb her hair, or let him see the ravages? Should she greet him with frosty composure, or let her tears come forth to accuse him? Before she could find her voice, the door was hesitantly opened. It was Sabina, pale as death. "Jane has been arrested."

She told Isobel the whole story: How she didn't want the baby, how Pratt botched the abortion, how Jane had saved her life. "I didn't know it was witchcraft," she cried, wringing her hands.

As Sabina became more and more agitated, Isobel's mind turned hard and clear as an icicle. "You must testify," she said.

Sabina had good reason for her reluctance. Her abortion would be public knowledge. Henry might never forgive her—for doing away with the child, for bringing on this notoriety. But what troubled her most was the notion of betraying her friend. "If it weren't for Jane, I would be dead," she kept sobbing.

"She saved your life, aye, but she has endangered your soul. Witchcraft is a mortal sin. And you're as guilty as she if you withhold this evidence."

She said no more than that. For much as she believed Jane deserved to be convicted, she could not bring herself to insist that her sister-in-law face such public devastation. Would I, in her place? she wondered. She thought not, and when at last Sabina resolved to go to court, Isobel was impressed with her courage.

The crisis eclipsed her personal grief, and she was surprised to find herself almost cheerful. Henry, knowing nothing of his wife's intention, had already gone to Saint Mary's to vouch for Jane if they'd let him. That left Isobel in charge of the inn. She aired all the bedding, got a stew going for lunch, even saw to the return of the Swindlestock's barrels.

As she tidied the guest rooms, she came upon Jacques's bag, still sitting where he'd left it on the undisturbed bed. She struggled a moment with her conscience, then locked the door. One by one she drew out his things. Two silk shirts and a linen one. A red and violet tunic. A comb. A bit of stale cake. A packet of peppermint leaves. Three pairs of particolored hosen—one badly ripped at the knee. She would mend it for him. She would forgive him. As she caressed the torn fabric she allowed herself, finally, to weep.

Henry and Sabina returned early in the afternoon. Now it was Henry who looked pale. He wrote "Closed due to illness" on a plank with a bit of charcoal and hung this makeshift sign on the gate. Then he went up to the bedroom, where Sabina lay dazed and exhausted.

Jacques had not returned with them. She wondered where he was. The discovery that he had lain with a witch must have shaken him. She would tell him it didn't matter. Nothing mattered but their love. "Was ever a woman so merciful?" he would say, deeply touched. "My darling, I don't deserve you." She sat on the steps to the gallery, waiting.

After an hour or so, Henry emerged, looking haggard. "How is she?" Isobel asked.

"Sleeping." No action had been taken against her. Walerand had been kind, he thought. Told her to see her confessor and to carry out her penance without fail. That was it. Pratt was being arrested.

"And Jane?"

"I don't know. He didn't seem to put much stock in the witchcraft nonsense. He's talking to her in private now. I think it will be all right. Feel like I've been through a bloody war, though." He went into the pub, downed a quart of ale, then retreated once more to the bedroom.

The children, knowing something was wrong, were miserable. They had been wailing and whining and beating each other up all afternoon. After a while she gave up trying to manage them. She sat on the steps and waited.

It was evening when he came. "Let me in!" he shouted, banging impatiently on the bolted wooden gate. "I need my horse."

She smoothed her skirt and checked her hair with fluttering hands before undoing the lock. But he scarcely seemed to see her. His shirt was limp with sweat and his face was hard with some purpose he did not seem ready to confide. "Bring me a pint of stout, will you?" He kept moving as he said it, almost running toward the stable. By the time she returned with the ale, he had his horse saddled. He accepted the cup without thanks and drank thirstily. She stood there uncertainly, wondering how to tell him that she forgave him, that they could go on. When he lowered the cup she thought he would speak to her. Instead, he did something very strange. He poured ale into his hand and sprinkled it over his clothing. Then he wet his hand again, this time running it into his hair.

"Jacques, I want you to know that—"

He dumped out the rest of the ale and thrust the cup at her. Without another word he was gone.

She ran, sobbing, to her room and threw herself on Jane's bed because it was nearer the door. That was how she came upon it—the small painted spicebox under the pillow. Once, when she'd come in unexpectedly, she'd seen Jane shove it hastily out of the way. At the time she had taken this furtiveness as just another of the girl's eccentricities, like her waking every night at midnight, and the Latin she murmured in her sleep. Now it came to her as a certainty: The evidence to convict Jane was in that box.

She dried her tears and sat up, balancing the box on her lap. Still sniffling, she lifted the hinged lid. A crumpled yellow scarf and a tangle of red ribbon. She removed them. Underneath was a jumble of trinkets and—yes! She gasped. Beeswax and a needle. She must have disturbed it as she rummaged in the box—the needle had fallen out. Still, there was no doubt. She felt a thrill of horror and righteous indignation.

The wick was a little misleading—one might take this for an ordinary candle. Better cut it off. Still holding the wax, she crossed the room in search of the small knife she used to trim her fingernails. The wick was a bit resistant. As she struggled with it, the heat of her hand softened the wax. She kneaded it in her excitement. When she realized what she was doing she stopped at once. Well, no harm done. In fact, now it looked even more like a man. She pinched it near the top to define the head better. But, oh dear . . . the initials had melted away. Yes, she was sure there had been initials. She supposed it would be all right to restore them. Since they'd been there to begin with. Since she'd erased them by accident. On the back, weren't they? She set the image on the bed so as not to damage it further and carved carefully with the needle. S. M. Then she plunged the needle where it belonged—in the heart.

Six

After the inquest Walerand invited Wycliffe back to his rooms at Merton so that the two of them could work together at putting the transcript in order. It was hot. The younger man's face was more florid than usual, and he had opened the top of his gown a bit. No doubt he would have liked to have stripped down to his limp shirt, but Walerand's presence—impossibly cool in his own black robe—inhibited him. Walerand had the rare elegance of never seeming to be inconvenienced by his own flesh. He did not sweat, did not yawn, did not even acknowledge the possibility of farting. No matter how late the hour or heavy the wine, he maintained the alert posture of a surveying eagle, and when he did sleep it was with an efficiency that scarcely wrinkled the sheets. Other men felt themselves to be more mortal than he and thus inferior, as if his lack of secretions placed him nearer the angels. Wycliffe, hunched over his work and perspiring from the effort of propelling the quill, was conscious of the pustule throbbing on his hot neck, the odor of his armpits and the grumbling of his empty stomach.

Walerand was taking what seemed to the registrar a fanatical interest in the accuracy of the transcript. The first thing he had said to Ingrid once the church was cleared and the three of them were alone was that other authorities would read it and that she herself would have an opportunity to review it. "So you see," he had continued. "You are not entirely at my mercy."

She had received this information without interest, for the worry he was addressing was not her worry. Perhaps she had never heard of the abuses that occurred in *ex officio* proceedings, where the inquisitor (in this case, Walerand) acted as both prosecutor and judge. To conduct such an inquest in private went against his English sense of justice, yet to question her in public was unthinkable. A fair transcript was one of the few protections he could offer.

The first few pages, in which she confessed to apostasy and fornication, were flawless, for Ingrid had responded in brief, forthright sentences, plain and slow as chant. The crucial words, though, the confession of sorcery, had been sobbed out nearly three hours later. Wycliffe's exhausted hand had dashed to keep up with the outpouring of Ingrid's exhausted spirit, and the final pages were a mess of scrawling, blottings and gaps.

Now Walerand sat back in his straight chair, his eyes closed and his fingers forming a steeple as Wycliffe read that section back to him: *"You keep asking me about Sabina. Why do you not ask me about the healings at Greyleigh? They were no different. If I am a sorceress now, I was then, too. People said they could feel God there, when the miracles happened. But I never felt him. Never. He never would show himself to me, never would—"* Wycliffe broke off and for some reason blushed. "It sounded like 'enter me.'"

"Yes, I believe so. 'Never would enter me.'"

"—though I begged him. Others knew him but I couldn't. Not ever. I think . . . I think God does not love me. Through my hands he loves others and it is a—" Wycliffe looked up. "'Torrent'? 'Torment'?"

"'Torment.'"

"—and it is a torment. Then she said something like, 'What am I saying? I cannot say this.'"

Walerand nodded. "Yes. I remember that."

"But do you not think it cruel how he healed others, always others in front of me, through my hands, and never me? Never me? Why did he not love me when I loved him so?"

She had been weeping as she spoke these words, and it was queer now to hear her anguish repeated in the registrar's tired monotone. As he read on, Wycliffe's tone became even flatter, more neutral, as if he were a physician maintaining a professional indifference to the patient's nudity. Perhaps he feared a contagion. Walerand did. She had been doubled over, clutching her waist, and something had convulsed under his own ribs.

Wycliffe continued. *"You felt him, didn't you, that day? Everyone who was there said they felt God's presence. But I did not. I felt only this horrible chill. They were all so colorful, there was so much color in the chapel and I was gray. Not even gray. Transparent. I hoped their color would fill me. I wanted to suck up all that faith—"* Wycliffe looked up apologetically. "There was something else, but I didn't get it."

"She said, 'I was so cold. I was so cold, and I wanted them to make me warm.'"

The young man took it down. "By this time she was crying so hard I missed a lot of what she said. There was something that began 'Oh God, how could I go on believing—'"

"No. It was 'How could *they* go on believing when I left them unhealed?'"

He made the correction. "And then, *I began to wish they would all go away. I hated their sores, and the stink, and the trusting looks that—that made me feel such a fraud. The truth is I hated them.*"

Walerand winced. "Yes," he said softly. "That is what she said."

"And then the confession: *Oh God, it is true. I am a sorceress. I have been Satan's all along.* I'm certain I got that part exactly."

He was right, but Walerand resented his certainty, his little moment of pride in having cataloged the fragments so accurately as Ingrid broke. But no, that's not fair, he thought. Wycliffe's big thumb, twitching against the edge of the parchment as he read, and the drop of perspiration that rolled from his temple to the hinge of his tense jaw, told Walerand he was being unfair.

"You must be thirsty," he said, to make amends, and rang for his servant. "I'll order up some wine." And then, as an afterthought, he added, "Would you like something to eat?"

"Well, if you're having something." In fact, Wycliffe was famished, for they had missed the midday meal, but he was loath to admit this to Walerand.

The magistrate was not hungry, but he professed great appetite and ordered up cold meat, bread and fruit. "Let's go on while we're waiting, shall we? I think we're almost finished."

Encouraged by the prospect of supper, the scribe took up his pen with renewed energy. "*I have been Satan's all along,*" he recited. "*That is why . . .* Something inaudible. The next thing I got was *the man recognized me.* Stress on the word 'recognized.'"

"Yes. Go on."

"*He recognized me. He knew. He saw through me right away. I was his. I was Satan's. I knew . . .*" Here the scribe's voice dropped. It pained him to repeat what was written. "*I knew he was the devil and I gave myself to him.*"

"Wait. She screamed at one point. Do you remember?"

"Yes. In fact, I know exactly where because I was so startled— you can see here, there's a blot. She screamed right before 'He recognized me.'"

"Yes. As if she were realizing it for the first time."

"Shall I go on?"

"Yes."

"*I knew he was the devil and I gave myself to him. I didn't care. I adored him.*"

Wycliffe looked up suddenly. "Do you think it's true?"

"That this man she slept with was the devil? No. In fact, we know who he is. A troubadour. Goes by a preposterous name—Voleur des Cœurs or something of the sort."

"But you believe she is a sorceress?"

Walerand tapped his fingers together thoughtfully. "She has said so. Do you doubt it?"

For a moment Wycliffe hesitated, for it was not his place to have an opinion on the proceedings he recorded. But then he committed himself with an eagerness that made his body seem very large. "Well, it is strange that she admitted to apostasy right off—"

"She could hardly deny it."

"Yes, but she admitted that she left of her own free will. She made no attempt to excuse herself. And with the charge of fornication it was the same, and unless I'm mistaken, we had no proof of that one."

"No, we hadn't." Walerand was looking at him with interest.

"So she owns up to two of the charges without a struggle, but the third, the sorcery charge, she denies vigorously, for hours. I must say, when she was denying it, I found her very convincing. I believed her."

"And when she confessed it?"

"I believed her then, too."

Baldwin would have smiled and shrugged while making this

admission. But Wycliffe's brow was furrowed, because he believed that there was a truth to be gotten at and that getting at it mattered. Walerand was glad that his servant arrived at that moment with their supper: He wanted to offer the young man something as a tribute.

It was as Wycliffe said: Ingrid's denials had been so vehement, so consistent, that he, too, had been ready to give way to them when she suddenly reversed herself and confessed. Now, as the registrar tore eagerly into his bread and beef, Walerand took up the transcript and returned to the part that gave him the most discomfort.

Q: Your employer, Mistress Greene, stated that when you put your hands upon her you muttered some words which she could not understand.

A: No, I did not speak at all.

Q: You called upon neither God nor Satan?

A: Neither.

Q: Did you think that by putting your hands on her you would heal her?

A: I don't remember thinking it. But I suppose I must have. Yes.

Q: You thought, Now I shall work a miracle, or something of the sort.

A: Well, no.

He remembered that she had smiled then as if the question struck her funny.

Q: According to your previous testimony, you were at that time in a state of mortal sin. You had lain with a man, you had renounced your vows and neither of these sins had been confessed or absolved. Considering the state of your soul, whatever made you think your touch could heal this woman?

A: Milord, there was blood all over. I wasn't thinking about my soul.

He blushed now to read this. Seldom had he been made to feel so foolish. He had rushed for the safety of a higher authority.

Q: You have studied Aquinas, have you not? Do you recall his teaching on magic?

A: Natural events follow the laws of reason. Irrational events have supernatural causes.

Q: Such as?

A: Such as divine intervention. Or the action of demons.

Q: Are we agreed that Mistress Greene's recovery was an irrational event?

A: My knowledge of medicine is limited. There may be a natural cause. But in all honesty, yes, I thought Sabina was dying and when she recovered it seemed to me a miracle.

She might have eluded me there, he reflected. If she had made up a pseudo-medical explanation, would I have been the wiser?

Q: An irrational event, then, supernaturally caused. Either by God or by demons. You say by God. But let us consider the possibility of demons for a moment, shall we?

A: There were no demons.

Q: Let us speak hypothetically. Can you tell me how one obtains the assistance of demons?

A: I don't know. I've never done it.

Q: According to Aquinas.

A: According to Aquinas, one requests it.

Q: Explicitly?

A: I would suppose so.

Q: Do not suppose. Recall your studies.

A: There could be an implicit request.

Q: Yes. Very good. Go on.

A: Aquinas believes that the very act of attempting magic implies a request for supernatural assistance.

Q: Precisely. I congratulate you on your mastery of the *Summa.* Now, does not Aquinas go on to say that any act of magic which fails to invoke God explicitly invokes Satan implicitly?

A: He does not say that, does he?

Q: He does, indeed.

A: Then he is mistaken.

Q: You presume to contradict Aquinas?

A: In all humility, I must. God cannot be prevented from intervening simply because a sinner no longer dares to speak his name. He cannot be prevented by our theology from aiding the sick and the dying. I swear to you, I have never called upon Satan. This healing came from God. It was a *healing*, milord—where is the evil in it?

Q: To save the life of a woman who murders her unborn child—

A: —is an act of awesome mercy. I dare not think of such mercy. My soul flinches from it as the damned hide their faces from the light. But even I, a wretched sinner, would not put such an act beyond God's love.

During that last exchange she had been suddenly very close to him. He was seated and she was standing, but the dais put them eye to eye, and her eyes were full of appeal. Her forearms had rested on the table—he remembered noticing the sunburn on them—and her fingers curved inward toward her breast. At Greyleigh she had seemed to be made of nothing but light. Now her nose was peeling, and her hair—she was so close he could smell it—her hair had the warm sleepy fragrance of damp hay. But something about her, something empty, tremulous and brave, recalled the saint, so that he had been embarrassed by the role of judge.

He set down the transcript and poured himself some wine. A cool breeze was coming in through the casement now. He wandered over and sat with one hip propped on the sill, looking out over the deserted quad. It was that time of evening when all the colors the sun has bleached from the day come back, rich and golden as sherry. In the distance he heard a woman calling her children in, and rowdy masculine singing spilling from some tavern. Trees rustled and sighed. The air was fragrant with soft nostalgia.

"I was there, you know, for the Pentecost miracles," he mused aloud. "None of us who saw her then doubted that she was a saint. It is true, what she said, John—one felt the presence of God. It seemed so simple. A matter of touch. Looking at one's fellow men with compassion and touching them. As Christ did. Nothing more than that." He gave a nervous, self-mocking laugh. "On the journey home I resolved to give away all my books, join an order and devote myself to lepers."

"Why did you not?" Wycliffe asked seriously.

He shrugged his elegant shoulders. "Well it was just a thought. It went the way of such thoughts."

"Now that she's confessed, everyone who had a hand in making her a saint will be rushing to shovel dirt on her grave," the young man observed, between bites.

Walerand shot him a fierce look, wanting to object and at the same time recalling how Bishop Locke had remarked to him, shortly after Ingrid's disappearance, "It might be better for everyone if she were not found."

"She won't be executed. Not now that she has confessed."

"But she'll never be seen again."

"No. I shouldn't think so. We'll put the word out that she died while on retreat and then lock her up somewhere. Probably not even a prison. If she's willing to cooperate, it can be more like a hermitage."

"People will want a body," Wycliffe pointed out. "Relics. Posthumous miracles."

"Bones are not hard to come by. Oh, don't look so shocked. We made a dreadful mistake. If it comes out, people will be hurt by it. Innocent people, uneducated people may lose faith."

"Maybe that sort of faith ought to be lost."

"That is a dangerous thought, John. That is abandoning the sheep to the wolves."

Wycliffe was staring at the queue of bread crumbs he'd made on the tablecloth. His heavy lips were pushed out with the sullen stoicism of a boy who has decided he is too old for tears. "You are the most honorable man I know," he said mournfully, in the North Country accent of his childhood.

The gentleness of the rebuke sharpened its sting. Walerand felt chastened. "The Church is dearer to me than my honor," he said. And though it was true, as he said it he regretted it a little.

"I suppose that itself is a kind of honor," the young man allowed.

"No. Better to call things by their proper names. A lie is a lie."

There was a knock then, and the porter stood in the doorway with an air of apology. "There is a man downstairs who demands to see you at once," he said.

Walerand suppressed his irritation before speaking—a discipline so habitual with him that the effort of it never showed. "You told him we were not to be interrupted?"

"Aye, milord. He told me to tell you that if you won't hear what he has to say, he'll stand at Carfax and sing his tale for all of Oxford to hear. Those were his exact words, milord," the servant added, to make sure he was not held responsible for such an impertinence. At the same time Walerand became aware of loud singing below.

> A nun is complaining,
> Her tears are down raining—

"Show him up at once," he said.

Seven

Though Walerand's study was illumined only by the last nod of a retiring sun, Jack experienced the sense of strong white light, the dazzlement that accompanied performance. He squinted a little as he looked at the magistrate and his scribe, who were seated at a table littered with parchment and the remains of a cold supper. Walerand was looking back in an alert, curious way, just as he had first looked at Ingrid that morning. There was an impartiality about him, a decency that Jack found hard to reconcile with his impression that Ingrid had been persecuted during her interview with him.

He ambled over to them with the careful walk of a drunk who is trying to appear sober and, without waiting to be invited, slouched into an empty seat, extending his legs so far under the table that his toes touched the legs of Walerand's chair.

He held his purse over the table and let it fall with a thud. "See that? That's one hour's wages. I made it in the Saracen's Head tonight. Not bad, eh? But then I thought to myself, I thought, Jack, you're a damned fool. You're a damned fool singing yourself hoarse for small change when there's a judge down the street who'll pay you a hundred times that just for keeping quiet. By the way, I suppose I should introduce myself. I go by the name of Jacques Brigand des Cœurs."

Walerand did not look surprised.

"Naturally I don't expect you to fall all over yourself in enthusiasm, not knowing what it is that I propose to be quiet about," Jack continued. "So let me come right to the point. That girl you've got in Castle Gaol—the one who calls herself Jane Basset—that girl is none other than Ingrid Fairfax, the miracle worker of Greyleigh. Ha! Of course, you know that. But it occurred to me that's not something you fellows want the world to know."

He looked shrewdly at his adversary, saw the little ridge appear in Walerand's cheek as his jaw tensed. With calculated rudeness he reached across the table, helped himself to Walerand's empty goblet and filled it to the rim with wine. He chugged it all down, exhaling loudly at the end the way children do when they have drunk fast.

"So," he went on. "Aren't you going to ask me how I know? Never mind, you don't have to ask. I'll spill the whole story for free. It's the *not* telling that'll cost you dear." He settled back in the chair, taking his time, eyeing them smugly as he rolled the goblet back and forth between his hands. "I had her, you see. At Greyleigh. Right under the nose of that ugly abbess."

Walerand could not help emitting a little gasp of dismay. Encouraged, Jack continued. "I don't mean to boast, but I have rather a way with women. I know how they think. When a woman says nay it could mean nay or it could mean aye. Very tricky that. But this one meant aye, no doubt about it." He shoved his hand inside his shirt and scratched energetically. Walerand's nose was lifted and pinched as if a bad smell had come into the room, while Wycliffe's blunt face was plainly aghast.

Jack chuckled as if savoring the memory. "She's a hot one, that Ingrid. Had to keep a hand clapped over her mouth the whole time or the whole convent would've heard her, screaming and moaning and carrying on."

He paused to pour more wine into his goblet. There was only a dribble left. "The thing I couldn't stand about her, though, was the way she tried to take up the sainthood theme again right afterward. 'May God forgive you,'" he mocked in falsetto imitation. "'I shall pray for you.' The little hypocrite!"

It was working. He caught the significant look that flickered between the two clerics. "John, will you go ask Sturges to send up another pitcher?" Walerand asked.

"Yes sir, right away." Wycliffe's chair made a loud scraping noise as he pushed it back, and he left the room in haste, as if on a mission of great importance.

He peered at the magistrate over the rim of his goblet. Walerand's elbows rested on the arms of his chair, and his fingers formed a spire. From time to time his two front teeth would alight on the very tip of this spire, bouncing there with a faint click against the fingernails. They were precise, even teeth, intelligent-looking teeth. When he saw that Jack was staring at him, he feigned a smile.

"I heard you made an appearance at Greyleigh after Ingrid left there," he remarked, affecting casualness.

Jack coached himself—a wary look and then a shrug. Take your time. Make him work for it. He'll believe it if he thinks he's wormed it out of you. "Aye," he responded. "To bring her a present. They didn't want to let me in."

"You got in, nevertheless." Another click—tooth against nail.

"Well, they couldn't really stop me, could they? All women. No men about."

Walerand led him on. "You must have been surprised when she wasn't there."

He glowered. "Aye. Fool that I was." He slammed the goblet down on the table. Leaning forward, he wagged a drunkard's finger in Walerand's face. "It's those sweet-faced ones you've got to watch out for."

"I'm afraid I don't know what you mean." Click.

"Well, it's obvious, isn't it? I wasn't the only one."

"You know that for a fact?"

"Oh come, man!" he blustered. "How else did she get away? How else would a girl who'd been sheltered like she was survive on the road? Or maybe you think God extended special protection to his little saint. Maybe she's got you believing that drivel she gave me when I finally caught up with her last night." He halted there. Make him ask, he reminded himself.

Walerand obliged. "Why—what did she say last night?"

He shrugged. "You know how she talks. Said she forgave me. Imagine that—she forgives me for the best time she ever had! Then she tried to save my soul. Luckily, Malverthorpe came along and interrupted. What an absurd fellow! You should have seen him with his sword drawn. To defend her virtue, he said. I'll lay odds he's had a piece himself. 'Twas probably Malverthorpe that fetched her out of Greyleigh in the first place."

He glanced at the window. It was nearly dark. His horse was tied up outside, but if he didn't get out of here before the gates closed at curfew, he would be trapped in town. Better conclude this quickly.

"Funny he charges her with witchcraft the next day," Walerand said.

This was not the direction Jack wanted the conversation to take. He rolled his eyes. "We both know the witchcraft charge is a cartload of manure, don't we? Ingrid's no witch. A bitch maybe, but not a witch." He laughed too loud and too long. "A bitch, not a witch," he repeated. "Ha!"

Walerand was giving him a look to freeze the very blood in his veins. Christ, he'd better escape, or he would never see the light of day again! With a tremendous effort of will he forced himself to keep slouching. "Actually," he resumed. "She's a sweet girl in her way. Took good care of me when I was sick. She can't help it if they've stuffed her head with a lot of rubbish about being a saint. So what I propose is a modest fee—say, ten crowns—and I'll not say another word about her. My lips will be sealed for life."

Walerand ignored this. He had dropped all pretense of nonchalance. "Why did you go back to Greyleigh?" he asked, in the manner of a prosecutor.

Jack pretended to have noticed no difference in tone. He could feel the sweat beading under his moustache. "I told you—to bring a gift. Look, I understand if you don't have that much money at hand. There's no hurry. I'll be staying at the Crossroads all week. You can send a messenger with it." He pushed his chair back, preparing to leave.

"Tell me the whole story, and then I'll decide what it's worth. Why did you go back to Greyleigh?"

Damn! Clearly Walerand was trying to detain him till the registrar came back. Jack thought of his knife, and the very thought of thinking of his knife made his forehead break out in sweat. This whole scheme was out of hand. When it first came to him it had seemed so elegant in conception, so perfect in its exploitation of his unique talents, that he had been carried away with his own cleverness, never even considering that he might not be able to escape.

"I see you're nobody's fool," he said. "So I'll tell you, as one man of the world to another. We were going to run off together, Ingrid and I. She was supposed to meet me by the gate. And I told her 'Ingrid, don't be late, or I'll have to come in for you and that damn abbess of yours is sure to make a scene.' I said 'I don't want to have to draw my sword in a nunnery. It just isn't fitting.' You might not guess it, but I'm a patient man, and I can't stand violence. So I waited all night before I went in. And that's when I found out she'd played me for a fool."

A church bell had started to ring while he was speaking. Now others took up the chorus. Curfew. "Look, I know you're a busy man," he said, rising. "I won't keep you any longer." He heard heavy feet on the stairs. More than one pair, from the sound of it. Maybe the window. They were on the second story—it was a survivable jump.

"Not at all," Walerand was saying. "By all means stay. John should be back any minute with more wine."

"Well, the fact is, I've got a girl waiting for me at the Saracen's Head. You know how it is."

Bolt the door. Gain time. As he spun round to face it, it was flung open with a cracking sound, as if someone was angry or meant to be dramatic. An enormous red-haired man filled the doorframe, the one who had escorted Ingrid from Saint Mary's. Jack went for his knife. The next thing he knew the man's big hand was clamped around his wrist and his arm was being twisted till he doubled over and howled with indignation. "It gives me great pleasure to inform you that you are under arrest," Walerand said.

Eight

Nothing in Jack's life, not even the first days at Greyleigh with his broken leg and fever, equalled the sheer physical misery of that night. Walerand had ordered him gagged to ensure that his story would spread no further. They had used Wycliffe's napkin, which tasted of linen and beef fat. To keep him from removing it, his hands were bound behind his back, and when they threw him in the cell, they left the handcuffs and gag in place. The linen drew all the moisture from his mouth—his tongue and throat felt coated in chalk. He could only lie on his side and that was tolerable at first. But as the night wore on, thin cold fingers of pain shot up from his shackled wrists and dug their grip into his shoulders. His head was heavy and his neck, by comparison, seemed frail. The strain cut a wedge between his shoulder blades. Beneath his cheek was a muck of rotted straw. The scratching of rodents was too near his face.

Walerand had threatened to have his tongue cut out if he ever told his story to anyone else. He wondered whether that was how they would punish him, ultimately. Maybe he would have a choice between that and life in prison. He spent much of the night trying to decide which was dearer to him—his tongue or his freedom—as if he would really have to answer that question in the morning.

He assumed they would come for him in the morning. But what if they didn't? What if he had to lie there till afternoon, till evening, till the following day? What if they simply forgot him? He was helpless as a baby. It was not something he could stand for long— that helplessness. If he was given a long sentence he would have to find a way to escape. But it was impossible to think about escape with his hands bound behind him, as though part of his intelligence dwelt in his hands and was cut off by the manacles. He was very much afraid.

Jack might have consoled himself with the knowledge that his plan had succeeded. Walerand now strongly suspected that Ingrid had been raped and that she had run away from Greyleigh to avoid abduction.

"But why did she not tell us so?" Wycliffe wondered.

"Because she does not see it that way. She blames herself. Perhaps she imagines she enticed him. You must realize how sheltered Ingrid had been. This fellow was probably the first man, apart from elderly priests, that she had ever spoken to. On the other hand," he continued, more to himself than to Wycliffe, "she may know full well that she was wronged. She may simply be protecting him."

"At such a cost to herself?"

Walerand shrugged with a faint smile. "Saints are notorious for their excesses of mercy."

"What of the confession of sorcery then?"

He sighed. "I don't know. I don't know. Perhaps . . . God help me, John, perhaps I forced it."

"It did not seem so to me."

"Well, certainly that wasn't my intent. But she may have become confused, pressured by my questions." All at once his vague misgiving took a distinct shape and he exclaimed with the enthusiasm of sudden insight, "You see, one thing is certain—Ingrid does not believe she is a saint. So when I implied that if she is not a saint she must be a sorceress, I trapped her."

He had an impulse to run to the Castle Gaol and release her at once. But bursting in and waking her in the middle of the night would only alarm her. And where could he put her? Better to go at dawn. They could clear up the charges first thing and get to Greyleigh before nightfall tomorrow. He told Wycliffe to meet him in St. George's vestry shortly after sunrise, then excused the young man.

Wycliffe nodded gratefully—it had been a long day— stretched, suppressed a yawn and began to gather up the sheets of parchment. "There's one thing I can't help wondering, sir," he said as he rolled them up together. "Her confession was so emotional. She said she could never feel God and . . . I think she meant that."

Walerand looked at him seriously, considering this. " 'How long O Lord? Wilt thou forget me forever? How long must I bear pain in my soul and have sorrow in my heart all the day? How long wilt thou hide thy face from me?' Do you recognize that?"

"It's a psalm, isn't it?"

"Yes. Ingrid could probably tell you the number." He gazed at the wall behind Wycliffe's head, as if reading off of it. " 'I am like a vulture of the wilderness. Like an owl of the waste places. I lie awake. I am like a lonely bird on the housetop . . . I eat ashes like bread, and mingle tears with my drink . . . for thou hast taken me up and thrown me away. My days are like an evening shadow. I wither away like grass.' That one's 102, I believe."

Wycliffe closed his robe as if to defend himself from a sudden chill. If Walerand had been reading from a psalter, if he had been reading in Latin, it would not have been so disquieting. It was his knowing these words by heart, speaking them in this stark English . . . "So you are saying that such an outcry is not incompatible with faith," he concluded, wanting to sum up quickly and escape.

The older man's wry shrug did little to mitigate his troubling response: "We have forgotten, I suppose, that God is vulnerable to these accusations."

Isobel had thought Malverthorpe, on his daily visits to the Crossroads, looked as terrible as it was possible for a living man to look. She was wrong. Here in his dim room he was like something dredged up from the grave. He lay on a wad of soiled bedding, his face pocked by shadows, his limbs so disordered they seemed to have lost all connection to his trunk. The room was stifling, and it stank.

A young man rose to greet her as she entered. "Reginald Baldwin, Doctor Malverthorpe's counsel." He gave a small gallant bow and offered her the room's only chair.

"I can't stay," she said. "It's almost curfew."

"You!" Malverthorpe croaked from the bed. "You are that girl from the Crossroads. Were you in on it too? Were you in on the little joke?"

"Please excuse my client, madam. He is unwell."

"It is no joke, Doctor," Isobel said, turning to face Malverthorpe from a safe distance. "Alas, I believe the charges you have made against Jane Basset are true."

Baldwin glanced uneasily at his client. "Perhaps we should step outside, Mistress uh—"

"Greene. Isobel Greene. I've come with some evidence which may support your case. Something I found among her things."

Malverthorpe raised himself on one elbow. "What is it? Give it to me."

Isobel was reluctant to go near him. "Maybe Master Baldwin should have a look at it, to see if it's really what I think it is." She placed her parcel on the plank table and with nervous fingers untied the knot in the yellow silk wrapper.

Delicately, Baldwin picked up the lump of wax and held it up to the oil lamp. "'Twould appear to be a sorceress' doll."

"Give it here!" Malverthorpe insisted.

Baldwin affected a shrug as he proferred the image. "I wouldn't make too much of it."

Malverthorpe turned it over and over, examining it from all angles. "What's this?" he exclaimed. "S. M. My initials!"

"So it would seem," Baldwin agreed, with an air of detachment.

"And the needle—look how it stabs the heart." He clasped the bedclothes to his chest as if protecting it. "She kills me. I am doomed."

"I don't think it means that," Isobel said in alarm. "A needle to the heart is a love spell. Isn't that what it means—a love spell?"

She appealed to Baldwin for confirmation. Beneath his studied nonchalance, he looked uneasy, out of his depth. "Well, that would depend," he began, then paused to clear his throat. "That would depend. As the emotions are commonly believed to reside in the heart, a symbolic blow to it would seem to imply love, yes. But if the sorceress wishes to engender a sexual obsession, the more logical target would seem to be the—uh—genitalia. Still—"

"Fool!" Malverthorpe rasped from his bed. "Fool! 'Twas never my love she wanted. It is my death."

"The evidence of that is inconclusive, Doctor. We would have to examine her state of mind at the time she—"

"State of mind! Ha! She hates me. From the moment we met she has been plotting my doom."

Baldwin cleared his throat again. "With all due respect, Doctor—"

"Ask this woman if it is not so. Tell him, girl. Tell him how she hated me. Tell—" He drew a terrible rattling breath. "—how she has wished me dead."

She was frightened now. Malverthorpe's eyes had a queer, triumphant light that looked to her like madness. He still clutched the bedclothes in one gnarled hand while the other pointed at her ghoulishly. She wished she had not come.

"I don't think . . . It was more a matter of vanity. She enjoyed the way you were always—"

"You lie!"

Her shoulders jumped, and she felt the blood rush to her face. "Well, no," she amended. "No, she didn't like you following her but she . . . " How could she explain it—the way Jane wanted to take without having to give? Her secret joy in bringing him down. This morning she had been so sure, but now . . . it was all so confusing.

"She hated me. Admit it—do not spare me. I am a dead man."

She remembered Jane in the hayrick with Jacques sprawled across her. The way his fingers were wrapped around a strand of her hair.

"You are right," she answered. "Jane hated you."

His face relaxed, and he nodded slowly. "Yes. Do not spare me. Tell me she wished me dead."

She remembered Jane's smile, that cruel victorious smile.

"It is true," she said. "I heard her say so once. She wished you would die."

Malverthorpe's eyes closed, and he fell back on the pillows, exhausted. "So be it."

Nine

Oxford Castle was uninspired from the start, a utilitarian structure thrown up in a hurry by the Norman invaders. If they had meant it to be awesome, they would have put it at Carfax, the highest point in town. Instead, they had chosen a low, swampy, smelly area near Fisher's Row, where the river formed a natural defense. (Though no one had ever been much interested in attacking Oxford.) Parts had been allowed to fall to ruin, for nobody had lived there for generations, but the little church inside, Saint George's, had been kept up, and the blunt ugly tower served as a prison. Jack was being held in an airless cell at the top of it, while Ingrid was isolated underground.

Walerand had never been in the dungeon before, though he had sent many a prisoner there. Perhaps this was just as well, for more knowledge might have weakened his resolve. In horizontal space it was vast. Beyond a sphere of light cast by the jailer's torch were crypts of darkness that a solitary imagination could populate with monsters. The ceiling was so low that a tall man had to be mindful of his head. It was supported by the thickest columns he had ever seen: two people reaching around one could scarcely have joined hands. Because they were so thick, one imagined they were holding up a great weight and that they might fail. Tons of stone would fall. You would be crushed to death.

Ingrid was tethered to one of these pillars by a single chain attached to her ankle. The little pile of straw on which she huddled was like a campsite in a stone forest. She sat clutching her drawn-up knees and looked at her liberators without comprehension. He spoke her name gently. When he put his hand on her shoulder she flinched.

"Gone mad," the guard explained with cheery detachment. "Screamed half the night, but I guess she's tired out now."

Walerand's mouth went dry. The sense of having done wrong overpowered him. "Bring something for her to drink," he ordered with less than his usual courtesy.

He crouched beside her. "Ingrid, do you remember who I am?"

She blinked. A long moment passed. Then she lifted the hem of her skirt to show him her fettered ankle. "I am caught in a trap," she said hoarsely.

His scalp prickled. "Ingrid . . . "

She tugged at his hand, then pointed to her ankle and repeated, "I am caught in a trap."

"We'll get you out," he said, patting her foot. "Don't worry." The guard returned with a cup of cider, and Walerand demanded the key.

When they freed her leg she wanted to inspect the shackle. She looked up with a surprised expression. "I thought it had teeth."

He gave her the cider. She wrapped both hands around the cup like a child and drank in diligent little sips. "That's better," she said when she had finished, and tried to smile.

He helped her to her feet and she clung to his arm, wobbling a little as they went up the stairs and emerged into the sunlight. "Don't worry," she startled him by saying. "I'm all right."

A sharp glance found her face wan but composed, her intelligence quite present, quite accessible. Such a rapid transformation was hard to believe, and he did not know which phase to distrust.

"The jailer said you were screaming."

She looked away, shamefaced, but said nothing.

"*Were* you screaming?"

"I'm sorry," she mumbled.

They walked on in silence until they reached the entrance to Saint George's. His fingers closed around the door handle, but he did not open it. He turned to confront her. "Why were you screaming?"

"I was afraid the devil would come for me in the dark," she said. "But he didn't."

The vestry was a modest room but for the lace-trimmed robes, embroidered stoles and chasubles that hung from pegs, exuding an odor of incense and authority. The early sun, coming in through the single arched window, threw diamond-shaped panes of light over the floor and the table at the center of it. Wycliffe, who had just arrived, was arranging things: two chairs on one side of the table for himself and Walerand, two more on the other side, a little removed, for the prisoners. Quills, penknife, ink and parchment were arrayed in military formation at his place. The registrar himself looked crisp and austere but for the small fresh bloodstain where yesterday's pimple had burst—oddly festive that red spot on his white collar.

They all sat down and were struck by a shyness, because the intimacy of the small room contrasted with the gravity of the proceedings. Ingrid's hair was bushy and snarled, and there was a smudgy bruised look about her eyes, but she sat erect, disdaining the backrest, her hands folded in her lap.

Then Jack was brought in. As the handcuffs and gag were taken off, there was an explosion of sound from him. He rubbed his wrists and set his shoulders right with an air of resentment. Walerand offered him cider, and he drank noisily, without pause, ignoring everything but his thirst. When the cider was gone, he thrust the cup forward. "More," he demanded breathlessly.

Ingrid had risen to her feet. "Why is he here?" she kept saying, wringing her hands.

"Wait," the magistrate cautioned. He dismissed the jailer and waited for the sound of his footsteps to diminish.

"I should not have said he was the devil," Ingrid was crying. "That was a stupid, wicked thing to say and it isn't true. I don't know why I said it. It isn't true . . . "

"Ingrid, please, be seated."

"What I said yesterday was wrong. I—"

"We know," he soothed. "Please. Sit down."

She sank back into her chair, looking troubled. "You know? But why—"

"We know that this man forced you into his bed and that you fled Greyleigh to avoid abduction."

Her eyes widened. "No. That isn't true."

He had anticipated her resistance, had prepared arguments to jar her memory and lead her to revise her interpretation of events.

"You do this man's soul no good if you protect him from the consequences of his crime," he pointed out.

"But I wanted him, you see." She blushed as she said this, and that blush drained him of some of his conviction. He noticed a lack of resonance in his voice as he spoke now.

"You may have felt desire," he allowed. "That is only human. There is no blame in it if you resisted."

"I didn't."

"My dear, I know this is painful, but think back. He covered your mouth to muffle your screams. He has admitted it."

"He told you that? Jack, you told them that?" She and the troubadour exchanged a speaking look. Walerand had a bad feeling about that look. And then—this was the most curious thing—she seemed to become aware of her snarled hair for the first time. She pushed it back on the right side, the side nearest Jack, with a gesture that was very feminine, almost erotic. He was beside himself then, remembering the callous boorish way the man had spoken of her the night before. *She's a hot one, that Ingrid.* It was as if a hundred Saracens were looting the holy sepulcher. One could hardly be expected to remain objective.

"Think back. You tried to push him away."

"Yes. At first."

"He persisted."

"Yes, but—"

"And he overpowered you." She was beginning to look confused. He pressed his advantage. "The night you left Greyleigh, he was coming back for you. When you left you were fleeing him."

"In a way, yes, but—"

"You were afraid of him."

"Not in the way you mean."

"Not in the way I mean, but in some way you were afraid."

"No . . ."

He could see her confusion growing, and this gave him confidence. "No? Yes, Ingrid. You have already said so."

She had covered her eyes with her palms and was shaking her head back and forth. "You're going too fast. I can't think."

He lowered his voice, which had been rising to a shout, but

did not let up. "When you didn't meet him, he broke into the cloister, just as he had threatened to do."

"He did?" She turned to question the troubadour with her eyes. He muttered "aye" with a little smirk. "Oh, Jack, how foolish!" There was a caress in her voice. Slowly, thoughtfully, she said to Walerand, "I could have taken refuge in another convent. Or I could have confided in Dame Agatha. But I did neither." He had the impression that she was trying to discover the truth not by recalling it but by inferring it logically. As if convinced by her first, tentative argument, she continued with more confidence, speaking rapidly now and without emotion. "He held me off and asked 'Are you sure this is what you want?' Those were his exact words. I remember them because—because I didn't want to have to decide. I wished he *would* force me. Then I would have been blameless. But it was my decision. If you have any doubts, I can prove it. We lay together again the night before last. There was a witness."

"Who?" Jack said, obviously surprised.

"Isobel. She was on the gallery. You were asleep."

Walerand sighed. He envisioned all the loose leaves of his learning being blown away by that sigh. Truth was a vapor, the intellect a net, and the futile weaving of nets was the principal industry of Oxford. I should have been a carpenter, he thought. I should have been a plowman.

"If you did not leave Greyleigh to avoid abduction, why did you leave?"

He saw it in her look—the same weariness, the same impatience. Her look said, Why do you ask me these silly questions? But she answered, "I had broken my vows. I no longer belonged there."

"You yourself have spoken movingly of God's mercy. Would he not have extended his mercy to you?"

"Yes. Of course. To doubt it would be heresy."

"Then why did you not confess?"

There was no defiance in the way she met his gaze. Just a modest, steady candor. "I was not sorry."

Wycliffe's harsh nervous laugh ripped through the vestry. A purple flush was creeping up his neck. He was mortified. But he could not stop himself from laughing. It was ungovernable, delicious. Walerand, though he glared, felt the glee of it.

Not sorry. Oh, to dance a not-sorry dance, rise up and proclaim her patron saint of the unrepentant! How had he come to be here, robed in humorless black, her tedious judge, while all this time summer had its freckled nose pressed to the window? Ingrid was waiting to see what he would say next, her head tilted like a sympathetic listener's. He did not know what to say next.

At this moment Baldwin exploded into the room. His face was very red, and he was panting. The contrast with his usual bland composure made his agitated entrance doubly shocking. Walerand half expected him to announce the end of the world.

"Malverthorpe is dead."

Until then the judge had forgotten all about Malverthorpe. His first guess was suicide.

"No, milord." The young lawyer cast a dark accusing look at Ingrid. "It was not suicide, was it, Mistress Basset?"

She flushed—it was particularly noticeable because earlier she had been so pale. The recollection of that guilty reddening supported Walerand later, when doubts about his verdict kept him awake. "Tell me," she whispered. "What happened?"

"You know."

She shook her head. "Nay."

"What happened, Baldwin?"

The younger man blotted his perspiring face daintily with the end of his sleeve, catching his breath before he began his narrative. "Yesterday evening I went to see him, to tell him how the proceedings had gone. He was in bed. He complained of pains in the chest and said he had been very tired all day. While I was there another visitor came, the younger Mistress Greene—Isobel, I believe her name is. She said she had some evidence that would help him convict Jane Basset." He took a small parcel from his sleeve and placed it on the table in front of Walerand, unfurling the yellow silk it was wrapped in. Ingrid gasped. Inside the cloth was a crude male figure, modeled in wax, about the size of a finger. The initials S. M. were carved on it, and a silver needle had been driven through its heart.

"She said she found this under Jane's pillow. She said that Jane hated Malverthorpe and wished him harm. Malverthorpe—when he saw the image he cried out, 'She has killed me!' He was alive when I left him. But this morning I had a premonition. I ran to his lodgings and found that he had died during the night. They were just removing the body."

"Oh, Isobel! You wretched girl!" Jack said. "Don't you see? It is because she saw us. She was just getting back at Ingrid."

"Who is Ingrid?" Baldwin asked. No one bothered to answer.

"Tell them," Jack was urging her. "Tell them it isn't yours." But Ingrid did not seem to hear. All the blood had drained from her face.

"Thank you, Reginald," Walerand said. "I must ask you to leave us now." When the lawyer had withdrawn and closed the door, he asked Ingrid, "What have you to say about this?"

Her answer was inaudible. He had to ask her to repeat it.

"It is true."

"Ingrid, what are you doing?" Jack cried.

"It is true. I have killed him."

"But you didn't make that image!" he shouted. She shrugged as if this detail were of no importance.

"It is my duty to warn you that an act of sorcery which causes a death is punishable by death," Walerand heard himself recite mechanically.

She acknowledged this with a slight nod. The color had gone from her lips, as if she were already a corpse. "But you will not excommunicate me?" she asked anxiously.

"No. Not if you make a full confession."

"Do you want me to write it?" she offered.

Jack was out of his chair now. "This is insane! Don't let her do this! She doesn't realize—"

"Please say no more," Ingrid admonished him. "This has nothing to do with you." Then she asked Walerand, "Can you let him go? None of this was his fault."

Her brow was smooth as still water. He knew it would be cool to the touch. Beneath the turbulence of fear and doubt and confusion, the transitory screams and tears, had lain this cool. Purer than fire it was. You could not save her soul at the stake. No more than the moon would she burn.

"Ingrid, this is monstrous!" her lover cried.

"Nay," she said softly. "I am the monster."

Jack rubbed his face with both hands and groaned.

"Can you excuse him now?" she appealed to Walerand.

"Aye, you'd better get rid of me," he taunted. "Because you can't do this with me watching, can you? You couldn't put on the hair shirt again, and you can't do this."

She looked at him for a long moment. The dispassion in her gaze must have cut him to the quick, for the man was fighting for her life as if he loved it more than she did.

The diamonds of light on the floor had changed shape, foreshortened as the sun climbed toward noon. For an instant it seemed to Walerand that it was the floor that had shifted, and he wondered how he could be expected to judge anything on this moving earth.

Ingrid turned from Jack and pulled her chair closer to the table. Wycliffe set the parchment, ink and pen before her. Though she seemed quite composed—unnaturally composed—when she took up the quill her hand shook so violently that she had trouble guiding it to the inkwell. All at once Jack lunged forward and seized her wrist.

"Look. Look!" the troubadour demanded. "What is this trembling? It is your life, Ingrid." He slid one captured fingertip over his lower lip, stroked the whole helpless hand over his beard. "It is your life."

"Nay," she said, in a voice that must have chilled him. "It is only my fear. My flesh is cowardly."

He dropped the hand as if the life had already gone from it and it fell, limp, to her lap.

"All these months I risked dying in a state of mortal sin, yet I did not tremble," she said. "So what can trembling mean?" Still, she concealed the telltale hand in the folds of her skirt.

"Look at me in the eye, then, and tell me you made that image. Tell me that and I will trouble you no further."

"The wish behind it was mine. I wished him dead."

"You are not looking at me."

"I—"

He grabbed her shoulders, twisting her around and half lifting her from the chair. "Say it to my face."

"You're hurting me," she said mildly. Walerand might have rescued her but did not. His sympathies had deserted Ingrid and gone over to Jack, who was wrong, certainly, but alive with a pulse you could hear halfway across the room. Momentarily forgetting his authority, the judge had become a spectator intent on the outcome.

Ingrid struggled a little, and when she could not get free her expression suddenly changed. She smiled—a smile he could only describe as witchy. "You hate Isobel now, don't you?"

Jack was startled by that smile into releasing her and she sank back into the chair. "Aye," he said.

"I wanted you to hate her. And I was glad when she saw us, even more glad than when Malverthorpe saw us."

"That doesn't make you a witch."

She ignored this. "You believed I was good, that's why you can't understand. You thought I was an innocent you were seducing. But you are the real innocent, Jack. You think our Lady is going to smuggle you into heaven—and I daresay she will. It cannot be that way for me.

"Do you know what I did when you left Greyleigh?" she continued. "There were all these letters from sick people, people whose lives I might have saved. I burned them. As I recall, I was laughing. Tell me now that I am not a witch."

Before he could reply she grabbed his long sleeve. "Your leg, Jack. I could have healed it on the spot—"

"Nay, that isn't true."

"I made you suffer through six weeks of convalescence because I didn't want you to leave."

"Nay, that's not the way it happened."

She turned abruptly back to the table and took up the quill. "Let's do this quickly." Jack was left standing there, repeating. "That's not the way it happened." No one seemed to heed him.

"Wycliffe can write it if you prefer," Walerand offered, for her hand still trembled.

She shook her head and bore down hard to steady the pen. "I, Ingrid Fairfax—"

"No, I'm sorry," he interrupted. "This is for the public record. It must be Jane Basset."

"Yes. Of course." She took her hand away while Wycliffe substituted a fresh sheet of parchment. Then, almost as an afterthought, she turned back to Jack. She scooped up the wax figure and held it in her open palm. "This is mine, Jack."

Ten

The portress recognized him at once. This time she did not open the gate: She had learned from past experience. Part of her face peered out through the tiny grillwork window, her little nose quivering like a rabbit's. "What do you want?"

He took a step backward to show that he had reformed, swept off his cap and bowed. "Would you kindly tell Dame Agatha that Jacob Rudd is waiting outside and requests an interview?" Her face disappeared. He had heard no reply, and as he stood on shifting feet, idly rotating his cap with little taps of his fingers, he wondered whether she would return at all.

He did not know why he was doing this. Certainly not for love of Ingrid, for there was no warmth in his heart when he thought of her. She had looked at him with soulless eyes, chilly and gray as a winter sea. "This has nothing to do with you," she had said. At great risk to himself he had tried to save her and then she'd given up without a fight, saying "This has nothing to do with you," as if she lived in a moral universe he was too simple to enter.

With Agatha's help she might still be saved—against her own wishes—but he had no desire to see her again. As soon as this business was cleared up he was going away. Maybe to France. He'd been making the circuit of England for so long now that he couldn't even think of it as travel. It was just the monotonous exercise of a penned animal— round and round. The pen was large. It had been years before he noticed the fences. But now that he'd seen them, he could never forget they existed, could never recover that tang of freedom he had first tasted on the road.

"Don't wait till it's too late to settle down and have a family," Chevalier had advised him. "I've fathered a dozen in my time," he boasted. "A dozen that I know of. But they all go by other men's names. I daresay it's the same with you, lad, and you couldn't care less now. When you're my age though, you'll wish you had a home." Jack had said what was expected of him: "Enough of this sentimental hypocrisy, Chevalier. Admit it—you had the best part of fathering. Leave it to lesser men to wipe the brats' snotty little noses and shitty little bottoms." How the old man had guffawed at that—completely cheered up he was. Hell.

Roland Chevalier—né Ralph Wigan—was the most famous troubadour in England, Jack's idol till they finally met this winter at court. The first time Jack laid eyes on him, all he could think was, Who is that absurd fellow? He'd been fooled by the timeless virility of Chevalier's lyrics into expecting a young man. Instead, here was this old fart in a skimpy red tunic—an unfortunate choice of color, for his great, vermillion-clad stomach and scrawny legs brought to mind a giant red-breasted robin. He'd combed long strands of hair from a low side part over the crown of his head in an attempt to conceal his baldness. Involuntarily Jack's hand had flown to his own head, exploring it for the first signs of thinning, and he'd glanced down to make sure he could see his own belt. Never, he thought: I shall never look like that. I'll wear a long robe when I'm old, and dark colors. I'll have some dignity. But how would he know when it was time? Wouldn't he think, I've another year or two, maybe even three? Maybe he was deceiving himself even now. He checked his stomach again, just to make sure.

They had become friendly, Chevalier paternal, Jack playing the son. On poetry the older man's advice was brilliant—no one could touch him as a poet. But on the subject of women—Christ, was he tedious! It was like listening to an old soldier recounting past campaigns. Neither soldiers nor troubadours age with any grace, he thought. Their glory is in their youth, and once it's past all they can do is dwell on it.

Wincing, Jack rotated his shoulders and rubbed the back of his neck, trying to work out the knot that the night in handcuffs had tied at the top of his spine. It was late in the afternoon now, and he was worn out from the sleepless night, the hearing and the breakneck ride to Greyleigh. He needed a bath and a nap.

Chevalier took a nap every afternoon. He took defeat lying down, snoring in his own stale breath while the best of the day went on without him.

He had fallen for one of the queen's ladies-in-waiting, Julia Bradegare. A real charmer—Jack wanted to court her himself, but he kept his distance in deference to the older man. Though, God knows, Chevalier never stood a chance with her. Julia's special claim to beauty was her forehead—a high round brow, demarcated by a delicate widow's peak. On Ash Wednesday she, like everyone else, had gone about besmudged. *Dust thou art and to dust thou shalt return.* That grimy reminder of mortality on Julia's lovely forehead inspired the most haunting ballad Chevalier had ever composed. Jack would have given his soul to have written it. But the fair Julia was unimpressed. He saw that she could hardly suppress her laughter. The whole thing put him in a rotten mood, and he'd quietly left the hall and gone up to the ramparts for a private sulk. Julia followed him there.

"Is something wrong?" she asked. "You went off so abruptly."

"You shouldn't have laughed at Chevalier," he said, scowling.

"He didn't see, did he?" she asked, with real concern. "He's such a sweet old man. I wouldn't want to hurt his feelings."

Let me die a violent death, Jack thought. Any death will do. Just don't let me live to be called a sweet old man.

"Still," she went on. "It's rather silly to write a whole poem about a part of a person."

"Nonsense. It was a great poem. You should be flattered. I wish I'd written it myself."

She lowered her head and looked up at him through her lashes, shyly daring. "I do, too. Wish you'd written it."

She desired him. Cruel nature still unfairly favored him. This only made Jack angrier. "Because I'm not old?" he challenged. "In twenty years I shall be."

"Well, in twenty years no one will be writing poems about my 'alabaster forehead,'" she retorted. "And anyway, why should I be flattered? My forehead has nothing to do with *me*."

He had seized her skull in both his hands and pressed his open lips to her brow with such vehemence that she gasped. Later he discovered that his lips were black with her ashes.

Jack sought out a pebble on the ground and gave it a vicious kick. Where was that damned portress? If they thought they could get rid of him by ignoring him . . . hell, he'd ring the bloody bell all afternoon if he had to. He was reaching for the cord when the gate opened. "Dame Agatha will see you now," the nun said, as if it surprised her. As he followed her up the path, he heard the familiar creak of the well and caught a whiff of that detested fishy smell. The memory brought a distinct ache to his leg. "Lean on me, you are not heavy," she had said in a voice like milk, and he'd felt her fingers at his waist, warm through the layers of wet clothing. They had been right to call it holy, that touch. Such comfort could bring a soul to grace. Oh, Ingrid . . .

The cloister had been menacing that swollen night, the corridors dark, damp and wind slammed, the stone saints wrathful. Now a sunny breeze blew in through the green tangle of the courtyard, and the statues were harmless in their niches. Their heads were large in proportion to their bodies so that they looked rather like children. Saint Lucy was holding up a small plate on which rested two eyeballs—presumably her own, which had been gouged out by the Romans. She might have been serving boiled eggs. Saint Sebastian's pointing finger drew one's attention to the arrows poked in his breast—as if such a detail could be overlooked. His expression was probably meant to be serene resignation, but the sculptor was not first-rate. Sebastian looked peevish, and perhaps a little bored. Was it any wonder that Ingrid, who had grown up with these images of painless martyrdom, was herself so eager to die?

Agatha received him in her own room. She was standing by the window, her shape cast in a long shadow across the tiled floor. The shadow overtook him first as she approached, and its length made him notice how, by contrast, she was small. Her short stature must have vexed her: she must have hated looking up to him literally when metaphorically she looked down on him. The top of her head seemed to strain upward as if to gain an inch or two by sheer force of will, and the taut aggressiveness of her stance reminded him of certain small dogs.

"They have found her," he stated without preamble. "In Oxford. She's been sentenced to death for sorcery."

Her black-lined nostrils flared, her mouth tensed, but she did not exclaim. She sat down at her desk, indicating that he should sit on the other side. When she placed her folded hands on the desk top, between two neat weighted stacks of parchment, the knuckles showed white. "Tell me."

It took some ten minutes to relate the whole story and during that time she did not once interrupt, nor did she move. When he finished she asked, "Will she be allowed the sacraments?"

This query seemed to him so much beside the point that he almost snapped, "I don't know." But then he remembered that Ingrid had asked the same thing of Walerand. "Aye," he said. "Walerand said he'd send her a priest."

"And she requested this?"

"Aye."

The abbess leaned back in her chair. She exhaled slowly, obviously much relieved.

"She is to *die,* madam," Jack was compelled to remind her.

"But she will die in a state of grace."

He felt a drop of sweat rolling down his back. Dame Agatha was saying, "All this time I have been afraid that she would die in mortal sin. But now she is reconciled. God has been merciful." He could not believe what he heard. He thought she must be dwelling on this triviality because the shock of the whole was too much to absorb at once, just as a person who has lost all in a fire will at first bewail some small, easily replaced item—a button or a spoon.

"This is *Ingrid* we are talking about! The Ingrid you raised since she was a little girl. At this moment she is chained to the wall of a dungeon, trying to scare off the rats. Tuesday morning, while you're in the chapel chanting, men will be leading her to the gallows, there to be strangled."

Her eyebrows had gone up and she was looking at him as if he were behaving strangely and distastefully and she was too polite to bring this to his attention.

"Death will come fast," he continued. "But before it comes, she will hear her own neck snap. And however resigned she is to dying, she will not be able to help gasping for one last breath."

This is unbearable, he thought, and he wanted to stop. But Agatha's impassive face moved him to fury. He chose each word as if it were a nail and drove it home with a sharp whack of his voice. "Have you ever been to an execution, madam? There are people who never miss one. Believe it or not, there are people who are aroused by such a thing, men whose cocks will swell as they watch her die."

"Stop this," she whispered.

He sprang to his feet and, with his hands braced on the desk, leaned over so that his face was inches from hers. "They won't cut her down right away. Her body will swing back and forth, limp as a sack of rags. Her head will loll to one side. Flies will gather in her open mouth, and birds will feast on her open eyes."

She pushed her chair back to escape him. "For pity's sake . . . "

"Aye, madam, it is for pity's sake that I say these things. Uncaring hands will cut her down. Uncaring hands will fling this child you raised into a shallow grave. Dirt will be shoveled over her, and the name on the grave will not even be her own."

"But it will be a Christian grave." He rolled his eyes, incredulous, but she went on. "You think that is nothing, but it is everything. I did not raise a child, I raised a soul. I would kill the child myself if I had to, to save that soul."

His arm, shaking with the urge to strike her, flew across the desk, sweeping everything to the floor. "You bitch! You heartless bitch!" Unable to bear the sight of her, he strode to the window and looked out, pressing his hot face to the stone frame. He saw a flock of sheep in the pasture beyond the convent wall and wondered how they could breathe in their heavy coats in this thick August air.

"Anyway," she said with a surprising mildness, letting the insult pass as the utterance of a madman. "What do you suppose I could do about it?"

"You could persuade Walerand to reverse himself. Or you could persuade the bishop to overrule him."

"You overestimate my influence. Even if I believed she should be acquitted, I doubt I could get it done."

"But surely you do believe it!" he said, aghast once more.

"It is not for me to judge."

"But she is innocent. You know that."

"I know no such thing. She has confessed, after all."

"She was pressured to do so."

"Pressured how? Was she tortured? Threatened?"

Jack shrugged. "For all I know."

"No. She was not. I know Walerand."

Do sheep suffer? he wondered as he watched their passive procession across the meadow. Or are they too stupid to suffer? Broken horses and domesticated dogs one could still imagine having come from the wild, but it was impossible to imagine sheep in the wild. Shepherds had invented them. They were born to be victims.

"Perhaps Ingrid confessed to sorcery because her real crime cannot be confessed," Agatha was saying.

"Her real crime? Ingrid's only crime is that she is not a saint. Admit it—you all want her dead before your fraud can be discovered. She's got to die to cover your mistake."

"Master Rudd, she confessed," the abbess said sharply. "You may deplore the Church's decision, but Ingrid has embraced it. Do not interfere."

Say no more. This has nothing to do with you. 'Twas the sin itself she wanted and you she took on to get it . . . Far off there was a sorrowful bleat and it grew as other sheep joined in the outcry. Louder and louder it grew, piercing and tremulous, every sheep on earth bleating to heaven, and he knew to his horror he was weeping. He saw Anne—she was weeping, her fatherless baby weeping against her breast. *Oh, Lamb of God* . . . He saw Elaine, wiping her cheeks with her childish hand, and Isobel on the gallery—oh yes, something tragic about Isobel—and Ingrid, dry-eyed and dead being shepherded to the gallows. *Agnus Dei* . . . Ingrid, dry-eyed and dead, who'd wept when he tongued her sores, who'd wept when he tongued her sex, now dry-eyed and dead, and he didn't exist for her, he'd never existed for her. Let him go, she said. This is not his fault, this has nothing to do with him. Tears poured from his eyes and he sobbed, great gulping sobs.

Agatha must be appalled. Agatha, dry-eyed and dead. Oh, how had he ever sung in this world? Small, pathetic little man, dwarfed by the sky, bellowing so importantly, braying his silly songs against the crushing heavens. The angels must look down and laugh to see him, vainglorious little man with his "morality of beauty" and his swagger and his lips all black with ashes. *Miserere* . . .

He shuddered and wiped his face on his sleeve. He couldn't look at the abbess. The books and papers from her desk were jumbled on the floor and spilled ink bled over the tiles. Seeing the mess, he felt ashamed. Who did he think he was? He crouched and started to gather the loose papers together, but he had no idea how to restore them to their original order. His fingers were fumbling and inept. He thought of his name—Brigand des Cœurs—and felt like snickering. Who did he think he was?

"Did she lie with you every night?" Agatha asked suddenly.

He looked up, startled, realizing what it had cost her to ask him that. "Nay," he assured her. "Only the last."

"But you did not force her." It was not a question.

"With a girl that lonely . . . " He was going to say, "Only a very clumsy man would have needed force," but the boastful sound of it disgusted him. He hadn't forced her. Nay, he'd been a bloody pharisee, holding his blameless hands aloft while Ingrid shouldered her damnation. Ingrid, fumbling with the hooks of her gown—*Why must you make this so hard for me?* Because you must choose, he'd thought. You must choose me over God. Oh, who did he think he was?

"She was lonely and naive," he said. "I took advantage."

"You knew who she was," Agatha said, her voice bitter. "I suppose you thought it a fine feather in your cap, knowing who she was."

Jack sighed. "I thought I knew who she was. You thought you knew. Ingrid has made fools of us both." He was still crouched beside her desk, and he stayed there, on one knee as befitted a suppliant. "Madam, I entreat you—write to Walerand. Ask him to release her into your custody."

"So that you can carry her off?" she demanded with a cynical smile.

"Nay. I won't see her again."

"You say that now. But who's to prevent—"

He interrupted. "I will be in a monastery."

His statement startled him as much as it startled Agatha: He seemed to have spoken the words without ever thinking them. And once they were out, he felt a rush of elation, as if taking up a dare that had only been issued in jest. You think I won't? Watch me.

He stood up, his arms folded, one hip thrown out—a rakish, gambler's stance. "That would please you, wouldn't it? The famous libertine shorn and repentant in a monastery. Admit it, madam, you've coveted my soul from the moment you set eyes on me. Now it's yours for the taking. All it will cost you is a letter."

"I am not answerable for your soul," she said.

"Aye, but you are. If you won't lift a hand to save Ingrid, I'll know there's no mercy to be found in this Church. I'll go to the devil then, and go gladly. It's in your hands, madam."

"I've told you already my letter won't help. Walerand is bound by the law. If Ingrid has confessed to this crime, he cannot reprieve her. Even if he wants to, he can't."

"Ask him to question her again. Perhaps when she has had time to think she will retract the confession."

"And if she doesn't?"

"You will have fulfilled your share of the bargain. And I shall fulfill mine." The elation was gone now and he felt his resolution, cold and cutting and costly as a diamond. Whatever the outcome, he would stake all. He dared heaven to laugh at him now.

But Agatha doubted him. She took up her pen, tracing her jawline reflectively with the idle end of it. "You would be willing to leave tonight?"

"I will leave as soon as I know what has happened to Ingrid."

"No. You must leave for the abbey the moment the letter is dispatched. Those are my terms."

"My mind will never be free of it then," he protested.

"Nor should it be. You have done a wicked thing, Master Rudd. I mean for it to haunt you the rest of your days."

He shook his head. "That is too hard."

"Then no letter." She set down the pen.

Jack was defeated. He ran the fingers of both hands through his hair and groaned. "There should be a special hell for you, Agatha."

"Accept my terms and you can look down laughing from heaven."

Heaven, he thought. What did he care for heaven?

Ingrid's face was sunburned. In the vestry this morning her nose had been peeling. It would still be peeling when she mounted the gallows. And that dear detail would win her no mercy: They would hang her anyway.

Scowling, he pulled a clean sheet of parchment from the heap on Dame Agatha's desk and set it before her. "Tonight then," he said. "You have my word."

Eleven

Matthew stared bleakly at the ceiling, wide awake. Gillian and Bartholomew breathed softly in the bed beside him. Jocelyn and Celia, in the next room, had long ago cried themselves to sleep.

That afternoon he'd gone with the hangman to inspect the gallows, and then to the Crossroads, where he downed four pints in brooding silence. At supper he'd yelled at the children. When Gillian laid a soothing hand on his, he'd yelled at her too. He'd smashed the milk jug and stormed out—to the Chequer this time.

She had forgiven him when he staggered in drunk, well after curfew. "I know this is hard for you. You always liked Jane. To conduct her to her execution—oh Matty, I know it must be terrible."

"It's my job," he said curtly, rummaging in the pantry for something more to drink. All he could find was half a jug of forgotten claret, long gone sour. He drank it anyway.

What Gillian couldn't know, what she must never know, was

that he was one of Jane's victims. All of his will was braced against her spell. He could feel it right now, pulling at him from half a mile away. He would have no peace until she was dead.

When he first heard the charge against her, it came less as a shock than as a terrible confirmation. He thought of her in Pratt's barbershop with her wild hair and her weird detachment, slitting open the vein in her arm. No wonder it had not hurt! No wonder he had been compelled to follow her, compelled later to stare at her just as Malverthorpe was compelled to stare. When Jane looked at him, the skin of the earth peeled back to reveal a hot, swarming chaos—this, he knew now, was bewitchment.

He had argued against it, saying to himself as he had said to Gillian, She is too nice. For she was a kind, clean, industrious girl. But what did that mean? People thought *him* nice—upright, reliable, the most solid of citizens. Jane knew better. Jane had seen his demons, and they answered to her. We know what the others do not, her eyes had always said to him. We are alike, you and I.

There were certain fantasies, things he'd heard of, things no man would ask of his Christian wife. He'd always tried to leave Gillian out of them, substituting a faceless abstraction of a woman. But since he'd met Jane, it was her face he saw, her long supple body.

Her height was marvelous to him, for nothing in Matthew's world was built to his scale. He was forever ducking, pulling in his arms to keep from knocking things over, shortening his stride so that others could keep pace, lowering his booming voice. He was afraid of killing things by accident. And Gillian was so delicate, it was like making love to a quail. It must be suffocating for her to lie beneath him, his vast shoulders blocking out the moon and stars. But Jane was tall, and there was something resilient about her spine. She looked as if she could withstand him. He imagined thrusting against her with the full power of his body, nothing held back.

He felt the power now, wakeful and unruly in his thick arms and legs, in his sex. Just once in his life, he'd like to unleash it. Just once, he'd like to let go. Brought to words, it might not seem a perverted wish. But Matthew never put it into such words. His desire skulked in some sewer world where the sun of language never shone. It kept company with demons.

A good man restrained himself. If you loved your wife, you learned restraint. He remembered his wedding night—God, what an oaf he'd been! They had grown up together, he and Gillian: She was like a little sister. He'd been deluded by this into thinking that the door of her virginity would be left ajar for him, had not foreseen that he would have to break it down. When she lay on their nuptial bed, wearing a new shift and that inquisitive look of hers, her closed thighs had seemed an insurmountable problem. As her husband, he might command her to open them. But she was *Gillian*, no mere wife. And he could not part them himself. To do so would be to flaunt his physical advantage over her, to rub it in that he was big and she was small. (Her indignant four-year-old fists pattering against his five-year-old ribs had first educated him about this.) He ended up muttering a request in her ear, but clear, plain English eluded him. She didn't hear or didn't understand and had to ask him what he'd said. To repeat it was out of the question, so he'd pushed her knees apart after all, rushing to get past his embarrassment, trying not to let himself know that this was Gillian. "Matty, don't!" she'd complained, as if he were yanking her braids, but he rushed on in some lost hope that speed would keep her from seeing him. He glimpsed her helpless, indignant face—so like that streaky four-year-old's—just glimpsed it, then plowed on, loosing her blood and his seed in a single stroke.

To say that his pleasure had come at the expense of her pain is a mere sketch made by the intellect. His teeth had broken the skin of the original apple: Every nerve of him knew sin.

He lay awake that night making rules for himself. He would have her only once a month. Twenty-nine abstainings to one indulgence. He would keep a count of them—not counting the temptations, for there were sometimes twenty-nine of those in a single day, but numbering the sunrises after chaste nights.

The first month was very difficult. His bride, who was used to sharing a room with her sisters, tormented him with her careless immodesty. When she went to the window at dawn, he could see the shadow of her body through her shift. When she pulled on her stockings, her thighs leered at him. She didn't understand it was for her own protection that he scolded her about these lapses. She took offense. In bed it was worse: The heat of her body pressed against his felt like a prod from Satan's pitchfork. The only way to withstand it was to turn his back.

In those first weeks, they became estranged from one another—Matthew restless and uncommunicative, Gillian sulky. By the time the thirtieth day arrived, the day when, according to his own rules, he could have her, Gillian suspected she was pregnant. By the fortieth day she was sure of it. With as much relief as dismay, he realized the matter was out of his hands, for to have a woman in pregnancy was unlawful. He stopped counting. As Gillian's belly grew, so did the ease between them. In fact, they seemed to get along best when she was carrying a child. It settled things.

Her first labor began on a Sunday night and did not end till Tuesday morning. Later she swore she did not mean the terrible things she had shrieked at him—the curses, the hate, the blame. She said she did not even remember any of it. But he carried the memory in his flesh. When he walked in a crowd he would reflect that every person in it had come into being through a woman's anguish. It seemed incredible to him that the earth was populated at all.

Oh, would morning never come? Jane was pulling on his blood as the moon drags the sea. His sex ached, and his will was giving way—what was the will of an ordinary man against the wiles of Satan?

He looked at Gillian, wanting to fall on her as if he were a drowning man and her body the shore. He could carry Bartholomew back to his own bed, wake her . . . No. These demons had no place in the bed he shared with his wife.

With a moan he got up and went to the window. Still dark. Somewhere, he knew, there was a wax doll with his initials, black smoke rising as its groin was held to the flame.

Twelve

Once, when she was walking out to Port Meadow, Ingrid encountered an assembly of cows. They were listening thoughtfully to a sermon preached by an emanciated youth in dusty friar's garb. His call to repentance seemed to puzzle them, but they were too polite to leave.

"Why are you preaching to the cows?" she asked, when he came to a natural pause in his discourse.

"Cows are easier than birds," he replied.

Thinking this a joke, she had laughed and immediately was sorry, since her laughing seemed to hurt his feelings. His tonsure had not been groomed for a long time, for there was a round patch of short hairs standing on end, while all around it drooped long, greasy spears.

"Will you bless me?" she asked, to make amends for having laughed.

His smile was sweet and sinless, though lacking in several important teeth. "What is your name, my child?"

"Ingrid," she replied, forgetting her new identity.

"I am Brother Francis."

She knelt, and he placed his hands on her head, his fingers curving to embrace it. "Thy sins are forgiven thee, Sister Ingrid. Go in peace."

It felt like a true absolution and only the strong odor of urine emanating from his robe prevented her from burying her face there.

About a month later, in the Crossroads, she overheard Matthew telling Henry about a poor demented youth he had arrested. Evidently the fellow believed he was Saint Francis. At the time of the arrest he was walking up St. Ebbe's nude, having given his robe to a beggar.

This beggar was soon found, but he was no longer in possession of the robe. The thing was so jumpy with lice, he said, that he had thrown it in Trill Mill Stream. "Why did you ask for it, then?" Matthew had demanded. "Nay sir, I never asked for it, nor for anything else. The young friar was so skinny, see, I felt sorry for him, and that's why I stopped him—to offer him a bit of some bread I'd got. But he wouldn't have it, and he wouldn't let me go till I took his robe."

She met him again in the spring. Brother Francis was huddled in a niche in the town wall, crying. Bits of grass and twigs were woven into his tangled hair. A white bird dropping adorned his shoulder. She crouched beside him and asked what the trouble was. "I was sitting here so that the birds could build a nest on my head," he told her. "At first they didn't trust me, but I sat very still for two days and two nights and finally one started. It took another two days, I think. She would come and go, but I never moved. Then she laid her eggs. It was so wonderful—the heat from my head was warming them. But . . ." he sobbed. "I . . . I fell asleep and, and my head dropped and the nest fell off and the eggs are bro-broken."

Poor Brother Francis—he would squander the whole of his love on a beggar or a bird, and the small miracle of a sparrow egg was all he ever asked of heaven. This was worth crying about. The death of someone who had been given great miracles, who had thrown away her gift to grasp at—at what? She couldn't even remember now—this was not worthy of sympathy. For her own fate, she would not shed a tear.

Walerand had come to see her. He said Dame Agatha had written to intercede for her and because of this he was offering one last chance to retract her confession. He said that if she were pleading guilty when in fact she was innocent, she was committing the sin of suicide and would be damned for it. What a pang of remorse it had given her to see him looking so grave and concerned! The pockets of weariness under his eyes spoke of troubled sleep. Finally she could think of nothing to do but to clasp his hand between hers and say, "Be at peace. You are doing God's will." Pronouncements about God's will were a habit left over from the old days. Realizing that such a statement could carry no weight coming from a felon, she added, "I am indeed guilty."

At the door of her cell he turned back to ask her bluntly, "Did you make that image?"

"I have already admitted it," she said.

"No. You haven't. Not in so many words."

She had not wished to lie, but she saw that for his peace of mind she must, and that her lie was more true than the literal facts. For she knew that she alone was responsible for Malverthorpe's death. As her compassion once healed, so her hatred had killed. She might have been the instrument of his redemption. God had given her this opportunity even after her great sin. And she had cast it aside, refusing to be so used, refusing to see the man as anything but ridiculous and burdensome. So Malverthorpe had died, embittered, betrayed, despairing of God's grace. She could only hope that by giving her own life she might win his salvation. Isobel, like Judas, had been nothing but God's unwitting pawn.

She said, "Yes, I made it." Walerand, as he left, looked less relieved than she had hoped.

He had given her his own psalter and she chanted her way through it twice a day, the cadences familiar and comforting. Apart from that there was nothing to do, and, hardworking as she had always been, she found this idleness trying. She would have paced, if only to tire herself and earn the consolation of sleep, but the chain around her ankle made this impossible.

Poor Matthew had looked so apologetic as he clamped the shackle on. She felt ashamed to have let him down, Matthew who had always been so kind to her, who trusted in her innate goodness as he trusted in everybody's. She imagined how he would feel, escorting her to the gallows, and she kept trying to think of some little joke she could make, so he would feel better. She prayed—for his sake, for Walerand's and for the hangman's—that she would be brave. As for Jack, she prayed ardently that he would not be present.

On the last evening the jailer told her she could have anything she wanted for supper. She thought this odd: If food was meant to sustain life, any meal at all was quite pointless. Despite her refusal, he brought her a cup of wine and some beautiful apricots. To her surprise, she was able to consume both with genuine pleasure, filling her mouth with this last taste of life's sweetness, the juice sticky and warm on her lips. She left some fruit on the pits and tossed them into the darkness beyond her little lamp, to be finished by the mice. Then she set herself once again to prayer. Only now was she learning to pray properly—simply and humbly. What she used to call prayer—all that emoting on the chapel floor—now seemed to her the equivalent of Jack's singing: overblown, conceited, a sexual display, a dazzling nothing. God had been right to remain silent. Now she would not even presume to ask for an answer. If he should forgive her someday, after long years of exile and purging fire, this would be enough. This would be infinitely more than she deserved.

Though she was wide awake, the rattling of the key startled her. She had not expected it to be so soon. She jumped to her feet, flustered with trivial anxieties. She was not yet dressed. She had taken off her gown to keep it clean and had on nothing but her shift. She had meant to comb her hair and wash before Matthew came for her. And she had meant to think of a joke.

She was not afraid, no, she wasn't afraid, but she seemed to be floating in the viscous atmosphere of nausea. What if she threw up? She grabbed her dress and tried to put it on, but couldn't figure out where it opened, what was the top and what was the bottom of it, and her fingers were vibrating in a way that made them useless. They reminded her of something . . .

Jack. They reminded her of Jack, holding them to his beard saying, "It is your life, Ingrid." Matthew's heavy rapid tread coming down the stairs and the jumpy light from his torch were rushing her heartbeat. Something had got hold of her windpipe and was squeezing it.

"I'm sorry. I'm not quite ready." Her voice sounded breathless and off-key. He must think she meant she was not ready to die. "I'm having trouble with my dress," she explained. "It's—can you help me?" She turned one quivering hand palm up, to show him that it was only this minor problem.

He plunged the torch into the nearest sconce and in two strides he was standing over her. Something was wrong with the way he looked, but before she could tell what it was he snatched the gown and threw it aside. He mumbled some words she did not understand but knew to be obscene. At first she thought this must be part of the

263

procedure for executing criminals: They were dungeon words and seemed to go with killing. But then it occurred to her that he had misinterpreted her request. "I'm sorry. I didn't mean—"

He said it again. Still she did not comprehend. Some kind of demand it was, made up of crude words, ugly words, words that reminded her of mud and gravel. The oddness of such an utterance coming from wholesome Matthew Sturges tickled her overwrought nerves. She giggled.

His huge hand crashed across her face, knocking her to the ground. She shouldn't be laughing like this. It was unseemly. No wonder he was angry. And she shouldn't have lost her balance. He might think she had fallen to reproach him, to exaggerate the force of the blow. Blood from her split lip was crawling down her chin. She took a swipe at it with the back of her hand. It made her feel slatternly to be sprawled on the floor in her shift with her hair in her eyes and her lip bleeding. If only she could stop laughing!

He cursed and raised his arm again. She slid backward very fast, as far as the chain would allow. "No, please, please don't hurt me. I'll be good."

Ancient words, more ancient than the Psalms. Long before the age of reason there had been this taut attention, this fear pounding against the walls of her veins. Don't hurt me: I'll be good.

He was standing astride her, moaning. Then she saw what was wrong: His clothing gaped around his exposed sex, which stood alone against gravity, undefended and pink. She feared for him, wondering what could have brought him to this awful vulnerability. Somehow she was to blame. That was why he was angry. "Witch," he groaned. "Whore." She loosened the drawstring of her shift in a gesture of submission.

"Matthew?"

He struck her again. A star of white light burst before her eyes. She heard cloth tearing, the dull clank of a chain. The sight of her bare thighs alarmed her. If only he would pause a moment—she just needed a moment to remember him from somewhere else and then he could go on, it would be all right. Somewhere else she had been fond of him, could be fond of him now if only he would stop a minute and show her the face she was fond of.

But this was not Matthew's face. It was an absolute face, a face beyond thought, a face as terrible as the Red Sea. It blazed with the unmotivated wrath of an Old Testament God, a God who would not be bound by covenants, a God you could not tame by being good.

He flipped her over and took her face down, grinding her against the stone floor. All his weight seemed to be between her shoulder blades: She could not breathe. She slapped the floor with her palms, trying to alert him, but he pounded on. The pressure of his sex was pushing her insides upward, turning them inside out as one turns a long sock by pushing on the toe. *"I am poured out like water, and all my bones are out of joint . . ."* She could not breathe—her lungs were ripping, a spinning darkness overtaking her eyes. *"My tongue cleaves to my jaws. I am utterly spent and crushed . . ."* The smell of earth. Cold stone and no color, no color for all eternity. This was death and she had made it.

She had made it, she alone. A mean death, wrought by cowardice and stupid, lifeless thoughts. God had never willed it. *"For thou hast no delight in sacrifice . . ."* Oh, she knew now, she knew so much! But too late. *"Oh Lord, open thou my lips and my mouth shall show forth thy praise. For thou hast no delight in sacrifice . . ."*

Suddenly her scalp was bright with pain. Her head jerked back and the floor stopped crushing her chest. Matthew had her by the hair: the pain sparkled like joy. A great roar came from him. Splitting earth, lava, the just and the unjust perishing together. *"Deep calls to deep at the thunder of thy cataracts . . ."* Ingrid gulped air till she was drunk on it.

The dungeon still echoed with his cry as Matthew subsided and heaved himself off of her. His breathing was troubled and raw. She wanted to turn to him, but she could not work out how to move— her body felt mashed like a seed in a mortar.

She closed her eyes to savor her breathing, so nearly lost. Soon to be lost again. As it deepened and slowed, she floated back to a sunny meadow, the clean starchy smell of Sister Pipp's apron, the pillowy cloud of her bosom. "Aren't you a daft one, with all your frettin'! God loves you, child, same as he loves all his creatures. You mustn't forget it." A warm comfort spread over her, settling with a sigh like a down coverlet after it's shaken. She looked at her hands, still tensed around wads of dirty straw, and she felt affection for them, as someone would who loved her. Poor, dear hands—what had they ever done that they should have to die? What cruelty in her had begotten this notion—that a daft and fretful child ought to be killed on a summer morning? She recoiled from the ugliness of it—the harsh rope, the hangman's hood, the misguided solemnity of the gallows. God had no delight in it.

This cannot be, she thought. I must think what to do. She stirred, and the aching of her body reasserted itself. Her face hurt, and her ribs when she drew breath. Something was biting into her abdomen, bruising her hipbone. Gingerly she pried her belly from the floor, reached under and grasped the offending object.

It was a ring of keys.

Oh, merciful God! Oh lawless, mischievous, marvelous God "*Open thou my lips and I shall show forth thy praise.*"

She knew it must be done in one swift motion, with n hesitation. Roll over while feeling for the smallest key—it would b the smallest key. Bend to the ankle, release it, clamp the open shackl on Matthew's leg. Throw the keys out of reach before he could wre them from her. The difference between living and dying was only thi And she accomplished it.

Matthew was lying on his back, weeping soundlessly. Tea poured from his open eyes, rolled with ceremonial majesty down h temples to dampen his hair. Ingrid was awed. He was like the ear itself, mirroring the sorrow of heaven. Who would have dared consc him?

She stood up, her legs wobbling like a foal's. Any minute he would recover and start to yell for the jailer. Her blood, hot and urgent with the will to live, so stressed the fabric of her veins that she would not have been surprised to hear them rip. She cast aside her ruined shift and pulled on her gown, then looked again.

He was sitting up now, his back resting against the column he was chained to, one knee raised, monumentally still and no more likely than a mountain to shout out. There had always been something abject in Matthew's expression—she realized it only now because it was gone. In its place was a quiet gravity, a sorrowful intelligence that Ingrid found very handsome. God had used him strangely. She hoped he would know peace.

266

"All of the gates are locked for the night, but there is a gap in the wall at the top of the Turl," he said slowly. Maybe it was just because her own pulse was racing that his speech seemed so slow. He spoke as if a century was nothing to him. "Stay off Cornmarket and the High. If anyone sees you, don't wait for them to raise hue and cry—run into a church. As long as you are within the sanctuary you cannot be removed by force. If you hold out long enough they'll commute your sentence." He paused, and she had the feeling there was more he wanted to say, but he only added, "I'll count to a hundred before I call for the jailer."

She needed no further encouragement to start running.

She felt a creature's joy of lung and limb as she sped through the crabbed lanes and alleyways, spanning open sewers, ducking laundry lines, clearing obstacles without ever breaking her stride. Her feet fell silently, her blood thundered. She felt maned and defiant. She felt like God's true intention.

Walerand had just finished dressing and was about to make his way to the gallows when the sexton of St. Michael's Church came to summon him. The man had spotted Ingrid from the tower and raised the alarm. At first she had gone on running, for a crumbling of the wall, well known to curfew violators, was within sight. But when she heard the clamor rising on Horsemonger Street, she changed her mind and turned back to the church. The keeper of the north gate had nearly tackled her on the threshold—as he told it, she slipped right through his hands. She was sitting now in the sanctuary and would not move from it. Mass had been delayed. The civil authorities were helpless.

A little demon in Walerand's mind whispered, "Good girl!" but he put on a grim face. "How did she escape?" he asked, as they hurried up the High.

"No one knows, milord. Must have been a struggle though—she's all banged up."

He was glad to hear it, for bruises argued that, however improbably, Ingrid had escaped by natural means. He was not at all eager to delve again into the question of who—God or Satan?—assisted her in the marvelous.

By the time they reached the church, Thomas Burgh, the Hustings magistrate, was there as well. The two judges held a hasty conference. "Banish her and be done with it," was Burgh's solution, for he knew her only as Jane Basset, and it was clear that he'd never considered her much of a threat to the king's peace. For Walerand, matters were not so simple. If Ingrid was no longer marching meekly to her death, the Church had lost control of her. She was unpredictable and there was no guessing what harm she could do. He went in to the church.

She was sitting cross legged on the floor, her back against the altar, and when he came toward her she greeted him as if he were her guest. There was the queerest feeling of friendship and ease between them. He wanted to fight it and could not.

"What happened?" he asked her.

"I want to live." She said it trustingly, confidingly, fully expecting him to encourage her in this endeavor. It pained him that he could not.

"Ingrid, you confessed. No one forced you. I—"

"I know," she interrupted, putting a soft pacifying hand on his arm. "But here we are."

There it was again: that slippage, that sensation of the ground shifting beneath him, as if the earth were a horse trying to throw him off its back. He clung to the silver crucifix hanging from his neck as if it were the reins.

"I shall be obliged to excommunicate you," he said stiffly.

"I know."

"You will lose your soul."

"That is in God's hands."

The left side of her face was swollen and discolored, the eye flinching a bit from the light. Even so, she gazed at him with angelic serenity. The earth had thrown him off after all. He was drifting weightless in blue space. Somewhere a man was speaking urgently, trying to reason with an angel. "Don't be foolish," he argued. "You will be anathema. No one can aid you without themselves being excommunicated. No one can feed you or shelter you or speak to you. You will be a double exile—banished by the state, sent forth barefoot to fend for yourself. You will not survive and when you die you will be damned for all eternity."

" 'Now we see through a glass darkly, but then face to face,' " she replied.

There was nothing more to be said. He went out and reported his failure to Burgh. The proclamation of banishment was drawn up at once. It directed Jane Basset to proceed by the shortest route to the nearest seaport and to leave England by the first available ship. In the event that she was unable to obtain immediate passage, she must show good faith by wading waist-deep into the sea each day of the delay, which was not to exceed two months. If she was seen in the realm at any time after this period of grace, she would be summarily executed.

A slight hitch developed in the banishment ceremony, which called for the outlaw to be stripped of exterior garments. With much embarrassment Ingrid confided that she was not wearing a shift. A messenger was dispatched to the Crossroads to fetch one. Then six women had to stand in a circle around her, forming a sort of dressing room with their skirts so that she could take off her dress, put on the shift, and put the dress back on, only to have it yanked off again— this time with due solemnity—as the banishment proclamation was read aloud.

The bystanders who had gathered outside the church were asked to file inside to witness her excommunication. The candles would be snuffed out, the missals and crosses laid on the floor and from the pulpit Walerand would damn her soul. Already the sexton had begun to toll the funeral bell as Ingrid set off, barefoot and alone, for the Abingdon Road, the sun white on the sighing sail of her underdress. "Arrayed in splendor," Walerand thought, "like the lilies of the field." Well the bells should toll, for common sense said she would not survive. Yet Walerand, whose heart was as breezy and light as that gauzy linen, knew that she would live, and live in a state of grace. "No one knows what faith we have, Ingrid and I," he mused.

Which was a queer thing to be thinking as one mounted the pulpit to pronounce anathema. "It is true. She is a witch. She has bewitched me. I am mad," he said to himself as an experiment. But even as he said it, he knew that he was saner than he dared know, so sane he could carry the world's madness in his pocket and walk up High Street whistling.

PART FOUR

One

After the jailer released him from his ignominious captivity, Matthew could not bring himself to go home. He left town by the south gate and spent the day wandering in Bagley Wood. His skin had that itch one gets from staying up all night and there was a rawness to his senses. The humid, sun-streaked forest had a sadness and a softness like a face on the verge of tears, but when he sighed and relaxed into a tender melancholy its beauty would turn on him, stabbing his heart with its piercing green and the cries of outraged birds. He remembered Jane's face as he had seen it through the tangle of her hair, half squashed against the dungeon floor—so very like his children's faces on their safe pillows, the mouth moist, open, abandoned, just like his sleeping children's. At the moment of climax he had seen her face and known that she was not a witch but a suffering creature and oh, such grief had rushed out with his seed! Such grief and a knowledge, a knowledge he imagined belonged only to the moment of death. He heard again the heavy dull clank of the chain skidding across the floor, the low clanking complaint it made every time he slammed into her. I am like those boys who tear the wings off flies, he thought. I am like those boys who torture cats.

He hiked to Cowley, intending to have a meal and perhaps to drink there, where no one knew him. But as soon as he sat down in the pub he realized he was not carrying any money. Hunger drove him home.

By then it was night. He let himself in quietly. Gillian was sitting by the open window of the kitchen in her shift. Her hair—which she kept neatly braided even in childbirth—was loose and somehow deranged. She knows, he thought.

From his great height he took in the little room, his precious lost kingdom. The shelves with which he had buttressed the walls were losing their battle against chaos: they, the tabletop, the floor, all a-jumble with toys and tools, dishes, mismatched socks and the little collections children make of shards and scraps and unremarkable stones.

Gillian spoke first. "Are you safe, then?" she asked carefully.

"Aye, of course."

She fidgeted with the ends of her hair, not looking at him. "They're saying she bewitched you, that that's how she escaped."

"Nay. I am not bewitched."

"Then how . . . ?" Her voice was soft with fear.

"I raped her, Gill."

Her lips formed an "oh," but no sound came out. Why had he never noticed before how fine-faceted her face was, like a jewel? He stood there hypnotized, dazzled by the way a different expression seemed to glint from each facet: disbelief, hurt, dread—of course—but also curiosity and a sort of wonder. What was on his own face, he could not guess. His lungs, which he had always imagined ending with his ribs, now seemed to reach all the way to his groin. He felt strangely light.

At last she stood and said in a brittle voice, "It's late. I'm going to bed."

Shrieks and teeth and nails could not have punished him as her silence did. "Gill," he entreated, "please say something."

"What should I say, Matthew? You know what you did."

"But tell me what you feel. Say you hate me if you do."

She stood there uncertainly and he saw that she was trembling. "I know . . ." she began. "I know you have never . . ." Her tongue rejected the next word and she averted her face.

"Never what?"

"Never—" Again she faltered.

"Say it, Gill. For heaven's sake."

He head jerked in defiance. "Never *desired* me. I know my body—my breasts—if they're worn out it's from suckling your children. But even years ago, when they were good—and they *were* good once—you never looked. God, Matthew, why did you marry me if you find me so ugly? You thought it was enough to love my soul? We were such friends and you thought that was enough and now you find that it isn't and you are bound to me and it's too late, neither of us can get out of it. Oh, don't think—don't think I have no sympathy for a man who can't desire his wife. I do. I know you love me, that's the awful thing. You have always been so . . . good." The good dangled at the end of her outburst like an unresolved chord, muted and disquieting.

He gaped at her, utterly dumbfounded. What on earth was she talking about? Her response struck him as immoral, and he almost felt betrayed, as if it were she who had been hoarding a dark secret. Here he had confessed to a heinous crime and there was not a word of condemnation, not a trace of horror or sympathy for his victim. Just this strange talk about her breasts. Her breasts? He could see the tops of them now through the loose opening of her shift, the lovely heavy flesh falling droopily from a frame too delicate to support them. The fragile neck and shoulders, the exquisite collarbone, and then that plunge into plush shadows, calling to his open hand. What could he possibly say?

She was turning toward the stair, deeply embarrassed and anxious to escape before her tears started to flow.

"Gillian, come here."

She shook her head and moved faster. He couldn't think what to say: There were no tools in his plain, blunt vocabulary tempered for this job. He lunged and caught her on the first step. "No!" she cried furiously as he peeled the shift from her shoulders. "Don't patronize me, Matthew!"

"Be quiet," he muttered. "Just be quiet." He knelt and pressed his face between her breasts, covering and caressing them with her long, fragrant hair.

"Oh, God, stop it," she pleaded, weeping now, miserable with need and injured pride. But he held her fast. Like a knight holding the grail in blood-stained hands, he felt sullied, and sanctified. He gathered her shuddering body into his arms and carried her easily up the narrow stairs: He was strong and graceful. When he laid her on the bed, she rolled herself into a ball and hid her face in the pillows, sobbing. He lit the lamp.

"No light," she whimpered. "Please, no light."

Gently he rolled her to her back so he could look at her as he scrambled out of his clothes. "Gillian. Gillian, my dearest . . ." It was no good. Such talk was foolish on his lips.

"Gill, look at me."

She opened her eyes. Her expression was soft, lost. She chewed her fingers in a worried way. "Matthew?"

"Aye, my darling, what is it?"

"You've never called me that—'my darling.'"

"What is it, my darling?"

"Your face . . . It scares me."

He held hers still between his hands as he entered her. "Don't look away."

Two

Eventually, she knew, there would be hard, practical problems to solve. Her feet would start to bleed, and she would have to find some shoes. At night her shift would not be warm enough, and when it rained the thin fabric would cling, tempting men to mischief. She would have to come up with the fare for the Channel crossing, though as an excommunicate she could neither work nor beg.

But to find oneself alive on a day when one had expected to be dead tends to put a person in a good mood. Ingrid felt herself to be walking barefoot on a island paradise. Things plump, sweet and nourishing drooped from the trees and hedges. Grace chirped and buzzed all around her; grace was warm on her shoulders and hair. Funeral bells had tolled for her soul and her soul had been alive to hear them. The leaves fluttered like a million green flags, proclaiming "This is the kingdom of heaven."

Midafternoon she stopped to rest in the mottled shade of an oak and fell asleep. She was awakened by the sound of an animal breathing nearby. When she opened her eyes, she saw a horse—a war horse, higher and broader than any she had ever seen—and astride it a tall, broad, well-dressed man. His eyes matched the sky so exactly that she fancied his head was transparent, that she was seeing the sky through two little windows. His hair was gold and silver mixed, and his ruddy face was handsome with health and good cheer. She blinked at him.

"Are you all right?" he asked.

"Yes. Quite." She sat up groggily and pushed the hair back from her face, collecting herself.

"I saw you lying there—"

"I was just taking a nap."

His gaze made her aware that her shift had ridden up a bit, and she tugged it back down over her calves.

"What happened to you?"

She did not understand.

"Your face," he said, touching the side of his own.

Her fingers explored her cheek, rediscovering the tenderness and swelling. "Does it look bad?" she asked.

"Rather."

Now fully awake, she stood up defensively, trying to smooth her wrinkled shift and finger-comb her hair.

"Were you robbed?" he asked.

"No. I'm an outlaw."

This seemed to amuse him. "I see. What'd you do?"

"I killed a man." Earlier she had decided that this was the best way to present herself to men encountered on the road, that it might turn the odds a little in her favor. But this one did not seem very much impressed.

"What—just now?"

"No. Before."

The horse was dancing in place, as if impatient to be off. He reined it in a bit, soothing its mane with his gloved palm. "Can I offer you a ride somewhere?"

"No. Thank you, though."

He frowned. "If you're afraid—"

"Oh, no," she assured him hastily. "I know you mean to help. Thank you. Really." With a polite nod, she turned back toward the road. The heavy gloved hand fell on her shoulder. She felt the power in it but felt also its kindness.

"Let me at least give you something to wear. My wife—"

"Have care for your soul," she warned. "I am anathema."

He chuckled. "I'll take my chances."

"I'm serious."

"Never said you weren't. I was excommunicated myself once. You learn to take these things with a grain of salt." He slipped his foot out of the stirrup so that she could use it to mount. "Come on. Up you go," he encouraged.

"*Surely goodness and mercy shall follow me all the days of my life.*" She climbed up behind her rescuer, clasping his thick waist.

"So," he said over his shoulder, once they were on their way. "Outlawed and excommunicated and not even dry behind the ears. That's something. You must be famous."

"I don't know."

"What's your name?"

"Jane Basset."

He reflected a moment. "Nay. Never heard of you. Sorry. I'm Roger Fleming, by the way."

"*Roger Fleming?*"

"Aye."

"*I've* heard of *you!*"

"Oh?"

"At Greyleigh. They talk about you all the time."

He laughed from deep in his belly. "Is that a fact? What do they say?"

"You broke all the windows."

"Not all of them," he amended modestly. "What were you doing at Greyleigh? You were a student, I suppose."

"Yes."

"So of course you know Agatha, the abbess. We were married once. But I don't suppose she ever talks about that."

"No."

They rode on in silence. Ingrid, who had never been on horseback before, was relishing the luxury of this effortless locomotion, letting her sore feet dangle and enjoying the view from this high vantage. It delighted her to think that her benefactor was the dreaded, the legendary Roger Fleming.

"Agatha was very intelligent, too smart for me, really," he said after a while. "Not so pretty in the face, but Lord, what a sweet little body she had! She was—what would you call it? Fiery. She'd give me a good chase and then let me catch her. I lost my nerve at the chapel door, though. Too bad."

Ingrid tried to connect this account with the Dame Agatha she had known, and her mind reeled. There was no taking it in.

"Got a new wife now," Fleming continued. "Well, not that new. Fifteen years it's been. Church doesn't recognize it of course, but everyone else does. Two boys, too. You'll meet them."

And so it was that Ingrid, who first expected to be dead and later expected to shiver alone through an unsheltered night, found herself couched in the noisy splendor of Fleming Manor, dining on fowl and sleeping on a featherbed. Roger's wife, Madeleine, had a lush, blowsy kind of beauty and a disposition like well-turned, sun-warmed earth. In the sons, lads of twelve and fourteen, Ingrid could see the side of their father which Agatha must have despised: loud, competitive, naively friendly. About twenty people shared the family's supper table. She never figured out who they all were, and no one seemed curious to know who she was. The random, sloppy generosity of the household reminded her of an unweeded garden. If they didn't dig up your roots it was because you looked all right to them.

Madeleine gave her the most wonderful dress—a dark green velvet with slashed sleeves lined in apricot silk. "It's much too fine for me," she protested, but Madeleine pointed out that the hem was stained and the elbows worn and that Roger had never much liked her in it. All evening she would catch herself caressing the marvelous fabric, admiring the gleam and shadows of the folds falling over her lap. It was the sort of dress she had wished for as a child.

Roger told her she could stay as long as she liked under his protection, but Ingrid thought it best to leave the country as ordered. He insisted on escorting her to the coast. It would be pleasant to visit the seaside with the boys, he said. An easy two days on horseback, but four or five on foot, and dangerous at that. Madeleine backed him up. "You'll be getting these fellows out of my hair for a few days," she said. So they set off the next morning, Ingrid riding with Adam, the younger and lighter son. Both horses and riders were in high spirits. Ingrid, well-rested and clad in the same mossy green that clothed the summer day, felt blessed and happy.

Late in the afternoon, when they were only a few miles from Southampton, they were assaulted by a terrible odor. It was so bad that they had to cover their noses and mouths with their sleeves and as they rode on it got stronger. When they came out of a blind of trees into the open sky, they discovered its source: At least a hundred sheep lay dead in a field. The odor of decay was so strong and disgusting that even the birds stayed away. "Murrain," Roger muttered, and spurred his horse. The stench lingered in their nostrils till they reached the coast.

Ingrid had never seen the sea before. She had always imagined it to be like a pond only much bigger. The salt breeze, the gulls, the sand, the enormous sky, the slow heavy churn and the blue of it—none of this had entered into her picture. She was astonished.

"You're lucky," Adam sighed, squinting wistfully at the great creaking ships which bucked a little in their moorings, their masts aspiring toward the sun.

They tied up their horses and bought some ale at a dockside concession. Roger left them there while he went to arrange her passage. When he returned, a quarter of an hour later, he was frowning. "Our timing was good," he announced. "*The Phillippa Regina* sails tonight. The captain's agreed to take you aboard." Ingrid wondered how much he had paid for this favor, but by now she did not even try to protest Fleming's generosity. Still, his face was clouded and she wondered what was worrying him.

"Listen, Jane," he cautioned, putting a hand on her shoulder. "If you hadn't told me you were excommunicated I would never have known it. Keep that in mind when you get to France. The French aren't like us, you see. Whatever the priests tell 'em they take right to heart."

She agreed to heed this advice, but his face did not brighten. "Roger, what's wrong?"

"Remember the sheep we saw? Well, it's not just sheep. There's a plague in town. We've got to ride on to Portchester. I'm afraid we've got to go right away or we won't make it by nightfall." He took a coin from his purse and closed her hand around it. "That's for your supper."

And then they were gone. Ingrid felt suddenly very alone. As she walked where the sea met the sand she thought, This is the very edge of England. And these were her last hours there. She wondered what that meant, whether it meant anything at all, exploring this notion of "exile" as if it were a wound, touching it tentatively to see how much it hurt. Her convent education had not instilled patriotism. At Greyleigh she had seldom even spoken English, and England was nothing to her but an abstraction. Yet she was uneasy, feeling that she should be doing something to make these final hours count. Tonight as she watched the sails unfurl, the anchor being pulled up, her thoughts would be going out with the tide. But later, when the sun came up, she would look backward and see the shore, the shape and outline of this island, England. Then she would know what it meant. Too late. Reaching out, she would grasp nothing but the sea air. Every loss in her life had been like that, every grief postdated, every love a fog-shrouded coast, receding. Her father had slipped away without a good-bye. Greyleigh, her childhood home, she had abandoned without a backward glance. Nick, Nigel and Tom would bound into the Crossroads when they returned from the long vacation, expecting to celebrate their reunion with a night of drinking, and they'd be greeted instead with the strange and sobering tale of her excommunication. There would never be a chance to explain. There would never be a chance to tell Jack she lived after all, and that she loved him. She loved him.

The sea stole her footprints, quietly, indifferently. Lapped by that rhythmic indifference, her sorrow would not hold its shape. God is vast, she thought. God is far. God is blue.

The God of Greyleigh had been sallow, jealous, preoccupied, always hovering over one's shoulder, poring over one's accounts. She had rejected that God as false, and longed for the God who longed for man. And then, in the dungeon, he had come to her ablaze, a fire

281

so voracious even good and evil were consumed. But here God was at rest, a God neither for her nor against her, a God who had nothing to say. Only that truth which withstood the blaze could sail on this vast blue God. This was the method of grace. How many times she had prayed for it. But a prayer of thanksgiving was only a footprint. Thanks had no meaning if God had no will. She was dumb.

In the cool arc of space there was mercy, inscrutable mercy. But in the ever-receding horizon there was terror. Once before she had known this terror: a longing without object, a weightless anchor that would not take hold. God does not hide from us, she thought. It is we who shield our eyes. The truth is too gorgeous to bear. And I will forget, she thought. I will forget.

She took one last breath of her vision, then turned and walked toward Southampton.

From the outskirts, all appeared well. Southampton was a white-washed, clean-swept, seaside town, tidier than Oxford. At first, the only sign that anything was amiss was the incessant tolling of funeral bells. Then she began to notice clumps of loose earth where one didn't expect them, odd bits of uprooted grass from churchyards disheveled by grave digging. Gradually she noticed, too, that every fourth or fifth shop was closed and that many of the more prosperous homes were firmly shuttered and looked abandoned. In the poorer quarters the humid air carried sickroom smells down from second-story windows, brought private cries, whimpers, even deathbed confessions indecently close, so that one breathed an atmosphere of soiled mattresses, tear-stained pillows and limp wrinkled sheets. In this unnatural intimacy the eyes of passersby were politely unseeing, like the eyes of strangers in a public bathhouse.

Ingrid walked aimlessly for a long time as the shadows length-ened and the breeze grew chillier. Her ship sailed at nightfall—she had better hurry back. Having lost her bearings, she went into a tavern to ask the way. "'Tisn't far," the publican told her. "Turn right and take the first road you come to down the hill. You'll make it with time to spare."

She thanked him and started to leave, but turned back at the door to ask, "Do you know of a good doctor?"

He sniffed. "Not a lot to choose from. Most of 'em have gone. Now Parmenter, he's a good man, but—"

"Where does he live?"

"Top o' the hill. Big stone house with the ivy growing up the front. But he won't have time for you, miss."

"Why not?"

"You're not sick enough. Not if you're still on your feet."

"Same road, then?"

"Aye, same road."

She paused on the road and looked down toward the waterfront. In the dusky light she could see workmen loading cargo onto the *Phillippa Regina*. For a moment she hesitated. Then she turned and walked briskly up the hill.

There was no response to her initial rap on the front door. She knocked harder. Still no answer. But gold light showed through the casement window, which was ajar. She stood below it and called out, "Hello?" A stout matron appeared at the opening. Her head was swathed in a white coif that came down low on her forehead, accentuating the roundness of her face. Her expression was unfriendly. "He can't come out any more tonight," she said crossly. "He just got in, and he's not going out any more."

"Pardon me, ma'am. I only wanted to speak with him. Just briefly."

The woman shook her head. "Not tonight. No more tonight. Tell me the address, and he'll go there in the morning."

"I'm afraid I have no address," Ingrid admitted. "I only wanted—"

"For pity's sake, can't you all leave him alone? He's seen thirty patients this one day. Can't you let him rest?"

Accepting defeat, Ingrid backed up a step. "Yes, of course," she apologized. "I'm sorry to have disturbed you. Do you think if I come round early in the morning, before he goes out—"

But the doctor himself came up behind his wife, laying a pacifying hand on her shoulder. "No, I'll come now. Just wait a moment while I change my clothes."

Ingrid was heartened by his kind manner. "I only came to speak with you," she explained. "But I can come back tomorrow."

"Tomorrow will be very much like today. Come in. We can talk now." He left the window and a moment later the door opened. "Come in," he repeated, standing aside.

The interior glowed with tasteful affluence—polished furniture, Turkish rugs, a tiled floor, everything scrubbed and fresh. There was no fire in the hearth—the night was warm—but a dozen candles illuminated the parlor. Parmenter, a tall man stooped with fatigue, was in his shirt, the sleeves rolled up to the elbows, the front open, revealing graying chest hair. "I stink, I'm afraid. Come into the dispensary and talk to me while I wash up."

She followed him into the next room, to his wife's displeasure. Once there she felt right at home, for the dispensary's strong, herbal smell brought back memories of Greyleigh infirmary. She admired the array of neatly labeled jars and the gleaming instruments—expensive, clearly the best. Strips of gauze were stewing in a greenish infusion. She sniffed, trying to identify its components, wondering what it was for. With a gesture he invited her to take the room's only chair while he poured vinegar from a jug into a steaming washbasin.

"Never thought I would like the smell of vinegar," he remarked. "Now when I'm out there it's all I can think of—coming home and washing in vinegar." He scrubbed his hands and forearms, splashed the pungent wash water over his face and finally dunked his whole head. When he raised it, he paused a moment, eyes closed, exhaling slowly. He reached for a towel and patted himself dry in the same unhurried way. "I'm trying to place you," he said. "Have we met?"

"No. I'm from out of town."

"You picked a bad time to visit us." He pulled his shirt over his head and slipped into the clean robe that had been hung on a peg, awaiting him. Then he went back to toweling his hair. All his movements were sluggish, bespeaking great weariness.

"There is an epidemic here?"

He nodded.

"How long has it been?"

His arms dropped, too tired to work the towel any longer. He left it draped over his shoulders and lowered himself to the edge of the cot used for examining patients. "The first case here was at the beginning of August."

"And the disease is elsewhere?"

"It hit Melcombe Regis in July. On the Continent they've had it for some time. There is talk of half the population . . . We don't know."

"Half the population ill?"

"Dead."

Ingrid crossed herself. "What is it?"

"A new disease. Something I haven't seen before. It kills within a week. Five days, usually. It kills . . . invariably."

Parmenter's wife hovered in the doorway. "Your supper's getting cold. Shall I have Agnes reheat it now or—"

"I'm not hungry, Meg."

"You *are* hungry. You just haven't any appetite."

"Yes, well, the end result is the same. I don't want supper. Maybe—" He looked at Ingrid. "I didn't catch your name."

"Ingrid."

"Maybe Ingrid would like something. Have you had supper?"

"I have, yes," she fibbed.

"Let's have some wine, then," he suggested. "Can you bring it in here, lass?"

"You haven't eaten all day," Meg said stubbornly.

"I had breakfast. Remember? And a very good breakfast it was."

"Look at you. Your face is as gray as your hair. Your bones grind into me now when we—" She broke off, mindful of their guest. "I'll not have you anymore!" she concluded, folding her arms and making a fist of her face. Ingrid could see tears starting in her narrowed eyes.

" 'Alas my love you do me wrong . . .' " he sang lightly. It must have been some old joke between them, for a grudging smile softened her worried, stubborn face.

"Go to the devil."

"Soon enough. I want to get drunk, Meg. Bring us some wine, there's a good lass."

"This has been hard on her," he confided when his wife was out of earshot. "But tell me, what have you come to see me about?"

"I wondered if you needed an assistant."

"Good Lord, I need twenty assistants. Tyler and DeBacton, my esteemed former colleagues, have taken off on holiday. There's only Hastings and me left."

"How are you treating people?"

He sighed. "Ineffectively. Nothing helps."

"You bleed them?"

"Bleed them, leech them, purge them. It's all worse than useless. No one recovers."

"But still you go out."

He turned his long hands palm up, his fingers spread in a shrugging gesture. "I'm the doctor. When people are sick, they call the doctor."

His wife came in and set a pitcher and two goblets down on the table beside the washbasin. "Are you finished with this?" she asked, tapping it.

He nodded. "No wait. I forgot to soak the shirt."

Meg wadded the garment into a ball and plunged it into the vinegar and water solution. She poured the wine, serving her husband first. He gulped his portion down so fast that by the time Ingrid was served he was proffering his goblet for a second helping.

"Come sit by me, lass," he urged his wife, patting a spot beside him on the cot's thin mattress.

She shook her head. "I'm going to bed. And that's where you should be."

"In a bit. This young lady seems to know of an assistant for me."

Meg glanced at Ingrid. "That right? Well, praised be. He surely needs one."

"Actually," Ingrid said when she had gone, "the assistant I had in mind was myself."

Perhaps the past few weeks had robbed him of the capacity for surprise, or perhaps he was just too tired or too tactful to register it. In any case, the neutral way he asked "What can you do?" encouraged Ingrid to be candid.

"I was infirmarian in a convent," she told him. He did not react to this either, but she could feel him looking at her with interest, sizing her up as she went on to outline her training and experience. When she had finished, he began to quiz her.

"Tell me the seven types of fever."

"Ephemeral, putrid, hectic, tertian, quotidian, quartan and . . . what is the other?"

"Sinochus. In spring you draw blood from which side?"

"The right. In autumn the left."

He nodded, impressed. "If the cephalic vein swells?"

"Apply oil or roses and water, warm in the summer, cold in winter."

"Good. Where do you bleed for a sore throat?"

"The neck."

"And for a swelling in the groin?"

"The toe."

He got up and poured himself another glass of wine. "More?"

She shook her head.

"It's very contagious, you know."

She kept her face impassive.

"Right," he said, with weary irony. "You're not afraid of death. So let us talk about the smell."

"I know about the smell. It hits you as soon as you come into town."

"Wait till you're at a bedside. When I visit the latrines of the healthy, that is refreshment. That smells good to me now. Everything that comes out of these people—sweat, breath, piss—is fouler than the winds of hell. A young man can't bear to be near his bride if he is sound and she is sick. A mother can't bear the stench of her own baby." The words were heavy as quarried slabs to judge from his labor in heaving them from his mouth. "You hear of people being drawn together by disasters . . . communal sufferings . . . In the siege of Calais for instance . . ." His eyes clouded over so that, while he was looking in her direction, Ingrid was sure he no longer saw her. He had already forgotten what he meant to say about the siege of Calais. "You don't see much heroism here, nor even much charity. Today . . . I found two sick children alone in a tenement. The parents had fled."

"No! How could they abandon their own children?"

"You are outraged, then."

"Of course. Just as you are."

"Am I? Do you think so?" He grasped at it like a hope. "I'm trying to be."

He paused and took two long, deliberate drafts from his goblet, working at getting drunk as if it were a job, as if in talking he had been slacking off. "I will tell you the worst thing," he said to the dregs in his cup. "People die saying there is no God."

She wanted to comfort him, but confronted with the depth of his discouragement and fatigue she felt too young, too fresh. All she could do was get up and pour the last of the wine into his cup. He looked at her with far more gratitude than this small gesture warranted. "You'd have to dress as a man," he said.

She plucked ruefully at the loose bodice of her dress. "I shouldn't have any trouble passing."

"Well, your height will help. And the mask. You see that gauze soaking over there? You wear it over your nose and mouth to keep out the humors. Helps a bit with the smell, too. I suppose you'll have to cut your hair, though."

She sighed. "It was only just getting long."

"And it's such pretty hair," he commiserated. "Maybe we can think of a way to hide it instead." She could tell that he was puzzling over it, trying to think of a way, and she was touched that he could muster so much sympathy for her trivial complaint.

"It grows fast," she assured him.

Parmenter turned his attention back to his cup, draining it in a few fast swallows and plunking it down on the table. "There now," he concluded with satisfaction. "Thoroughly pickled and ready for bed. You can sleep here in the dispensary, if that's all right. I'll knock at dawn to see if you've come to your senses. There's a spare blanket in the cupboard." He got up heavily from the cot. "So . . ." he added with a vague, drunken wave. "God bless."

The blessing reminded her. "Doctor Parmenter—"

"My name's Hugh, by the way."

"Hugh. I've been excommunicated."

"I didn't hear you."

"I said—"

"I didn't hear you," he repeated sharply. "Good night, and God bless."

Three

To read God's signature in a coincidence is a habit of mind that dies hard. Ingrid could not help seeing his hand in the events that brought her to Southampton. She who could heal with her touch had been guided to this place of sickness. She had been given a second chance. No more would she stand aloof from her gift. What God wanted of her she would do without reservation.

They got an early start the next day. Though Parmenter's features still sagged with weariness that sleep could not erase, he spoke and moved with such vigor that she revised her earlier estimate of his age. Meg served them an enormous breakfast. Ingrid, who was accustomed to nothing but bread and cider in the morning, was a little daunted by it. Hugh ate as he had drunk the night before, without particular relish but with great determination. "Eat as much as you possibly can," he encouraged her, "because once we get started, we may not have time to stop. And you probably won't have much appetite."

Once outside they were dazzled by the beauty of the morning. The sun teased the horizon, the edges of leaves, the corners of a whitewashed house. It was sweet on the breast of the calm sea, flamboyant on the wings of swooping gulls.

"Oh, Hugh!" she cried, startled by the day's freshness.

"Yes," he smiled. "Thank God for the mornings."

That first day Hugh showed her what to look for in diagnosing the disease. The earliest symptom was a bubo in the armpit or groin, the size of an egg or a small apple and purplish black in color. This

289

swelling brought unremitting pain and if one touched it—even grazed it with the fingertips—the patient screamed in agony. More lumps followed, and later small black patches marred the skin. "Death's fingerprints," Hugh called them, for the patient inevitably expired within two days of their appearance. The urine of the afflicted was dark—nearly black—and thick as syrup. The mind was affected as well: sometimes running wild as a rabid dog, more often drained of all meaning and feeling, unable to remember love, unable to believe that there was ever such a thing as pleasure.

Parmenter carried spare masks in his bag and gave them out to priests, gravediggers, the carters who hauled away the dead—anyone whose work put him at particular risk. Having observed that the disease flourished in squalor, he was adamant about cleanliness. Uninvited, he would visit tenements, urging the residents to throw out the filthy rushes—sometimes decades old—that covered their floors, to air their bed linens and change the straw in their mattresses. He was a tactful man by nature, but he did not hesitate to be blunt with people whose bodies were hospitable to fleas.

Around midday they were accosted by a tearful woman who begged them to come at once. Her son, a blacksmith's apprentice, had taken sick. "The buboes—he woke up with them, under his arms. And fever. Oh, hurry!" And though speed could make no difference for the unfortunate smith, Hugh did pick up his pace for the mother's sake. At the bedside he introduced Ingrid as his assistant, then folded back the sheet, carefully lifting the young man's arms to check the swelling. Lumps were indeed discernible, but there was no discoloration. He stood back and invited Ingrid to have a look. She brushed the lump almost imperceptibly with one finger, and the patient did not cry out, did not even grimace. Gradually she increased the pressure, probing till he winced. "Is that sore?" she asked. "Yes, doctor, fearful sore." Hugh was still standing back, waiting to see what she would do. She put her hand to the youth's forehead: There was fever. "How is your throat?" she asked. "Fearful sore," he replied. She felt his neck just beneath the jaw. More lumps. She put her ear to his chest and instructed him to breathe deep while she listened for congestion.

"Catarrh," she concluded, looking to Parmenter for confirmation. He was beaming.

"It's not the plague," he told the mother. "It's a simple catarrh. Keep him in bed, and give him plenty to drink. Give him an infusion of elder flowers with plenty of honey and a bit of vinegar—have him gargle with it every two hours or so. I'll look in on him later in the week."

There was a lilt to his step as they clattered back down the stairs and out to the street. "Catarrh!" he repeated, shaking his head with a bemused smile. "Let's celebrate."

They went into the same pub where Ingrid had asked directions the night before. She was relieved to sit down and quench her thirst, for they had been working for seven hours without stop. As her eyes adjusted to the tavern's comforting darkness, she noticed a young man sitting isolated from the rest of the customers. A mask similar to her own hung loose around his neck, and he was staring into space with a glazed, dull expression. Parmenter called out to him across the room— "Hastings!" and he sprang to life. The two men embraced joyously. Then Hugh presented her. "This is my new assistant, Fairfax. Marty Hastings, our sole remaining colleague."

He acknowledged her with a friendly nod, but there was an amused lift to his brow. "Been brawling?"

Ingrid took a moment to realize that he was referring to her bruised face. Parmenter, with his characteristic delicacy, had never mentioned it, but he came to the rescue now. "You should see the other fellow!"

They ordered a round, the two men talking shop, catching each other up on who among their acquaintances had been taken ill, who had died and who had left town—all of this related with a sort of blithe fatalism.

"You know the widow Tanner? I was by there today," Hastings told them. "My nose led me there. The old man, her father-in-law, was lying in the shed in the biggest pile of shit you've ever seen. Been there for four days, at least. I say, 'Maude, what the hell . . . ,' and she says to me, 'Look, I've got five children and they've no one but me.' Won't go near the man. He only had a few hours left at most, but hell, a dog shouldn't die like that. So I get her to bring me water and towels and a clean blanket, and I haul him out and start cleaning him up. You know that black shit and that black piss they all have. It's caked all over him. And flies—Christ, it was a bloody fly festival! Anyway, I go behind the shed and have a good puke, then come back and get him more or less clean. I'm just wrapping him up in the blanket when he shits again." Hastings rolled his eyes. "So I throw away that blanket, wash away the new arrivals and yell to Maude to bring another blanket. We get him all wrapped up—she helps this time—and damn if he doesn't shit again. It became a sort of contest: Will the old man kick off before Maude runs out of blankets?"

"Well?"

"Aye. He died on the fourth blanket. And I'll have you know the man was *clean*. Don't tell me we doctors are useless!" He saluted them jauntily with his mug. "Cheers."

"You know, the one thing I can't stand about this disease," he went on, "is the way those that get it are never those that can afford to pay your fee. Sweet Jesus, I'm out fourteen hours a day, I go home with nary a shilling to show for it. If I didn't stink so by the time I get home the wife'd accuse me of spending the whole day in the pub. Of course, there's a bright side to everything. Annie thinks I'm going to keel over any day now, so she's making every night count." He winked. "It's Annie that'll be the death of me."

"Count your blessings, man," Hugh put in. "Meg doesn't like me now. Says I'm too skinny."

"How 'bout you lad?" Hastings asked Ingrid. "How do you fare with the ladies these days?"

She looked to Hugh for rescue, but none was forthcoming. He was hiding a smile. "Not so well," she muttered.

The young doctor leaned forward confidingly. "It's your whiskers, son. Ladies don't like 'em. Ought to visit a barber now and then." He gave her shoulder a playful punch, then called for another round.

A week later he was dead.

On the thirtieth of September the funeral bells stopped tolling, at the mayor's order. People felt bad enough, he argued, without that infernal din. Two days later a field at the edge of town was hastily consecrated and turned into a mass grave. So many priests had succumbed to the plague that people were dying without the sacraments. The bishop decreed that in an emergency any Christian might hear a deathbed confession and grant absolution. This became one of the few useful services Ingrid and Parmenter were able to perform.

They went out every day, working separately but staying close, he on one side of the street, she on the other. Though Ingrid's disguise was not very convincing, no one ever questioned her. In Southampton there were only the sick, the dead and the walking dead. No one saw anyone elese. After a while she didn't even bother to pitch her voice low.

So far there had been no miracles. Often she felt the physical symptoms that had accompanied them in the past. She would become dizzy and queasy and she would vomit. She vomited once or twice a day—it had become almost routine—and she would think each time that she had managed to draw the sickness out of her patient and into herself. But after a few minutes her own strength returned, while the patient remained unchanged.

She tried to recall the state of mind that had preceded the healings in the past, to replicate it deliberately. The trouble was she had never been particularly conscious of herself at those times. Her hands would get hot—she remembered that. But otherwise it was rather ordinary. It would seem to her that she was doing something quite obvious—as obvious as picking up a baby when it cries. As obvious as kissing a skinned knee to make it better. She doubted herself before and after, but while she was touching someone there was no doubt.

Perhaps working a miracle took more compassion than she could muster now. The relentlessness of Southampton's misery was so heavy and dull that neither faith nor hope nor charity could penetrate it. There was a sameness after a while to the deathbed confessions, the grief of families, the first terrifying discovery of a bubo and the agony of the last hours. The bereaved felt it too, and hardly anyone wept anymore. Now when a person realized he was sick, he took quietly to his bed and died without fuss, knowing there was no drama in his personal demise. As she trudged through the streets, doing what she could, vomiting uneventfully and refilling her stomach with flavorless bread, Ingrid's heart was an inert lump.

Every night Hugh drank himself into oblivion, but in the

morning she would awake to the sound of bellowed love songs as he tried to woo his wife. He would shave, dress meticulously, bolt down his big breakfast, hug the resentful Meg so hard her feet left the floor, and set off down the road with his bag of hopeful supplies. He seemed as immune to despair as he was to the disease itself. Though Ingrid could not recall a single patient paying him, he never failed to present a bill at the end of his visit, as if this were all just business as usual. Once they heard an odd yelping sound coming from an alley. Discovering its source in a quick glance, he gripped her arm, trying to steer her past it. "Don't look," he muttered, with a grim angry set to his features. She could not help craning her neck. A couple was fucking in plain view, the woman's splayed white legs and the man's upturned buttocks a gruesome parody of the half-clad corpses one saw piled on carts and dumped in the street like household refuse. She imagined the parallel was not lost on the couple themselves. She did not know whether to be touched or exasperated that Hugh should still wish to protect her modesty after all they had seen together.

By mid-October hopelessness was the town's only comfort, and then even that was taken away, for two of the plague's victims inexplicably recovered. In both cases the buboes had burst, oozing black pus. The stink surpassed all previous stenches, but the patients lived for days afterward, gained strength and were seen walking about a week later. The resignation that had grown like a scab over the town's grief was torn off. The doctors were sent for with new urgency: They were expected once more to *do* something.

The sky was low and sulky, leaking a cold, unsatisfying drizzle. The open sewers were clogged for lack of a downpour and the street sweepers had died or given up so that one had to weave around the piles of human waste, garbage and offal and take care not to trip over the stiff elongated bodies of dead rats. Hugh went to call on the stricken pastor of Saint Mary Magdelene's and sent Ingrid to Will and Alice Taylor, who had already buried two of their children and were about to lose the third, a three-year-old girl. When she arrived, the child was sleeping in the arms of her mother, who sat cross-legged on the couple's bed, red eyed and listless, her back slumped against the wall. "It won't be long now," Taylor whispered. "The black spots came last night."

"May I have a look?"

"Can you not let her sleep?" Alice asked softly. "She was up crying all night."

"Aye," her father agreed. "She's out of pain for now and I'd sooner let her be."

"Please," Ingrid insisted. She sat down on the edge of the bed and Alice passed the small feverish body to her. The child stirred but did not wake. Lifting aside the blanket, Ingrid touched the little girl's chest on the pretext of inspecting the spots, praying all the while that the magic would come into her hands.

"We know there's nothing you can do," Alice said. "We don't blame you, doctor."

That tone of resignation: "nothing you can do." She hated it. She refused to believe it. God had healed through her hands: She must have faith.

"If the buboes break, she may recover. She *will* recover."

Will was skeptical. "I never heard of 'em breaking."

"I want to try lancing them." Both parents winced. "I know, I know. But it will give her a chance," she urged.

"Do you know this for certain?"

Ingrid hesitated. Doubt was her enemy. There must be no doubt. "Yes," she said, firmly. "Yes, I am certain."

Will crouched beside the bed and took his wife's hand. "What do you think, Alice?"

She closed her eyes, too tired even to shrug. "You decide it, Will."

"Aye, then," he said to Ingrid. "Do what you can."

On her orders, he cleared the dirty breakfast dishes from the table and moved it to the window for light. Ingrid set the child down on it. The movement woke her, and as soon as she saw the doctor she began to wail.

"It's the mask," her mother said. "It scares her."

Ingrid tugged the gauze down over her chin, revealing her face. Taylor gave her a close look but said nothing. The child was still crying as she unwound the blankets, crooning comforting nonsense and smoothing the damp hair away from the hot forehead with a tender, womanly touch. The child continued to look at her with distrust, her eyes glassy, and when Ingrid raised the girl's arm to examine the swelling she thrashed wildly. "No, no, no!" she screamed.

"I'll need you to hold her down." Taylor took his daughter's feet and Alice stationed herself at the baby's head. "No, change places," Ingrid told them, for she wanted the mother's view to be obscured. At her instruction, Will raised the child's arms and pinned the diminutive hands. "Papa's here," he soothed.

She fished the lancet and a wad of clean gauze from her bag. When she wrapped the cloth around the bubo, taking great care to apply no pressure, the child struggled, trying to twist free. "No Mama! No Mama!" she screamed. Taylor had gone pale, his mouth a tight thin line. Ingrid's teeth sank into her lower lip. The lancet trembled in her fingers, then fell to the table with a clank. She crossed herself and closed her eyes as the memory came back to her: the fearful eyes of the little girl, the cautery iron falling from her grasp. Crossing herself, then pressing the scorching metal into her palm. What if now she took up the lancet and plunged it into her own flesh? Nothing. She would bleed. The child would die. That was all. *"My God, my God, why hast thou forsaken . . ."*

In a rage of clarity she opened her eyes, raised the instrument and stabbed the black tumor. She heard the sharp indrawn breath of the mother and the piercing scream of the child. The bubo was supposed to spurt bloody pus—that was why she held the gauze around it—but nothing came out. Her lancet was lodged in something solid and tough. Still the child was shrieking. Ingrid broke into a cold sweat. She maneuvered the steel, searching for some part of the tumor that would yield, but it was a solid mass. Brown urine trickled over the child's thighs. Her ribs seemed to be straining to escape the confinement of her soft, black-smudged skin. She shuddered and was still.

Blindly, Ingrid hurled herself toward the window and heaved, her vomit splattering to the pavement two stories below. Her knees buckled, and she clung to the sill, retching and shivering for what seemed like a long time. When her trembling subsided, she spat twice and wiped her forehead with her sleeve. She thought: When I turn around, I will see the child and parents smiling, and we will fall on our knees in thanksgiving.

It was the last time she ever imagined such a thing. Stumbling to her feet, she turned to find the child lifeless, the handle of the lancet still protruding from her armpit. Will was consoling his wife. She could not meet his eyes. She yanked out the lancet and wiped it clean but did not put it back in her bag. She pulled the sheet up over the child's face and went out without a word.

Hugh found her on the beach, her back against a large rock, her knees drawn up, her gaze going far out to sea. Her hair was damp with the drizzle that fell from the low sky, her face wet with tears she did not notice she was crying. He dropped down next to her.

"You'll catch cold."

She gave a short laugh. "That's a good one."

He settled beside her, and they sat together for a long time without speaking. The gray water made a hushing sound. Gulls circled and cried in a worried way.

"Hugh."

He waited.

"I used to be able to heal with my touch. It's why I came to you."

He looked at her with interest. "Truly?"

"Yes. When I was younger they thought I was a saint."

"What happened?"

"Oh, I was so stupid. So stupid! All I wanted was to be like everyone else. I would always say it wasn't my doing, as if I were just an innocent bystander at all these blessed accidents."

"But you didn't really believe it."

His acuteness gave her a small unpleasant shock. "No, I suppose not."

"You came here thinking you could cure the plague."

"Yes. Oh God, Hugh, if only I could start over!" She was weeping harder now, keening like the gulls, her face turned up to the opaque sky, her nose and eyes running unchecked.

Hugh passed her a strip of gauze. "You shouldn't take it so personally, you know," he said.

"What do you mean?"

"No one is working miracles these days. How many patients

have we seen die with the relics of a favorite saint clutched to their chests? It seems the age of miracles is past."

"You think God has turned his back on us, then?"

Hugh threw the pebble he'd been fiddling with out toward the water. "I've never pretended to know what God was up to," he said, in a way that discouraged further discourse. "Look, we're getting soaked out here. Do you want to get back to work?"

"What's the use?"

"All right then—shall we spend the afternoon in the pub? We should get out of this rain in any event."

She sighed. "I think a pub would be even sadder."

"Yes," he agreed with a tired gentle smile. "That's how I see it too." He got up, shouldering his bag, and helped her to her feet. "Come, Fairfax," he encouraged, thumping her on the back. "Be a man."

Four

In his Rule, Saint Benedict cautions against being too eager to accept new brothers into the monastery. Obstacles are to be placed in a candidate's way, to "try the spirits and see if they be of God." The first obstacle is a long wait at the door.

Jack had never read the Rule. He did not know what to make of his reception at Abingdon. The sun was already going down as he rang the bell, having ridden from Greyleigh at great speed. The porter, a rotund and red-faced fellow, greeted him through a small hatch in the gate. "Oh! Jolly good!" he exclaimed, when Jack announced his intention to join them. "Would you be so kind as to wait? Stay right there, now. Don't budge from the spot."

The spot was a stone stoop under the arching gateway. Jack

stood there on shifting feet for the better part of an hour, toying with his cap as he had outside Greyleigh. He was bone tired—the previous night without sleep had caught up with him—and his neck and shoulders still ached. He was also very hungry. After a while he concluded that he must have been forgotten. He rang again.

"Ah, you! Yes! Lovely that you're still here," the porter said cheerily. "That your horse? It'll be needing water, I expect. Don't worry—we'll see to it right away." The hatch snapped shut.

Soon afterward, a young hooded monk came out and went straight for Damascus' bridle. "Look, I'm extremely tired," Jack said to him. "Could you tell that porter of yours to open up?" The monk put a finger to his lips, signifying that he was not allowed to speak. Before the troubadour could protest, his horse was led away.

Baffled, he sat down on the steps, wearily rubbing his face. Another hour passed before the hatch screeched open again. By now, night had fallen, and Jack was getting angry. "Warm enough?" the fat monk asked with a friendly smile.

"Now see here—" he began.

"I can send you out a blanket if you'd like."

"I don't want a bloody blanket. I want—"

"Oh. Jolly good. Sweet dreams then." The door closed with a click.

Jack grabbed the bell rope and pulled hard. No answer. He pulled again—kept ringing for a good ten minutes. At last the round face appeared, untroubled as ever. "I say, could you stop pulling on the bell? We're trying to sleep, you know."

"What have you done with my horse?"

"Why, he's in the stable. All tucked in for the night. You don't want him now, do you? A bit dark for traveling I should think."

This was true. He was stuck now till dawn. "Look," he said, struggling to keep his anger under control. "I've had a rotten day, and a rotten night before it. I would very much like to sleep. So if you could see your way clear to—"

"Oh, by all means sleep. Yes, absolutely. I'll see that you're not disturbed till late in the morning. Fact is, it's time I turned in myself. So then—nighty night."

The portal closed before Jack could say another word. Cursing, he settled himself as best he could on the hard step. He might have used his saddle bag for a pillow, but it was gone with his horse. Cursing some more, he took off his tunic and wadded it under his head.

He did sleep, finally: a thick, dreamless sleep from which he awoke at sunrise, stiff and aching. Recollection dawned bleakly on him. He was here, waiting to become a monk, and Ingrid was in prison, awaiting death. It did not seem fair that things should have become so consequential. Somehow the rules had been changed in the midst of a contest he'd been winning. He veered between indignation and remorse.

The letter would have reached Walerand by now. Perhaps he was talking to Ingrid at this very moment. She might yet recant. For the first time in many years, Jack began to pray. *Make her recant. Don't let her die.* Tears clotted behind his eyes and refused to fall.

After a while, he stood up and stretched, trying to work the kinks out of his muscles. He reeked. His stained and wrinkled shirt was the same one he'd put on to breakfast with Ingrid at the Cross-roads. That seemed a lifetime ago. Combing his matted curls as best he could with his fingers, he wandered off to piss. When he returned, there was a hunk of bread and a tall mug of cider on the step.

All day he waited in a state of tired resignation, punctuated with flashes of irritation. The porter reappeared at three-hour intervals, always with the same infuriating good cheer. At noon, he passed more food through the little door, and at mid-afternoon a pint of beer. At sunset, the gate was opened. The porter stood there with his arms folded over his great stomach, beaming. "The abbot will see you now, if you'd like."

"Are you sure? I wouldn't want to rush him."

The monk smiled amiably. "It *is* a bit soon, in fact. Five days is more the usual thing." He clapped a hand on Jack's back and led him through the gate.

The abbot was not what Jack expected. He was a tall skinny man, no older than Jack, and he moved with a loopy, almost comical grace, as if he had no joints. The Adam's apple was prominent in his long neck, his chinless face homely but for the eyes. The most beautiful eyes Jack had ever seen on man or woman: huge, pale, long-lashed and full of soul.

He introduced himself as Father Ambrose and settled weight-lessly on a chair across from Jack, his bony hands dangling over the arms, his habit forming a valley between his jutting knees. His attentive look conveyed a detached friendliness, but little curiosity. For once in his life, Jack didn't know what to say. A silence grew.

"Do you know what you are doing?" the abbot asked at last.

"Nay," Jack admitted.

This drew a smile. Father Ambrose smiled not only with his face but with his hands, twirling the palms out with a sort of musical gesture, the fingers spread. Then the palms turned down again and he said, with relaxed seriousness, "You will have plenty of time to find out. You begin as a lay brother, living as a monk but free to leave at any time. There is no shame at all in changing your mind."

"I won't."

"Ah." He nodded thoughtfully. "Why is that?"

Jack fidgeted with his cap, unable to answer.

"Would you like to make your confession at this time?"

He flashed a foolish grin. "There are enough sins to keep us at it all night. You'll find it very entertaining." Father Ambrose gazed steadily at him, and the grin faded. He began again. "It has been many years since my last confession. Even now I don't know if I feel repentant or just . . . sad. I have—" His thoughts ran in a vague, shushing current that slipped through the net of words. The ache had returned to his throat. He swallowed with difficulty. "I'm sorry. I can't do this right now."

The abbot did not insist. Jack was escorted to the washroom and then to a clean narrow bed in the guesthouse. In the morning he found that his clothes had been taken away and a monk's habit placed at the foot of the bed. He put it on.

After breakfast in the refectory, he was sent to a bare quiet room and given the Rule to read. He had learned reading late in life and could only do it slowly. By the time he struggled to the end of one of Saint Benedict's long sentences, he could no longer remember how it had begun. Hours passed. On the second page, a drop of moisture fell on the word "humility," the "hum" floating blearily on its surface. He touched his face in wonder. It was covered with tears. Quietly he closed the book and went to look for Father Ambrose.

The abbot heard his confession with remarkable dispassion. If he was shocked by what he heard, he gave no sign. To tell the whole story did little to relieve the burden of it, and Jack could not believe himself absolved by the formulaic forgiveness at the end. Still, Father Ambrose did him a great kindness. "You say the execution is to happen on Tuesday? Brother Timothy, the cellarer, has an errand in Oxford on Monday. If you like, I can ask him to make inquiries."

Sunday and Monday were long and miserable with suspense. Jack spent most of the time sequestered, trying to read the Rule. Late Monday evening, he was summoned to the abbot's room.

Father Ambrose leaned forward, his huge eyes soft with sympathy. "I'm sorry, Jacob."

His lips felt bloodless. "Tell me."

"Brother Timothy found the constable as he was . . . making things ready. If there was a stay of execution, he had heard nothing of it."

Jack felt like a prisoner hearing the pronouncement of his life sentence. A hundred years of sorrow, and another hundred, to be served consecutively. Time turned hostile. There was no appeal.

That night he lay awake, knowing that Ingrid, too, was awake. By now it would be real to her. She must be so scared! If only he could go to her, hold her. His muscles felt sore from fighting the bonds of circumstance that held him to the bed.

Morning was unwelcome, terrible. In the refectory he sat dazed, unable to chew his bread. The morbid description of hanging that he'd hurled at Dame Agatha rebounded now to hurt him. When the dishes were cleared and the monks rose with a scraping of benches to say the concluding prayer, Jack remained seated, his face buried in his hands. Father Ambrose came up behind him and placed a hand on his shoulder. He stayed there a long time. Jack was glad he kept silent, for no words could have consoled him. Yet the blessing conveyed by that hand flowed into his heart. And he was consoled.

Days turned to weeks, and the grief came in waves, receding for a time then crashing back on the crest of a nightmare or an unbidden memory. He did not fight it. In fact, he sometimes wanted to cling to it as the only thing that belonged to him. When it ebbed he found himself adrift, lost in the vast impersonal peace of the cloister.

The longer he stayed in the monastery, the less he knew who he was. All the accoutrements of Jackness had been taken away—his showy clothes, his lute, even his beard. His glib and colorful speech was hushed by the rule of silence. For a while it continued to chatter in his head, but gradually even that was subdued.

He had imagined that monastic life would be idle and boring, but in fact it was relentlessly active. Besides the seven daily offices, there was a great deal of hard physical labor, especially at harvest time, for the monks worked their own farm. When he wasn't in the fields, he was serving a shift in the kitchen, the brewery, the laundry or the latrines. The work brought a welcome exhaustion and good appetite. Happily, the food was better here than at Greyleigh.

The monks were allowed to converse only one hour a day, and Jack usually had to spend that hour in remedial study of Latin. Nevertheless, he came to know his brothers with an instinctive knowing that owed nothing to lanugage. By their gestures, their faces, the way they arose from bed or drank their beer, he knew the spirit of each man, and was content to be so known. There were no secrets.

In the silence was much kindness. When he struggled under the weight of a huge keg in the brewery, extra hands came under it without ostentation, letting him know that no plight went unobserved. He was deboning fish in the kitchen once, making an awful muddle of it. The cook touched him lightly on his back, inquired with his eyes whether he might take the knife, took it and showed him how to do the job better. He smiled when Jack got it right. There was an elegance in such moments too subtle to be articulated, a sweetness that fed his love of beauty and of love. He would never have imagined this.

For the first few weeks, he went about dazed, too empty of will to resist anything that was asked of him. He conformed readily. But as the first shock of grief and dislocation wore off, gusts of his old high spirits blew through him. He was moved to clown in the silence— pulling faces, enacting mimes—and given to outbursts of loud laughter. It was then that the discipline became a hardship. Father Ambrose seemed intent on effacing even those aspects of Jack's personality that were harmless or charming. He was forbidden to sing, not only at work but also in the chapel where everyone else was singing, because, explained the abbot, his voice was a source of pride. "The time will come when you forget you are a singer. When that time comes, you will entertain us on holidays, and we will be delighted."

Jack lost his temper then, and he was given a penance for it. He had to prostrate himself at the chapel door before and after each service. Another monk had been given this punishment during Jack's first week at the abbey, and Jack had recoiled at the idea of stepping over the poor fellow's prone body. It had seemed to him then that such a mortification could not be endured. But even this was different than he had imagined. Stretched out on the cool stone floor, he felt the sigh of each man's robe brushing over him. The sight of all those sandaled feet was rather comical, and he became absorbed in trying to guess which feet were who's. Everyone was careful not to kick him. They had all been there once and knew they might be again. When the last man had crossed over him, Jack sprang to his feet and dusted himself off with good humor. Father Ambrose, observing him from just inside the doorway, flashed a friendly smile. Jack smiled back— without irony, without defiance, without any self-consciousness at all. He simply smiled.

He would find himself watching Father Ambrose, trying to make him out. There was something cutting in the man: His clear, impartial gaze had the power to wipe the entertainer's seduction right off Jack's face, making him feel false and foolish. At times the abbot seemed an enemy, an ascetic ghoul who wished to rob him of his nature. This man has never known a woman, he would think. Easy to be holy when you have no appetites. But the abbot's way of moving, at once gawky and strangely beautiful, a grace at the very edge of clumsiness, made these arguments seem brutal and stupid. Here was a soul in full possession of its body, a dancer to music Jack did not yet know how to hear.

He thought often of that consoling touch in the refectory. There was mystery in it. Jack, who styled himself a lover, had never achieved anything like the power of that simple touch. It seemed to him now that he'd only been playing at love, imitating it as a child imitates what he only dimly understands of the adult world. Ambrose was the real lover.

Gradually, unevenly, and with many second thoughts, Jack found himself surrendering. Not for conventional reasons: he didn't care much about being good, didn't care at all what God thought of him. Nor could he love a Church that would send a girl to the gallows, a Church that had forbidden him, long ago, to lie with his wife.

To Father Ambrose, he confessed this ancient resentment. "When the priest said your childlessness was a cross, you took him to mean it was a penance," the abbot observed. "A penance imposed unjustly for no sin you could discern. But you see, a cross might also be understood to be an opportunity."

"An opportunity? Well, if that's what it was, I made the most of it." He was not boasting. His many liaisons now seemed sinful, not for their sterility, but for their heartlessness. He had been as heartless in his own way as the Church.

"I meant that the imposed restraint might have been an opportunity," the abbot replied.

"An opportunity to do what?"

"To do the only thing you really care to do, even now."

Love. That was all he cared to do. Perhaps he was meant to love as Ambrose did: with a touch that conferred blessing and took nothing in return. Perhaps that is why he had been created without seed. If he surrendered more and more to monastic discipline it was only because he aspired to this: to penetrate the mystery of passionless love.

But if he had been made for this, why was he so randy? His dream life conceded nothing to his celibate condition. The bell for matins seemed always to wake him on the verge of joy, and he cursed it. He hoped Ingrid did not watch his dreams, did not know how often they desecrated her.

He believed she was in heaven now. Her spirit came to him when he called: gentle, untroubled, unwilling to engage in regret. When he begged her forgiveness, her presence left him. It seemed she only came to keep him company. Knowing that she watched him, he wanted to do well. Whether the Church would ever canonize her was a matter of indifference to him. Jack venerated Ingrid as a saint.

He became devoted, also, to the Virgin Mary. There was a beautiful statue of her in the chapel. Her sweet oval face was tilted slightly, as if listening, and her long, graceful fingers reminded him of Ingrid's. In fact, he got the two of them mixed up sometimes. It didn't seem to matter. He began to compose secret hymns to her against that day when he forgot he was a singer and was allowed, at last, to sing.

One day he was in the scullery, scrubbing a pot. Burnt porridge was stuck to the bottom, and he had dedicated himself single-mindedly to scouring it away. He scrubbed and scrubbed, then rinsed. A ring of blackish scum remained. He would have to scour some more. There were bits of oat stuck between the bristles of his scrub brush. It seemed they should each have a name, so distinct was his awareness of them. And he thought: Is this all there is? Bits of burnt oatmeal, bent bristles, dark hairs on his wet arm. Thirty worn stairs from chapel to dorter, a chip in the fifth from the bottom. Into bed and out, twice every night, night after night, prayer after prayer, candles dripping on the altar, drip after drip, sandals off and on and off and on, pots shiny then blackened then shiny then black. Nothing but bits, precise and dazzling bits that amounted to nothing. Nothing happened. He could run away, bed a hundred women, take another wife and leave her, seduce another nun and see her killed. And still, nothing would happen. A few burnt oats, lodged in the worn bristles of a scrub brush—it could plunge a man into bottomless despair.

He laughed. He laughed until he cried.

And then he finished cleaning the pot.

Five

When Ingrid fainted one day shortly after she and Parmenter set off on their rounds, she tried to pass it off as nothing, as fatigue or the bad air. Hugh said, "You're not eating enough," and she insisted that she was, that in fact she was growing fat. As evidence, she drew his attention to the slight convexity of her usually flat abdomen, and her breasts which were, well, in evidence. "Forgive me, Fairfax," he ventured, the inimitable Parmenter tact straining, "but can we rule out pregnancy as a diagnosis?" When she reflected back on the past ten weeks she realized they could not. Why had she not thought of it herself?

Hugh insisted that she stop working, that it was one thing to risk her own health but quite another to endanger this unborn child. Ingrid had to admit she was relieved. She spent her days in luxurious boredom at home with Meg. The concern she had lavished on all the inhabitants of Southampton was now directed exclusively toward this unmet being who, so far, was indistinguishable from her own body. To her shame, she had become sublimely indifferent to the plague. She ate and slept with a resolute and concentrated selfishness, and on the rare occasions when she left the house, she felt like a priest carrrying the viaticum through a battlefield.

For Hugh, her belly became a sort of shrine. The moment he came home each night, he rushed to check on her condition—taking her pulse, pressing his ear to her abdomen, demanding to know what she had eaten, how long she had slept. All the weariness vanished from his face: He beamed; he laughed; he addressed baby-talk to her apron. His wife and Ingrid found this hilarious. "You'd think this babe was heir to the throne, for all your fussing!" Meg would exclaim. "Goodness, you'd think it was the Christ child!"

Ingrid was grateful neither of the Parmenters asked about the father. Hugh, remembering her bruised condition when he met her, had drawn his own conclusion. He had even wondered whether he ought to express sympathy for what Ingrid might consider an unhappy predicament. But his heart wasn't in it. To anticipate new life in the midst of so much death seemed to him an unmitigated joy. Hope dwelt under his roof. And Ingrid herself could not conceive of needing sympathy: She was placid, happy and, most of the time, sleepy.

Meanwhile, the epidemic was abating. There were fewer new cases, more recoveries. Now and then Hugh was coming home with a little money, a chicken or some cake bestowed in lieu of a fee. The market reopened and traveling merchants began to return. Hugh thought it an especially good sign when, late in November, a troubadour came to perform at the White Hart.

A troubadour! "Did you catch his name?" she asked eagerly.

"It was something French."

"It wasn't Jacques Brigand des Cœurs, was it?"

He shrugged, "I don't know. Might have been."

In her idleness she had had much time to brood over Jack, to miss him and wonder how she would ever find him again. She consoled herself with the thought that some day his wayfaring would bring him here as it had brought him to the Crossroads. But so soon! She bolted up from the supper table and ran all the way to the White Hart.

The tavern was packed. She would not have thought there were enough people left alive to crowd a place so. These were the uneasy survivors, sated with loss and taking a sabbatical from mourning. The rafters rang with harsh laughter, but no music.

"Has the troubadour gone?" she asked anxiously.

"Just out taking a piss, love."

She pushed her way to the back, where the stage was. There was a lute resting on a stool, but she couldn't tell whether it was Jack's. A baldish man with a huge stomach mounted the stage. Someone shoved a drink at her, and she accepted it absently. The fat man took up the lute and began to sing. His name was Chevalier, someone said.

She wanted to leave then, but she was wedged in by the crowd.

As it turned out, this was lucky. She heard a voice behind her say, "Aye, he's good, they say he's the best, but I think Jacques is better. Now there's a man who can rip the heart right out of your chest."

Jacques? Did they mean *her* Jacques?

"Alas, his singing days are over," said another. "He's entered a monastery, you know."

"Nay!"

"Aye. Hard to believe, I know. Wouldn't have believed it myself, but I heard it from a silk merchant who saw him there. He's with the Black Friars at Abingdon."

"Jacques Brigand des Cœurs?"

"Aye. The very same."

Jack in a monastery? It couldn't be! The second speaker echoed her next thought. "Surely he was just lodging there for the night."

"Nay. He had on the robes. Shorn like a lamb he was."

"It's the times, I guess. The God-fearing fall away, and the sinners get religion. Bloody shame in his case. There's some folks God made to be sinners, and you have to feel when they repent that they're going against his intentions."

She set off for Abingdon the next morning. The Parmenters tried to dissuade her, of course. She told them she had located the father of her child, that she'd thought he was dead. When Hugh saw that she was determined to go, he closed her hand around a purse full of coins. "No, don't thank me," he said. "It's your wages." The money allowed her to travel in relative safety and comfort. She wore her physician's robe, fell in with a party of merchants and reached the monastery in three days, tired but unmolested.

The abbot at Abingdon had taken precautions to make sure the plague did not spread to his monks. The guesthouse was open but quarantined. No one was allowed inside the monastery itself. The porter, Brother Richard, slept in the guesthouse and was not allowed to leave it, lest he carry the disease back to his brothers. He was a jovial man of middle years who seemed to be enjoying his peculiar exile, chatting up the guests like a good innkeeper. As soon as she got a moment alone with him, Ingrid asked about Jack.

"Aye, of course I know him. You couldn't miss him."

"And how does he fare as a monk? Having seen him on the stage, it's hard to imagine."

Brother Richard laughed. "Well, he got off to a rocky start, it's true, but he's settled down some. Lately he's become very devoted to Our Lady."

"They say she has a soft spot in her heart for troubadours."

"From what I hear, lots of ladies have a soft spot for Brother Jacob. I shouldn't be at all surprised if one day an old love snuck in disguised as a man and tried to woo him out."

He winked, and she blushed. "You know what really gave him trouble though," the porter went on, mercifully gliding over her discomfiture, "was the chanting. This one day at vespers—oh, saints be praised, I thought I'd die from holding back the laughter!" He laughed now, a silent, strenuous wheeze that jiggled his stomach and brought on a fit of coughing. He had to pause to wipe the tears from his eyes and mop his flushed forehead before he could continue. "We're all chatting merrily along—you've heard chanting before?—a low respectful sort of hum, you know, all of us trying to sound like one voice. Well, all of a sudden we hear this bellowing, and it's all over the place. Where we're sustaining a note, he's making these curlicues. I can hardly describe it—you had to be there—but the likes of it have never been heard before or since. So after the service the abbot takes him aside and asks what in the name of heaven he thinks he's doing. And he says, he says—" Brother Richard's stomach shook and he wheezed some more. "He says 'Pardon me, father, but it's bloody boring the way you fellows sing. Why don't I give you all a few lessons? You won't believe the difference a little harmony can make, a little trilling.' Well, the poor fellow. The abbot had to sit him down and explain the whole idea of humility. For the next fortnight he made our Brother Jacob mouth the words without any sound at all. You've never seen a glummer man."

"Anyhow," the monk concluded, wiping his eyes again. "You'll be able to see him in the morning when the brothers go out to work. From the window, I mean."

She hardly slept that night, and at dawn she was up and stationed by the second floor casement. In the distance she could hear the low rolling of the morning chant like the lapping of a calm sea, sound of the womb, of her soul's cradle. She longed to bury her face in it as in a mother's skirts, and she felt a stab of jealousy that Jack was lovingly adopted while she, the natural child, was disowned.

Brother Richard came in quietly, bearing a bowl of steamed milk and a small parcel. "A little something to sustain you on your journey."

She took the hint. "I'll be off within the hour."

He laid a kind hand on her shoulder. "That's for the best."

Sudden tears smarted her eyes. "I only want to see for myself that he is well . . ."

"Well, now, a few more minutes—he'll come out that little door there, with the others, and you'll see that he's fine, just fine.

"You'll be fine, too," he added as he left. "You're a good girl."

Huddled in her cloak—for the thin fog that drifted in through the open shutters was cold—she comforted herself with the milk and waited. She wondered whether she would even recognize him in a guise so unlike him and from this distance.

The door to the cloister split open, and a score of hooded monks queued out. Jack's cowl was raised too, concealing his face, but he still had that loose, swaggering walk, and he wore his habit with a certain flair, the rope belt slung low on his hips. The sight of his lean, cocksure figure moved her in a way she had not expected.

The monks dispersed to the barns and various outbuildings. Jack was heading off alone toward a copse that lay just outside the abbey wall, an ax swinging at his side. She watched till she lost sight of him, and then, greedy for more, sped down the stairs and out of the gatehouse. She ran full speed down the road that skirted the wall, and when it ended she slipped in among the trees. And there he was— not twenty yards from her. He was hacking kindling with an easy rhythmic curve of his arm and singing an *Ave*.

The cowl was down now, and as she crept nearer, picking her way carefully lest a cracking twig betray her presence, she saw that he had shaved his beard and that his hair, though not yet tonsured, was cut very short. His face looked rounder, younger than she had remembered it, and there was a dimple in his chin that she had not known about. His fresh-shaven jaw had a slightly blue cast, and his eyes, above it, were very blue, the whites very white above the white fog of his breath. And all the woe of the world was nothing beside this one glimpse of her lover's face.

He paused in his work, looked around. It seemed he felt someone there. She pressed herself close to a tree trunk and held her breath, certain it was her pounding heart that had alerted him. Jack shrugged and went back to his singing and chopping.

He is happy, she thought. This life has brought him peace. Well, why should she be surprised? Monastic life was meant to bring peace. It hadn't for her, but she was not made for lasting peace. She would always be a desert voice, howling at the inscrutable heavens. A stanza of longing followed by a stanza of despair, a stanza of acceptance, a stanza of wild praise. And then, a few hours later, a new song in the ancient pattern, the despair sung as if there had never been acceptance, the praise as if there had never been despair, each sung forgetfully, as though it were the only song on earth. Now and then you held the whole Psalter in your hands, saw the pattern and the peace in it, like the world breathing its seasons. An hour later your throat was full of dust.

She had no complaint about this, not at the moment. Looking at Jack, she had no complaint about anything. He is happy, she thought. I should leave him in peace. She could imagine him, rapt before the Virgin's altar, all that rambunctious passion refined to a sweet devotion. He would make beautiful hymns, and his jaunty spirit would gladden the cloister.

She should leave him in peace. It was wicked to go seducing people out of cloisters, selfish and wicked to endanger someone's soul just because you longed to have him in your bed. Just because your arms ached to hold him, and your eyes wanted to burn through his habit and your blood beat so loud you couldn't hear your conscience . . .

She stepped out into the clearing, the frosty ground crunching beneath her feet. Jack looked up again, and this time the ax fell from his hand. She thought he would run to meet her. Instead, he dropped to his knees and crossed himself. "Saint Ingrid!"

For an instant she was dumbfounded. Then it dawned on her: He thought he was having a vision. The temptation to mischief was too strong to resist.

"You used to be sarcastic when you called me that," she pointed out.

He lowered his head. "Forgive me. I was a fool."

"And now you're repenting of it. And you are repenting of lying with me. Is this not so?"

"Yes, my lady."

"Tell me, Brother Jacob, are you truly sorry?"

"Lady," he implored. "Do not tease me. You see from heaven how I do."

"Yes. We see that you are making musical innovations. All the saints are vastly amused."

She thought he would smile at that, but he just stared at the ground, chastened.

"Don't be sad, Brother Jacob. It could not have been otherwise. Somewhere in your heart you must know this."

He looked up at her, his eyes brimming with tears. "But you died."

"And if I had not? Would you still be sorry?"

"Nay," he admitted. "Then I would have gone on sinning. You have redeemed my soul with your death, Saint Ingrid."

It was like a blow to the chest. He was lost to her. She meant more to him dead than she ever could alive. I have nowhere to go, she thought. She felt so breathless she might float off into the dim cold sky. A ghost.

"You are happy as a monk," she said at last. That he did not hear the pain in her voice made her feel lonelier than she had known possible.

"I am at peace. I try to be at peace."

"You do not find the discipline taxing?"

"You see me, lady. You know what a poor monk I make. Still . . . I am trying to subdue my passion. Someday I may learn to love."

"To love without passion? That isn't like you, Jack."

There was a flash of surprise, or doubt. But he bowed his head again. "Then help me, I beg you."

"I'm not sure I want to help."

He misunderstood. With a look of dejection he said, "Nay, I

313

have no right to ask anything of you. You have every reason to tell God to send me straight to Hell."

She chuckled. Jack used to laugh this way, with dry, secret amusement and an edge of anger. "God has never asked my opinion in the matter. If he did . . . Oh, Jack, do stand up. Look at me."

With evident misgiving he tottered to his feet. She took a step forward and he stepped back in alarm. "You look so real," he said, pale with awe. "Your cheeks are bright as if you felt the cold."

"I do feel it. If you touched me, I would feel that too."

Jack frowned. "Is this a temptation?" he asked suspiciously.

She laughed, heartened by the tinge of irritation in his voice. This was the old Jack, unwilling to be pushed around by nuns or saints or God himself. "I hope it is, my love."

Now he was looking at her, really looking, and she was no longer a ghost. She felt herself there on the earth, a thin green blade, trembling.

"Ingrid." Wonder and joy flooded his face. "Are you . . . ?"

She thought he would laugh then, exclaim, "Damn you!" But he came to her without a word and held her fast in his arms, held her long, tightening his embrace when she tried, halfheartedly, to pull away. It almost hurt, this return of feeling—like the flow of blood in frostbitten extremities, a network of fine cracks spreading over her skin. His fingers searched for her, spaded and dug through the wool, the flesh, for the very bone, her little cracking cry in response saying yes, I am, I am alive. Their kiss, finally, was soft, like the soft spot on a newborn's skull.

Later, when they found their voices, when wonder had given way to plain curiosity and facts were exchanged, she told him she was carrying a child. She watched his face carefully to see whether the faintest flicker of pleasure was mingled with his puzzlement and surprise. And it was. He was trying to frown, but his smile leaked out all over.

"How can that be?"

"You have forgotten so soon? Our night in the hayrick?"

"Nay, nay, of course not. But you know I cannot . . ."

She pressed her fingers to his lips, hushing him. "Shame on you, Jack. All these months in a monastery and still so little faith?"

A deception that brought such gladness was worth whatever it cost Ingrid in remorse. And who could be sure that this was not Jack's child? For there are miracles wrought neither by the firm white hand of God nor the devil's wagging cock, miracles too shrewd, too subtle to be explained to children, and wonders that were never worked by virgins.

Epilogue

When the plague came to Oxford in November, it hit hard and fast. There were new, more virulent strains: One, settling in the lungs, killed in just two or three days, and another, aiming straight for the heart, dispatched its victims in a matter of hours. Poor scholars, undernourished and overcrowded in their rickety lodgings, were especially vulnerable. Passing by Cary's Inn, Matthew saw a horseless cart overflowing with the bodies of dead boys.

In these circumstances law and order broke down. There was much looting, random violence. Small violations of the sanitation code—which were rampant—had ominous implications. The citizens of Oxford had elected him because they knew he could be counted on in a crisis, and he did not let them down. In the first days of the epidemic he worked without rest: breaking up fights, arresting looters, trying to get the streets cleaned and directing mass burials.

Townspeople were a little better off than clerics, but the Greenes, exposed early because of the travelers they lodged, were stricken in the first weeks. Matthew was so much occupied that he did not visit them for several days, and when finally, guiltily, he let himself into the closed inn, he found Henry unconscious from drink and all the rest of them dead. Sabina had gone first. Her body was already starting to decompose. Maggots teemed in the black holes that had been her eyes and mouth, and a rat strolled down her torso, sniffing with mild curiosity. Matthew ran retching into the yard. He sat there for some time, his head in his hands, telling himself that he must bury them. He was their friend; there was no one else.

He thought of his wife's body, which it seemed he had only just come to know. The children had been banished from the conjugal

316

bed, which was mussed so frequently these days that Gillian had given up making it. After his pub lunch, he would loom in his own doorway with a certain look that warned her to send the children outside. "Undo your hair," he would command her. She would complain of having to comb and braid and pin it up again twice in the same day, but she would obey him. And he would wish once again that he were a poet. All he could do was stand there with a besotted look and say, "You're so pretty." Perhaps that, and the testimony of his body, was enough. For she had acquired the gestures of a woman who knows her power to captivate.

If he buried Sabina, he might carry the contagion home to Gillian. His duty as a Christian and a citizen was clear: He could not dispell it rationally. But Matthew no longer thought of himself as a good man. He went out of the Crossroads and started looking for a cart to buy. With so many people fleeing town, a vehicle could not be had for any sum of money. So he stole one, and a horse to pull it. In great haste he loaded it up with his tools, his inventory of shoes and leather, the children's favorite toys and a jumble of clothes and bedding. He could not believe he had waited this long. They were on the road by dusk, the children giddy at the adventure, Gillian fretting about the house, things left behind, milk for the children, the impending rain. Instinct told him to travel north, that there was safety in the cold. Without a backward glance, he abandoned Oxford to its lawlessness.

During the plague many monasteries and convents refused the hospitality they had traditionally extended to travelers, and in this way protected themselves from contagion. Dame Agatha had always been grudging of Greyleigh's hospitality, feeling that visitors contaminated the cloister with worldliness. But when the plague came, she reversed herself. It scandalized her that other houses should be turning people away for such a selfish reason. As a matter of principle she opened Greyleigh to all comers. The nunnery was soon infected.

She nursed the victims herself, and by the time she succumbed, there was no one left healthy enough to care for her. She retired to her room, where she spent many days in agony. But Agatha was too stubborn to die. When she finally emerged, the cloister was silent in a way that made its previous silence seem loud. In every room she found corpses. They were sprawled over the beds, the floor, even the pews of the choir. There was not even a rodent left alive. She wrote the bishop and awaited his instructions. He sent her to Godstow where, no longer an abbess, she was able to practice the devotions she had long postponed. She was as content there as her nature allowed her to be, and lived to the age of ninety.

Greyleigh's lands were sold to neighboring estates, and the convent itself was demolished. The infirmary, of more recent construction and relatively solid, was left standing, and a few years later was turned into an inn. The inn's name is indicative of the sacrilege that came into vogue during that post-plague period: It was called The Randy Nun. Ingrid bristled at this, but her husband found it jolly amusing. Jack, who had stopped touring by then and was employed as the Flemings' bailiff, sang there often. And his son, after him.